PRUSSIAN BLUE

Also by Philip Kerr

PHILIP KERR

PRUSSIAN BLUE

A BERNIE GUNTHER THRILLER

Quercus

First published in Great Britain in 2017 by

Quercus Editions Ltd
Carmelite House
50 Victoria Embankment
London EC4Y 0DZ

An Hachette UK company

A CIP catalogue record for this book is available
from the British Library

HB ISBN 978 1 78429 648 3
TPB ISBN 978 1 78429 649 0
EBOOK ISBN 978 1 78429 650 6

10 9 8 7 6 5 4 3 2 1

Typeset by CC Book Production

Printed and bound in Great Britain by Clays Ltd, St Ives plc

The book is for Martin Diesbach,
who is no relation but a very good friend,
to whom I am always indebted

I am not so weak as to submit to the demands of the age when they go against my convictions. I spin a cocoon around myself; let others do the same. I shall leave it to time to show what will come of it: a brilliant butterfly or maggot.

– Caspar David Friedrich

CHAPTER 1

October 1956

It was the end of the season and most of the hotels on the Riviera, including the Grand Hôtel Cap Ferrat, where I worked, were already closed for the winter. Not that winter meant much in that part of the world. Not like in Berlin, where winter is more a rite of passage than a season: you're not a true Berliner until you've survived the bitter experience of an interminable Prussian winter; that famous dancing bear you see on the city's coat of arms is just trying to keep himself warm.

The Hotel Ruhl was normally one of the last hotels in Nice to close because it had a casino and people like to gamble whatever the weather. Maybe they should have opened a casino in the nearby Hotel Negresco – which the Ruhl resembled, except that the Negresco was closed and looked as if it might stay that way the following year. Some said they were going to turn it into apartments but the Negresco concierge – who was an acquaintance of mine, and a fearful snob – said the place had been sold to the daughter of a Breton butcher, and he wasn't usually wrong about these things. He was off to Bern for the winter and probably wouldn't be back. I was going to miss him but as I parked my car and crossed the Promenade des Anglais to the Hotel Ruhl I really wasn't thinking about that. Perhaps it was the cold night air and the barman's surplus ice cubes in the gutter but instead I was thinking about Germany. Or perhaps it was the sight of the two crew-cut golems standing outside the hotel's grand Mediterranean entrance, eating ice cream cones and wearing thick East German suits of the kind that are mass-produced like tractor parts and shovels. Just seeing those two thugs ought to have put me on my guard but I had something important on my mind; I was looking forward to meeting my wife, Elisabeth, who, out of the blue, had sent me a letter inviting me to dinner. We were separated, and she was living back in Berlin, but Elisabeth's handwritten letter – she had beautiful Sütterlin handwriting (banned by the Nazis) – spoke of her having come into a bit of money, which just might have explained how she could afford to be back on the Riviera and staying at the Ruhl, which is almost as expensive as the Angleterre or the Westminster. Either way I was looking forward to seeing her again with the blind faith of one who hoped reconciliation was on the cards. I'd already planned the short but graceful speech of forgiveness I was going to make. How much I missed her and thought we could still make a go of it – that kind of thing. Of course, a part of me was also braced for the possibility she might be there to tell me she'd met someone else and wanted a divorce. Still, it seemed like a lot of trouble to go to – it wasn't easy to travel from Berlin these days.

The hotel restaurant was on the top floor in one of the corner cupolas. It was perhaps the best in Nice, designed by Charles Dalmas. Certainly it was the most expensive. I hadn't ever eaten there but I'd heard the food was excellent and I was looking forward to my dinner. The maître d' sidestepped his way across the beautiful Belle Époque room, met me at the bookings lectern, and found my wife's name on the page. I was already glancing over his shoulder, searching the tables anxiously for Elisabeth and not finding her there yet, checking my watch and realizing that I was perhaps a little early. I wasn't really listening to the maître d' as he informed me that my host had arrived, and I was halfway across the marble floor when I saw I was being ushered to a quiet corner table where a squat, tough-looking man was already working on a very large lobster and a bottle of white Burgundy. Recognizing him immediately, I turned on my heel only to find my exit blocked by two more apes who looked as if they might have climbed in through the open window, off one of the many palm trees on the Promenade.

'Don't leave yet,' one of them said quietly in thick, Leipzig-accented German. 'The comrade-general wouldn't like it.'

For a moment I stood my ground, wondering if I could risk making a run for the door. But the two men, cut from the same crude mould as the two golems I'd seen by the hotel entrance, were more than a match for me.

'That's right,' added the other. 'So you'd best sit down like a good boy and avoid making a scene.'

'Gunther,' said a voice behind me, also speaking German. 'Bernhard Gunther. Come over here and sit down, you old fascist. Don't be afraid.' He laughed. 'I'm not going to shoot you. It's a public place.' I suppose he assumed that German speakers were at a premium in the Hotel Ruhl and he probably wouldn't have been wrong. 'What could possibly happen to you in here? Besides, the food is excellent and the wine more so.'

I turned again and took another look at the man who remained seated and was still applying himself to the lobster with his cracker and a pick, like a plumber changing the washer on a tap. He was wearing a better suit than his men – a blue pinstripe, tailor-made – and a patterned silk tie that could only have been bought in France. A tie like that would have cost a week's wages in the GDR and probably earned you a lot of awkward questions at the local police station, as would the large gold watch that flashed on his wrist like a miniature lighthouse as he gouged at the flesh of the lobster, which was the same colour as the more abundant flesh of his powerful hands. His hair was still dark on top but cut so short against the sides of his wrecking ball of a head it looked like a priest's black zucchetto. He'd put on some weight since last I'd seen him, and he hadn't even started on the new potatoes, the mayonnaise, the asparagus tips, the *salade niçoise,* sweet cucumber pickles, and the plate of dark chocolate arranged on the table in front of him. With his boxer's physique he reminded me strongly of Martin Bormann, Hitler's deputy chief of staff; he was certainly every bit as dangerous.

I sat down, poured myself a glass of white wine, and tossed my cigarette case onto the table in front of me.

'General Erich Mielke,' I said. 'What an unexpected pleasure.'

'I'm sorry about bringing you here under false pretences. But I knew you wouldn't have come if I'd said it was I who was buying dinner.'

'Is she all right? Elisabeth? Just tell me that and then I'll listen to whatever you have to say, General.'

'Yes, she's fine.'

'I take it she's not actually here in Nice.'

'No, she's not. I'm sorry about that. But you'll be glad to know that she was most reluctant to write that letter. I had to explain that the alternative would have been so much more painful, for you at least. So please don't hold that letter against her. She wrote it for the best of reasons.' Mielke lifted an arm and snapped his fingers at the waiter. 'Have something to eat. Have some wine. I drink very little myself but I'm told this is the best. Anything you like. I insist. The Ministry of State Security is paying. Only, please don't smoke. I hate the smell of cigarettes, especially when I'm eating.'

'I'm not hungry, thanks.'

'Of course you are. You're a Berliner. We don't have to be hungry to eat. The war taught us to eat when there's food on the table.'

'Well, there's plenty of food on this table. Are we expecting anyone else? The Red Army, perhaps?'

'I like to see lots of food when I'm eating, even if I don't eat any of it. It's not just a man's stomach that needs filling. It's his senses, too.'

I picked up the bottle and inspected the label.

'Corton-Charlemagne. I approve. Nice to see that an old communist like you can still appreciate a few of the finer things in life, General. This wine must be the most expensive on the list.'

'I do, and it most certainly is.'

I drained the glass and poured myself another. It was excellent.

The waiter approached nervously, as if he'd already felt the edge of Mielke's tongue.

'We'll have two juicy steaks,' said Mielke, speaking good French – the result, I imagined, of his two years spent in a French prison camp before and during the war. 'No, better still, we'll have the Chateaubriand. And make it very bloody.'

The waiter went away.

'Is it just steak you prefer that way?' I said. 'Or everything else as well?'

'Still got that sense of humour, Gunther. It beats me how you've stayed alive for this long.'

'The French are a little more tolerant of these things than they are in what you laughingly call the Democratic Republic of Germany. Tell me, General, when is the communist government going to dissolve the people and elect another?'

'The people?' Mielke laughed, and breaking off from his lobster for a moment, placed a piece of chocolate into his mouth, almost as if it were a matter of indifference what he was eating just as long as it was something not easily obtained in the GDR. 'They rarely know what's best for them. Nearly fourteen million Germans voted for Hitler in March 1932, making the Nazis the largest party in the Reichstag. Do you honestly believe they had a clue what was best for them? No, of course not. Nobody did. All the people care about is a regular pay packet, cigarettes, and beer.'

'I expect that's why twenty thousand East German refugees were crossing into the Federal Republic every month – at least until you imposed your so-called special regime with its restricted zone and your protective strip. They were in search of better beer and cigarettes and perhaps the chance to complain a little without fear of the consequences.'

'Who was it said that none are more hopelessly enslaved than those who believe they are free?'

'It was Goethe. And you misquote him. He said that none are more hopelessly enslaved than those who *falsely* believe they are free.'

'In my book, they are one and the same.'

'That would be the one book you've read, then.'

'You're a romantic fool. I forget that about you, sometimes. Look, Gunther, most people's idea of freedom is to write something rude on a lavatory wall. My own belief is that the people are lazy and prefer to leave the business of government to the government. However, it's important that the people don't place too great a burden on those in charge of things. Hence, my presence here in France. Generally speaking I prefer to go hunting. But I often come here around this time of year to get away from my responsibilities. I like to play a little baccarat.'

'That's a high-risk game. But then you always were a gambler.'

'You want to know the really great thing about gambling here?' He grinned. 'Most of the time, I lose. If there were still such decadent things as casinos in the GDR I'm afraid the croupiers would always make sure I won. Winning is only fun if you can lose. I used to go to the one in Baden-Baden but the last time I was there I was recognized and couldn't go again. So now I come to Nice. Or sometimes Le Touquet. But I prefer Nice. The weather is a little more reliable here than on the Atlantic coast.'

'Somehow I don't believe that's all you're here for.'

'You're right.'

'So what the hell do you want?'

'You remember that business a few months back, with Somerset Maugham and our mutual friends Harold Hennig and Anne French. You almost managed to screw up a good operation there.'

Mielke was referring to a Stasi plot to discredit Roger Hollis, the deputy director of MI5 – the British domestic counterintelligence and security agency. The real plan had been to leave Hollis smelling of roses after the bogus Stasi plot was revealed.

'It was very good of you to tie up that loose end for us,' said Mielke. 'It *was* you who killed Hennig, wasn't it?'

I didn't answer but we both knew this was true; I'd shot Harold Hennig dead in the house Anne French had been renting in Villefranche and done my very best to frame her for it. Since then the French police had asked me all sorts of questions about her, but that was all I knew. As far as I was aware, Anne French remained safely back in England.

'Well, for the sake of argument, let's just say it was you,' said Mielke. He finished the piece of chocolate he was eating, forked some pickled cucumber into his mouth, and then swallowed a mouthful of white Burgundy, all of which persuaded me that his taste buds were every bit as corrupt as his politics and morals. 'The fact is that Hennig's days were numbered anyway. As are Anne's. The operation to discredit Hollis really only looks good if we try to eliminate her, too – as befits someone who betrayed us. And that's especially important now that the French are trying to have her extradited back here to face trial for Hennig's murder. Needless to say, that just can't be allowed to happen. Which is where you come in, Gunther.'

'Me?' I shrugged. 'Let me get this straight. You're asking me to kill Anne French?'

'Precisely. Except that I'm not asking. The fact is that you agreeing to kill Anne French is a condition of remaining alive yourself.'

CHAPTER 2

October 1956

I estimated once that the Gestapo had employed less than fifty thousand officers to keep an eye on eighty million Germans, but from what I'd read and heard about the GDR, the Stasi employed at least twice that number – to say nothing of their civilian informants or spylets who, rumour had it, amounted to one in ten of the population – to keep an eye on just seventeen million Germans. As deputy head of the Stasi, Erich Mielke was one of the most powerful men in the GDR. And as might have been expected of such a man, he'd already anticipated all my objections to such a distasteful mission as the one he had described and was ready to argue them down with the brute force of one who is used to getting his way with people who are themselves authoritarian and assertive. I had the feeling that Mielke might have grabbed me by the throat or banged my head on the dinner table and, of course, violence was a vital part of his character; as a young communist cadre in Berlin he'd participated in the infamous murder of two uniformed policemen.

'No, don't smoke,' he said, 'just listen. This is a good opportunity for you, Gunther. You can make some money, get yourself a new passport – a genuine West German passport, with a different name and a fresh start somewhere – and, most important of all, you can pay Anne French back, with interest, for the way she used you so ruthlessly.'

'Only because you told her to. Isn't that right? It was you who put her up to it.'

'I didn't tell her to sleep with you. That was her idea. Either way she played you like a piano, Gunther. But it hardly matters now, does it? You fell for her in a big way, didn't you?'

'It's easy to see what the two of you have in common. You're both totally unprincipled.'

'True. Although in her case she was also one of the best liars I've ever met. I mean a real pathological case. I really don't think she knew when she was lying and when she was telling the truth. Not that I think the immorality of subterfuge really mattered to her. Just as long as she was able to maintain that cool smile and satisfy her own greed for material possessions. She managed to convince herself that she wasn't in it for the money; the irony is that she thought she was quite principled. Which made her an ideal spy. Not that any of this previous story really matters a damn.

'What's important – at least to me – is that now someone has to kill her. I'm afraid that MI5 would be very surprised if we didn't at least *try* to kill her. And the way I see it is that this someone might as well be you. It's not like you haven't killed people before, is it? Hennig, for example. I mean, that just had to be you who put a bullet in him and made it look like she'd done it.'

Mielke paused as our steak arrived and the half-eaten lobster was swept away. 'We'll carve that ourselves,' he told the waiter gruffly. 'And bring us a bottle of your best Bordeaux. Decanted, mind. But I want to see the bottle it comes from, right? And the cork.'

'You don't trust anyone, do you?' I said.

'That is one reason I have stayed alive for so long.' When the waiter had gone, Mielke cut the Chateaubriand in two, forked a generous half onto his dinner plate, and chuckled. 'But I also look after myself, you know? I don't smoke, I don't drink very much, and I like to keep fit because at heart I'm an old street fighter. Even so, I find that people are more inclined to listen to a policeman who looks as if he can take care of himself than one who doesn't. You wouldn't believe the number of times I've had to intimidate people in the SED Central Committee. I swear, even Walter Ulbricht is afraid of me.'

'Is that what you call yourself now, Erich? A policeman?'

'Why not? It's what I am. But why should that bother a man like you, Gunther? You, who were a member of Kripo and the SD for almost twenty years. Some of those so-called policemen you reported to were the worst criminals in history: Heydrich. Himmler. Nebe. And you worked for them all.' He shook his head, exasperated. 'You know, one day I really am going to look into your RSHA record and see what crimes you perpetrated, Gunther. I've a shrewd idea you're nowhere near as clean as you like to make out. So let's not pretend there's anything separating us as far as moral superiority is concerned. We've both done things we wish we hadn't. But we're still here.'

Mielke fell silent as he cut his own steak into smaller squares.

'Having said all that, I don't forget that it was you who saved my life, on two occasions.'

'Three,' I said bitterly.

'Was it? Perhaps. Well, like I say. Killing her. This is a good opportunity for you. To make a fresh start for yourself. A chance to come back to Germany and get away from this irrelevant place on the edge of Europe where a man of your talents is wasted, quite frankly. Assuming you're wise enough to understand that.'

Mielke forked a square of steak into his big mouth and started chewing furiously.

'Am I arguing?' I asked.

'No. You're not, for once. Which in itself is strange.'

I shrugged. 'I'm willing to do what you ask, General. I'm broke. I have no friends. I live alone in an apartment that's not much bigger than a lobster pot, and I work at a job that's about to be folded away for the winter. I miss Germany. Christ, I even miss the weather. If killing Anne French is the price I have to pay to get my life back, then I'm more than willing to do it.'

'You were never easily influenced, Gunther. I'll be honest. I expected more opposition. Perhaps you hate Anne French more than I thought. Perhaps you really do want to kill her. But in this case, to be willing is not enough. You must actually go to England and kill her.'

The waiter came back with a decanter of red wine and placed it on the table in front of us. Mielke took it from him, sniffed at the cork, and then nodded at the empty bottle of Château Mouton Rothschild that had been presented for his inspection.

'Taste it,' he told me.

I tasted it and, predictably, it was as good as the white I'd been drinking; perhaps better. I nodded back at him.

'As a matter of fact I do hate her,' I said. 'Much more than I expected to hate her. And yes, I will kill her. But if you don't mind I'd like to know a bit more about your plan.'

'My men will meet you at the railway station here in Nice, where you will be given your new passport, some money, and tickets on the Blue Train to Paris. From there you can transfer to the Golden Arrow for Calais and then to London. Upon arrival you'll meet more of my men. They will brief you further and accompany you on your mission.'

'Is that where she's living? London?'

'No, she's living in a little town on the south coast of England. Fighting extradition, but without much success. MI5 seems to have abandoned her, more or less. My men will provide you with a detailed diary of the woman's movements so you can accidentally meet her, and arrange to have a drink with her.'

'Suppose she doesn't want to meet with me again? When we parted it was hardly on the best of terms.'

'Persuade her. Use a gun if you have to. We'll give you a gun.

But make her come with you. Somewhere public. That way she'll be more trusting.'

'I don't quite understand. Don't you want me to shoot her?'

'Good Lord, no. The last thing I want is for you to be arrested so you can spill your guts to the British. You need to be a long way away from Anne French when she dies. Hopefully you'll be back in Germany by the time that happens. Living under a new name. That will be nice for you, won't it?'

'So, what, I'm to poison her tea, is that it?'

'Yes. Poison is always best in these situations. Something slow that doesn't leave much trace. Recently we've been using thallium. Really, it's a formidable murder weapon. It's colourless, odourless, and tasteless and doesn't make its effect felt for at least a day or two. But when it does – it's devastating.' Mielke smiled cruelly. 'For all you know, you might have ingested some in that wine you're enjoying. I mean, you really wouldn't know if you had. I could have had the waiter put the stuff in the decanter, which is why I let you taste it and not me. You see how easy it is?'

I glanced uncomfortably at the glass of Mouton Rothschild and made a fist on the table.

Mielke was clearly enjoying my obvious discomfort. 'At first she'll think she's got a stomach upset. And then – well, it's a very long, painful death, you'll be glad to know. She'll puke for a couple of days, and that will be followed by extreme convulsions and muscular pain. After that comes a complete personality change – hallucinations and anxiety; lastly there's alopecia, blindness, a lot of agonizing chest pain, and then the end. You want to see it. Believe me, it's a living hell. Death, when it comes, will seem like a mercy.'

'Is there an antidote?' I still had one eye on the wine I'd been drinking, wondering how much of what Mielke had told me was true.

'I'm told that Prussian blue, orally administered, is an antidote.'

'The paint?'

'Effectively, yes, it is. Prussian blue is a synthetic pigment that works by colloidal dispersion, ion exchange, something like that. I'm not a chemist. However, I believe it's one of those antidotes that's only marginally less painful than the poison, and the chances are that by the time an English hospital wakes up to the fact that poor Anne French has been poisoned with thallium and tries to give her any Prussian blue it will already be too late for her.'

'Jesus,' I said, and picked up my cigarettes. I put one in my mouth and was about to light it when Mielke snatched it away and threw it into a planter without apology.

'But like I said, by the time she's dead you'll be safely back in West Germany. Only not in Berlin. You're no good to me in Berlin, Gunther. Too many people know you there. I think Bonn or maybe Hamburg would suit you better. More important, it would suit me if you went there.'

'You must have hundreds of Stasi agents all over West Germany, General. So what possible use could I be?'

'You have a particular skill set, Gunther. A useful background for what I have in mind. I want you to set up a neo-Nazi organization. With your fascist background this shouldn't be difficult. Your immediate task will be to desecrate or vandalize Jewish sites throughout West Germany – cultural centres, cemeteries, and synagogues. You can also persuade or even blackmail some of your old RSHA comrades to write letters to the newspapers and the federal government demanding the release of Nazi war criminals or protesting against the trial of others.'

'What have you got against the Jews?'

'Nothing.' Mielke tossed another piece of chocolate into his omnivorous mouth alongside the piece of steak that was already in there; it was like having dinner with some Prussian farmer's prize pig as it dined on swill that was made from the family's choicest leftovers. 'Nothing at all. But this will only lend credibility to our own propaganda that the federal government is still Nazi. Which it is. After all, it was Adenauer who denounced the entire denazification process and who brought in an amnesty law for Nazi war criminals. We're just helping people see what is already there.'

'You seem to have thought of everything, General.'

'If I haven't, someone else has. And if they haven't, they'll pay for it. But don't let my jovial manner fool you, Gunther. I might be on holiday but I'm deadly serious about this. And you'd better be as well.'

He pointed his fork at me as if he was contemplating shoving it in my eye and I felt somewhat reassured that there was a piece of meat on the end of it.

'Because if you're not, you'd better learn to be right now, or you'll never see tomorrow. How about it? Are you serious about this?'

I nodded. 'Yes, I'm serious. I want that English bitch dead every bit as much as you do, General. More, probably. Look, I'd rather not talk about what passed between us in any detail, if you don't mind. It's still a source of some grief to me. But I will tell you this, my only regret about what you've told me so far is that I won't be there in person to see her suffering. Because that's what I want. Her pain and her degradation. Now, does that answer your question?'

CHAPTER 3

October 1956

I returned to my flat in Villefranche, satisfied only that I'd managed to convince Mielke that I was actually going to carry out his orders and travel to England to poison Anne French. The truth was that while I hated the woman for all the pain she'd given me, I didn't quite hate her enough to murder her, and certainly not in the monstrous way that Mielke had described. I very much wanted a new West German passport but I also wanted to stay alive long enough to use it, and I had no doubt that Mielke was quite prepared to have his men kill me if he even half-suspected I was preparing to double-cross him. So it was that for a few moments I contemplated packing a suitcase immediately and leaving the Riviera for good. I had a bit of money under the mattress and a gun, and the car of course, but there was a good chance that his men would be watching my flat, in which case flight was probably futile. That presented the hair-raising prospect of my cooperating with Mielke's plan long enough to get hold of the passport and the money, and then looking for an opportunity to give his men the slip, which left me somewhere between the tree and its bark. Most of the men in the Stasi had been trained by the Gestapo and were experts at finding people; giving them the slip would be like trying to evade a pack of English tracker hounds.

In order to see if I was under surveillance I decided to take a walk along the seafront, hoping that this might make the Stasi reveal themselves and also that the cool night air would help to clear my head enough to think of a solution to my immediate problem. Inevitably my feet took me to a bar in the correctly named Rue Obscure, where I drank a bottle of red and smoked half a packet of cigarettes, which achieved exactly the opposite result from the one I was hoping for. And I was still shaking my head and pondering my limited options when I walked, a little unsteadily, home again.

Villefranche is a strange warren of alleys and narrow back-streets and, especially at night and at the close of the season, resembles a scene from a Fritz Lang movie. It's all too easy to imagine yourself being followed by unseen vigilantes through this dark, meandering catacomb of French streets, like poor Peter Lorre with a letter M chalked onto the back of your coat, especially when you're drunk. But I wasn't so drunk that I couldn't spot the tail that had been pinned to my arse. Not so much spot it as hear the stop-start, clip-clop sound of their cheap shoes on the cobbled alleyways as they tried to match the erratic pace of my own foot-steps. I might have called out to them, too, in mockery of their attempts to keep eyes on me but for the sense – the good sense, perhaps – that it might be best not to give them, and more impor-tant, the comrade-general, even the vaguest impression that I was anything but subordinate to him and his orders. The new Gunther had a much shorter spout than the old one, which was probably just as well; at least it was if I wanted to see Germany again. So I was surprised when I found my way back down to the esplanade blocked by two human bollards, each with absurdly blond, master-race hair of the kind that Himmler's favourite barber would have put up on his hero-haircut wall. In the shadows behind them was a smaller man with a leather eye patch, whom I half-recognized from a long time ago but failed to remember why, if only because the two human bollards were already busy gagging my mouth and tying my wrists in front of me.

'I'm sorry about this, Gunther,' said the man I'd half-recognized. 'It's a shame that we have to meet again in these circumstances but orders are orders. I don't have to tell you how that works. So nothing personal, see? But this is just how the comrade-general wants it.'

Even as he spoke the two blond bollards lifted me off my feet by the forearms and carried me to the end of the vaulted blind alley like a shop-window mannequin. Here a single street-light singed the evening air a sulphurous shade of yellow until someone killed it with a silenced pistol shot, but not before I saw the wooden beam that crossed the vaulted roof and the plastic noose that was dangling off it with obviously lethal intent. The realization that I was about to be hanged summarily in that dim, forgotten alley was enough to lend a last spasm of strength to my intoxicated limbs and I struggled hard to escape the iron grip of the two Stasi men, but to no avail. Like Christ ascending into heaven I felt myself already rising up from the cobbled ground to meet the noose, where another obliging Stasi man, wearing a grey suit and a hat, was holding on to a street lamp like Gene Kelly to help lasso my neck with it.

'That's it,' he said, when the lasso was in place. The Leipzig accent. The same man from the Hotel Ruhl, perhaps? Must have been. 'Okay, boys, you can let go now. I reckon this bastard will swing like a church bell.'

As he steadied the noose under my left ear I sucked a quick breath and the next second the two human bollards let me go. The plastic noose slipped tight, the world blurred like a bad pho-tograph, and I stopped breathing altogether. Desperately trying to find the uneven ground with the toecaps of my shoes, I only managed to turn myself around in space like the last ham in a butcher-shop window. I caught a brief glimpse of the Stasi men watching me hang and then pedalled some more on my invisible bicycle before deciding that it might go easier for me if I didn't struggle and, in truth, it didn't really hurt that much. It wasn't pain

I felt so much as a tremendous sense of pressure, as if my whole body might actually explode for want of an airhole. My tongue was like a baccarat pallet, it was so big, which was probably why most of it seemed to be outside my mouth, and my eyes were looking at my ears, as if trying to determine the source of the infernal racket I was hearing, which must have been the sound of the blood pounding in my head, of course. Most curious of all, I felt the actual presence of the little finger I had lost years before, in Munich, when another old comrade had cut it off with a hammer and chisel. It was as if all my being were suddenly concentrated in a part of my body that no longer even existed. And then 1949 and Munich and poor Vera Messmann seemed like ten minutes ago. The phantom finger swiftly spread and became a whole limb and then the rest of my body and I knew I was dying, which is when I pissed myself. I remember someone laughing and thinking that maybe, after all these years, I had it coming anyway and that I'd done pretty well to get this far without mishap. Then I was at the bottom of the cold Baltic Sea and I was swimming hard up from the wreck of the MV *Wilhelm Gustloff* to reach the undulating surface, only it was too far, and with bursting lungs I knew I wasn't going to make it, which is when I must have passed out.

I was still up in the air but looking down on myself as I was lying on the cobbles of the Rue Obscure. I seemed to be hovering above the straw-dog heads of all those Stasi men like a cloud of gas. They'd cut me down and were trying to loosen the ligature around my neck but they gave up when one of the agents produced a pair of wire cutters and clipped it along with some of the skin under my ear. Someone stamped on my chest, which was all the first aid I was about to receive from the Stasi, and I started to live again. One of them was applauding my performance on the high wire – his words, not mine – and now back in my body I turned over on my stomach to retch and drool onto the cobbles and then to haul some air painfully into my starved lungs. I touched something wet on my neck, which turned out to be my own blood, and heard myself mumble something with a tongue that was only just accustomed to being inside my mouth again.

'What's that?' The man with the wire cutters bent down to help me sit up, and I spoke again.

'Need a cigarette,' I said. 'Get my breath.' I put a hand on my chest and willed my heart to slow down a bit before it packed up altogether after the excitement of what I'd assumed were my last few minutes on earth, or near it anyway.

'You're a game one, uncle, I'll say that for you. He wants a nail, he says.' He laughed and fetched a packet of Hit Parades from his pocket and stabbed one between the lips of my still trembling mouth. 'There you go.'

I coughed some more, and then sucked hard when his lighter sparked into life. It was probably the best cigarette I'd ever tasted.

'I've heard of a last cigarette,' he said. 'But I never saw the condemned man smoke one *after* the execution. Tough old bastard, aren't you?'

'Less of the old,' I said. 'Feel like a new man.'

'Get him on his feet,' said another man. 'We'll walk him home.'

'Don't expect a kiss,' I croaked. 'Not after you've pulled me through the cocoa like that.'

But they'd made a pretty good job of hanging me half to death, and when I was on my feet I almost fainted and they had to catch me.

'I'll be all right,' I said. 'Give me a minute.' And then I puked, which was a shame after the nice steak I'd eaten with Mielke. But it's not every day you survive your own hanging.

They half-carried, half-walked me home and along the way the man I'd recognized before explained why they'd tried to make me hand in my spoon.

'Sorry about that, Gunther,' he said.

'Don't mention it.'

'But the boss feels that you weren't taking him seriously. He didn't like that. Reckons that the old Gunther would have put up a bit more resistance to the idea of killing your old girlfriend. And I have to say I agree with him. You always did have a lot of hair on your teeth. So for him not to see any – well, he thought you were taking the piss. We were going to just mix you up a bit but he said we should impress on you what would happen to you for real if you try to give him the fucking basket. Next time, our orders are that we leave you dangling. Or worse.'

'It's nice to hear a German voice again,' I said wearily – I could hardly put one foot in front of the other. 'Even if you are a bastard.'

'Aw, don't say that, Gunther. You'll hurt my feelings. We used to be friends, you and me.'

I started to shake my head but thought better of it when the pain kicked in. My neck felt like I'd had a chiropractic session with a gorilla. I began coughing again and paused to retch into the gutter once more.

'I don't remember. Then again, my brain's been starved of oxygen for several minutes so I can only just remember my own name, let alone yours.'

'You need some pain expeller,' said my old friend and, producing a little hip flask, he put it to my lips and let me take a substantial bite of the contents. It tasted like molten lava.

I winced and then uttered a short, staccato concerto of coughs. 'Christ, what is that stuff?'

'Gold Water. From Danzig. That's right.' The man grinned and nodded. 'Now you're getting there. You remember me, don't you, Gunther?'

In truth I still hadn't a clue who he was, but I smiled and nodded back at the man; there's nothing quite like being hanged to make you anxious to please, especially when it's your own hangman who's genially claiming your acquaintance.

'That's right. I used to drink this stuff when we were both cops at the Alex. You probably remember that, don't you? Man like you doesn't forget much, I reckon. I was your criminal assistant in '38 and '39. We worked a couple of big cases together. The Weisthor case. Remember that bastard? And Karl Flex, of course, in '39. Berchtesgaden? You certainly wouldn't have forgotten him. Or the cold air of Obersalzberg.'

'Sure, I remember you,' I said, tossing my cigarette away and still without a clue as to who he was. 'Thought you were dead. Everyone else is these days. People like you and me, anyway.'

'We're the last of them, you and me, true enough,' he said. 'From the old Alex. You should see it now, Gunther. I swear, you wouldn't recognize the place. Railway station's there, like before, and the Kaufhaus, but the old Police Praesidium is long gone. Like it was never there. The Ivans demolished it on account of the fact of it being a symbol of fascism. That and the Gestapo HQ on Prinz Albrechtstrasse. The whole area is just one enormous wind tunnel. These days the cops are headquartered over in Lichtenberg. With a smart new building on the way. All the modern conveniences. Canteen, showers, crèche. We've even got a sauna.'

'Nice for you. About the sauna.'

We reached my front door and someone helpfully fetched the keys from my pocket and let me into the flat. They followed me inside and, being policemen, had a good poke around in my stuff. Not that I cared. When you've nearly lost your life everything else seems of little importance. Besides, I was too busy looking at my cadaver's face in the bathroom mirror. I looked like a South American tree frog; the whites of my eyes were now completely red.

My anonymous friend watched me for a while and then, stroking a chin that was as long as a concert harp, he said, 'Don't worry, that's just a few burst blood vessels.'

'I'm a couple of centimetres taller, too, I think.'

'In a few days, you'll find the eyes are back to normal. You might want to wear some sunglasses until they calm down a bit. After all, you don't want to frighten anyone, do you?'

'It sounds like you've done this before. Half-hanged someone, I mean.'

He shrugged. 'It's lucky we've already got your picture on your new passport.'

'Isn't it?' I touched the livid crimson mark that the plastic cord had left on my neck; anyone would have been forgiven for thinking my head had been stitched onto my shoulders by Dr Mengele.

One of the other Stasi men was in my kitchen, making coffee. It was odd how the men who'd tried to hang me were now looking after me so carefully. Everyone was just obeying orders, of course. That's the German way, I guess.

'Hey, boss,' said one, to the man standing next to me in my bathroom. 'His phone's not working.'

'Sorry about that,' I said. 'Since no one ever calls me I hadn't noticed.'

'Well, go and find a pay phone.'

'Boss.'

'We're supposed to call the comrade-general and tell him how things went.'

'Tell the general I can't say it's been one of my best evenings,' I said. 'And be sure to thank him for dinner.'

The Stasi man went away. My friend handed me the hip flask again and I took another bite of Gold Water. There's real gold in that stuff. Tiny flecks of it. The gold doesn't make the stuff expensive, but it does make your tongue look semiprecious. They should give it to all men who are about to be hanged. It might brighten the proceedings up a bit.

'No initiative,' he said. 'You have to tell them what to do. By the numbers. Not like it was in our day, eh, Bernie?'

'Look, Fridolin, no offence,' I said. 'I mean, I'm not anxious to repeat tonight's experience, but I really haven't a fucking clue who you are. The chin I recognize. The bad skin, the leather eye patch – even the pimp moustache. But the rest of your ugly mug is a mystery to me.'

The man touched the top of his bald head self-consciously. 'Yeah, I've lost a lot of hair since last we met. But I had the eye patch. From the war.' He held out his hand affably. 'Friedrich Korsch.'

'Yeah, I remember now.' He was right; we had once been friends, or at least close colleagues. But all that was in the past. Call me petty but I tend to hold it against my friends when they try to kill me. Ignoring his hand, I said, 'When was that? The last time we met?'

'Nineteen forty-nine. I was working undercover for the MVD on an American newspaper in Munich. Remember? *Die Neue Zeitung*? You were looking for a war criminal called Warzok.'

'Was I?'

'I bought you lunch in the Osteria Bavaria.'

'Sure. I had pasta.'

'And before that you came to see me in '47, in Berlin, when you were looking to get in touch with Emil Becker's wife.'

'Right.'

'Whatever happened to him, anyway?'

'Becker? The Amis hanged him, in Vienna. For murder.'

'Ah.'

'What's more, they finished the job. Those cowboys weren't doing it for kicks like you guys. My kicks, that is. I never thought it would feel so good to have my feet firmly on the ground.'

'I feel bad about this,' said Korsch. 'But—'

'I know. You were only obeying orders. Trying to stay alive. Look, I understand. For men like you and me, it's an occupational hazard. But let's not pretend we were ever friends. That was a long time ago. Since then you've become a real pain in the neck. My neck. Which is the only one I've got. So how about you and your boys get the hell out of my place and we'll see each other at the train station in Nice, the day after tomorrow, like I agreed with the comrade-general?'

CHAPTER 4

October 1956

The Gare de Nice–Ville had a forged-steel rooftop, an impressive stone balcony, and a big ornate clock that belonged in purgatory's waiting room. Inside were several grand chandeliers: the place looked more like a Riviera casino than a railway station. Not that I'd visited many casinos. I was never much interested in games of chance, perhaps because most of my adult life had felt like a reckless gamble. All bets were certainly off as far as the next few days were concerned. It was hard to imagine working for the Stasi having anything but a negative outcome for Gunther. Undoubtedly they were planning to kill me as soon as the job in England was complete. Whatever Mielke said about working for him in Bonn or Hamburg after Anne French was safely silenced, it was on the cards that I would be the last loose end from the Hollis operation. Besides, my eyes looked like the two of diamonds, which isn't ever much of a card to play in any game. Because of them I was wearing sunglasses and I didn't even see the two Stasi men as I came through the station entrance. But they saw me. The GDR gives those boys radioactive carrots to help them see in the dark. They ushered me to the platform, where Friedrich Korsch was waiting beside the Blue Train that would take me to Paris.

'How are you?' he asked solicitously as I handed my bag to one of the Stasi men and let him carry it onto the carriage for me.

'Fine,' I said brightly.

'And the eyes?'

'Not nearly as bad as they look.'

'No hard feelings, I hope.'

I shrugged. 'What would be the point?'

'True. And at least you've got two. I lost one in Poland, during the war.'

'Besides, it's a long way to Paris. I assume you are coming to Paris. I hope you are. I haven't got any money.'

'All in here,' said Korsch, patting the breast pocket of his jacket. 'And yes, we are coming to Paris with you. In fact, we're going all the way to Calais.'

'Good,' I said. 'No, honestly, it will give us a chance to talk about old times.'

Korsch narrowed his eye, suspicious. 'I must say you've changed your tune since last we met.'

'When last we met I was not long hanged by the neck until I was almost dead, Friedrich. Jesus might have managed to forgive his executioners after an experience like that, but I'm a little less understanding. I thought I was history.'

'I suppose so.'

'You can suppose all you like. *But I know*. Frankly, I'm still a bit sore about it. Thus the silk foulard scarf and the sunglasses. God only knows what they'll make of me in the dining car. I'm a little old to be passing myself off as a Hollywood movie star.'

'By the way,' he asked. 'Where did you go yesterday? You gave my men the slip. We had an anxious morning before you came back again.'

'Were you watching me?'

'You know we were.'

'You should have said. Look, there was someone I needed to see. A woman I've been sleeping with. She lives in Cannes. I had to tell her I was going away for a few days and, well, I didn't want to do it on the phone. You can understand that, surely.' I shrugged. 'Besides, I didn't want you people knowing her name and address. For her own protection. After the other night I've no idea what you or your general are capable of.'

'Hmm.'

'Anyway, I was only gone for a few hours. I'm here now. So what's the problem?'

Korsch said nothing, just looked at me closely, but with my eyes hidden behind the dark glasses he had nothing to go on.

'What's her name?'

'I'm not going to tell you. Look, Friedrich, I need this job. The hotel's closed for the season now and I just have to get back to Germany. I've had it with France. The French drive me mad. If I have to stay here for another winter I'll go crazy.' That much was certainly true; and almost as soon as I said it I regretted my sincerity and did my best to cover it with some nonsense about wanting my revenge on Anne French. 'What's more, I really want to get even with this woman in England. So leave it, will you? I've told you all I'm going to tell you.'

'All right. But next time you're thinking of going somewhere, make sure you keep me informed.'

We climbed aboard the train, found our compartment, left some luggage there, and then the four of us went to the dining car to eat some breakfast. I was ravenously hungry. It seemed we all were.

'Karl Maria Weisthor?' I asked affably as the waiter brought us coffee. 'Or Wiligut. Or whatever the murdering bastard used to call himself when he wasn't convinced he was an ancient German king. Or even Wotan. I can't remember which. You mentioned him the other day and I meant to ask. Whatever became of him, do you know? After we collared him in '38? Last I heard he was living in Wörthersee.'

'He retired to Goslar,' said Korsch. 'Protected and cared for by the SS, of course. After the war the Allies permitted him to go to Salzburg. But that didn't work out. He died in Bad Arolsen, in

Hesse, in 1946, I think. Or was it 1947? Anyway, he's long dead. Good riddance, too.'

'Not exactly justice, is it?'

'You were a good detective. I learned a lot from you.'

'Stayed alive. That says something, under those circumstances.'

'It wasn't so easy, was it?'

'Not much has changed for me, I'm afraid.'

'You'll be around for quite a while yet. You're a survivor. I knew it then and I know it now.'

I smiled, but of course he was lying; old comrades or not, if Mielke told him to kill me he wouldn't hesitate. Just like in Villefranche.

'This is quite like old times, you and me, Friedrich. You remember that train we took to Nuremberg? To interview the local police chief about Streicher?'

'Almost twenty years ago. But yes, I remember.'

'That's what I was thinking of. Just came into my mind.' I nodded. 'You were a good cop, Friedrich. That's not so easy, either. Especially under those circumstances. With a boss like the one we had back then.'

'You mean that bastard Heydrich.'

'I do mean that bastard Heydrich.'

Not that Erich Mielke was any less of a bastard than Heydrich, but I thought it best to leave this left unsaid. We ordered breakfast and the train began to move, west towards Marseilles where it would turn north for Paris. One of the Stasi men groaned a little with pleasure as he tasted the coffee.

'This is good coffee,' he muttered as if he wasn't used to that. And he wasn't; in the GDR it wasn't just freedom and toleration that were in short supply, it was everything.

'Without good coffee and cigarettes there would be a revolution in this country,' I said. 'You know, maybe you should suggest that to the comrade-general, Friedrich. Exporting revolution might be easier that way.'

Korsch smiled a smile that was almost as thin as his pencil moustache.

'The regime must trust you a lot, Friedrich,' I said. 'You and your men. From what I hear it's not every East German who gets to travel abroad. At least, not without snagging his socks on the barbed wire, anyway.'

'We've all got families,' said Korsch. 'My first wife was killed in the war. I remarried about five years ago. And I have a daughter now. So you can see there's every reason to go home again. Frankly, I can't imagine living anywhere else than Berlin.'

'And the general? What's his incentive to go home again? He seems to enjoy things here even more than you do.'

Korsch shrugged. 'I really couldn't say.'

'No, perhaps it's best you don't.' I glanced sideways at our two Stasi breakfast companions. 'You never know who's listening.'

After breakfast, we went back to the compartment and talked some more. All things considered we were getting on very well now.

'Berchtesgaden,' said Korsch. 'That was a hell of a case, too.'

'I'm not likely to forget. And a hell of a place, too.'

'They should have given you a medal for the way you solved that murder.'

'They did. But I threw it away. The rest of the time I was only ever a few steps ahead of a firing squad.'

'I got a police medal towards the end of the war,' admitted Korsch. 'I think I still have it in a drawer somewhere in a nice blue velvet box.'

'Is that safe?'

'I'm a party member now. The SED, that is. Everyone who worked in Kripo was re-educated, of course. It's not for pride I keep the medal but to remind me of who and what I was.'

'Talking of which,' I said, 'you might like to remind me who I am, old friend. Or at least who I'm supposed to be. Just in case someone asks me. The sooner I get used to my new identity, the better, don't you think?'

Korsch removed a manila envelope from his jacket pocket and handed it to me. 'Passport, money, ticket for the Golden Arrow. There's a legend that comes with the passport. Your new name is Bertolt Gründgens.'

'He sounds like a communist.'

'Actually, you're a travelling salesman from Hamburg. You sell art books.'

'I don't know anything about art.'

'Nor does the real Bertolt Gründgens.'

'Where is he, by the way?'

'Doing ten years in the crystal coffin for publishing and distributing rabble-rousing propaganda against the state.'

The crystal coffin was what prisoners called Brandenburg Prison.

'We prefer to use real people if we can when we give someone a new identity. Somehow it gives the name a little more weight. In case someone decides to do some checking.'

'What about the thallium?' I asked, putting the envelope in the pocket of my trousers.

'Karl will hold on to it until we get to Calais,' Korsch explained, indicating one of the Stasi men. 'Thallium is easily absorbed through the skin, which means that certain precautions are required to handle it safely.'

'That suits me very well.' I took off my jacket and threw it onto the seat beside me. 'Aren't you warm in those wool suits of yours?'

'Yes, but ministry expenses don't run to a Riviera wardrobe,' said Korsch.

We talked more about Berchtesgaden and soon we'd almost forgotten the unpleasantness that had been the occasion for our renewed acquaintance. But just as often we were silent, smoking cigarettes and staring out the carriage window at the blue sea on our left. I'd become fond of the Mediterranean and wondered if I would ever see it again.

Once we were through Cannes the train started to pick up speed and within less than ninety minutes we were halfway to Marseilles. A few kilometres east of Saint-Raphaël I said I had to go to the toilet and Korsch ordered one of his men to accompany me.

'Frightened I'll get lost?' I said.

'Something like that.'

'It's a long way to Calais.'

'You'll survive.'

'I hope so. At least that's the general idea.'

The Stasi man followed me along the Blue Train to the washroom and it was about then, as the train entered the outskirts of Saint-Raphaël, that it started to slow. Fortunately they hadn't searched me back in Nice and, alone in the washroom, I removed a leather blackjack from my sock and slapped it against my hand. I'd confiscated the sap off a visitor to the hotel a month or two before and it was a beauty, nice and flexible, with a wrist lanyard and enough heft to give you some real striking power. But it's a nasty weapon – a villain's tool because it often relies on a smile or a friendly enquiry to catch its victim unawares. When I was a young uniformed cop in Weimar Berlin, we took a dim view of it whenever we caught some Fritz with one in his pocket because those things can kill you. Which is why sometimes we'd use the Fritz's own blackjack to save a bit of paperwork and dole out a bit of rough justice – on the knees and on the elbows, which is bad enough. I should know; I've been sapped a few times myself.

I kept it behind my back as, smiling, I emerged from the toilet a few minutes later with a cigarette in my other hand.

'Got a light?' I asked my escort. 'I left my jacket in the compartment.' My villain's smile faltered a little as I remembered he was Gene Kelly – the Leipzig man who'd lassoed my neck with the noose. This bastard had it coming, with all the strength in my shoulder.

'Sure,' said Gene, bracing himself against the carriage wall as the train began to brake noisily.

I put the cigarette between my lips expectantly as, glancing down at his jacket pocket, Gene started to retrieve his lighter. It was all the opportunity I needed and I had the blackjack swinging like a juggler's wooden club in the blink of an eye. He saw it before it hit him the first time, but only just. The spatula-shaped weapon struck the top of his straw-coloured head with the sound of a boot kicking a waterlogged football and Gene collapsed like a derelict chimney but, while he was still on his knees, I hit him hard a second time because I certainly didn't forget or forgive his laughter as he'd watched me hang in Villefranche. I felt a spasm of pain in my neck as I hit him but it was worth it. And when he was lying, unconscious – or worse, I didn't know and I didn't care – on the gently moving corridor floor, I took his gun. Then, as quickly as I was able, because he was heavy, I dragged him into the washroom and closed the door, after which I ran to the opposite end of the train, opened a door, and waited for it to stop at a signal, right next to the Corniche in Boulouris-sur-Mer, as I knew it would. Over the years I'd taken that train to Marseilles several times; just the previous day I'd sat in my car after I'd given the Stasi the slip for a few hours and watched the train come to a halt at the very same light.

I jumped off the train onto the side of the tracks, reached up, slammed the carriage door shut, and ran in the direction of the Avenue Beauséjour, where I'd parked my car. Running away is always a better plan than you think; just ask any criminal. It's only police who will say that running away doesn't solve anything; it certainly doesn't solve crimes or make arrests, that's for sure. Besides, running away was a much more appealing idea than poisoning some Englishwoman I'd once slept with, even if she was a bitch. I've got more than enough on my conscience as it is.

CHAPTER 5

October 1956

The train would not stop again until it reached Marseilles in a little over an hour's time. I breathed a sigh of relief, almost. There wasn't a cloud in the sky and it promised to be a perfect late October day. A few French families with children on half-term holidays were walking down to the beaches of Saint-Raphaël, careless, relaxed, laughing, in search of some autumn sun before the long winter, and I looked at them with envy, wishing for a life more ordinary and less interesting than mine. Nobody paid me any attention but just in time I remembered the gun under my waistband and pulled my already sweat-stained shirttail out of my trousers to hide it. Then I climbed a low wooden picket fence and crossed a piece of dry waste ground onto the Avenue Beauséjour. My heart was beating like a small animal's and if the bar on the corner had been open I might have gone in and swallowed a large one just to keep a lid on my fear, which was growing by the minute. When I was standing right next to my car I uttered a deep, desperate sigh and stared into the bright, prickling atoms of existence and asked myself if there was any real point to what I was doing. When you go on the run you have to believe it's worth it, but I really wasn't sure about that. Not anymore. I was already tired. I had no real energy left for life, let alone escape. My neck still ached and my eyes were two acid burns on my face. I just wanted to go to sleep for a hundred years, like Friedrich Barbarossa deep inside his mountain lair at Obersalzberg. Nobody cared if I lived or died – not Elisabeth, and certainly not Anne French – so why was I even doing this? I had never felt more alone in my life.

I lit a cigarette and tried to smoke some sense into those suddenly feeble organs that were shrinking inside my chest.

'Come on, Gunther,' I said. 'You've been in some tight spots before. All you have to do is get in that crappy French car and drive. Do you really want to give those Bolshevik swine the satisfaction of catching you now? Stop feeling sorry for yourself. Where's that Prussian backbone people are always on about? Only, you'd better hurry up. Because any minute now someone is going to go looking for you on that train and who knows what will happen when they find Gene Kelly reading the insides of his eyelids. So finish that cigarette, climb in that damn car, and get going before it's too late. Because if they find you, you know what's going to happen, don't you? Hanging is going to sound like a picnic next to thallium poisoning.'

A few minutes later I was driving west along the Route Nationale, towards Avignon. I give a good pep talk even though I say so myself. It was now decided: I was going to survive if only to spite those communist bastards. I had a full tank of fuel and a Citroën that had recently been in the workshop – a four-hundred-franc grease-and-oil change – so I was confident it wouldn't let me down, or as confident as you can be when it's not a German car. In the boot was some money, some warm clothes, another gun, and a few meagre possessions from my flat in Villefranche. For a while I kept glancing seawards, where I now had the moving Blue Train in sight on my left, hoping that none of the Stasi were looking out of the compartment window. The road I was on ran parallel to the track. This gave me an anxious half an hour's driving, but I had no choice about the route if I wanted to pick up the main highway north, along the Rhône. I didn't really relax until I reached Le Cannet-des-Maures, where the rail track and the DN7 went in different directions, and it was there I finally lost sight of the train altogether. But despite the head start I'd made on my countrymen I didn't fool myself that it would be beyond their abilities to find me again. Friedrich Korsch was smart, especially with a man like Erich Mielke driving him hard with the threat of what might happen to his wife and five-year-old daughter if he didn't catch me. Like the Gestapo before them, the Stasi had been finding Germans who didn't want to be found for almost a decade. That was what they were good at, perhaps the best in the world. The Mounties might have had a reputation for always getting their man but the Stasi always got the men and the women and the children, too, and when they got them they made them all suffer. There were thousands locked up in Berlin's notorious Stasi prison at Hohenschönhausen, not to mention several concentration camps once run by the SS. Almost certainly they would now proceed to fabricate some reason to force me out of France, whether I wanted to leave the country or not. I had a shrewd idea I might have seriously disabled Gene Kelly with the blackjack, in which case Korsch might finish the job, leaving me wanted for murder by the French police. So I knew I had to get out of France, and soon. Switzerland was more or less impossible to get into, of course, England and Holland were too far away, and Italy probably wasn't quite far enough. I might have tried Spain but for the fact that it was a Fascist country and I'd had enough of fascism to last me a lifetime. Besides, I'd already more or less made up my mind where I was going even before I'd jumped off the train. Where else could I go but Germany? Where better for a German to hide than among millions of other Germans? Nazi war criminals had been doing it for years. Only a few thousand had ever bothered to escape to South America, or ever needed to. Every year they seemed to find some wanted man who'd re-invented himself in some shithole no-account town like Rostock or Kassel. Once I was across the French border I could find a small town in Germany and disappear for good. Not being anyone particularly important, that had to be a reasonable possibility. Once I was in West Germany, I might get by without either one of my passports. I'd stand a better chance there than almost anywhere. But I bitterly regretted telling Korsch how much I wanted to return home, even if it had been done to convince him we were friends again; he wasn't stupid and almost certainly he would put himself in my shoes and arrive at the same conclusions I had.

Where else could Gunther go but the Federal Republic? If he stays in France the French police will find him for us and then, when he's in custody in some small provincial town, we'll poison him with thallium just like we'll poison Anne French. There is only West Germany for Bernhard Gunther. He's been chased out of almost everywhere else.

I put my foot down hard on the accelerator in an attempt to gain some time because every minute was precious now. As soon as he was at the station in Marseilles, Friedrich Korsch would telephone Erich Mielke at the Hotel Ruhl in Nice and the comrade-general would mobilize every one of those Stasi agents working undercover in France and Germany to start looking for me all along the border. They had my picture, they had the registration number of my car, and they had the almost limitless resources of the Ministry of State Security, not to mention a capacity for ruthless efficiency that would have been the envy of Himmler or Ernst Kaltenbrunner.

Not that I was without resources myself; as a detective with the Berlin Kripo I'd learned a thing or two about evading the law. Any cop will tell you that being one is excellent training for how to be a fugitive. Which is exactly what I was. Until a few days ago I'd been nothing more than a steady source of simple information wearing a tail coat behind the concierge's desk at the Grand Hôtel in Cap Ferrat. I wondered what some of the guests would have thought if they'd seen me slugging a Stasi agent with a blackjack. The thought of what Gene's friends might do if ever they caught up with me made me step harder on the accelerator and I sped north at a hundred kilometres an hour, until the memory of the sound of his thick skull receiving the hard blow began to fade a little. Perhaps he would live after all. Perhaps we both would.

I love driving, but France is a big country and its endless roads hold no pleasure for me. Driving is fine if you're along-side Grace Kelly and in possession of a nice blue convertible Jaguar on a picturesque mountain road with a picnic basket in the boot. But for most people, motoring in France is dull, and the only thing that stops it from being routine are the French, who are among the worst drivers in Europe. Not without some justification, we used to joke that there were more Frenchmen killed by bad motorists during the fall of France in the summer of 1940 – as the French desperately tried to escape the German advance – than there were by the Wehrmacht. For this reason I tried to keep my mind on my driving but, in almost inverse proportion to the relentless monotony of the road ahead, my mind soon began to wander like a lost albatross. It's said that the prospect of being hanged concentrates a man's mind won-derfully and I'm sure that's true; however, I'm here to report that the actual experience of being hanged, and the lack of oxygen that a noose tightening against the two carotid arteries occasions, affects a man's thinking in all sorts of adverse ways. It had certainly affected mine. Perhaps that was Mielke's inten-tion: to make me more dumbly compliant. If so, it hadn't worked. Dumb compliance was never my strong suit. My head was full of mist and clouded with what had been long for-gotten, as if the present was now obfuscated by the past. But that wasn't quite it, either. No, it was more like everything below my line of sight was shrouded in mist and, beyond the desire to return to Germany, I could not see where I had to go and what I had to do. It was as if I were the man in that pic-ture by Caspar David Friedrich and I was a wanderer above a sea of fog – insignificant, deracinated, uncertain of the future, contemplating the futility of it all, and, perhaps, the possibility of self-destruction.

Old and once familiar faces reappeared in the far distance. Snatches of Wagnerian music echoed between half-glimpsed mountaintops. There were smells and fragments of conversation. Women I'd once known: Inge Lorenz and Hildegard Steininger, Gerdy Troost. My old partner Bruno Stahlecker. My mother. But, gradually, as I left the French Riviera behind and headed determinedly north towards West Germany, I started to recall in detail what I'd been prompted to remember by Korsch. It was all his fault – reminiscing like that, in what was obviously, in retrospect, an attempt to put me off my guard. He'd been a decent cop back then. We both were. I thought about the two cases we'd worked together after I'd been drafted back into Kripo on Heydrich's orders. The second of these cases had been even stranger than the first and I was obliged to investigate just a few months before Hitler invaded Poland. Clearly, as if it were yesterday, I remembered a dark and wintry night in early April 1939, and being driven halfway across Germany in the general's own Mercedes; I remembered Berchtesgaden, and Obersalzberg, and the Berghof, and the Kehlstein; I remembered Martin Bormann and Gerdy Troost and Karl Brandt and Hermann Kaspel and Karl Flex; and I remembered the Schlossberg Caves and Prussian blue. But most of all I remembered being almost twenty years younger and possessed of a sense of decency and honour I now found almost quaint. For a while back there, I think I sincerely believed I was the only honest man I knew.

CHAPTER 6

April 1939

'It's high time they arrested you, Gunther,' said a sharp voice from on high. 'There's no place for lefties like you in this city's police force.'

I looked up and caught sight of a familiar uniformed figure descending the wide stone stairs like a late arrival at the Leader's Ball; but if Heidi Hobbin had ever owned a glass slipper she'd have taken it off and stuck the heel in my eye. There weren't many women in the Berlin police force: Elfriede Dinger – who subsequently married Ernst Gennat, not long before he died – and Police Commissioner Heidi Hobbin, who was also known as Heidi the Horrible, but not because she was ugly – she was actually quite a looker – it was just that she enjoyed bossing men around, mercilessly. At least one of them must have enjoyed it, too, because I later learned that Heidi was the mistress of Kripo boss Arthur Nebe. Dominant women: that's one particular perversion I've never really understood.

'I hope you're taking him straight to Dachau,' Heidi told the two Gestapo men who were escorting me down the back stairs towards the Police Praesidium's Dircksenstrasse exit. She was accompanied by an ambitious young district court councillor, a friend of mine from the Ministry of Justice, called Max Merten. 'It's the very least that he deserves.'

After Hitler became the chancellor of Germany in January

1933, I was never what you'd call popular around the Alex. When Bernhard Weiss was purged from the Kripo because he was a Jew it was inevitable that the men from his Murder Commission were always going to be regarded with suspicion by our new Nazi bosses – especially if they were centre-left SPD supporters like me. All the same, hers was an easy mistake to have made; even with the Gestapo on their best behaviour and summoning me politely – almost – on Reinhard Heydrich's orders, to their headquarters, they still managed to give the appearance of two men making an arrest. But Heidi didn't know this and was still labouring under the misapprehension that I was being taken into custody. Considering she was supposed to be a cop, she never was very observant.

Enjoying the prospect of her imminent disappointment, I stopped and touched the brim of my hat. 'Kind of you to say so, ma'am,' I said.

Heidi's eyes narrowed as she regarded me as if I were an unflushed lavatory. Max Merten tipped his bowler hat politely.

'You're a troublemaker, Gunther,' said Heidi. 'And you always have been, with your smart remarks. Quite frankly I have no idea why Heydrich and Nebe believed they needed you back at the Alex in the first place.'

'Someone has to do the thinking around here now that the police dogs have been sacked.'

Merten grinned. It was a joke I'd heard him make on more than one occasion.

'That's exactly the kind of remark I'm talking about. And which I for one will certainly not miss.'

'Will you tell the commissioner the good news?' I asked one of the Gestapo men. 'Or shall I?'

'Commissar Gunther isn't actually under arrest,' said one of the Gestapo men.

I smiled. 'You hear that?'

'What do you mean, "not actually"?'

'General Heydrich has summoned him to an urgent meeting in his office at Prinz Albrechtstrasse.'

Heidi's face fell. 'What about?' she asked.

'I'm afraid I can't tell you that,' said the Gestapo man. 'Now, if you'll excuse us, Commissioner. We don't have time for this. The general doesn't like to be kept waiting.'

'That's right,' I said, and looking at my watch, I tapped it urgently. 'We really don't have time for this. I've got an important meeting to attend. With the general. Perhaps later, if there's time, I'll drop by your office and tell you what it was he wanted to consult me about. But only if Heydrich thinks it appropriate. You know what he's like about security and confidentiality. Then again, perhaps you don't. It's not everyone he takes into his confidence. By the way, Commissioner Hobbin, where is your office? I've forgotten.'

The Gestapo glanced at each other and tried, without success, to suppress a grin. Despite all evidence to the contrary, they had a sense of humour, albeit a dark one, and this was the sort of status-conscious joke that any power-minded Nazi – which was more or less all of them – could understand and appreciate. The young magistrate – he couldn't have been much more than thirty – Max Merten, was trying harder at not smiling. I winked at him. I liked Max; he was from Berlin-Lichterfelde and at one stage he'd been considering a career in the police, until I talked him out of it.

Meanwhile Heidi Hobbin made a small, tight fist that strongly resembled her pugnacious personality, turned abruptly away, and then started back up the stairs and, reasoning that my laughter would only make her even more angry, I let out a loud guffaw and was pleased to hear my escorts do the same.

'Must be nice, working for Heydrich,' said one, slapping me on the back by way of congratulation.

'Yes,' said his partner, 'even the bosses have to go careful with you, eh? You can tell them to go where the pepper grows, right?'

I smiled uncomfortably and followed them both down to the side door of the Alex. I wouldn't ever have described the secret security service boss as my friend. Men such as Heydrich didn't have friends; they had functionaries, and sometimes myrmidons, such as I was, for I had little doubt that Heydrich had another unpleasant job that he thought only Bernhard Gunther could do. No one ever had to go more carefully in Germany than former SPD members who now worked for Heydrich – especially now, given the recent invasion of what remained of Czechoslovakia after Munich, which had made another war seem almost inevitable.

Outside, on Dircksenstrasse, I lit my last cigarette and hurried into the backseat of a waiting Mercedes. The morning air was freezing due to a fall of spring snow but the car was warm, which was just as well as I'd forgotten my coat, such was the urgency of the summons; one moment I'd been staring out of my corner office window at the model train set below that was Alexanderplatz and the next – with no explanations needed or supplied – I was sitting in the back of the car, heading west along Unter den Linden and rehearsing a form of words that might enable me to body-swerve the particular job Heydrich had in mind for me. I was just a bit too scrupulous and questioning to make a good myrmidon. Intransigence was futile, of course; like Achilles, the general was not someone who could easily be deflected. You might just as well have tried to fend off a Greek hero's javelin with a Meissen dinner plate.

Unter den Linden was choked with traffic and pedestrians and there were even a few cars parked in front of the government buildings on Wilhelmstrasse, but Prinz Albrechtstrasse was always the quietest street in Berlin and for much the same reason that the remoter parts of the Carpathian Mountains were avoided by all sensible Transylvanians. Like Castle Dracula, number 8 Prinz Albrechtstrasse contained its own pale-faced prince of darkness, and whenever I approached the neo-baroque entrance I couldn't help but think that the two naked ladies who adorned the broken segmental pediment were actually a pair of vampire sisters married to Heydrich who wandered the building at night in search of some clothes and a good meal.

Inside, the huge building was all high-arched windows, vaulted ceilings, stone balustrades, swastikas, busts of the Antichrist, and bare of much in the way of furniture and human feelings. A few wooden seats were arranged along the plain white walls as in a railway station, and the only sounds were whispered voices, footsteps hurrying through the marble-floored corridors, and the reverberating echo of an occasional door slammed hard on hope in some remote corner of eternity. No one but Dante and perhaps Virgil went into that place of woe without wondering if they would ever come out again.

Located on the second floor of the building, Heydrich's office was not much bigger than my flat. The room was all grand space, cold white simplicity and neat order – more like a parade ground than an office; with no discernible personal touches, it had the quality of making Nazism seem clean and stainless and, in my eyes at least, summed up the moral void that lay at the heart of the new Germany. There was a thick, grey carpet on the polished wooden floor, some decorative inlaid pillars, several high windows, and a bespoke rolltop desk that was home to a regiment of rubber stamps and a switchboard. Behind the desk were two sets of tall double doors and between these a half-empty bookcase on which stood an empty goldfish bowl. Immediately above the goldfish bowl was a framed photograph of Himmler, almost as if the bespectacled Reichsführer-SS was himself a strange species of creature that could live in and out of water. Which is another word for a reptile. Beside a large map of Germany on the wall was an arrangement of leather sofas and armchairs and it was on one of these that I found the general with three other officers, including his adjutant, Hans-Hendrik Neumann, Kripo boss Arthur Nebe, and Nebe's deputy, Paul Werner – a

beetle-browed state prosecutor from Heidelberg who hated me
no less than Heidi Hobbin hated me. Heydrich and Nebe were
both possessed of stronger profiles, but while Heydrich's was
the kind of head that belonged on a banknote, Arthur Nebe's
belonged in a pawnshop. Nazi racial experts were keen on using
calipers to measure noses to scientifically determine Jewishness
and I wasn't the only cop at the Alex who wondered if either
man had ever submitted himself to a test and if so, what the
result had been. Hans-Hendrik Neumann looked like a cut-price
Heydrich. With his fair hair and high forehead, he possessed an
interesting nose that was sharp but still had some growing up
to do before it could ever match his master's beaky schnozz.

No one got up from their seats and no one but me gave the
Hitler salute, which Nebe must have especially enjoyed, given
how long we'd known and distrusted each other. As usual, giving
the salute made me feel like a hypocrite but hypocrisy has its
positive side – what Darwin or one of his early followers would
have called survival of the fittest.

'Gunther, at last you're here,' said Heydrich. 'Sit down, please.'

'Thank you, sir. And may I say, General, what a great pleasure
it is to see you again. I've missed these little talks we used to
have.'

Heydrich grinned, almost enjoying my insolence.

'Gentlemen, I must confess that there are times when I do
believe in a providence that protects idiots, drunkards, children,
and Bernhard Gunther.'

'I think you and I might just be the directors of that providence, sir,' said Nebe. 'If it wasn't for us, this man would have
bitten the grass by now.'

'Yes, perhaps you're right, Arthur. But I can always use a useful
man, and he's nothing if not that. In fact, I think his greatest
virtue is his usefulness.' Heydrich stared up at me as if he was
genuinely looking for an answer. 'Why is that, do you think?'

'Are you asking me, sir?' I sat down and glanced at the silver cigarette box on the coffee table in front of us. I was dying for a smoke. Nerves, I suppose. Heydrich could do that to you. Two minutes in his company and he was already on my cake.

'Yes. I rather think I am.' He shrugged. 'Go ahead. You can speak quite freely.'

'Well, I think that sometimes a harmful truth is better than a useful lie.'

Heydrich laughed. 'You're right. Arthur, we *are* the directors of providence where this fellow is concerned.' Heydrich flipped open the lid of the silver cigarette box. 'Do smoke, Gunther, please; I insist. I like to encourage a man's vices. Especially yours. I have a feeling that one day they might be even more useful than your virtues. In fact, I'm sure of it. Turning you into my stooge is going to be one of my long-term projects.'

CHAPTER 7

April 1939

I took a cigarette from the silver box, fired it up, crossed my legs, and directed my smoke at the moldings on the high ceiling of Heydrich's office. I'd said enough for the moment. When you sit down with the devil it's wise not to insult him more than you have to. The devil was wearing a uniform that was the same colour as his heart: black. So were the others. It was only me who was wearing a lounge suit, which helped to persuade me that somehow I was different from them – better, perhaps. It was only later on, in the war, that I formed the conclusion that perhaps I wasn't much better after all. For me, prudence and good intentions always seemed to take precedence over conscience.

'Correctly, you assume a certain licence because of your presence here in my office,' said Heydrich. 'I daresay you have already formed the conclusion that you are about to be useful to me again.'

'It crossed my mind.'

'I wouldn't make too much of that, Gunther. I find I have a very short memory where favours are concerned.'

Heydrich's voice was quite high-pitched for so large a man, almost as if his riding breeches were too tight.

'I've found it's generally wise to forget quite a bit I used to believe was important, myself, General. In fact, more or less everything I used to believe in, now I come to think about it.'

Heydrich smiled his thinnest smile, which was almost as narrow as his pale blue eyes. Otherwise his long face remained so devoid of expression he resembled a burn victim at the Charité.

'You'll have to forget quite a bit after this job, Gunther. Almost everything. With the exception of the men in this room you'll be forbidden to discuss this case with anyone. Yes, I think we must now call this a case. Don't you agree, Arthur?'

'Yes, sir. I do. After all, a crime has been committed. A murder. A very uncommon kind of murder, given the place where it has occurred and the absolute importance of the person to whom he will be reporting.'

'Oh? Who's that?' I asked.

'No less a figure than the Leader's deputy chief of staff, Martin Bormann himself,' said Nebe.

'Martin Bormann, eh? Can't say that I've heard of him. But I assume he must be someone important, given the man he works for.'

'Please don't allow that ignorance to interfere with your appreciation of the paramount importance of this case,' said Heydrich. 'Bormann may not occupy any governmental position, but his close proximity to the Leader makes him one of the most powerful men in Germany. He has asked me to send him my best detective. And since Ernst Gennat is not well enough to travel any distance, right now that would appear to be you.'

I nodded. My old mentor, Gennat, had cancer and was rumoured to have less than six months to live although, given my present situation, that was beginning to seem like a long time; Heydrich was not someone who had a tolerance of failure. Once before, he'd sent me to Dachau, and he could easily do it again. It was time for my body-swerve. 'What about Georg Heuser?' I asked. 'Aren't you forgetting him? He's a good detective. And altogether better qualified than I am. For one thing, he's a Party member.'

'Yes, he is a good detective,' agreed Nebe. 'But right now

Heuser has some explaining to do about those qualifications he's claimed. Something to do with pretending to have a PhD in law.'

'Really?' I tried to tamp down a smile. I was one of the few detectives at the Alex who was not a doctor of law, and so this news was rather satisfying to someone who only had his *Abitur*. 'You mean he's not a doctor after all?'

'Yes, I thought that would please you, Gunther. He's suspended, pending an inquiry.'

'That is a pity, sir.'

'We could hardly send a man like that to Martin Bormann,' said Nebe.

'Of course, I could send Werner here,' said Heydrich. 'It's true his skills lie more in crime prevention than in detection. But I shouldn't like to lose him if he screws this up. The plain fact of the matter is you're expendable and you know it. Werner is not. He's essential to the development of radical criminology in the new Germany.'

'Since you put it like that, sir, I can see your point.' I looked at Werner and nodded. He was the same rank as me – a commissar, which meant I could speak to him with greater licence. 'I think I read your paper, Paul. Juvenile delinquency as the product of criminal heredity – wasn't that your last offering?'

Werner removed the cigarette from his mouth and smiled. With his dark, shifty eyes, swarthy features, and trophy-handle ears, he looked no less criminal than almost anyone I'd ever arrested.

'So you do read these things in the Murder Commission? I'm surprised. Actually, I'm surprised you read anything at all.'

'Sure I do. Your papers on criminology are essential reading. Only, I seem to remember that most of the juvenile delinquents you identified were Gypsies, not ethnic Germans.'

'And you disagree with that?'

'Maybe.'

'On what basis?'

'It's not been my experience, that's all. Berlin criminals come in all shades and sizes. In my eyes, poverty and ignorance always seemed to be a better explanation for the reason why one Fritz picks the pocket of another than his race, or how big his nose might be. Besides, you look like you've got a touch of the Gypsy yourself, Paul. How about it? You a Sinti?'

Werner kept smiling, but only on the outside. He was from Offenburg, which is a city in Baden-Württemberg on the French border, famous for burning witches and the home of a notorious metal chair with spikes that could be heated until it was hot. He had the face of a Swabian witch finder and I suspect he'd have cheerfully seen me burned to death.

'I'm just joking.' I looked at Heydrich. 'We're just swelling necks here, like a couple of tough guys. I know he's not a Sinti. He's a smart fellow. I know he is. You've got a doctorate, too, haven't you, Paul?'

'Keep talking, Gunther,' said Werner. 'One day you'll talk yourself onto the guillotine at Plötzensee.'

'He's right, of course,' said Heydrich. 'You're an insolent fellow, Gunther. But as it happens this is all to the good. Your independent spirit bespeaks a certain resilience that will come in handy here. You see, there's another reason Bormann wants you in preference to Werner, or even Arthur here. Since you've never been a Party member he believes that you're not anyone's man, and more importantly, that you're not my man. Only, please don't make that mistake yourself, Gunther. I own you. Like your last name was Faust and mine was Mephisto.'

I let that one go; there was no arguing with Heydrich's fat pants but it was still comforting to believe that God in his grace might yet persuade a few angels to interfere on my behalf.

'Anything that you can find out about that bastard while you're in Obersalzberg, I want to know about it.'

'I take it you mean the Leader's deputy chief of staff.'

'He's a megalomaniac,' said Heydrich.

I didn't offer an opinion on that one. I'd already let my mouth run a bit too much.

'In particular I want you to see if there's any truth in an intriguing rumour here in Berlin that he's being blackmailed by his own brother, Albert. Albert Bormann is adjutant to Adolf Hitler and chief of the Leader's Chancellery in Obersalzberg. As such he's almost as powerful down there as Martin Bormann himself.'

'Is that where I'm going sir? Obersalzberg?'

'Yes.'

'That'll be nice. I could use a little Alpine air.'

'You're not going there for a holiday, Gunther.'

'No, sir.'

'Any opportunity to get some dirt on that man – on either man – you take it. You're not just a detective while you're there, you're my spy. Is that clear? When you're there you'll think that yours is a choice between pestilence and cholera. But it isn't. You're *my* Fritz, not Bormann's.'

'Yes, sir.'

'And in case you might still be labouring under the misapprehension that your miserable soul is still your own, then you might like to know that the police in Hannover are investigating the discovery of a body in a forest near Hamelin. Remind me of the details, Arthur.'

'He was a fellow called Kindermann – a doctor who ran a private clinic in Wannsee, and who was a colleague of our mutual friend Karl Maria Weisthor. It seems he was shot several times.'

'Now, given Kindermann's connection to Weisthor, I daresay he deserved it,' added Heydrich. 'But all the same, it might be awkward if you were to have to explain your own acquaintance with this man to the police in Hannover.'

'When am I leaving?' I asked brightly.

'As soon as our meeting is concluded,' said Heydrich. 'One of my men has already been to your apartment and packed some of your personal things. There's a car waiting downstairs to drive you straight to Bavaria. My own car. It's faster. You should be there well before midnight.'

'So what's it all about, sir? You mentioned a murder. Who's dead? I assume it's nobody important, otherwise we'd have heard the bad news on the radio this morning.'

'I'm not sure, exactly. Bormann wasn't too clear about that on the telephone when we spoke earlier. But you're right, it was nobody important, thank God. A local civil engineer. No, it's *where* this person was murdered that makes it important. The victim was shot with a rifle on the terrace of Hitler's private home in Obersalzberg. The Berghof. The killer, who remains at large, must surely have been aware that the Leader was making a speech in Berlin last night. Which means it's highly unlikely that this could have been a botched attempt to assassinate Adolf Hitler. But naturally Bormann is worried how this will make him look in the Leader's eyes. The very fact that *anyone* could be shot at Hitler's own home away from home – the one place where he can go to relax and retreat from the cares of state – this will be a matter of great concern to everyone who has anything to do with the Leader's security, which is why Bormann wants this killer apprehended as soon as possible.

'It's unthinkable that the Leader could go there until the assassin has been caught. If he's not caught, this might even cost Bormann his job. Either way it's a situation which is good for the SD and Kripo. If the murderer isn't caught, then Martin Bormann will very likely be fired by Hitler, which will please Himmler enormously; and if he is caught, then Bormann will be substantially in my debt.'

'It's comforting to know that I can't fail, sir,' I said.

'Let me make one thing quite clear to you, Gunther: Obersalzberg is Martin Bormann's domain. He controls everything there. But as a detective given the power to ask questions on Hitler's mountain, you have a perfect opportunity to turn over a few rocks and see what crawls out from underneath. And you will certainly have failed me if you don't come back here with some dirt on a stick about Martin Bormann. Clear?'

'Clear. How much time do I have?'

'Apparently Hitler plans to visit the Berghof immediately after his birthday,' said Nebe. 'So there's no time to lose.'

'Remind me,' I said. 'When is that? I'm not very good at remembering birthdays.'

'The twentieth of April,' said Nebe patiently.

'What about the local police? Gestapo? Will I be working with them? And if so, who's in charge? Me or them?'

'The local leather tops have not been informed. For obvious reasons Bormann wants this kept out of the newspapers. You'll be in sole charge of the investigation. And you'll report directly to Bormann. At least in principle.'

'I see.'

'Be careful of him,' said Heydrich. 'He's not half as dumb as he looks. Don't trust the telephones at the Berghof. Life down there isn't a place for riding miniature ponies. Quite possibly Bormann's men will be listening to every word you say. I know because it was my men who installed the secret microphones in several of the rooms and all of the guest houses. The telex you can probably rely on; telegrams, too, but not the telephones. Neumann here will accompany you in the car as far as Munich. He'll explain precisely how you can stay in touch with me. But I already have a spy in the RSD at Obersalzberg. Hermann Kaspel. He's a good man. Just not very good at finding out things he shouldn't know about. Unlike you. Anyway, I've provided you with a letter of introduction, signed by me. The letter states that he's to assist you in every way he can.'

I knew Hermann Kaspel. In 1932, I'd helped to get him fired from the police when I found out that he'd been leading an SA troop during his off-duty hours; this after a police sergeant called

Friedrich Kuhfeld was murdered by Nazi thugs. We hadn't been sending each other any Christmas cards since then.

'I've heard of the SD, sir,' I confessed. 'But I'm not sure what the RSD is.'

'The Leader's personal security guard. Affiliated to the SD but not under my command. They report directly to Himmler.'

'I'd like to take along my own criminal assistant at the Alex, sir. Friedrich Korsch. He's a good man. You might remember that he was very helpful with the Weisthor case last November. If solving this case is as urgent as you say it is, then I might have need of a good criminal assistant. Not to mention someone I can trust. Hermann Kaspel and I have a little bit of ancient history that goes back to his time as a Schupoman, before the government of von Papen. In 1932, he was the leader of a Nazi cell at Station 87 here in Berlin, which was a matter about which we disagreed.'

'Why does that not surprise me?' said Heydrich. 'But you can rest assured. Whatever feelings of antipathy you might have for each other, Kaspel will carry out my instructions to the letter.'

'All the same, sir. Korsch is a proper detective. A bull with a good head on his shoulders. And two heads are better than one with an urgent case like this.'

He glanced at Nebe who nodded back. 'I know Korsch,' said Nebe. 'He's a bit of a thug, but still, a Party member. Might make inspector one day. But he'll never make commissar.'

'Bormann won't like it,' said Heydrich, 'and you may have to persuade the deputy chief of staff to let you keep the man, but take him, yes.'

'One more thing, sir,' I said. 'Money. I might need some. I know fear is the Gestapo's proven method. But in my experience a bit of cash works better than the Offenburg hot stool. It helps to loosen tongues when people get a smell of it. Especially when you're trying to work discreetly. Besides, it's easier to carry money about than instruments of torture.'

Heydrich nodded. 'All right, but I want receipts. Lots of receipts. And names. If you bribe anyone I shall want to know who, so I can use them again.'

'Of course.'

Heydrich looked at Nebe. 'Is there anything else we need to tell him, Arthur?'

'Yes. Kaltenbrunner.'

'Oh yes. Ernst Kaltenbrunner. We mustn't forget him.'

I shook my head. This was another name I hadn't heard before.

'Nominally at least, he's the head of the SS and the police in Austria,' explained Nebe. 'He's also a member of the Reichstag. It seems he has a weekend home in Berchtesgaden, just down the hill from Obersalzberg. Neumann will provide you with the address.'

'It's nothing more than a crude attempt to put himself within the Leader's inner circle,' said Heydrich. 'Nevertheless I should like to know more about what that lard-assed subaltern is up to. Let me explain. Until recently Kaltenbrunner and some others were trying to create an island of governmental autonomy in Austria. That could not be allowed. Austria is soon to disappear altogether as a political concept. Practically, all key police functions have already been brought under the control of this office. Two men loyal to me – Franz Huber and Friedrich Polte – have been appointed as Gestapo and SD leaders in Vienna, but it remains doubtful if Kaltenbrunner has quite accepted this new administrative reality. In fact, I'm more or less certain he hasn't. So his influence in Austria requires that he be subject to constant scrutiny. Even when he's in Germany.'

'I think I get the picture. You want some dirt on him, too. If there is any.'

'There is,' said Heydrich. 'There most certainly is.'

'Kaltenbrunner has a wife,' explained Nebe. 'Elisabeth.'

'That doesn't sound so dirty.'

'He also enjoys the favours of two aristocratic Upper Austrian women.'

'Ah.'

'One of them is the Countess Gisela von Westarp,' said Heydrich. 'It's uncertain if any of their liaisons take place at the house in Berchtesgaden but if they do it's certain the Leader would take a very dim view of this. Which is why I want to know about it. Hitler places great store on family values and on the personal morality of senior Party men. Find out if this Gisela von Westarp is ever at the house in Berchtesgaden. Also if any other women go there. Their names. It shouldn't be beyond your powers of investigation. That's how you used to make a living, isn't it? As a private detective, one of those shabby little men who snoop around hotel corridors and peer through keyholes looking for evidence of adultery.'

'In retrospect it doesn't seem so shabby,' I said. 'As a matter of fact I used to quite enjoy snooping around hotel corridors. Especially the good hotels, like the Adlon, where there are thick carpets. It's easier on the feet than goose-stepping across a parade ground. And there's always a bar close at hand.'

'Then this should be easy for you. And now you may go.'

I grinned and got to my feet.

'Something amusing you?' asked Heydrich.

'It was only something Goethe once said. That everything is hard before it's easy.' I got up and walked to the door but not before nodding Paul Werner's way. 'I might not have a doctorate. A real one. But I do read, Paul. I do read.'

CHAPTER 8

April 1939

It was 750 kilometres from Berlin to Berchtesgaden, but in the rear seat of Heydrich's own car – a shiny black Mercedes 770K – with an SS-monogrammed cashmere rug across my knees, I hardly noticed either the distance or the cold. The car was as big as a U-boat and almost as powerful. The eight-cylinder supercharged engine throbbed like rush hour at Potsdamer Platz and even with snow on the autobahn the Mercedes just rolled up the road; it felt as if I were riding into the after-life Hall of the Slain with a chorus line of Valkyries, only in rather finer style. I'm not sure that Mercedes has ever made a better automobile. Certainly never one as big or as comfortable. A couple of hours in that limousine and I was ready to take charge of Germany myself. In the front seat, behind the enormous steering wheel, sat Heydrich's Easter Island statue of a driver, and next to him Friedrich Korsch, my criminal assistant from the Alex. Alongside me in the back of the car was Hans-Hendrik Neumann, Heydrich's pointy-faced adjutant. The rear seats were more like a pair of leather armchairs in the Herrenklub and during some of the journey I dozed off. We made Schkeuditz, just west of Leipzig in under two hours – which seemed remarkable to me – and Bayreuth in less than four, but with darkness falling and more than four hundred kilometres still to go, we were obliged to stop and refuel in

Pegnitz, north of Nuremberg. Filling the tanks of KMS *Bismarck* would have been quicker and cheaper . . .

1956

I could have used a big, powerful car like the Mercedes 770K on my escape through France. Certainly I could have used a nap. The Citroën was an 11 CV Traction Avant – which is French for an underpowered front-wheel-drive rust bucket; the eleven probably referred to the amount of horsepower the thing had. It was uncomfortable and slow and, driving it, I needed all my wits about me. After six hours behind the wheel I was exhausted; my neck and eyes hurt and I had a head that ached worse than Ptolemy's botched craniotomy. I wasn't any further north than Mâcon but I knew I was going to have to stop and take a rest, and thinking it might be better if I stayed under the radar, avoiding all hotels and even pensions, I pulled into a jolly-looking camping site. There are two million campers in France, a large proportion of whom are motorists. I had neither a tent nor a caravan but this hardly seemed to matter since I was planning to sleep in the car and, in the morning, to use the showers and cafeteria in that order. What I wouldn't have given for a hot bath and a dinner at the Hotel Ruhl. But when I offered the individual in the site office – a man with hooded eyes and a perfumer's fastidious nose – the fifty-francs charge for the space he asked to see my camping licence and I was reluctantly obliged to confess that I was unaware that such a thing even existed.

'I'm afraid it is a legal requirement, monsieur.'

'I can't camp here without one?'

'You can't camp anywhere without such a licence, monsieur. Not in France, anyway. It was created to give people insurance against damage caused to any third party by camping. Up to twenty-five million francs for damages arising from fire, and five million for damages arising from accident.'

'So wait, I don't need insurance to drive a car in France but do need it to pitch a tent?'

'That's correct. But you can easily get a camping licence from any automobile club.'

I glanced at my watch. 'I think it's a little late for that, don't you?'

He shrugged, indifferent to my fate. I daresay he was less than keen to have a suspicious character like me staying on his campsite; a man with a foreign accent wearing a scarf in October and sunglasses after dark isn't the type of carefree camper who encourages trust in the heart of Vichy. Even Cary Grant couldn't have pulled that off.

So I left the campsite and drove on for a few kilometres and found myself a nice quiet country lane under some tall poplars and then a field where I could shut my sore eyes for a while. But it was hard to sleep knowing that Friedrich Korsch and the Stasi were already on my trail. Almost certainly they would have hired some self-drive cars at the Europcar rental office next to the railway station in Marseilles and very likely they were only a couple of hours behind me on the N7. Eventually I managed to sleep a little on the backseat of the Citroën but not without Friedrich Korsch appearing in a dream that took place somewhere at the back of the double pain I now called my eyes.

It was strange the way he'd entered my world again after all these years, and yet not strange at all, perhaps. If you live long enough you realize that everything that happens to us is all the same illusion, the same shit, the same celestial joke. Things don't really end, they just stop for a while and then they start up again, like a bad record. There are no new chapters in your book, there's just the one long fairy story – the same stupid story we tell ourselves and which, mistakenly, we call life. Nothing is ever really over until we're dead. And what else could a man do who'd worked for the Reich Security Office except carry on working for the same lousy department under the communists? Friedrich Korsch was a natural policeman. Such continuity made perfect sense to the communists; the Nazis had been good at law enforcement. And with a different book – Marx instead of Hitler – a slightly different uniform, and a new national anthem, 'Risen from the Ruins', everything could carry on as before. Hitler, Stalin, Ulbricht, Khrushchev – they were all the same, the same monsters from the neurological abyss we call our own subconscious. Me and Schopenhauer. Sometimes being German seems to come with some serious disadvantages.

I could almost hear the voice of Friedrich Korsch now, seated in the front of the Mercedes 770K as we'd reached the outskirts of Nuremberg – effectively, the capital of Nazism in Germany – and he'd mentioned a good hotel, which was where I most wanted to be right now, with a comfortable bed, a hot bath, some eyedrops, and a good dinner . . .

1939

'The Deutscher Hof,' said Korsch. 'Remember that, sir?'

'Of course.'

'That's a nice hotel. Best I've stayed in, anyway. Always reminds me a bit of the Adlon.'

Korsch and I had stayed at the Deutscher Hof – rumoured to be Hitler's favourite hotel – on a trip to Nuremberg the previous September, when we'd been investigating a possible lead in a serial murder case. For a while we had suspected that Julius Streicher, the political leader of Franconia, might be the culprit and we had gone to Nuremberg to speak to the local police chief, Benno Martin. Streicher was Germany's leading Jew-baiter and the publisher of *Der Stürmer,* a magazine so crudely anti-Semitic that even a majority of Nazis shunned it.

I caught Korsch's eye in the side mirror mounted on the huge spare tyre beside his door and nodded.

'How could I forget?' I said. 'That was the night we first clapped eyes on Streicher. Totally blue with drink he was, but still boozing it up with a couple of stroke maidens like he was the Holy Roman Emperor himself. For a while I quite fancied him for it. The murders, I mean.'

'Hard to believe a man like that is still a gauleiter.'

'There's a lot that's hard to believe right now,' I murmured, thinking about the war that was probably just down the road; surely it wouldn't be long before the French and the British called Hitler's bluff and mobilized their armies. Rumour had it that Poland was next on Hitler's list for annexation, or whatever the diplomatic word is after Munich for invading someone else's country.

'Not for much longer,' said Neumann. 'Confidentially, Streicher's been under investigation since November, accused of stealing Jewish property seized after Kristallnacht, which was rightly the property of the state. Not to mention the fact that he's been libelling Göring's daughter, Edda.'

'Libelling?' said Korsch.

'He alleged in his newspaper that she was conceived by artificial insemination.'

I laughed. 'Yes, I can see how that would piss Göring off. How it would piss any man off.'

'General Heydrich expects him to be stripped of all his Party offices by the end of the year.'

'Well, that's a relief,' I said. 'Where are you from, Neumann?'

'Barmen.' He shook his head. 'It's all right. Franconia is a mystery to me, too.'

'It's wizard country,' I said. 'Stay on the path, that's what they always say there. Don't go into the woods. And don't ever talk to strangers.'

'Damn right,' said Korsch.

After a moment I said, 'Confidentially, you say. I suppose that means it's all going to be done in secret and then swept under the carpet, just like the Weisthor affair.'

'I believe Streicher is still protected by Hitler,' said Neumann. 'So yes, I imagine you're probably right, Commissar Gunther. But nothing's perfect, is it?'

'You noticed that, too, eh?'

'Speaking of secrets,' said Neumann. 'I suppose we'd better discuss how you're going to keep the general informed of what you're up to when you're in Obersalzberg, without alerting Martin Bormann.'

'I've been wondering about that.'

'While you're down there, I'll be based a few kilometres across the German border, in Salzburg. As a matter of fact, I do quite a lot of confidential work for the general in Austria. Close to Berchtesgaden is a little place called St. Leonhard. It's virtually on the border. And in St. Leonhard there's a discreet guest house called the Schorn Ziegler, which has a very good restaurant. Real home cooking. I'll be staying there. If you have anything to report or if you need anything from Heydrich's office in Berlin, that will be where you can find me. Failing that you can always find me at Gestapo headquarters in Salzburg. That's easy to find, too. Just look for the old Franciscan monastery on Mozartplatz.'

'I take it the monks are no longer there. Or did they all join the SS?'

'What's the difference?' said Korsch.

'Regrettably, they were thrown out of there last year.' Neumann looked sheepish for a moment. 'After the annexation, there were a lot of things that happened that could have been handled differently, better.' He shrugged. 'Me, I'm just an electrical engineer. I leave politics in the hands of the politicians.'

'That's the trouble,' I said. 'I have an awful feeling that the politicians are even worse at handling politics than the rest of us.'

'Drink?' Neumann lifted the armrest to reveal a small cocktail cabinet.

'No,' I said, taking hold of the red leather rope on the back of the seat in front of me, as if it might help me to hold on to that resolve. 'I do believe I'm going to need a clear head when I get to Obersalzberg.'

'You don't mind if I do,' he said, lifting a small crystal decanter clear of its purple-velvet-lined cocoon. 'The general keeps an excellent brandy in his car. I think it's almost as old as I am.'

'Go ahead. I look forward to reading the taster's notes.'

I lowered the window a centimetre and lit a cigarette, if only to chase off the faintly intoxicating smell of hot oil and warm rubber and expensive alcohol and male body odour that filled the elegant interior of the big Mercedes. Icy fog shrouded the road ahead, dissolving other headlamps and rear lamps like something soluble at the bottom of your glass. Small forgotten towns came and went in a blur as the fallen angel's car tunnelled its rumbling way south through the uncertain dark. Yawning and blinking and registering what was always twenty metres behind us, I sank deeper into my seat and listened to the sharp-toothed wind as it whistled a melancholy banshee tune beside the freezing-cold glass of the window. There's nothing like an extended road trip at night to steal thoughts from your past and your future both, to make you think that coming is no different from going, and to persuade you that a hoped-for long journey's end is merely another bloody beginning.

CHAPTER 9

April 1939

It was almost midnight when we reached Berchtesgaden in the southeast corner of Bavaria. In the dark, it looked like a typical Alpine valley town with several tall church spires, a high castle, and many colourful wall murals, although most of these were of recent origin and illustrated a childish devotion to one man that bordered on idolatry. Living in the capital of Germany, I suppose I ought to have been used to a bit of apple polishing and arse grovelling, but for Berliners a hero always comes with a dirty mark on his white vest, and it's unlikely that any of my fellow citizens would ever have decorated the outside wall of his home with anything more than a kitsch name board or a street number. I wasn't sure why Adolf Hitler had chosen a cosy little tourist town as his unofficial capital – which is what it was – but he'd been visiting Berchtesgaden since 1923, and in the summer it was impossible to open a German newspaper without seeing several pictures of our avuncular Leader with local children. He was always seen hand in hand with children – the more German-looking, the better – almost as if someone (Goebbels, probably) had decided being seen with them might make him seem like less of a belligerent monster. For me, the opposite impression always prevailed. Anyone who'd read the Brothers Grimm could have told you that big bad wolves and wizards, wicked witches and greedy giants had always enjoyed the taste of a hot pie stuffed with the succulent meat of small boys and girls who were dumb enough to go off with them. I wondered about some of those little girls in pigtails and dirndls who were taken to meet Hitler as a birthday treat, I really did.

We'd arrived in Berchtesgaden with a river to the left and the town on our right, and almost immediately the Mercedes turned east to cross a small bridge over the Ache and head up a winding, snowy mountain road towards Obersalzberg. Looming above us in the moonlight was the Göll massif, which rises to a height of more than two thousand metres and straddles the border between Austria and Germany like an enormous thundercloud. A few minutes later we came upon our first security checkpoint, and while we were expected, nevertheless we were obliged to wait while the semi-frozen SS guard telephoned his headquarters for our permission to proceed any further. After Berlin's poor excuse for an atmosphere, the cold air through the open window of the car tasted as pure as glacier melt. Already I felt healthier. Maybe that was why Hitler liked the place so much; he wanted to live forever. Our permission came through and we drove on for a few kilometres until, just short of another sentry gate, which marked the boundary of the so-called Prohibited Area, we pulled into the driveway of the Villa Bechstein, a three-storey Alpine-style chalet, and stopped next to another giant Mercedes-Benz.

'This is where you and Criminal Assistant Korsch will be staying,' Neumann told me. 'But it's also as far as the rest of us can go, Commissar. From here on you're in the hands of the RSD. Another staff car will take you to the deputy chief of staff.'

We got out of the car and found ourselves surrounded by five bandbox RSD officers who inspected our credentials carefully and then invited me but not Korsch to climb into the second Mercedes. The wind was getting up and there was a strong smell of wood smoke coming from the villa's chimneys that made me yearn for the sight of a roaring fire and a cup of hot coffee with someone warm holding it.

'If you don't mind, gentlemen,' I said, 'I'd like a few minutes to wash my hands. And unpack.'

'There's no time for that,' announced one of the RSD officers. 'The Boss doesn't like to be kept waiting. And he's already been waiting all evening for your arrival up at the Kehlstein House.'

'The Boss?' For a moment I wondered just who it was that I was about to meet.

'Martin Bormann,' said another.

'And what's the Kehlstein House?'

'The Kehlstein is the northernmost peak on the Göll massif. Not the highest, and the house – well, you'll see.' One of the officers had opened the door of the Mercedes while another had taken charge of my bag and was carrying it into the villa. And minutes later I was heading further up the magic mountain with three men from the RSD.

'Captain Kaspel, isn't it?' I asked.

'Yes,' said the man now sitting next to me. He pointed to the man seated alongside my new driver. 'And this is my superior, Major Högl. Major Högl is the deputy head of the RSD in Obersalzberg.'

'Major.'

We stopped to negotiate another checkpoint, after which Högl finally turned and spoke to me. 'We're now in the Prohibited Area, better known among everyone who works here as the Leader's Territory. An FG1 level of security is only fully operational when the Leader is actually here, however, but given the special circumstances, we thought it best to step things up to FG1, for the time being anyway.'

Kaspel was, I knew, from Berlin, but there was no mistaking Högl's Bavarian accent or his pompous manner. I'd seen it before, of course; anyone who comes into contact with a god often enough starts to believe in his own self-importance.

'What special circumstances are those, Major?'

'The murder, of course. This is why you're here, isn't it? To investigate a homicide? That's what you're good at, I'm told by General Heydrich.'

'He's never wrong about very much,' I said. 'Care to give me a small advance on what's happened?'

'That would not be appropriate,' Högl said stiffly. 'Really, it's up to the deputy chief of staff what you're told.'

'By the way, who's the chief of staff around here? With all these deputies sometimes it's a little hard to keep up with who's who in Nazi Germany.'

'The deputy of the Leader. Rudolf Hess. As a matter of fact he's going to be staying at the Villa Bechstein when he gets here from Munich the day after tomorrow. But if you see him you can call him sir, or General.'

'That's a relief. Deputy of the Leader is a little bit of a mouthful.'

I lit a cigarette and yawned. It was safer than making a joke.

'But to all intents and purposes it's Martin Bormann who runs the show up here,' said Kaspel.

I folded my arms across my chest and pulled hard on my cigarette, which seemed to bother Högl. He waved the smoke back at me.

'Just to let you know, smoking is not permitted anywhere on the Kehlstein,' said Högl. 'The Leader has a very keen nose for tobacco and doesn't care for it in the least.'

'Even when he's not here?'

'Even when he's not here.'

'That really *is* a keen sense of smell.'

Finally we reached the top of the road, where an impressive sight awaited me. In a large stone-clad entranceway at the bottom of an almost sheer mountain slope was a pair of arched bronze doors as big as an African elephant, and they opened as we pulled up to them. Of course, like any German, I knew the legend, that the Emperor Friedrich Barbarossa (although some said it was Charlemagne) was asleep inside these mountains awaiting the great battle that would herald the end of the world, but I hadn't ever thought to discover if he was expecting visitors. This was another joke I kept to myself. I couldn't have felt more intimidated if I'd been summoned to meet the troll king to discuss his daughter's unfortunate condition.

The open doors revealed a long, perfectly straight tunnel which might easily have admitted the passage of the big Mercedes but I was told we had to get out and walk.

'Only the Leader is permitted to drive to the end of this tunnel,' explained Högl. 'For everyone else, it's the shoemaker's penny.'

'I'm happy to stretch my legs a bit,' I said bravely. 'It's ten hours from Berlin. Besides, all pilgrimages should end on foot, don't you think?'

I finished my cigarette quickly, tossed it onto the road and followed Högl and his deputy down the length of the brightly lit marble tunnel. I ran my hand along the wall and glanced up at the cast-iron light fittings as we walked; everything was new and spotlessly clean. Even the U-Bahn station at Friedrichstrasse wasn't as new or well made as this place.

'Is this where the Leader lives?' I asked.

'No, this is the way up to the tea house,' explained Kaspel.

'The tea house? I can't wait to see what the ballroom looks like. Not to mention the cocktail bar and the master bedroom.'

'The Leader doesn't drink,' said Kaspel.

This information was enough to restore my faith in at least two of my bad habits. Maybe they weren't such bad habits after all.

At the end of the tunnel Högl looked up. 'The tea house is one hundred and thirty metres above our heads,' he said, and then announced our presence into a microphone that was built into the wall.

We were standing in a large, round, vaulted chamber, the sort of place where you might have expected to find a priceless sarcophagus or perhaps a treasure belonging to at least forty thieves, but instead there was a set of lift doors, which could have been gold they were so brightly polished, but even as I was assuring myself that they were more probably brass, I began to feel uneasy in a way I'd never felt before. It was, perhaps, the first time I realized the true extent of Adolf Hitler's apparent divinity: if this was a representative example of the way our chancellor lived, then Germany was in a lot more trouble than even I had realized.

The lift doors parted to reveal a mirrored cage with a leather bench seat and its own RSD operator. We stepped inside and the brass doors closed again.

'Powered by two engines,' said Högl. 'One electric. And a backup diesel engine that was taken from a U-boat.'

'That should come in handy if there's a flood.'

'Please,' said Högl, 'no comedians. The deputy chief of staff doesn't have a sense of humour.'

'Sorry.'

I smiled nervously as the lift cage rose up the shaft. It was the smoothest lift ride I'd ever taken, although I had the strong idea that it should have been travelling in the opposite direction. Then the doors opened and I was ushered through a doorway and what looked like a main dining room, down some steps, and straight into the presence of Martin Bormann.

CHAPTER 10

April 1939

He wasn't tall and at first I didn't see him. I was too busy staring in wonder at the Kehlstein reception hall, where everyone was waiting for me. It was a large round room, perfectly proportioned, made of grey granite blocks, with a coffered ceiling and a marble fireplace that was the size and colour of an S-Bahn train. Above the fireplace was a Gobelin tapestry featuring a couple of bucolic lovers and on the floor was an expensive crimson Persian rug. In front of the red fireplace a circular table was surrounded by comfortable armchairs that made me feel tired just looking at them. There were no curtains on the big square windows that provided an unimpeded mountaintop view of a dark and stormy night. Light snow was dusting the glass and outside the window I could hear the lanyard shifting in the wind on a tin flagpole like the clapper in a tiny bell. It was a good night to be inside, especially on top of a mountain. A log the size of the Sudetenland was smoking in the grate and on the walls were several electric candelabra that looked as if they'd been placed there by a mad scientist's faithful retainer. There was a mahogany grand piano and a small rectangular table and some more chairs, and in another doorway a man wearing a white SS mess jacket with a silver tray under his arm. It was a room with the kind of rarefied atmosphere in which some men might have thought they could decide the future of the world, but it made my ears feel as if someone had pulled a cork out of my skull, although that could as easily have been the sight of an open flask of Grassl on the table, prompting the sudden realization that I needed a drink that wasn't tea. Only one of the five men around the table was in uniform but I knew he couldn't be Bormann, as the man had only a colonel's helping of cauliflower on his SS collar badge; he was also the one man who got to his feet and returned my Hitler salute, politely. The others, including the pugilistic-looking type who now took charge of things in the tea house, and whom I guessed was probably Martin Bormann, remained firmly seated. I didn't blame any of them much for not wanting to get up to greet me – sudden movements like that at such high altitude can give you a nosebleed. Besides, the chairs really did look very comfortable and, after all, I was just a copper from Berlin.

'Commissar Gunther, I presume?' asked Bormann.

'How do you do, sir?'

'You're here, at long last. We would have had you flown here, but there wasn't a plane available. Anyway, sit down, sit down. You've come a long way. I expect you're tired. I'm sorry about that, but it really can't be helped. Are you hungry? Of course you are.' He was already snapping his fingers in the air – strong, fat fingers that were wholly unsuitable for something as delicate as a tea house to summon the man in the SS mess jacket. 'Fetch our guest something to eat. What would you like, Commissar? A sandwich? Some coffee?'

I couldn't place the man's accent. Perhaps it was Saxon. It certainly wasn't an educated sort of voice. He was right about one thing, however: I was as hungry as a threshing machine. Högl and Kaspel had sat down at the table as well, but Bormann didn't offer them anything. I soon realized that he was wont to treat the men who worked for him with open contempt and brutality.

'Perhaps a slice of bread with mustard and some sausage, sir. And maybe a cup of coffee.'

Bormann nodded at the waiter, who went to fetch my dinner.

'First of all, do you know who I am?'

'You're Martin Bormann.'

'And what do you know about me?'

'From what I've been told you're the Leader's right-hand man here in the Alps.'

'Is that it?' Bormann uttered a scornful laugh. 'I thought you were a detective.'

'Isn't that enough? Hitler's no ordinary leader.'

'But it's not just here, you know. No, I'm his right-hand man in the rest of Germany, too. Anyone else you've ever heard of as being a person who's close to the Leader – Göring, Himmler, Goebbels, Hess – believe me, they don't amount to shit when I'm around. The fact is that if any of them wants to see Hitler, they have to come through me. So when I talk, it's as if the Leader were here now, telling you what the fuck to do. Is that clear?'

'Very clear.'

'Good.' Bormann nodded at the bottle of schnapps on the table. 'Would you like a drink?'

'No, sir. Not when I'm on duty.'

'I'll decide if you're on duty, Commissar. I haven't yet made up my mind if you're the real deal or not. Until then, have a drink. Relax. That's what this place is all about. It's brand-new. Even the Leader hasn't seen it yet, so you're very privileged. We're here tonight because we're field-testing the place. Seeing that everything works before he gets here. That's why you can't smoke, I'm afraid. The Leader always knows when someone's been smoking, even in secret – I've never known a man with such heightened senses.' He shrugged. 'Not that I should be surprised, of course. He's the most extraordinary man I've ever met.'

'If you don't mind me asking, sir, why a tea house?'

Bormann poured me a glass of schnapps and handed it to me with those fat fingers of his. I sipped it carefully. At fifty per cent proof, it rated a bit of caution, just like the man who'd poured it. There was a largish scar above his right eye and, with his plus-four trousers and thick tweed jacket, he had the look of a prosperous farmer who didn't mind kicking his prize pig. Not fat, but a burly middleweight going to seed, with a proper double chin and a nose like a parboiled turnip.

'Because the Leader likes tea, of course. Stupid question, really. He already has a tea house just across the valley from the Berghof – the Mooslahnerkopf. Which he enjoys walking to. But it was thought that perhaps something more spectacular was fitting for a man of such vision. In daylight the views from this room are breathtaking. You might almost say that this tea house is designed to help provide him with some necessary inspiration.'

'I can imagine.'

'Do you like the Alps, Herr Gunther?'

'They're a little too far off the ground for me to feel quite comfortable. I'm more of a city boy. The beanpole – that is, the Berlin radio tower – is quite high enough for me.'

He smiled patiently. 'Tell me about yourself.'

I sipped some schnapps and leaned back in my armchair, and then sipped some more. I was dying for a smoke and a couple of times I even reached for my cigarette case before I remembered how health-conscious they were in Obersalzberg. I glanced at the faces of the other knights seated at this particular round table and perceived that perhaps I wasn't the only one who needed a cigarette.

'I'm a Berliner, through and through, which means I'm just naturally opinionated. Not necessarily in a good way. I got my *Abitur* and I might have gone to university but for the war. Saw enough in the trenches to persuade me that I like mud even less than snow. I joined the Berlin police right after the armistice. Made detective. Worked in the Murder Commission. Solved a few cases. Was on my own for a while – a private investigator, and I was doing all right for myself, making good money, until General Heydrich persuaded me to come back to Kripo.'

'Heydrich says you're his best detective. Is that really true? Or are you just some Fritz he's sent down here to spy on me?'

'I know how to work a case by the book when that's what's required.'

'And what book might that be?'

'The Prussian General Code of 1794. The Police Administration Law of 1931.'

'Ah, that kind of book. The old kind.'

'The legal kind.'

'Does Heydrich still pay attention to that sort of thing? To the letter of the pre-Nazi law?'

'More often than you might think.'

'But you don't like working for Heydrich, do you? At least that's what he tells me.'

'It has its interesting side. He keeps me around because, for me, work is the best jacket. I don't like to take it off until I've worn it out and then some. Tenacity – and a stolid propensity to obstinacy – are forensic qualities the general seems to appreciate.'

'He tells me you've got a lot of snout, too.'

'I certainly don't mean to be that way, sir. To other Germans, we Berliners seem to be insolent when we're not. About a hundred years ago we worked out that there's no point in being friendly and polite if no one else appreciates it. No one in Berlin, that is. So now we please ourselves.'

Bormann shrugged. 'That's honest enough. But I'm still not convinced you're the right fist for this particular eye, Gunther.'

'With all due respect, sir, neither am I. With most murder cases I'm usually not required to audition for the job. On the whole, the dead don't mind much who gives them their last manicure. And I'm not about to convince a man as important as yourself of anything, probably. I wouldn't presume even to try. The kind of Fritz who can talk a hole through someone's stomach – that isn't me. These days there's not much of a market for what's laughingly called my personality. I certainly didn't bring any of my favourite music to put on your nice Bechstein.'

'But you did bring your own piano player, didn't you?'

'Korsch? He's my criminal assistant. In Berlin. And a good man. We work well together.'

'You won't need him while you're here. My men will give you all the assistance you need. The fewer people who know about what's happened here, the better.'

'With all due respect, sir. He's a good copper. Sometimes it helps to have another brain I can borrow – to add another tooth just when I need to chew something hard. Even the best men need a good deputy, someone trustworthy they can rely on, who won't let them down. That would seem to be as true here as anywhere else.'

It was supposed to be a compliment and I hoped he'd see it that way, but he had the most pugnacious jaw I'd seen outside of a boxing ring. I had the sense that at any moment he might grab me by the throat, or have me thrown from the battlements – if a mountaintop tea house has such a thing as battlements. This was the first tea house I'd been in that looked as if it could have kept the Red Army at bay. Perhaps that was the real reason it had been built and I didn't doubt that inside the rest of Hitler's mountain were other secrets I might prefer not to know about. It was enough to make me finish the schnapps a little more quickly than I ought to have done.

Bormann rubbed his roughening, midnight chin thoughtfully.

'All right, all right, keep the bastard. But he stays down at the Villa Bechstein. Outside the Leader's Territory. Is that clear? If you want to pick his brains, you do it there.'

CHAPTER 11

April 1939

Bormann leaned forward and poured me another drink. 'I would have preferred a Bavarian up here. The Leader thinks Bavarians have a better understanding of how things work on this mountain. I think you're probably just another Prussian bastard, but you're my kind of bastard. I like a man with some blood in his veins. You're not like a lot of these albino Gestapo types that Heydrich and Himmler grow on a petri dish in some fucking science lab. Which means you've got the job. You are acting with my full authority. At least until you screw up.'

I steadied the glass as he filled it to the top, which is the way I like my schnapps served, and tried to look like I was taking a compliment.

'Either way, when this is all over and you've caught this bastard, it never happened, do you hear? The last thing I want is for the German people to think that security here is so lax that every Krethi and Plethi can just stroll up the hill from Berchtesgaden and take a potshot at their beloved Leader outside his own front door. So you'll sign a confidentiality agreement, and you'll like it.'

Bormann nodded at the man next to him, who produced a sheet of printed paper and a pen and placed them in front of me. I glanced over it quickly. 'What's this?' I asked. 'Next of kin?'

'What it says,' said Bormann.

'I don't have a next of kin.'

'No wife.'

'Not anymore.'

'Then put your girlfriend down.' Bormann grinned unpleasantly. 'Or the name and address of someone you really care about in case you've screwed up or you're about to open your trap and we have to threaten to take it out on someone else.'

He made it sound entirely reasonable that this was how things were done – how a policeman who failed to catch a murderer would be treated by the state. I thought for a moment and then wrote down the name of Hildegard Steininger and her address in Berlin's Lepsiusstrasse. It had been six months since she'd been my girlfriend and I hadn't liked it very much when I found out that she was seeing someone else – some shiny-looking major in the SS. I hadn't liked it at all so I suppose I didn't give a damn if Bormann ever decided to punish her for my shortcomings. It was small-minded, even vindictive, and I'm not proud of what I did. But I wrote her name down all the same. Sometimes true love comes with a black ribbon on the box.

'So to find the hammer and the nails,' said Bormann, 'let's get to the reason why you've been brought all the way from Berlin.'

'I'm one big ear, sir.'

At this moment the SS waiter arrived back at the table with a tray bearing the food, and the coffee, for which I was especially grateful since the armchair was extremely comfortable.

'This morning at eight o'clock, there was a breakfast meeting at the Berghof. That's the Leader's own house. Which is next to mine, a few metres further down the mountain. The people present at this meeting were largely architects, engineers, and civil servants, and the purpose of the meeting was to consider what further improvements might be made at the Berghof and in Obersalzberg for the convenience, enjoyment, and security of the Leader. I suppose there must have been about ten or fifteen men who were present. Perhaps a few more. After breakfast, at about nine o'clock, these men went out onto the terrace that overlooks the area. At nine fifteen a.m., one of these men – Dr Karl Flex – collapsed onto the terrace, bleeding profusely from a head wound. He'd been shot, most probably with a rifle, and died at the scene. No one else was wounded, and curiously, no one seems to have heard a thing. As soon as it was established that he had been shot, the RSD cleared the building and conducted an immediate search of the woods and mountainsides that directly overlook the Berghof terrace. But so far no trace of the assassin has been found. Can you believe it? All these SS and RSD and they can't find a single clue.'

I nodded and kept eating my sausage, which was delicious.

'I don't have to tell you how serious this is,' said Bormann. 'Having said that, I don't think this was connected with the Leader, whose movements today and yesterday have been widely reported in the newspapers. But until the killer is apprehended, it will be quite impossible for Hitler to go near that terrace. And as you will doubtless be aware, it's his fiftieth birthday on the twentieth of April. He always comes here to Obersalzberg on or just after his birthday. *This year will be no exception.* Which means you have seven days to solve this crime. Do you hear? It's imperative that this murderer is caught before the twentieth of April because I certainly don't want to be the man who tells him he can't go outside because there's an assassin on the loose.'

I put down my sausage, wiped my mouth clean of mustard, and nodded. 'I'll do my best, sir,' I said firmly. 'You can rely on that.'

'I don't want your best,' shouted Bormann. 'I want better than your best, whatever that particular heap of shit amounts to. You're not in Berlin now, you're in Obersalzberg. Your best may be good enough for that Jew Heydrich but you're working for me now and that's as good as working for Adolf Hitler. Is that clear? I want this man under a falling axe before the end of the month.'

'Yes, sir.' I nodded again. Where Bormann was concerned, nodding silently was probably the best response. 'You have my word that I'll give it everything I've got. Rest assured, sir, I'll catch him.'

'That's more like it,' said Bormann.

'First thing in the morning,' I added, stifling a yawn, 'I'll get right on it.'

'Fuck that,' yelled Bormann, banging the tabletop. My white china cup jumped on the monogrammed blue saucer as if the Kehlstein had been hit by an avalanche. 'You'll get on it right now. That's why you're here. Every hour that we don't catch this swine is an hour too long.' Bormann looked around for the waiter and then at one of the men seated around the table. 'Bring this man some more hot coffee. Better still, give him a packet of Pervitin. That should help to keep him on his toes.'

The object of Bormann's command reached into his jacket pocket and took out a little metallic blue-and-white tube, which he handed to me. I glanced at it briefly, but all I saw was the manufacturer's name – Temmler, which was a Berlin pharmaceutical company.

'What is this?' I asked.

'Up here it's what we call Hermann Temmler's magic potion,' said Bormann. 'German Coca-Cola. Helps the workforce at the Obersalzberg keep up with the construction schedule. You see, they are only permitted to work when Hitler's not here – so as not to disturb him – which means that when he's somewhere else, they have to work twice as long and twice as hard. That stuff helps. Göring's considering giving it to bomber crews to help them stay awake. So. Take two with your coffee. That should put a bit more spring in your Hitler salute. Which looked like shit, by the way. I know you've had a long journey and you're tired but round here that's just not good enough, Gunther. Next time I'll kick your arse myself.'

I swallowed two of the tablets uncomfortably and apologized, but he was right, of course; my Hitler salute was always a bit slack. That's what comes of not being a Nazi, I suppose.

'Have there been any previous shooting incidents at the Berghof?'

Bormann glanced at the man wearing an SS colonel's uniform. 'What's the story, Rattenhuber?'

The colonel nodded. 'There was an incident about six months ago. A Swiss called Maurice Bavaud came up here planning to shoot the Leader. But he abandoned it at the last moment and made his escape. He was finally apprehended by the French police, who turned him over to us. He's now in a Berlin prison, awaiting trial and execution.'

But Bormann was shaking his head. 'That was nothing like a serious attempt,' he said scornfully, and then looked at me. 'Colonel Rattenhuber is head of the RSD with responsibility for securing the Leader's person, wherever he is. At least that's the theory. In point of fact, Bavaud was armed only with a pistol, not a rifle. And he planned to shoot Hitler when he came down to the bottom of his drive to greet some well-wishers. But Bavaud lost his nerve. So, Herr Gunther, I think the simple answer to your question is no. This is the first time someone has fired a shot at anyone in this vicinity. Nothing like this has ever happened here before. This is a harmonious community. This is not Berlin. This is not Hamburg. Berchtesgaden and Obersalzberg constitute a peaceful rural idyll in which decent family values and a strong sense of morality prevail. That's why the Leader has always enjoyed coming here.'

'All right. Tell me a bit more about the dead man. Did he have any enemies that anyone knows of?'

'Flex?' Bormann shook his head. 'He worked for Bruno Schenk, one of my most trusted people on the mountain. Both men were employees of Polensky & Zöllner, a Berlin company that handles most of the construction work in Obersalzberg and Berchtesgaden. Karl Flex wasn't RSD or political, he was a civil engineer. A diligent and much-admired servant who had lived here for several years.'

'Possibly there was someone who didn't admire him quite as much as you did, sir.' While Bormann was absorbing my jab I followed up quickly with a couple of punches to his body. 'Like the man who shot him, for instance. Then again, perhaps there was more than one man involved. To get past all the security up here must have taken some planning and organization. Which is to say we might be talking about a conspiracy.'

For once Bormann stayed silent as he considered this possibility. Me, I just hoped I'd spoiled the cosy concept of his tea house with its monogrammed china and its expensive Gobelin tapestry. How much had it cost to build this Nazi folly? Millions, probably. Money that could have been spent on something more important than the comfort of the madman who now ruled Germany.

'Witness statements?' I asked. 'Have they been taken?'

'I've had them roneoed for you,' said Högl. 'The originals have already been sent to Berlin. For the attention of the Reichsführer-SS. He's taking a personal interest in this case.'

'I shall want to read them all. And where is the body? I'll need to take a look at it.'

'At the local hospital,' said Rattenhuber. 'Down in Berchtesgaden.'

'There will need to be an autopsy, of course,' I added. 'With photographs. The sooner, the better.'

'The man was shot,' said Bormann. 'Surely that's obvious. What more could an autopsy tell you?'

'A thing can remain unknown even though it's obvious. Or, put another way, nothing evades our attention as persistently as that which we take for granted. That's just philosophy, sir. Nothing is obvious until it's obvious. So I shall have to insist on an autopsy if I'm to do my job properly. Is there a doctor at this hospital who might carry out such a procedure?'

'I doubt it,' said Rattenhuber. 'The Dietrich Eckart is set up to look after the living, not to take care of the dead.'

'No matter,' I said. 'I suggest you get Dr Waldemar Weimann, from Berlin. Frankly, he's the best there is. And from what you've already told me I can't imagine we want anything less than that for a case like this.'

'That's quite impossible,' said Bormann. 'As I said, I want to keep a tight lid on this. I don't trust doctors from Berlin. I shall ask one of the Leader's own physicians to carry out an autopsy. Dr Karl Brandt. I'm sure he's equal to the task. If you really think it's necessary.'

'I do. I shall have to be present, of course.' I was silent for a moment, seemingly lost in thought, but in truth I was just assessing the effect that the Pervitin was now having on me. Already I felt more alert and energetic, and bolder, too – bold enough to start taking charge and making demands. Bormann wasn't the only one who could sound as if he knew what he wanted.

'I should also like to visit the crime scene tonight. So you'd better arrange some arc lights and a tape measure. And I shall want to speak to everyone who was on the terrace this morning. As soon as is convenient. Also, I will need an office with a desk with two telephones. A filing cabinet with a lock. A car and a driver on permanent call. Coffee-making facilities. A large map of the area. Some lengths of dowel – the longer, the better. A camera. A Leica IIIa with a 50-mm F2 retractable Summar lens should be just fine. And several rolls of black-and-white film – the slower, the better. Not colour. Takes too long to process.'

'Why do you need a camera?' asked Bormann.

'With more than a dozen witnesses on the terrace when Dr Flex was shot, it will help me if I can put some faces to the names.' I could feel the stuff surging through me now. Suddenly I really wanted to find and catch the Berghof killer, and maybe tear his head off. 'And I'll need plenty of cigarettes. I can't work without them, I'm afraid. Cigarettes help me think. I appreciate that it's forbidden to smoke anywhere that the Leader is likely to be, so I shall smoke outside, of course. What else? Yes, some winter boots. I've only come with shoes, I'm afraid, and I may need to do some walking in snow. Size forty-three, please. And a coat. I'm freezing.'

'Very well,' said Bormann, 'but I shall want all of the prints and negatives to be handed over when you leave.'

'Of course.'

'Speak to Arthur Kannenberg at the Berghof,' Bormann told the man sitting next to him. 'Tell him that Commissar Gunther is going to use one of the guest rooms as his office. Zander? Högl? Make sure that everything else he wants is made available to him. Kaspel? You show him the Berghof terrace.'

Bormann stood up, which was everyone's cue to do the same. Except me. I stayed put in my armchair for a long moment, as if I were still lost in thought, but of course it was nothing more than dumb insolence, paying him back in kind for his bad manners. I already hated Martin Bormann as much as I'd hated any Nazi, including Heydrich and Goebbels. There is evil in the best of us, of course; but perhaps just a little bit more in the worst of us.

CHAPTER 12

April 1939

Once upon a time the Berghof – or the Haus Wachenfeld, as it was then called – had been a simple two-storey farmhouse with a long, sloping roof, overhanging eaves, a wooden porch, and a picture-postcard view of Berchtesgaden and the Untersberg. These days it was a much-expanded and rather less cosy structure, with a vast panoramic window, garages, a terrace, and a recently built low wing to the east of the house that resembled a military barracks. I wasn't sure who stayed in the east wing, but it probably wasn't the military, because a large contingent of SS already occupied a former hotel, the Türken Inn, less than fifty metres further to the east of the Berghof and immediately below Bormann's own house in Obersalzberg, which seemed to command a better position than Hitler's.

The Berghof's front terrace was about the size of a tennis court, with a low wall; it backed onto a larger, secondary terrace, which in turn bordered a lawn to the west. Behind the secondary terrace were what looked like additional living quarters, styled in the local vernacular, which is to say they looked like a row of cuckoo clocks. On my instructions, several SS men were erecting a number of arc lights on the front terrace so that I might inspect the crime scene, although the only evidence of a crime was the chalk outline of a man's fallen body just behind the low wall. On Bormann's instructions, any blood from Flex's corpse had been washed away. Playing the part of the dead man and muffled in his black SS greatcoat, Captain Kaspel took up a position on the terrace to help me understand where Flex had been standing when he'd been shot. The light snow and the wind did not encourage lingering and he stamped his boots to help keep warm, although he might just have been imagining he was stamping on my face. Not very tall, shaven-headed, hook-nosed, and with a wide mouth, Kaspel was a thinner, more sensitive, and better-looking version of Benito Mussolini.

'Flex was standing about here,' explained Kaspel. 'According to the witness statements, he was in a group of three or four men, most of whom were looking at the Reiteralpe, to the west. Several of the witnesses are sure that the shooter must have fired from a group of trees on a mountain slope behind the house, over there to the west.'

In the arc light I glanced over one of the witness statements and nodded. 'Except that no one seems to have heard a thing,' I said. 'The first any of them really know about the shooting is when the victim is lying on this terrace with blood pouring from his head.'

Kaspel shrugged. 'Don't ask me, Gunther. You're the great detective.'

I hadn't yet been alone with Kaspel, which meant I hadn't had a chance to give him Heydrich's letter ordering him to put himself under my command, so he was still treating me with understandable disdain. It was clear he hadn't forgotten or forgiven anything about 1932 and how I'd helped to get him fired from the Berlin police.

'What were the weather conditions like when Flex was shot?'

'Clear and sunny.' Kaspel blew on his hands. 'Not like this.'

I might have felt the cold more myself except for the fact that the pills I'd taken seemed to be having an effect on my body temperature, too. I was as warm as if I'd still been in the car.

'Were any of these men wearing a uniform?'

'No, it seems they were all civilians.'

'Then I wonder how the shooter picked him out,' I said.

'Telescopic sight? Binoculars. A hunter, perhaps.'

'Perhaps.'

'Good eyesight? I don't know. Go figure.'

'It seems to have been at least a minute or two before any of them worked out that Flex had been shot. At which point they finally retreated indoors.'

For a moment I lay down beside the chalk outline and stretched out on the cold paving stones.

'Did you know the dead man? Flex?'

'Only by sight.'

'Seems as if he was tall.' I got up again and dusted the snow off my coat. 'I'm one hundred and eighty-eight centimetres but it looks to me as if Flex was possibly seven or eight centimetres taller.'

'Sounds about right,' said Kaspel.

'Have you ever used a rifle scope?'

'Can't say that I have.'

'Even the best Ajack rifle scope will only put you four times nearer your target. So perhaps the victim's height helped the shooter. Perhaps he knew that all he had to do was shoot the tallest man. But we'll have a clearer view of what happened when it's daybreak.' I glanced at my wristwatch, saw that it was two a.m., and realized I didn't feel the least bit tired. 'Which is in five or six hours from now.'

I took the tube of Pervitin out of my pocket and regarded it with some incredulity.

'My God, what is this stuff? I have to admit, it's kind of wonderful. I could have used some Pervitin when I was still pounding the beat.'

'It's methamphetamine hydrochloride. It packs quite a punch, doesn't it? Frankly, I've learned to be a bit wary of the local magic potion. After a while there are side effects.'

'Such as?'

'You'll find out soon enough.'

'Go ahead and scare me, Hermann. I can take it.'

'For one thing, it's addictive. A lot of people on this mountain have come to rely on Pervitin. And after two or three days solid on that stuff there's always the risk that you'll have violent mood swings. Heart palpitations. Or even cardiac arrest.'

'Then I'll just have to hope for the best. Now that Bormann's got my ears stiff about this I really don't see any other way of working around the clock, do you?'

'No.' Kaspel grinned. 'Sounds like Heydrich's really dropped you in the shit with this case. And I'm going to enjoy watching you fall on your ugly face, Gunther. Or worse. Just don't expect me to give you the kiss of life. The only people Mrs Kaspel likes me to kiss is Mrs Kaspel.'

Further up the mountain, or so it seemed, I heard what sounded like an explosion; and seeing my head turn, Kaspel said: 'Construction workers on the other side of the Kehlstein. I think they're digging another tunnel through the mountain.'

Somewhere a telephone was ringing and a few moments later an SS man stepped out onto the terrace, saluted smartly, handed me the Leica and several rolls of film, and announced that Dr Brandt was now awaiting our arrival at the hospital down in Berchtesgaden.

'We'd better not keep the doctor waiting,' I said. 'Let's hope he's using this stuff, too. I hate a sloppy postmortem. Will you drive me down the mountain, please?'

We walked down the steps of the Berghof terrace to where we'd left Kaspel's car parked in front of the garage. I thought about asking him to stop at the Villa Bechstein to pick up Korsch and then decided against it; if he had any sense he was in bed by now, which seemed a long way off for me.

'And don't expect me to hold a kidney dish, either,' added

Kaspel. 'I don't much like the sight of blood before bed. It keeps me awake.'

'Well, you're in the wrong Party, aren't you?'

'Me?' Kaspel laughed. 'My God, that's rich coming from a bastard like you, Gunther. How does an old social democrat like you come to be a police commissar working for a man like Heydrich, anyway? I thought you'd been fired in 1932.'

'I'll tell you sometime.'

'Tell me now.'

'No, but I'll tell you this. Something that directly affects you, Hermann.'

It was a twelve-minute drive back down the mountain to Berchtesgaden and, finally alone with Kaspel, I gave him Heydrich's letter and told him that in spite of our shared history, the general expected nothing less than the captain's total cooperation with my present mission. He pocketed the letter, unread, and said nothing for a while.

'Listen, Hermann, I know you hate my guts. You've got every reason to feel that way. But look here, you'll hate me even more if I have to tell Heydrich you were obstructive. You know how he hates to be disappointed in the people who work for him. If I were you, I'd forget how much you dislike me and throw in your lot with Gunther, for now.'

'You know, Commissar, I was thinking the same thing.'

'There's all that and there's this, too. You should remember from our time in Berlin that I'm cursed with being an honest cop. I'm not the type to take all the credit myself. So if you help me, I promise I'll make sure that it's recognized by Heydrich. Me, I couldn't care less if there's any career advancement at the end of this. But you might think differently about your own future.'

'That's fair enough. But honestly? I had nothing to do with what happened back then. I might have been a Nazi, and an SA organizer, but I'm not a murderer.'

'I'll buy that. So, then. We're looking out for each other. Right?

Not friends. No. Too much laundry there. But perhaps – perhaps we're *Bolle* boys from Berlin. Agreed?'

Bolle was a Berliner's word for the kind of pal you made when you were drunk, on a Kremser van day trip to Schönholzer Heide park in Pankow – the kind of pal that had inspired a dozen cruel folk songs mocking the Franz Biberkopfs of this world who put no limits on drinking or pleasure, or violence, or all three at once. Now, that's what I call a worldview.

'Agreed.' Kaspel stopped the car for a moment on a wider bend of the meandering mountain road and then offered me his hand. I took it. '*Bolle* boys from Berlin,' he said. 'In which case, as one *Bolle* boy to another, let me fill you in about our friend Dr Karl Brandt. He's Hitler's personal physician here in Obersalzberg. That means that he's a member of the Leader's inner circle. Hitler and Göring were the principal guests at his wedding, in 1934. Which means he's as arrogant as they come. Given that Bormann has asked Brandt to carry out this postmortem, he won't have had any choice in the matter, but he certainly won't like having to perform the procedure in the middle of the night. So you'd be well advised to handle him with velvet gloves.'

Kaspel produced a packet of cigarettes, lit us both, and then started driving again. At the foot of the mountain road, we crossed over the river and drove into Berchtesgaden, which was predictably deserted.

'Is he up to this? Brandt?'

'You mean is he competent?'

'Surgically speaking.'

'He used to be a specialist in head and spinal injuries, so my guess is yes, probably, given that Karl Flex was shot in the head. But I'm not so sure about the hospital. Really, it's not much more than a clinic. There's a brand-new SS hospital under construction at the Stanggass – that's what we call the Reichs Chancellery – but that won't open for another year.'

'What do you mean – the Reichs Chancellery?'

Kaspel looked at me and laughed. 'That's all right. I was the same when I got here. A typical Berliner. That's why this place is run by a Bavarian mafia. Because Hitler doesn't trust anyone but Bavarians. Certainly not Berliners like you and me who are automatically suspect in the Leader's eyes of leaning to the left. Look, there's something you have to understand right now, Gunther. Berlin isn't the capital of Germany. Not any longer. No, really, I'm perfectly serious. Berlin is just for showcase diplomacy and propaganda purposes – the big set-piece parades and speeches. This crummy little Bavarian town is the real administrative capital of Germany now. That's right. Everything is run from Berchtesgaden. Which is why this is also the largest construction site in the country. If you didn't already know that after seeing the Kehlstein House – which cost millions by the way – then let me underline it for you. There's more new building being done here in Berchtesgaden and Obersalzberg than in the rest of Germany put together. If you can't believe that, then just look through those witness statements and see who was on that terrace yesterday morning. All of the country's leading civil engineers.'

Hermann Kaspel drew up outside the only building in Berchtesgaden where the lights were on and stopped the engine. For someone who was in any doubt that this might be a hospital, they need only have looked at the wall and its mural of a woman wearing a nurse's uniform in front of a black Nazi eagle.

'Here we are.'

He took out his cigarette case, opened it, and then found a banknote, which he rolled into a tube.

'Give me one of those magic tablets,' he said. 'Time to go to work.'

'You're coming inside?'

'I thought I might help.'

'I thought you were squeamish about the sight of blood.'

'Me? Whatever gave you that idea? Anyway. We're *Bolle* boys, right?'

'Right.'

'Bit of blood is par for the course when you're out on the piss in Pankow, right?'

I nodded and handed him one of the Pervitin tablets, only he didn't swallow it; instead he crushed it on the flat metal of his cigarette case with the car key and then separated the powder into two small parallel white lines.

'One of the Luftwaffe pilots from the local airport showed me this little trick,' he explained. 'When they have to make a night flight and they need to wake up or sober up in a real hurry, the best and quickest way to do it is with a hot rail, like this.'

'You're full of surprises, do you know that?'

Kaspel laid the end of the tube in the powder and then inhaled it noisily through one nostril and then the other, at which point he shuddered, uttered a series of loud expletives, blinked furiously several times, and then hammered the steering wheel with the flat of his hand. 'Go and fuck yourself!' he yelled. 'Go and fuck yourself. I am on fire. I am on fire. Now, that's what I call a fucking air force.'

He shook his head and then let out a loud whoop that had me feeling more than a little alarmed and wondering what effect Hermann Temmler's magic potion was having on my own body.

'Now let's go and find the doctor,' said Kaspel, and hurried inside the hospital.

CHAPTER 13

April 1939

Karl Brandt, who met us in a cold room in the hospital basement, was already dressed for surgery but under his immaculate
white overalls he was wearing the black uniform of an SS major,
which looked like some sort of contradiction. He was a tall,
strikingly handsome, stern-looking man in his mid-thirties, with
high cheekbones, light brown hair, and a very neat parting he
touched nervously every so often with the side of his hand, as
if there might be a wind in the hospital that would cause him
to soon require the action of a comb. It was almost a leading
man's face – the kind of face that might have found him a starring role in one of Dr Goebbels's movies – except for the fact
that there was something lacking in the man's cold, dark eyes.
It was hard to think that this was the face of a healer. Rather it
seemed more like the face of a fanatic who might easily have
prophesied the coming of a biblical flood and a new Cyrus from
the north who would reform the Church, or perhaps foretell
the arrival of a new religion. A couple of years later, in Prague,
I would come across his name again, in connection with the
murder of General Heydrich, but at this particular moment, I'd
never heard of him. He blinked at me with slow contempt as
I stumbled my way through an apology, first for keeping him
waiting and then for the lateness of the hour.

'We came as soon as we heard you were here, Doctor. I apologize if you've been waiting for very long. If it had been up to me, I'd have said this could certainly have waited until first thing in the morning, but the deputy chief of staff was most insistent that an autopsy should proceed with all possible speed. Of course, the sooner we find out exactly what happened to Dr Flex, the sooner I hope to apprehend the culprit, and the sooner we can restore everyone's peace of mind and the Leader can return to his beautiful home. Sir, I don't know if you were acquainted with the victim, but if you were I would like to offer you my condolences and to thank you for agreeing to perform what might well be a distressing task. If you weren't acquainted with him I should like to thank you, anyway. I do appreciate that forensic medicine is not your usual field, however—'

'I assume you must have attended a postmortem before in your capacity as a Murder Commission detective,' he said, interrupting me with an impatient wave of his hand. 'In Berlin, wasn't it?'

'Yes, sir. More often than I care to remember.'

'It's been more than ten years since I was a medical student and did any real anatomy, so we may have need of that forensic memory. I might also require your assistance from time to time, to help shift the body. Can you do that, Commissar?'

'Yes, sir.'

'Good. Since you mention it, I did know the victim. But this will in no way affect my ability to carry out the autopsy procedure. And I am as eager to find a satisfactory conclusion to this tragic affair as anyone. For the sake of my friend, it goes without saying. And for the Leader's peace of mind, as you say. Well, let's get on with it. I haven't got all night. The body is this way. We don't have a pathology suite in this hospital. Sudden deaths are rare in Berchtesgaden and usually dealt with in Salzburg. The body is laid out in what passes for an operating theatre here, which is as good a place as any to carry out a postmortem.'

Brandt turned on the heel of a highly polished jackboot and

led the way into a brightly lit room, where the corpse of a very tall, thin man with a small beard, still dressed in his winter tweeds, was lying on a table. The apparent cause of death was immediately obvious: a large piece of skull, several centimetres square and still attached to his scalp, was hanging off the side of his blood-encrusted head like an open trapdoor and half of the man's scrambled brains seemed to have spilled onto the table and the floor tiles like fragments of minced meat in a butcher's shop. Karl Flex himself was staring up at the ceiling with open-mouthed astonishment, his wide blue eyes unflinching against the bright light, almost as if he had seen the marvellous sight of the Lord's angel of death come to fetch him from one world into the next. It was a shocking sight, even for a Murder Commission veteran like me. Sometimes the human body strikes me as more fragile than could reasonably be expected.

'Holy shit,' muttered Kaspel, and momentarily put his hand to his mouth. 'That's what I call a fucking head wound.'

'Best get all of the cursing done now, gentlemen,' Brandt said coldly, stretching some rubber gloves onto his hands.

'Sorry, sir, but – holy shit.'

'Smoke if it helps to keep your mouth busy, Captain. It certainly won't bother me. I much prefer the sweet smell of tobacco to that of antiseptic. Or the sound of your cursing. Just as long as you don't pass out.'

Kaspel needed no second invitation and immediately lit up, but I shook my head at his open cigarette case when it came my way. I certainly didn't want anything interfering with my understanding of how Karl Flex had met his death. Besides, I needed both hands for the camera, and was already taking pictures of the dead man with my expensive new toy.

'Is that strictly necessary?' complained Brandt.

'Absolutely,' I answered, focusing on the ruined skull, which looked very like the empty shell of the boiled egg I had eaten for breakfast that morning. 'Every picture tells a story.'

'I assume that all of the victim's personal effects have been removed from his pockets?' Brandt asked Kaspel.

'Yes, sir,' he answered. 'They're in a bag on a table in the dispensary next door, awaiting the commissar's inspection.'

'Good,' said Brandt. 'Then we needn't worry too much about how we remove the victim's clothes.' He handed me a pair of very sharp scissors. Then he fetched another pair, started to cut up the leg of the dead man's trousers, and invited me to do the same on the other side. 'All the same, it does seem a shame. I mean, look at this.' He opened Flex's jacket to reveal a label. 'Hermann Scherrer of Munich. If this suit wasn't already covered in blood then one might have tried to save it.'

I put down the Leica and took hold of a trouser leg and was about to start using the scissors when a rather sleepy bee crawled out of the turn-up.

'What about saving this chap, instead?'

'It's just a bee, isn't it?' said Brandt.

'I need a bag,' I said, allowing the bee to crawl on my hand for a moment. 'Or an empty pill bottle.'

'You'll find some in the dispensary,' said Brandt.

With the bee still attached to the back of my hand I went into the dispensary and found a small bottle. While I waited patiently for the bee to crawl inside, I glanced around, noting with some surprise that the dispensary seemed to be well stocked with Losantin and natron.

'Why don't you take its photograph?' Brandt said through the open door.

'Maybe I will if I can get it to smile.'

Once the bee was bottled I went back into the operating theatre and set about catching up with Brandt, whose sharp scissors had already progressed as far as the dead man's waist. Meanwhile, Brandt had invited Kaspel to remove the dead man's shoes, his thick socks, and his necktie.

'With a Raxon tie, you're always well dressed,' said Kaspel, repeating the company's famous advertising slogan. 'Unless it's like this one and covered with blood.'

'By the way,' said Brandt, slicing open the man's shirt like an impatient tailor, and then the vest that lay underneath. 'Beyond the obvious fact that he was shot in the head, what are we looking for? I'm not exactly sure. I mean, I could open his sternum and look for traces of poison if you want. But—'

'Back in the trenches, I had a friend who was shot through the neck,' I said. 'I kept pressure on it, with my hand, to stop him bleeding out, like you were supposed to do. Only to find that it was the second shot, in the chest, which I didn't even see, that killed him. Life's full of surprises like that. And death more so.'

'This man's been shot just the once,' said Brandt. 'And that's what killed him, too. I'll stake my reputation on it.'

'That's a shrewd guess now that you've got his shirt open, sir,' said Kaspel.

Kaspel had Flex's shoes off and was inspecting the maker's label on the insole.

'This fellow was a good German, all right.' Kaspel's constant chatter was drug-related, of course. I was feeling quite chatty myself. 'A real Nazi, I reckon.'

'Why do you say so?' I asked.

'Lingel shoes.'

Lingel shoes of Erfurt were fond of proclaiming their own Aryan purity, with the implication that other shoe manufacturers – Salamander, for example – were racially tainted. It was the sort of stunt that all sorts of German manufacturers had tried to pull since the enactment of the Nuremberg Laws of 1935.

I sliced through the dead man's underpants – for some reason Brandt had left them uncut – to expose his genitals.

'Does that look normal to you?' I asked Brandt.

'What do you want? A ruler?'

'I was thinking about the colour. His cock looks a bit red to me.'

Brandt stared momentarily at Flex's genitals and then shrugged. 'I really couldn't say.'

But there was something about the dead man's cock that made me fetch my camera again. Brandt winced and shook his head.

'You're a callous pair, I must say,' observed Brandt.

'I don't think he's feeling shy, sir,' I said, and took a picture of Karl Flex's cock. 'And I'm certainly not planning to publish these in the local newspaper.'

I put down the camera and turned back to the table, where the dead man's clothes were now hanging off him like a second skin. And finally we had arrived at the bloody ruins of Flex's head.

'This time we're looking for a bullet,' I said, feeling around in the dead man's matted blond hair. 'Sometimes you'll find one sticking to the scalp. Or under a man's shirt collar. Or even on the floor.'

I stirred the heap of brain matter on the table and on the floor with my forefinger, but there wasn't anything metallic in there, I was sure about that. I stood up and came back to the head. Brandt was staring into the hole like a child standing over a rock pool.

'We're also looking for a bullet hole,' I said.

'There's a hole all right,' said Brandt. 'As big as the Atta Cave, that one.'

'This looks more like an exit wound,' I said. 'I'm looking for a smaller one. An entry wound, perhaps.' I felt around the scalp for a moment. By now my hands were covered in sticky, day-old blood. There seemed to be only one pair of rubber gloves in that theatre. 'And here it is. About two or three centimetres below the exit wound.'

'Let me see,' said Brandt.

He let me guide his forefinger into a hole about the size of a pfennig, and then nodded.

'By God, you're right. It *is* a hole. Quite fascinating. Right on the occipital bone. The bullet enters here, just to the left of the lambdoid suture and exits a few centimetres higher up in an explosion of temporal bone and brain matter. The people standing next to him must have been considerably bloodied.'

'That's what I'm hoping,' I said.

'Sometimes it's easily forgotten just how destructive a bullet wound can be.'

'It is if you weren't in the trenches,' I said. 'For anyone who was, like me and Captain Kaspel here, this was an almost daily sight. Which is our excuse for what you call being callous.'

'Hmm. Yes. I take your point, Commissar. Sorry.'

'Can we get another picture, sir? Perhaps you could indicate this hole with a pen or a pencil?'

'You mean stick it in there?'

'If you would, sir. Makes it easier to know what's what in the photograph. And how big the hole is.'

I rinsed my hands and then collected up the Leica. And when Brandt was ready with his pencil, I took several pictures of the bullet hole.

'I suppose you would like me to search the skull cavity for any bullet fragments,' said Brandt.

'If you wouldn't mind, sir.'

Brandt put his hand inside Flex's head and began to palp what remained of the brain in search of something hard. It looked like someone scooping out a pumpkin for St Martin's Day.

'Given the state of the victim's cranium, it seems unlikely that we will find anything,' he said. 'Chances are that any bullet fragments are lying somewhere on the Berghof terrace.'

'Agreed, sir. Which makes it a pity that some helpful idiot thought to scrub the blood away.'

'Still, we'd best make sure, I suppose.' But after a while, Brandt shook his head. 'No. Nothing.'

'Thank you anyway, sir.'

'I suppose we'd better turn him over,' Brandt said helpfully, 'now that I've seen that entry wound. Just to make quite sure, as you say.'

We cut the remainder of the clothes off Flex's body and then turned him over in search of another bullet hole. His thin white body was quite unmarked but I took another picture anyway, for my own memory's sake. By now I was acutely aware of how much like a dead Christ Karl Flex actually looked. Perhaps it was the beard that did it, or the clear blue eyes; and perhaps all men look a bit like Christ when they're laid out for burial; then again, perhaps that's the whole point of the story. But of one thing I was quite certain: with a head wound like that it was going to take longer than three days for Karl Flex to be resurrected alongside the just and the unjust.

'That's going to be quite an album when you've finished,' observed Kaspel.

'Commissar, if you're in agreement with me,' said Brandt, 'I'm going to record the cause of death as gunshot wound to the head.'

'I agree.'

'Then I think we've probably finished, don't you?' said Brandt. 'Unless there's anything else you want me to do here?'

'No, sir, and thank you. I'm very grateful for everything.'

Brandt drew a sheet over the corpse, and moved the clothes into a neat pile under the table with the edge of his boot.

'I'll have a medical orderly come in and tidy up first thing in the morning,' he said. 'As for the body, what do you want to do with it? I mean, I imagine he must have some family some-where.'

I followed Brandt to the sink, where he washed his hands.

'That's up to Martin Bormann,' I said. 'I understand that there's a need for discretion here. That there's a need to prevent the Leader from being alarmed by this unfortunate event.'

'Yes, of course. Well then, I'll let you ask him what's to be done with the corpse, shall I?'

I nodded. 'There is just one more thing, sir. You say you knew the man well. Can you think of anyone who might have wanted to kill him?'

'No,' said Brandt. 'Karl Flex had lived in the area for several years, and although he wasn't from this part of the world – he was from Munich – he was very well liked by almost everyone in Obersalzberg. At least, that was my impression. He was my next-door neighbour, more or less. My wife, Anni, and I live in Buchenhohe, back up the mountain, and a little further east of the Leader's Territory. Lots of people who work in Obersalzberg live there.'

'What were his interests?'

'Reading. Music. Winter sports. Cars.'

'Any girlfriends?'

'No. Not that I know of.'

'But he did like girls.'

'I really couldn't say. I assume so. What I mean is, he never talked about anyone in particular. Why do you ask?'

'I'm just trying to paint a picture of the man and why someone shot him. Perhaps a jealous husband. Or the aggrieved father of some unfortunate local girl. Sometimes the most obvious motives turn out to be the right ones.'

'No. There was nothing like that. I'm certain of it. Now if you'll excuse me, Commissar. I really have to get back to my wife. She's not at all well.'

Brandt snatched off his overall and walked out without another word. I can't say he was much of a doctor but it was easy to see why Hitler kept him around. Ramrod-straight and with the solemn manner of a taper-bearer he looked good in his black uniform and while he didn't seem like the kind of doctor who had the cure for anything very much, he could certainly have frightened away a persistent cough or cold. He certainly frightened me.

CHAPTER 14

April 1939

'Well, he certainly wasn't much help,' objected Kaspel. 'The long streak of piss.'

It was three thirty in the morning and we were in the Berchtesgaden hospital dispensary, going through Flex's personal effects, which I'd already photographed, collectively, several times. Kaspel had compiled a list of the dead man's possessions, which I now had in my hand.

'It's cold fish like him that give the SS a bad name, right enough,' I said. 'But as it happens, Dr Brandt was a lot more help than you might think.'

'How? It was you who found the entry wound, wasn't it?'

'Not for what he told us, but maybe for what he didn't tell us. For example, Flex had a bad case of gonorrhoea. Brandt didn't mention that, although if it was obvious to me then it must have been obvious to him.'

'So that's why you took a photograph of his cock. And I thought it was for your own personal smut collection.'

'You mean the pictures I keep of your wife and sister?'

'So you're the Fritz who's got them.'

'A bad dose of jelly would certainly explain the presence of a bottle of Protargol on the list of Flex's personal effects. Except that there's no Protargol here now. It would seem that someone's already removed it. That and the Pervitin, which also appears on your list. On the other hand, the dead man's money clip – rather a lot of money, several hundred marks, wasn't it? – that's still here. Along with all his other valuables.'

'Oh, yes. You're right. The drugs are gone, aren't they? Pity. I was going to have that Pervitin myself.'

'My guess is that Brandt removed them. Certainly he had more than enough opportunity while he was waiting for us to get here. Obviously he didn't know that like any good copper, you'd already compiled this list.' I took one of Kaspel's cigarettes and let him light me with Flex's lighter. 'Now, as far as the Protargol is concerned, it may just be that as Flex's friend he wanted to spare him the embarrassment of us discovering the deceased was taking silver proteinate for a venereal disease. I suppose I can understand that. Just. I might do the same for someone I knew. If he was married, perhaps.'

'I can explain the meth,' offered Kaspel. 'There used to be a plentiful supply of the magic potion here in Berchtesgaden. They used to give it to the local P&Z workers to help them meet their construction deadlines. But lately the supply seems to have dried up. At least for anyone who isn't in a uniform. I've heard that right now there are lots of civilians in Berchtesgaden who are desperate for some magic potion. Like I said, Pervitin can be quite addictive.'

'So why has the supply dried up?'

'Unofficially the word around Hitler's mountain is that they're stockpiling the stuff for our armed forces, in case there's a war. That the German military is going to need methamphetamine to stay awake long enough to beat the Poles. And presumably the Ivans when they come in on the Polack side.'

I nodded. 'Then that would also explain the presence of Losantin and natron in this clinic.' I pointed these out on the shelves and, when Kaspel shrugged, I added: 'Losantin is used to treat skin burns caused by poison gas. Natron is used to neutralize chlorine gas. At least it was when I was in the trenches.

It looks like someone is preparing for the worst, even in Berchtesgaden.'

'I'll tell you something else that's missing,' said Kaspel. 'At least according to the list I made yesterday morning with Major Högl. There was a little blue notebook and a small set of keys on a little gold chain that was around his neck. They're gone, too.'

'Can you remember what was in the book?'

'Numbers. Just numbers.'

'So let's see what's left. Packet of Turkish 8—'

'Everyone in the Leader's Territory smokes them. Me included.'

'A set of house keys, some loose change, a tortoiseshell comb, a pair of reading glasses, a leather wallet, civilian driving licence, weapons permit, employment identification document, hunting permit, NSDAP Personal Identity Document, Aryan Family Tree Record, a Party badge, some business cards, a gold signet ring, a gold Imco lighter, a little gold hip flask, a gold wristwatch – this is a Jaeger-LeCoultre, which is really expensive – a pair of gold cufflinks, gold Pelikan fountain pen—'

'Karl Flex liked his gold, didn't he? Even the money clip is eighteen carat.' Kaspel unscrewed the top of the hip flask and sniffed the contents.

'And then there's this Ortgies .32 automatic,' I said. 'Where was he keeping this, anyway? Under his waistband? In his sock? Around his neck on a gold chain?'

'It was in his jacket pocket,' said Kaspel.

I tugged out the magazine and inspected it. 'Loaded, too. It would seem that our tall friend may have been expecting some trouble after all. You wouldn't carry this little hedge trimmer unless you thought you might actually need it.'

'Especially up here. If he'd been found carrying that at the Berghof he'd have been arrested, even with the civilian permit. Bormann's orders. Only the RSD are allowed to carry weapons in the Leader's Territory. And never inside the Berghof or the Kehlstein, where the only person allowed to carry a gun is Bormann himself. Check it out if you want. There's always a lump in the right-hand pocket of his jacket.'

I pointed at the hip flask. 'What's the poison?'

Kaspel took a bite from the hip flask and nodded his smiling appreciation. 'That's the good stuff. Same as Bormann drinks.'

I took a bite myself and then a deep breath. Grassl has that effect on you. On top of the methamphetamine it felt like a dose of electric current running down my insides. 'I do love a job that lets me drink the best schnapps when I'm on duty.'

Kaspel laughed and pocketed the hip flask. 'I think we'd better make sure this doesn't fall into the wrong hands.'

'A Hermann Scherrer suit, Lingel shoes, cashmere socks, silk underwear, a plutocrat's watch, and more gold than King Solomon's temple – he lived well, didn't he? For a civil engineer.' I shrugged. 'What does a civil engineer do, anyway?'

'He does very well, that's what he does.' Kaspel pulled a face. 'At least until he gets shot in the back of the head. That's right, isn't it? He was shot in the back of the head, not the front like everyone thought before. Which means the shooter could have been in the woods at the back of the Berghof, like everyone thought.' He shook his head. 'Beats me how we didn't find anything.'

'You were there? In the woods?'

'I commanded the search detail. You wouldn't get Rattenhuber or Högl getting their boots dirty. No, that was me and my men.'

'I'm going back there. Now that I've seen the body I want to read all the witness statements in my new office – supposing that I do have an office – and then take a closer look at that terrace.'

'I don't know what you expect to find. But I'll come with you.'

'Don't you want to go home, Kaspel? It's three thirty in the morning.'

'I do. But I'm flying now, since I snorted the magic potion. Like I was in an Me 109. It'll be ages before I can even close my eyelids, let alone get some sleep. Besides, we're *Bolle* boys, right?

From Pankow. We keep going until one of us collapses or gets thrown in jail. That's the way this thing works now. I'll drive you back up the mountain to the Berghof and along the way I'll give you a few hard lumps of truth about this place.'

CHAPTER 15

April 1939

It had stopped snowing and the night felt as if it were holding its breath. My own billowed in front of my face like a cloud over one of the mountaintops. Even at night it was a beautiful, magical place but as with all stories involving magic in Germany, there was always a sense that my lungs and liver were already on someone's menu – that behind the lace curtains of one of these quaint little wooden houses, a local huntsman was sharpening his ax and preparing to carry out his orders to have me quietly killed. I shivered and, still holding the Leica, I pulled the collar of my coat up and wished that I'd also asked for a pair of warm gloves. I decided to add gloves to my list of requirements. Bormann – the Lord of the Obersalzberg, as Kaspel had called him – seemed willing to let me have almost everything else. Kaspel opened the car door for me politely, his attitude now entirely different from that of the man I'd met an hour or two before. It was already clear that he'd changed a lot since leaving the Berlin police. The Nazis could do that to a man, even if he was Nazi. I was almost starting to like him.

'What's he like, Heydrich?' he asked.

'Haven't you met him?'

'Briefly. But I don't know him. I report direct to Neumann.'

'I've met the general several times. He's smart and he's dangerous, that's what he's like. I work for him because I have to.

I think even Himmler's afraid of him. I know I am. That is why I'm still alive.'

'It's the same all over. If anything, it's worse here than in Berlin.'

'So tell me how that works.'

He winced. 'Hmm. I don't know, Gunther. *Bolle* boys from Pankow and all that, yes. And I want to help you and the general. But I think we both know that there are things of which we cannot and should not speak. That's why *I'm* alive, too. It's not just P&Z workers who can end up having an accident. And if that doesn't work, Dachau concentration camp is less than two hundred kilometres from here.'

'I'm glad you mentioned Dachau, Hermann. Three years ago Heydrich sent me there to look for a man who was a convict, a fellow named Kurt Mutschmann, which meant I had to pose as a camp inmate myself. But after several weeks the pose felt real enough. I was only able to get out of there by finding Mutschmann, and not until. Heydrich thought it was all very amusing. But I didn't. Look, I think you know I'm no Nazi. I'm useful to him because I don't put politics before common sense, that's all. Because I'm good at what I do, although I wish I wasn't.'

'All right. That's fair enough.' Kaspel started the car. 'So, then. This is not the harmonious rural idyll that Martin Bormann has described to you, Gunther. Nor is the Leader popular here, in spite of all those flags and Nazi wall murals. Far from it. The whole of Hitler's mountain is riddled with disused tunnels and old salt mines. That's where the mountain gets its name, of course. From the salt. But the local geology provides a very good metaphor for how things are in Obersalzberg and Berchtesgaden. Nothing is what it looks like on the surface. Nothing. And underneath – well, there's nothing sweet going on here.'

Hermann Kaspel steered across the river and drove us back up the mountain to the Berghof. It was a winding road but in the moonlight we soon encountered a construction crew engaged in widening it to make things easier for anyone coming to see Hitler. Most of them were wearing traditional Tyrolean hats and thick jackets and one or two of them even gave the Hitler salute as we drove by, which Kaspel returned, but their expressions were churlish and wary.

'In the summer there are as many as three or four thousand workers like those around here,' explained Kaspel. 'But right now there are probably only about half that number. Most of them are accommodated in local work camps at Alpenglühen, Teugel-brunn, and Remerfeld. Only, don't make the mistake of thinking these men are forced into the work. Believe me, they're not. It's true that in the beginning the Austrian employment offices were ordered to refer all available workers to this site. The men they sent were wholly unsuitable to work in the Alps – hotel clerks, hairdressers, artists – and lots of them got sick, so now it's just local Bavarians who are used, men with experience of working in the mountains. Even so, we've had a lot of trouble at the work camps. Drinking, drugs, gambling. Fights about money. The local SS has its work cut out keeping order with some of these fellows. Still, there is no problem getting workmen. These Obersalzberg Administration workers are all very well paid. In fact, they're on triple time. And that's not the only attraction. Construction work in this area has been declared by Bormann to be a reserved occupation. In other words, if you work on Hitler's mountain, you won't have to serve in the armed forces. That's especially attractive right now, given that everyone thinks there's going to be another war. So you can imagine there's no shortage of volunteers. In spite of all that, the construction work up here is very dangerous. Even in the summer. Explosions – like the one you heard earlier – are often used to create tunnels through mountains and there have been lots of accidents. Fatal accidents. Men buried alive. Men who fall off mountaintops. Only three days ago there was a big avalanche that killed several men. Then there are the constant delays caused by Hitler's regular presence in the area – he likes to sleep late and doesn't care for the sound of construction work. That means the work, when it does take place, has, of necessity, been around the clock. God knows how many men were killed building that fucking tea house on the Kehlstein; considerable risks were taken to get it ready in time for his fiftieth birthday. So there are a lot more widows around here than there need have been. That's caused a lot of resentment in Berchtesgaden and the surrounding area. Anyway, Flex worked for P&Z. And just to work for that company around here might provide someone with a pretty good motive for murder.

'But here's another. Nearly all of the houses and farms you see up on the mountain have been the subject of government compulsory purchase orders. Göring's house. His adjutant's house. Bormann's house. The Türken Inn. Speer's house. Bormann's farm. You name it. In 1933 all of the houses on the mountain were in private hands. Today there's hardly one that isn't owned by the German government. It's what you might call real estate fascism and it works like this. Someone in the government now favoured by Hitler or Bormann needs a nice house to be near to the Leader. So Bormann offers to buy such a house from its Bavarian owner; and you might imagine, with so few houses left in private hands, that it's a seller's market and a high price for such a house could be obtained. Not a bit of it. Bormann always offers well below the market rate, and God forbid you should ever refuse his first offer, but if you do, here's what happens. The SS turn up out of the blue, block off your drive, and remove your roof. That is not an exaggeration. And if you still won't sell to the government, then you might easily find yourself sent to Dachau on some trumped-up charge, at least until you change your mind.

'Take the Villa Bechstein, where you're staying, Gunther. It was formerly owned by a woman who was a keen supporter of Hitler. She gave him a new car when he came out of Landsberg Prison, not to mention a nice new piano for his house, and probably quite a bit of money on top. But none of this mattered when the Lord of Obersalzberg decided he wanted her house for Nazi VIPs. She was obliged to sell just like everyone else. And for a knock-down price. That's how Hitler rewards his friends. It's a similar story for the Türken Inn. The fact is, the town of Berchtesgaden is full of small houses occupied by local Bavarians who used to own bigger houses on Hitler's mountain. And all of those people hate Martin Bormann's guts. In an effort to distance himself from this ill feeling, Bormann sometimes uses a man called Bruno Schenk to deliver his compulsory purchase orders. Or more often Bruno Schenk's man Karl Flex. You want a motive for murder? There's another one for you. An excellent one. Bruno Schenk and Karl Flex were two of the most hated men in the area. If anyone deserved a bullet in the head it was them, or Bormann's adjutant, Wilhelm Zander, whom you've already met at the Kehlstein. Which means you're going to have a hell of a problem solving this case without stepping on Martin Bormann's corns. It's my private opinion that the corruption here goes even deeper than that. Perhaps all the way through the mountain, if you see what I mean. Maybe as far as Hitler himself. I wouldn't be surprised if the Leader is getting his ten per cent of everything, because Bormann certainly does. Even from the Türken shop where the SS buy their smokes and their postcards. Seriously. Bormann always takes his lead from Hitler and my guess is that it was Hitler put him up to this little moneymaking game.

'But that's not just idle speculation. Let me tell you a little-known story about the house that Hitler bought. The Haus Wachenfeld. Now called the Berghof, on which many more millions have been spent. Of course, he's been coming here since 1923, after the putsch, when he couldn't afford to do much more than rent a room at the Haus Wachenfeld. But in 1928, as his situation started to improve, he was able to rent the whole house from the owner – a widow in Hamburg by the name of Margarete Winter. By 1932, Hitler was rich from the sale of his book, and so he decided to make the widow an offer to buy the place. Because she was living in Hamburg there was very little pressure he could apply to make her sell and, by all accounts, she didn't want to sell. But she was short of cash. Her husband had lost most of his money in the crash of '29, and they'd been obliged to sell his leather factory. Some local Jews bought it for a knock-down price. The widow hated those Jews even more than she disliked the idea of Hitler forcing her out of her house in Obersalzberg. So she offered *him* a deal. She'd sell the house to Hitler for 175,000 reichsmarks if he also did *her* a favour. The very next day, that same leather factory was struck by lightning and it burned to the ground, although it seems much more likely that it wasn't Mother Nature who destroyed it but some local SA men. On Hitler's personal orders. That's a true story, Gunther. So you see, Hitler always gets what he wants, by hook or by crook. And Martin Bormann does much the same.'

'So if I understand you correctly, Hermann, half of the people I speak to are going to tell me nothing because they're afraid of Bormann. And the other half aren't going to tell me anything because they're hoping the murderer is going to get away with it. Because they think that Karl Flex had it coming. In spades.'

Kaspel grinned. 'That's a pretty fair description of your investigative task, yes. You're going to need to keep your cards so close to your chest, you'll be lucky to see what suit they are.'

'Heydrich wanted me to find some dirt on Bormann. It sounds like this could be what he wanted. Have you told him any of this?'

'No. But none of this will come as a big surprise to Heydrich. It was Bormann who helped Himmler to buy his house. That's not in Obersalzberg but in Schönau, about fifteen minutes from here. The Schneewinkellehen. The place used to be owned by Sigmund Freud. Figure that one out. Anyway, Heydrich is certainly not going to try and take Bormann to task for doing something his own boss has done, too.'

'Good point. He did ask me to see if there's any truth in a rumour that Bormann's being blackmailed by his own brother. I imagine Heydrich wants to know what Albert has on his brother so he can blackmail him as well.'

'Now, what that might be, I don't know. All I know is that Albert Bormann has the other ear of Adolf Hitler, which means he is almost as powerful down here as Martin Bormann. You have to hand it to Hitler. He certainly knows how to divide and rule.'

We stopped at a checkpoint and once again presented our credentials to the frozen SS guard. A searchlight illuminating our car also showed me the size of the security fence.

'It wouldn't be easy to get over that,' I said. 'Especially with a rifle in your hand.'

'There's ten kilometres of that fence,' said Kaspel. 'With thirty separate gates, each with Zeiss-Ikon security locks. But the fence is often damaged by rock slides and avalanches and – well, sabotage. Even when it's undamaged this perimeter fence doesn't mean shit. Oh, it looks good and it makes the road secure enough and I expect it makes Hitler feel safe, but everyone in the RSD is well aware that all those tunnels and private salt mines mean there are plenty of locals who can come and go as they please inside the perimeter. And what's more, they do. It's like Swiss cheese inside this mountain, Gunther. Hitler banned all hunting behind the perimeter wire fence because he's fond of little furry animals but that doesn't stop people hunting there with total impunity. The best game to be had around here is in the Leader's Territory and the chances are that your shooter is some local peasant who accessed the area through an old salt mine tunnel that his fucked-up, inbred family has been using for hundreds of years. He was probably looking to pot a couple of rabbits or a deer but he settled for a rat instead.'

'Thanks for telling me all that, Hermann. I appreciate your honesty.' I grinned. 'Some beautiful scenery, a dead body, a lot of lies, and a dumbhead of a cop. You know, all we need is a pretty girl and a fat man and I think it's safe to say that we have the ingredients for a Mack Sennett comedy. That's why I'm here in Obersalzberg, I guess. Because the Almighty enjoys a damn good laugh. Believe me, I should know. They say there's a grace in this world and forgiveness, only I don't see it, because my own fucked-up, falling-over, full-of-shit life has been keeping my dear Father in heaven amused since January 1933. To be honest, I'm beginning to hope He chokes on it.'

Kaspel pursed his lips and shook his head. 'You know, I've been twisting my brain for the reason General Heydrich should have sent you down here to Obersalzberg, Gunther. And maybe I'm starting to get a glimpse of his reason. You might just be in possession of a darker spirit than any of us.'

'Hermann? You've been away from Berlin for too long. You ever wonder why we have a black bear on our coat of arms? Because he's got a sore head, that's why. Everyone in Berlin is like me. That's why everyone else in Germany loves the place so much.'

CHAPTER 16

April 1939

We arrived on the northern side of the Berghof, where we were greeted on the stairs leading up to the terrace by a man I'd first met many years before. Arthur Kannenberg had once owned a garden restaurant in Berlin-West, near Uncle Tom's Cabin, called Pfuhl's Weinund. But it went belly-up in the crash and the last I'd heard of Kannenberg he'd left Berlin and gone to work in Munich, managing the officers' mess in the Nazi Party HQ. A small, round man with pale skin, very pink lips, hyperthyroidic eyes, and dressed in a grey *Tracht* jacket, he greeted me warmly.

'Bernie,' he said, shaking my hand, 'it's good to see you again.'

'Arthur. This is a surprise. What the hell are you doing here?'

'I'm the house manager here at the Berghof. Herr Bormann told me to expect you. So here I am, at your service.'

'Thanks, Arthur, but I'm sorry if that meant you had to stay up so late.'

'Actually I'm used to it. The Leader is a bit of a night owl, to be honest. Which means I have to be one, too. Anyway, I wanted to make sure everything was arranged to your satisfaction. We've made an office for you in one of the spare rooms on the second floor.'

Kaspel made himself scarce while I followed Kannenberg

under a covered walkway and then entered a vestibule through a heavy oak door.

'Are you still playing that accordion of yours, Arthur?'

'Sometimes. When the Leader asks me to.'

With its low ceilings, dim lighting, red marble columns, and vaulted arches, the lobby area resembled the crypt in a church. Homely, it wasn't. Kannenberg led the way upstairs and we walked down an impressively wide corridor that was lined with pictures. He showed me into a quiet room with a cream-coloured tile stove painted with green figures. The walls were clad in sanded spruce and a wooden seat was built around a corner with a rectangular table. On the floor were several rugs and a wrought-iron basket full of logs for the wood-burning stove. There were two telephones and a filing cabinet, and everything I'd asked for, including fur-lined Hanwag boots. Seeing them I sat down and put them on immediately; my feet were freezing.

'This will do very nicely,' I said, standing up and stamping around the room for a moment to test my new boots.

Kannenberg switched on a table lamp, lowered his voice, and leaned closer.

'Anything you need while you're here – and I do mean anything – you come to me, all right? Don't ask any of these SS adjutants. You ask them a question, they'll want to clear the answer with someone else first. You come to me and I will sort you out. Just like we were back in Berlin. Coffee, alcohol, pills, something to eat, cigarettes. Only, don't for Christ's sake smoke in the house. The Leader's girlfriend, she smokes in her room with the window open and she thinks he doesn't smell it, but he does and it drives him mad. She's here now and just because he's away she thinks she can get away with it. But I can smell it in the morning. You're just across the hall from his private study so please, Bernie, if you want a cigarette, take it outside. And make sure you pick up your butts. Anyway, I'll take you around the house in the morning. But for now, let me show you how close you are to him. Just to make the point about the cigarettes.'

We were standing in the doorway and Kannenberg opened the opposite door and switched on a light to let me peek inside the Leader's study. It was a spacious room, with French windows, a green carpet, lots of bookshelves, a big desk, and a fireplace. On the desk was a pair of chest expanders, and above the fireplace was a painting of a pink-faced Frederick the Great when he was still a young man and probably just the crown prince. He was wearing a blue velvet coat and holding a sword and a telescope as if he were expecting to admire the view from the Leader's French window. I know I was.

'You see? You're just across the hall.'

Kannenberg picked up the chest expanders and put them in a desk drawer.

'He needs these because his right arm gets all the exercise,' he explained sheepishly. 'Makes his left arm weaker.'

'I know the feeling.'

'He's a great man, Bernie.' He glanced around the study, almost as if it were some sort of shrine. 'One day, this room, his study, will be a place of pilgrimage. Thousands of people already come here in the summer just to catch a glimpse of him. That's why they had to buy the Türken Inn, to give him some peace and quiet. This is what this place is meant to be all about. Peace and quiet. Well, it was, until yesterday morning's tragedy. Let's hope you can quickly restore things to how they were, before.'

Kannenberg switched out the light and stepped back into the hall.

'Were you there, Arthur? When Karl Flex was shot?'

'Yes, I saw the whole thing. Weber and the others were just about to adjourn to the new Platterhof Hotel to see how far things had progressed with the building work there, when it happened.'

'Weber?'

'Hans Weber, the lead engineer from P&Z. I was standing about a metre away from Dr Flex, I suppose. Not that I realized what had happened for a moment or two. Mainly because of the hat he was wearing.'

'Hat? I haven't seen any hat.'

'It was a little Tyrolean green hat with feathers. Like something a local peasant would wear. It was only when his hat fell off that anyone realized the extent of his injuries. It was as if his head had exploded from inside, Bernie. Like when an egg you're boiling just bursts open. I expect someone threw the hat away because it was soaked with blood.'

'Do you think you could find that hat?'

'I could certainly try.'

'Please do. Was anyone else wearing a hat?'

'I don't think so. And if they were it wouldn't have been like that one. It wasn't what you'd call a gentleman's hat. I think Flex wore it because he thought it made him look like one of the locals. Or a character.'

'And was he? A character?'

'I really couldn't say.' But Kannenberg caught my eye and, placing a forefinger over his lips, he shook his head meaningfully.

'I know it's very late, Arthur, but I'd appreciate it if you could accompany me onto the terrace for a few moments and explain exactly what happened. Just so that I can build a picture in my mind.'

We went downstairs.

'It's this way. Through the Great Hall.'

'How about that wife of yours? Freda. Is she here, too?'

'She is. And she'll fix you a big Berlin-sized breakfast in the morning. Whatever and whenever you want.'

The Great Hall was an oversized rectangle with a red-carpeted floor on two levels and a larger version of the hall on top of the Kehlstein. On one side was a red marble fireplace and on the northern side, the huge panoramic window. It was the sort of room where a medieval king might have given banquets and administered a rough kind of justice. Thrown a condemned man out of that window, perhaps; according to Kannenberg, the window was powered by an electric motor to wind it up and down, like a cinema screen. There was another grand piano, a huge tapestry of Frederick the Great, again, and by the window a marble-topped table and an enormous globe, which did little to assuage any fears I had about Nazi Germany's territorial ambitions. Hitler's devotion to the example of Frederick the Great persuaded me that he must have often stood beside that globe and wondered just where he might send Germany's armies next. We crossed the upper level, and exited the Berghof through the winter garden which, in stark contrast to the Great Hall, looked like my late grandmother's sitting room. Outside, on the freezing terrace, the arc lights were shining brightly and several RSD men, including Kaspel, were awaiting my arrival.

'So,' said Kannenberg, heading straight for the low wall that bordered the terrace, 'Dr Flex was standing here, I think. Next to Brückner. One of Hitler's adjutants.'

'Was Brückner wearing a uniform?'

'No. Everyone was looking at the Untersberg – that's the mountain that can be seen on the other side of the valley. Everyone except Dr Flex, that is. He was looking in the opposite direction. Straight up at the Hoher Göll. Like I am now.'

'You're sure about that, Arthur?'

'Absolutely. I know because he was looking at me. I wasn't really part of their discussion. I was just sort of hanging around waiting for Huber or Dimroth – he's the head engineer from Sager & Woerner – to tell me that they had finished breakfast. Or that they were ready to go to the Platterhof. But it could just as easily have been Flex who told me. And at the moment he fell I was looking right at him as if that's what he was going to say.'

'So he's taller than everyone else, right?'

'Yes.'

'And wearing a little green Tyrolean hat. Correct?'

'Correct.'

'And facing you, instead of down the valley.'

'That's right.'

'And you're standing where?'

Kannenberg crossed the terrace and stood in front of the winter garden's window. 'Here. Just here.'

'Thank you, Arthur. We'll take it from here. You go to bed, like a good fellow, and I'll see you later on today.'

'And if there's time you can tell me about Berlin. I miss it sometimes.'

'Oh, and Arthur? See if you can find me a pair of gloves. My hands are freezing.'

I went back inside to fetch the camera from my office on the first floor where I'd left it, and then returned to the terrace where Kaspel was now smoking a cigarette. Seeing me he stubbed it out very carefully on the wall and then placed the butt in his coat pocket. I smiled and shook my head. If I hadn't thought Hitler was crazy before coming to the Berghof, I did now. Where was the harm in a few lousy cigarettes? I took a short walk around the terrace and then came back to Kaspel.

'Hey, I just had a thought,' Kaspel said. 'If he was facing up the mountain and the shot hit him in the back of the head, then—'

'Exactly.' I pointed into the darkness that lay beyond the terrace, to the north, towards Berchtesgaden at the bottom of the mountain. 'The shooter was down there somewhere, Hermann. Not in the woods, or up there. No wonder you didn't find anything. The shooter was never there.' I glanced around the terrace and saw a neat stack of wooden dowelling in the corner. I fetched a length and carried it to the edge of the terrace. 'The question is, where exactly was he positioned? Where would a man with a rifle get the sort of cover he'd need to avoid discovery long enough to take a shot at this terrace?'

I handed Kaspel the wooden dowelling. 'Flex was taller than me. About the size of that man there.' I pointed at one of the sleepy-looking SS men awaiting our orders, who was also the tallest. 'You. You're about the same height as Flex. Come here. Come on, Germany awake, right?'

The SS man moved smartly towards the wall.

'What's your name, son?'

'Dornberger, sir. Walter Dornberger.'

'Walter, I want you to take off your helmet and turn to face away from the valley. And I want you to pretend to be the man who was shot. If you don't mind, I want to borrow your head for a moment. Hermann? You hold the dowelling in position alongside his head, where I tell you.'

'Right you are,' said Kaspel.

I put my finger at the bottom of the SS man's skull. 'Entry wound about here. Exit wound about six to eight centimetres higher. Perhaps more. But it's hard to be more accurate, given the skull damage. If we had the dead man's hat, of course, we would have an actual bullet hole, which might enable us to plot the bullet's trajectory.'

It was at this moment that Kannenberg returned carrying a hat with a four-cord rope band and a pin that was a fisherman's fly. Made of green loden wool, and with a two-inch brim, the hat was heavily stained with blood. On the inside especially it looked as if someone had used it as a gravy boat. But it was quite dry and a small hole was clearly visible in the crown where the assassin's rifle bullet had exited.

'This is the hat,' explained Kannenberg. 'I found it on the floor by the incinerator.'

'Well done, Arthur. Now we're getting somewhere.'

This time Kannenberg waited to see what I was about to do with the SS man and the dowelling and the gnome's hat I was holding. I pushed the dowelling through the hole and then asked the SS man if he wouldn't mind putting the hat on his head for a moment.

'Now, then,' I told Kaspel. 'Lower the end of the dowelling a few centimetres to where we thought the bullet entered Flex's skull. That's it.'

Quickly I took some photographs and then inspected both ends of the dowelling – one pointing up at the wooden balcony immediately above the terrace and the other pointing over the edge of the wall and down the valley.

After a moment or two I removed the green hat from the SS man's blond head and laid it on the ground.

'Arthur? I'm going to need you to show Walter here where you found the hat. Walter? I want you to go to the incinerator, get down on your hands and knees, and see if you can't find a spent bullet. And Arthur? I'm going to need a ladder so that I can climb up and take a closer look at that balcony.'

'Right away, Bernie,' said Kannenberg.

'We're going to see if we can find the spent bullet up there in the woodwork on that balcony,' I explained. 'One single silver bullet.'

'Why silver?' asked Kaspel.

I didn't answer but the truth was I couldn't see the point of anyone shooting a rifle bullet at the terrace of Hitler's private residence unless it was made of a melted-down silver crucifix.

CHAPTER 17

April 1939

We didn't find a single bullet lodged in the woodwork of the Berghof's second-floor balcony because by the time it was light, we'd found four of them. Before gouging out these bullets with my Boker knife I marked each of their positions with a piece of Lohmann tape and then photographed them. I was beginning to wish I'd asked for a photographer as well as a Leica, but the truth was I was hoping to pocket the Leica when the case was over and sell it when I was back in Berlin. When you're working for people who are mostly thieves and murderers, a little of it comes off on your hands now and then.

From the second-floor balcony at the Berghof it was clear exactly why Hitler had chosen this place to live in. The view from the house was breathtaking. It was impossible to look at this view of Berchtesgaden and the Untersberg behind it without hearing an alphorn or a simple cowbell, but not Wagner. At least not for me. Give me a cowbell any day to the high priest of Germanism. Besides, a cowbell only has one note, which is a lot easier on the backside than five hours in the Bayreuth Festival Hall. In truth I spent very little time admiring the postcard view from Hitler's mountain; the sooner I was away from there and back to the combusted blue air of Berlin, the better. And so with Hermann Kaspel holding one end of the measuring tape at the top of the ladder, I retreated to the wall at the edge of the terrace and the place where Flex had been shot, and positioned the length of dowelling like a rifle along the same descending angle.

'Would you agree,' I asked Kaspel, 'that the end of this piece of dowelling seems to be pointing towards those lights to the west of here?'

'Yes.'

'What is that building?'

'That is probably the Villa Bechstein. The place where your assistant is currently staying.'

'Yes, I'd forgotten about Korsch. I hope he slept better than me.' I glanced at my watch. It was almost seven o'clock. I'd been in Obersalzberg for seven hours but it felt like seven minutes. I suppose that was the methamphetamine. And of course I knew I was going to have to take some more, and soon. 'Well, we'll soon find out. Because that's where we're going just as soon as we've had breakfast in the Leader's dining room. To the Villa Bechstein. Korsch can go and find a ballistics expert to look at these bullets and tell us some more about them while I unpack my bag and clean my teeth. Maybe get this film developed, too.'

Kaspel came down the ladder and followed me through the winter garden, the Great Hall, and into the dining room, where there was too much knotted-pine panelling and a built-in display cabinet that contained various pieces of fussy-looking china with a dragon design. I hoped they might be fire-breathing dragons because for all its pretensions to grandeur the room was cold. There were two tables, a smaller round one in a bay window set for six, and a larger rectangular one set for sixteen. Kaspel and I took the smaller table, threw off our coats, drew up two terracotta-red leather armchairs, and sat down. Without thinking, I tossed my cigarettes onto the tablecloth. Somewhere I could smell fresh coffee brewing.

'Are you serious?' said Kaspel.

'Sorry. I forgot our orders.' Hurriedly, I put the cigarettes away, seconds before a waiter wearing white gloves appeared in the room, as if he had materialized out of a brass lamp to grant us both three wishes. But I had a lot more than three.

'Coffee,' I said. 'Lots of hot coffee. And cheeses, lots of cheeses. And meats, too. Boiled eggs, smoked fish, fruit, honey, plenty of bread, and more piping-hot coffee. I don't know about you, Hermann, but I'm hungry.'

The waiter bowed politely and went away to fetch our German breakfast. I had high hopes of the kitchen at the Berghof; if you couldn't get a good German breakfast at Hitler's house, then all hope was surely lost.

'No,' said Kaspel. 'I meant are you serious about an investigation at the Villa Bechstein? That place is for Nazi VIPs.'

'Is that what I am? That's interesting. Never saw myself that way before now.'

'They put you there because it's the nearest place to the Berghof that's not someone else's house. So you wouldn't have too far to go.'

'Very considerate.'

'I don't suppose Bormann ever considered that you might be looking for a gunman at the Villa Bechstein. The deputy leader, Rudolf Hess himself, is due to arrive any time now.'

'Doesn't he have his own house?'

'Not yet. And actually Hess doesn't really like it here. Even brings his own food. So he doesn't come that often. But when he does, he always stays at the villa, with his dogs.'

'I'm not fussy who I stay with. Or what I eat, as long as there's plenty of it.' I glanced around, disliking the dining room almost as much as I'd disliked the Great Hall. It was like being inside a walnut shell. 'I guess this must be the new wing we're in now.'

'Bormann isn't going to like it.'

'We'll burn that bridge when we come to it.'

'No, really, Bernie. Relations between Bormann and Hess are already poor. If we start poking our noses around the Villa

Bechstein, Hess is likely to view it as an attempt to undermine his authority as deputy leader.'

'Bormann's going to like it even less if I don't catch this shooter and soon. Look, Hermann, you saw where those bullets were. They're the angles we have to work with. Just like in billiards. Maybe someone who works there didn't like Flex. Who knows, maybe the butler got bored and stuck a rifle out of the master-bedroom window to see who he could hit on the terrace. I always like the butler for a murder. They've usually got something to hide.'

The coffee arrived and I took out my cigarettes *again* before putting them away, *again*. It's only when your habit bothers someone else that you start to notice how much of a habit it really is. So I swallowed a couple of Pervitin with the coffee and bit my lip.

'What happens to people who smoke in this fucking house?' I said. 'Seriously? Are they sent to Dachau? Or are they just hurled off the Tarpeian Rock by locals high on meth?'

'Give me a couple of pills,' said Kaspel. 'I'm starting to slow down. And I've a feeling I'm going to need to keep going for a while longer.'

'Could be.' I laid the four misshapen bullets on the tablecloth. They looked like the teeth from a witch doctor's kit bag. Who knows? Maybe they would enable me to divine the name of Flex's murderer. Stranger things had happened in the ballistics lab at the Alex. 'There are five bullets in a standard rifle magazine,' I said. 'That means either our murderer shot at Karl Flex four times and missed, or he tried to shoot more than one man on the terrace. But why didn't anyone hear anything? If the shots came from somewhere as close as the Villa Bechstein, someone must have heard shots being fired. Even the butler. This is supposed to be a secure area.'

'You heard the explosion,' said Kaspel. 'The one made by the construction workers. And especially first thing in the morning, shots are often fired to make small avalanches up on the Hoher Göll, in order to prevent larger ones. So it's possible that people did hear a shot and connected it with an avalanche. Equally, there are lots of historic shooters' clubs in Berchtesgaden that like to meet up on public holidays and discharge old black powder weapons. Blunderbusses and dragoon pistols. Any excuse. Frankly, we've tried to put a stop to them but it's no use. They pay no attention.'

The waiter returned with an enormous breakfast tray on which was a large piece of honeycomb, still attached to the wooden tray that had come out of the hive. Seeing it, I let out a groan of childish excitement. It had been a while since anyone in Berlin had seen honey.

'My God, that's what I call luxury,' I said. 'Ever since I was a boy I've never been able to resist honeycomb.' Even before the waiter had laid all the things on the breakfast table, I'd gouged off a piece, scraped off the beeswax capping with my knife, and started sucking the honey greedily.

'Is it local?' I looked at the label on the side of the wooden tray. 'Honey from the Leader's own apiary at Landlerwald. Where's that?'

'On the other side of the Kehlstein,' said Kaspel. 'The deputy chief of staff is an expert on agriculture. That's Bormann's background, you know. He trained to be an estate manager. The Gutshof is a farm that produces all sorts of produce for the Berghof. Including honey. When we drive up the mountain, the main farmhouse is on our left. There's eighty hectares of farmland. All the way around the mountain.'

'I'm beginning to see why the Leader likes it here so much. I'll want to talk to someone at that apiary.'

'I'll speak to Kannenberg,' said Kaspel. 'He'll fix it with Hayer, the fellow who's in charge of things at the Landlerwald. But why?'

'Let's just say I have a bee in my bonnet.'

Not long after we'd finished eating breakfast several of the other men who'd also been on the terrace when Flex was shot turned up. Freda Kannenberg came and told me 'the engineers' were waiting for me in the Great Hall.

'How many are there?'

'Eight.'

'Is anyone else likely to come in here for breakfast?'

'No,' she said. 'Frau Braun usually has breakfast in her own rooms upstairs, with her friend. And Frau Troost doesn't ever eat breakfast.'

'Very well,' I told Freda, 'I'll see them in here. One at a time.'

Freda nodded. 'I'll tell the waiter to bring some fresh coffee.'

CHAPTER 18

April 1939

The first man I spoke to was the state engineer August Michahelles. He was a handsome man wearing military uniform, who
bowed politely as he presented himself at the breakfast table.
I stood up, shook his limp hand, and then invited him to sit
down and help himself to coffee. I opened my file of witness
statements and found the list that Högl had compiled.

'You're the head of the state construction bureau for Deutsche
Alpenstrasse, is that right?'

'That's correct.'

'I thought there would be more of you out there. According
to my list there were twelve people on that terrace yesterday
morning. Including the dead man. And yet there are only eight
people here at the Berghof today.'

'Professor Fich, the architect – I believe he had to go to Munich
to meet with Dr Todt and Dr Bouhler. As did Professor Michaelis.'

I shrugged. 'How is it that people feel they can absent themselves so quickly from a murder investigation?'

'You'd have to ask them. And if you'll forgive me for saying
so, I'm not sure what else I can add to the statement I made to
Captain Kaspel yesterday.'

In spite of his uniform he seemed uncertain of himself. He
didn't even pour himself a coffee.

'Probably not much,' I said. 'Only your statement was about

what happened. What you saw. I'm more interested to hear what the meeting was all about. Martin Bormann was rather vague about that. All these very well-qualified engineers meeting up at the Berghof. I'm sure there must have been something of real importance that brought you all together. And I'd also like to hear more about Dr Flex.'

The state engineer looked thoughtful for a moment and played with a rather scabby-looking earlobe that he'd clearly worried before.

'So,' I said. 'What was the purpose of the meeting?'

'It's a regular meeting. Once a month.'

'And is this meeting well known about, generally?'

'There's nothing secret about it. In order to accomplish the transformation of the Obersalzberg in accordance with Herr Bormann's wishes, it's necessary that from time to time we meet to review the progress of construction work. For example, there's the construction of the new Platterhof Hotel, which has required the demolition of almost fifty old houses. Also the construction of new technical installations, such as an electricity supply station. The current from Berchtesgaden has proved to be unreliable. At present we are laying new electrical and telephone cables in the area, widening access roads, and digging new access tunnels. This requires skilled workers of course—'

'I'd like to take a look at this work sometime,' I said.

'You'll have to ask Bormann,' said Michahelles. 'Some of the work is for the security of the Leader and therefore secret. I should need to see something in writing and signed by him in order to answer a question like that.'

'So it's military then?'

'I didn't say that.'

'All right. That's fair enough. I *will* ask Bormann. So tell me about Dr Flex, instead. Did you know him well?'

'No, not well.'

'Can you think of a reason why anyone would want to kill him? Any reason at all?'

'Frankly, no.'

'Really?'

Michahelles shook his head.

'You know it's strange, Herr Michahelles, I've been here in Obersalzberg for less than ten hours. And yet I've already heard that Karl Flex was one of the most unpopular men in the Bavarian Alps.'

'I wouldn't know. But you're speaking to the wrong person.'

'So who should I be speaking to? Ludwig Gross? Otto Staub? Walter Dimroth? Hans Haupner? Bruno Schenk? Hanussen the clairvoyant? Who? Give me a clue. I'm supposed to solve a murder here. If everyone on this damn list is as uninformative as you, that might take a while. For obvious reasons I'd like to be gone before summer.'

'I don't mean to be unhelpful, Commissar Gunther. The two men who worked most closely with him and knew him best were Hans Haupner and Bruno Schenk. Schenk's the first administrator and had worked closely with Flex. I'm sure he could tell you more than I can.'

'That wouldn't be difficult.'

Michahelles shrugged, and suddenly I was having a hard job holding on to my temper, although quite possibly that was the magic potion kicking in again. My heart was already working like it was being paid treble time.

'A busy man, is he? Dr Schenk.'

'I should say so, yes. He's what we call the fire brigade man for sensitive situations involving local construction work.'

'Let's talk about you, Herr Michahelles. Are you popular in Berchtesgaden?'

'I have no idea.'

'Is it possible that someone would like to kill you, too? I mean, apart from me. Like someone who used to own one of those fifty houses you mentioned just now. The ones that were demolished.'

'No, I don't think so.'

'Has anyone ever threatened you? Perhaps even told you they were going to shoot you?'

'No.'

I spread the four spent bullets across the tablecloth like a waiter's crummy tip. 'You see these? These are four bullets we found in the woodwork of the balcony immediately above the terrace. So it's just possible the gunman took a shot at you, too. Maybe more than one. And missed. How about it?'

'No, I'm sure there isn't anyone.'

'I hope you're right, August. You're a brainy fellow, I can tell. And I'd hate to see those brains end up on someone's floor like Karl Flex's, just because you couldn't quite bring yourself to tell me if there's anyone you know who'd like to kill you, too. If the shooter did try to murder you, then he might try again, you know.'

'Is that all?' he said stiffly.

'Yes, that's all. Oh, ask Dr Schenk if he'd mind coming in here next, would you?'

Bruno Schenk was about forty years old with a high forehead and an even higher manner. He wore a grey suit, a neat white shirt and collar, and a tie with a Party pin. He wasn't much taller than his walking stick but he *was* the section head of Polensky & Zöllner, with responsibility, he quickly informed me, for building all of the connecting roads between the Kehlstein and Berchtesgaden, which made him feel taller, I suppose.

'I hope this won't take too long,' he added to the pompous sum total of that. 'I'm a busy man.'

'Oh, I know. And I appreciate you coming here to help me out with my questions.'

'What do you want to know, Commissar?'

'P&Z. That must be a rich company by now with all this construction work. Paid for by the state, I believe.'

'P&Z. Sager & Woerner. Danneberg & Quandt. Umstaetter. Reck brothers. Höchtl & Sauer. Hochtief. Philipp Holzmann. There are more companies contracted to do work here by the Obersalzberg Administration than you could possibly imagine, Commissar. And more work than anyone might reasonably conceive.'

I could tell that I was supposed to be impressed by all that. I wasn't.

'As first administrator, you must be an important man.'

'I enjoy the confidence of the deputy chief of staff in all matters affecting building development on the mountain, that's true. Between Martin Bormann and myself there's only the chief administrator, Dr Reinhardt, who's tasked with more responsibility.'

Schenk's voice and his grammar were no less correct than his appearance and most of the time he didn't even look at me, as if I were beneath his influence and concern. Instead he turned his coffee cup on its saucer, one way and then the other as if he wasn't sure which way the handle should face – towards him, or towards me – a bit like a snake trying to decide where it should park its rattle. He didn't know it yet but he was looking for a slap.

'So tell me about the work,' I said. 'I'm interested.'

'Perhaps another time,' he said. 'But today's my birthday. I have a number of appointments to keep before an important luncheon date. With my wife.'

'Congratulations,' I said. 'How old are you anyway?'

'Forty.'

'If you don't mind my saying so, you look older.'

Schenk frowned for a moment but tried to contain his irritation, the way I'd just contained my own. I was being given the runaround and getting tired of it; there seemed little point in my murder investigation having the full backing of Martin Bormann if no one else around the Berghof seemed to appreciate this. It was beginning to look as if I would have to get tough with someone – tougher than I'd been with August Michahelles – if I were to make some progress before Bormann saw me. Bruno Schenk looked made for a little rough-housing. I always say if you're going to get tough with someone, you might as well enjoy it.

'Then again,' I said, 'I expect with all of the responsibilities resting on your shoulders, the work takes its toll on a man.'

'Yes it does. We've had to accomplish some massive tasks in less time than was needed. The Kehlstein tea house, for example. That particular feat of engineering gave Herr Bormann's previous adjutant, Captain Sellmer, a heart attack. And as one thing ends another begins. The Platterhof-Resten Road has had to be entirely replanned, because a bridge has had to be built. And just consider this, Commissar – that all the work has to be achieved without damaging a single tree. The Leader is most insistent that trees are to be preserved at all costs.'

'Well, that's reassuring anyway, about the trees. We certainly need lots of those in Germany. Exactly what is the Platterhof, sir?'

'A people's hotel, formerly the Pension Moritz, that is being created using only the finest materials, to house the many eager visitors who come to see the Leader when he's here. Currently it's one of the largest projects in Obersalzberg. And when it's complete it will be one of the finest hotels in Europe.'

I wondered just how many would come when the whole of Europe was at war. Perhaps some, looking for Hitler's head on a stick, or perhaps none at all. Schenk looked at his watch, which reminded me that it was time for me to put him on the spot, or at least to try; he was slippery.

'Well, I won't keep you, sir. I can see you're a very busy man. I just wanted to ask you why you think that your assistant Karl Flex was one of the most hated men in the area. And if perhaps you might believe that someone local might have shot him out of revenge for being overzealous in carrying out your instructions. Such as serving a compulsory purchase order on the original owners of the Pension Moritz, perhaps. Or demanding more of your local workers than seemed at all reasonable. Men have been killed, I believe. Perhaps unnecessary risks were taken. That's the kind of thing that can easily produce a motive for murder.'

'I really couldn't speculate on such a distasteful thing. And I don't mean to teach you your duties, Commissar, but you shouldn't ask me to, either. You're the detective, not me.'

'I'm glad you understand that, sir. And I'm under a certain amount of pressure, too. From the same man as you, I believe. So please don't think I take my job any less seriously than you do yours. Or that it's any less important. In fact, right now, I rather think that my job may be more important. You see, last night when I met Martin Bormann he told me two things. One was this – and I'm quoting him here: "When I talk it's as if the Leader were here now, telling you what the fuck to do." And the other thing he told me was that I enjoyed his full authority to catch this man before the Leader's own birthday. Which is in a week's time, as I'm sure I don't have to remind you, Dr Schenk. His full authority. Isn't that right, Hermann?'

'That's right. Those were his exact words. His full authority.'

It was my turn to bang a tabletop, so I did and Schenk's coffee cup bounced pleasingly on its saucer, so I banged the table a second time and stood up to make my point even more forcefully. I might even have smashed a cup or a saucer on the engineer's carefully combed head but for the AH monogram on the pattern, which gave me a little pause for thought. The meth was coursing through me now and even Kaspel was looking surprised.

'His full authority,' I yelled. 'You hear that? So think again and think fast, Dr Schenk. I want some better answers than "Another time, today's my birthday" and "I really couldn't speculate" and "You're the detective, not me." What are you wasting my time for? I'm a policeman, and a commissar to boot, not some fucking toothless peasant with a pickaxe in his hand and a dumb look on his gormless face. It's a murder I'm trying to solve – a murder at the Leader's house – it isn't the crossword in today's newspaper. If Adolf Hitler can't come down here next week because I couldn't catch this maniac then it won't just be my guts hanging on the Leader's perimeter fence, it'll be yours and every other tongue-tied bastard's who calls himself an engineer on this fucking mountain. And as the first administrator, you'd better make sure they know that. Do you hear?'

It was all an act, of course, but Schenk didn't know that.

'I must say, you have a most violent temper,' said Schenk.

He flushed the same colour as the chair he was on and stood up, only I put my hand on his shoulder and shoved him back down. I could be a bit of a bully myself, when I tried; only I never once thought I'd be trying to pull it off in Hitler's own dining room. I was starting to like Dr Temmler's magic potion. Kaspel seemed to like it, too. At least, he was smiling as if he'd been wanting a chance to slap Schenk himself.

'Most violent and unpleasant.'

'You haven't seen anything yet. And I'll tell you when I'm through stiffening your ears, Dr Schenk. I want a list of names. People you've upset and pissed off. Maybe one or two of them threatened you and your boy Flex. You and he have done a lot of that, haven't you?'

Schenk swallowed uncomfortably and then raised his voice. 'Anything I have done has been done with the full knowledge of the deputy chief of staff himself, with whom I shall certainly be lodging a formal complaint regarding your egregious conduct.'

'You do that, Bruno. Meanwhile, I shall certainly call General Heydrich in Berlin and have the Gestapo take you into custody, for your own protection, of course. Salzburg, isn't it, Hermann? The nearest Gestapo HQ?'

'That's right. In an old Franciscan monastery on Mozartplatz. And a horrible place it is, too, sir. Even the spirits of the saints walk carefully past that monastery. We can have him there in half an hour.'

'You hear that, Bruno? And after you've had a few days in a cold cell on bread and water, we'll talk again and see how you feel then about my conduct.'

'But please, you've no idea how bad things had got here,' he bleated. 'For example, on the southern side of the Haus Wachen-feld there was a path for cows, which local sightseers were starting to use to catch a glimpse of the Leader, even in bad weather. Local farmers were charging visitors, some of whom would even bring binoculars to get a better look at him. This situation had become unacceptable – the Leader's security was becoming compromised – and in 1935, we began to purchase property around the house, piece by piece, lot by lot. But as, in the beginning, Hitler didn't allow us to apply pressure on these property owners, we were obliged to pay some outrageous prices. Local farmers – many of whom had been heavily indebted before – were now making a fortune from selling their little gold mines. This had to stop, and in due course it did. In order to establish the transformation of the Obersalzberg the way the Leader wanted it, we've had to demolish over fifty houses, and yes, it's true that some of these people were not happy with the price they received, in comparison with the price they were asking. Please, Commissar, there's no need to involve Himmler and Heydrich, is there?'

'They are involved,' I snarled back. 'Who do you think it was asked me to come here? Now go out there and speak to your colleagues waiting in the Great Hall and when I come back here, I want a list of names. Resentful workers, angry homeowners, sons of aggrieved widows, anyone with a grudge against you, Flex, or even Martin Bormann. Understood?'

'Yes, yes, I'll do as you say. Immediately.'

I grabbed my coat and walked out of the dining room. I'd enjoyed my breakfast but I'd eaten too much. Either that or talking to a Nazi like Schenk just gave me a rotten feeling in my stomach.

'I don't know where any of this is going to go,' said Kaspel, following me out of the Berghof and down the icy steps to the car. 'But I do like working with you.'

CHAPTER 19

April 1939

The Villa Bechstein was a five-minute drive down the hill from the Berghof and on the other side of a stone-built SS guardhouse that covered the entire road. Kaspel told me that after Helene Bechstein had been obliged to sell her house to Bormann, Albert Speer had lived there while his own house – and a studio – much further to the west, was being constructed to his own design. Having seen quite a bit of Speer's architectural talent on show in Berlin, I doubt it could have improved on the Villa Bechstein, which sat in a nest of deep snow like a fancy gingerbread house. It was a large, three-storey villa with two wraparound wooden balconies, a high mansard roof with a dormer window, and a bell tower made of marzipan and chocolate. It was the sort of house you could only have afforded if you'd been Martin Bormann or someone who sold a great many pianos to a great many Germans.

Almost immediately I got out of the car I turned and looked back up the mountain at the Berghof, only there were several trees in the way. From inside the hallway a butler had appeared, hovering silently in the doorway like a black-and-white dragonfly. He bowed gravely and then ushered me up the heavy wooden stairs to the second floor. The house might have been old but everything had been recently refurbished and was of the very highest quality, which is a style of interior decoration that always seems to suit the simple tastes of the rich and powerful.

'Has the deputy leader arrived yet?' I asked the butler, who answered – with a local accent – to the name of Winkelhof.

'Not yet. We expect him sometime this morning, sir. He'll be occupying his apartments on the upper floor, as usual. You'll hardly notice each other.'

I had my doubts about that. Top Nazis aren't known for being shy and retiring. At the top of the stairs was a long-case clock with a Nazi eagle on top and next to this a life-sized bronze nude of a bewildered woman who looked as if she was trying to find the bathroom. Winkelhof showed me into a large, chintzy bedroom with a green Biedermeier sofa, a single bed, and a small portrait of the Leader. My bag was already waiting for me on the bed and although a log fire was laid it wasn't lit and the room was cold. I was already wishing I hadn't handed over my coat. The butler apologized for the room's temperature and immediately set about trying to light the fire, only the chimney flap seemed to be firmly stuck, which caused him some irritation.

'I do apologize, sir,' said Winkelhof. 'Perhaps I'd better show you to another room.'

So we found another room, with another portrait of Hitler – this one was just a face on a black background, which was a little more pleasing to me, given that the Leader's head seemed almost to have been severed, in accordance with my earlier hopes and dreams. A big French window opened onto the wooden balcony and the fireplace worked. While the butler lit the fire with a candle match, I went onto the snow-covered balcony and inspected the view, which wasn't a view at all in that I could only see more of the same trees I'd already seen at ground level.

'This is east-facing, right?' I asked the butler.

'That's correct, sir.'

'So the Berghof is behind those trees.'

'Yes, sir.'

'Before the deputy leader gets here, I'd like to take a look out of the windows immediately above this room. And from that dormer window on the roof, too.'

'Certainly, sir. But may I ask why?'

'I just want to satisfy my own curiosity about something,' I explained.

We went upstairs. The deputy leader's apartments were predictably opulent and included several Egyptian artefacts, but his biggest window afforded no better a view of the Berghof than the one I'd seen from the floor below. It was only the dormer window on the floor above that gave me what I'd been hoping for, which was a clear, uninterrupted sight of the Berghof terrace about a hundred metres to the southeast of the Villa Bechstein. I looked at the butler and quietly sized him up for the murder, and it took just a second to see that he'd had nothing to do with the shooting; after twenty years in the job you get a nose for these things. Besides, the lenses in his horn-rimmed spectacles were as thick as the bottom on a glass-bottomed boat. He wasn't the most obvious sniper I'd ever seen. I opened the window – which took a bit of doing because of the ice – and poked my head outside for a moment or two.

'Winkelhof, is anyone staying in this room now?'

'No, sir.'

'Was anyone in it yesterday morning?'

'No, sir.'

'Could anyone have had access to this room that you don't know about?'

'No, sir. And you saw me unlock the door.'

'Are all the rooms in the villa locked like this one?'

'Yes, sir. It's standard practice at the Villa Bechstein. Some of our guests have sensitive government papers and they prefer to have a lock on the doors to their rooms and apartments.'

'Were you on duty yesterday morning at around nine o'clock?'

'Yes, sir.'

'Did you hear anything that sounded like a shot? A car back-firing? An avalanche charge, perhaps? A door closing loudly?'

'No, sir. Nothing.'

I went downstairs again and took a quick walk around the exterior of the house along a pathway that had been recently cleared of snow. The ground floor of the Villa Bechstein was made of rough stone with a covered terrace, where I found an armoury of snow shovels and a pile of logs that looked like enough fuel for a short ice age. Seeing this it crossed my mind that perhaps the Leader's pious wish to look after the local trees wasn't such a high priority after all. It didn't take very long to find what I was looking for: on the eastern side of the house there was a scaffolding tower, which went all the way up to the icicled eaves, about nine to twelve metres above the ground; beside it was a neat ziggurat of tiles, a bucket, and some ropes. Tied to the tower was a sign from a local roofing company but there were no ladders that might have enabled a man to climb up to the roof. Even with ladders it looked like a hazardous job in winter, but not quite as hazardous, perhaps, as going up there with a rifle to take a shot at Hitler's private terrace. I knew I was right about that now because I found an empty brass cartridge lying on the ground immediately below the dormer window. I spent another fifteen minutes looking for others but found only one.

In the villa's hallway, I summoned Winkelhof and asked him about the roofer.

'Müller? He's been repairing some tiles and a chimney pot that came off in a recent storm. He'd be working up there now but it seems that someone has stolen his ladders. But don't worry, sir, it won't disturb you. I'm certain of that.'

'Stolen? When?'

'I'm not sure, sir. He reported them missing about an hour ago, when he arrived here first thing this morning. But yesterday he didn't come at all. So really, there's no telling how long the ladders have been gone. Please don't concern yourself. Really, it's not important.'

But something made me think that I'd had something to do with this theft and so I picked up the telephone and asked the Obersalzberg operator to connect me with the Berghof; a few moments later the mystery of the missing ladders had been solved. Arthur Kannenberg had asked the RSD to find him a ladder so that I might have one on the Berghof terrace and they'd borrowed the roofer's ladders from the Villa Bechstein without telling anyone. If only all feats of criminal detection were so straightforward.

'They're bringing the ladders back now,' I said to the butler. 'Telephone Herr Müller and tell him I'd like to speak with him as soon as he gets here. The sooner, the better, Winkelhof.'

In the drawing room I found Friedrich Korsch warming himself in front of a large fire and reading a newspaper while he listened to the radio. In Berlin there was much outrage at the military pact the British had signed with Poland and I wasn't sure if this was good news or bad news – if this would deter Hitler from invading Poland, or bring about an immediate declaration of war by the Tommies if he did.

'I was beginning to think something might have happened to you,' said Korsch. 'I had a terrible feeling I might be kicking my heels here all day.'

I glanced around the drawing room and nodded appreciatively. Kicking your heels didn't look so bad in a room like that. Even the tropical fish in the aquarium looked warm and dry. Kicking arses felt altogether more hazardous; for all I knew, Bormann was going to be furious at the way I'd just treated his first administrator.

'As it happens, you're in luck, Friedrich. You're right in the centre of things after all. This villa is now a crime scene.'

'It is? It certainly doesn't feel like one. I slept like a top last night.'

'Lucky you.' I told him about Karl Flex, as much as I knew. Then I showed him the brass cartridges. 'I found these on the path outside. By the way, this is Captain Kaspel. I think you met, briefly, earlier on.'

The two nodded at each other. Korsch lifted a cartridge up to the firelight.

'Looks like a standard rimless bottleneck eight-millimetre rifle cartridge.'

'My guess is that we'll find more of these on the roof. Just as soon as the RSD comes back with the ladders.'

I explained about the roofer before handing Korsch the spent bullets we'd dug out of the balcony at the Berghof.

'Get someone to take a look at these. Might have to be the Police Praesidium in Salzburg. And I'm going to need a rifle with a telescopic sight. I also want these films developed and printed. And discreetly. Bormann wants this matter handled very discreetly. And you'd better warn whoever does it that these prints are for adult eyes only.'

'There's a photographer in Berchtesgaden who can do the job,' said Kaspel. 'Johann Brandner. On Maximilianstrasse, just behind the railway station. I'll organize a car for you. Although now I come to think about it, I'm not altogether sure if he's still there.'

'I'll sort it out,' said Korsch, and pocketed the films. 'There must be someone local who can do your dirty pictures. You have been busy, sir.'

'Not as busy as Karl Flex,' I said. 'By the way, Hermann. Where does a man go if he wants some female company in this town?'

'That's an unfortunate side effect of the magic potion,' said Kaspel. 'It does give a man the point.'

'Not me, Hermann. Karl Flex. He had a dose of jelly. Remember the Protargol? The question is, where did he get it? The jelly, I mean. If it comes to that, where did he get the Protargol?'

'There is a place,' said Kaspel. 'The P-Barracks. But it's supposed to be under the medical supervision of a doctor from Salzburg.'

'It's a barrack. You mean it's under the control of the Ober-salzberg Administration?'

Kaspel went to the drawing-room door and closed it carefully.

'Not exactly. Yes, it's the P&Z workers who are going to the P-Barracks, yes. But I really don't see someone like Hans Weber or Professor Fich running a bunch of whores, do you?'

'So who then?'

Kaspel shook his head.

'Keep talking,' I said. 'This is starting to get interesting.'

'It's about six kilometres from here, at the Gartenauer Insel, in Unterau, on the north bank of the River Ache. About twenty girls work there. But it's strictly workers only, and off limits for anyone in uniform. I'm not sure if that would have included Karl Flex. I haven't been there myself but I know some SS men in Berchtesgaden who have, if only because there's always trouble at the P-Barracks.'

'What kind of trouble?'

'The workers get drunk while they're waiting for a particular girl. Then they fight about which girl they want and then the local SS have to restore order. It's always busy, day and night.'

'If the place is making two hundred marks an hour, sixteen hours a day,' said Korsch, 'then that's three thousand a day. Twenty thousand a week.'

'Assuming that Bormann is keeping at least half—' I said.

'I didn't say that,' said Kaspel.

'Are you saying he doesn't know about it?'

'No. From what I've heard it was his idea. To set the place up. But—'

'Then perhaps it was Karl Flex who collected the cash from these girls for his master, the Lord of the Obersalzberg. As well as a little taste of what was on offer. Which in itself provides a possible motive for murder. Pimps get murdered all the time. Horst Wessel, for example. He was just an SA pimp murdered by a good friend of his whore's landlady.'

Kaspel was looking slightly sick.

'True story,' I said. 'Happened right on my patch, in Alexanderplatz. I helped my then boss, Chief Inspector Teichmann, crack that case. You can forget all the crap in the Nazi song. It was a simple dispute about an eighteen-year-old snapper. Wessel wasn't much older. So that's where we're going next. To the P-Barracks in Unterau.' I looked around as I heard the RSD men returning the ladders outside the window. 'As soon as we've had a look at the Villa Bechstein's roof.'

'I swear, you're going to get me killed, Gunther.'

'You'll be fine,' I said. 'Just watch where you're putting your feet. It looks slippery up there.'

CHAPTER 20

April 1939

Rolf Müller, the local roofer, was a primitive, round-shouldered, good-humoured sort of fellow with a full head of reddish hair that looked dyed but probably wasn't, glasses that were almost opaque with dirt and grime, and an abstracted manner that seemed to mark him out as one who was always alone on a rooftop. He seemed to have a propensity for conversations with himself from which he saw no reason to exclude anyone else who happened along, me included, and to this extent, he was like a character from a play by Heinrich von Kleist whose misunderstandings and detachment from reality are the stuff of comedy. Emil Jannings would have played him in a movie. His hands and face were covered in boils. He looked like a careless beekeeper.

'Don't get me wrong,' he told me when I found him tying one of the returned ladders to the scaffolding tower. 'It's not that they're bad. Not a bit of it. It's just that they don't give a second thought for anyone else. Which if they did, they wouldn't do it in the first place, see? It comes of being in uniform, I reckon. Not that I was like that myself when I was in uniform. But it's that particular uniform, I think. And that cap badge. The skull and crossbones. It's just like them Prussian kings and the old-life cavalry that guarded them. Nothing mattered to those cavalrymen except the person of the emperor. It's like they think the human part of you doesn't matter anymore, when it does. It really does, you know.'

Gradually I grasped that he was talking about the RSD men who'd borrowed his ladders and I offered him an apology for the inconvenience he'd suffered, not to mention a little of the money I'd had from Heydrich and a cigarette from my own case.

'I had no idea that the ladder they'd borrow would be yours. So there's five reichsmarks for you. And my regret for what happened this morning, Herr Müller.'

'Thank you, sir, I'm sure, but I'd rather not have the money and not have the extra work, nor the worry, any morning. Don't smoke. I know they're only ladders to a man like you, sir. But without them ladders I'm stranded, see? And suppose I'd been up there when they took them? Now where would I be?'

'Still on the roof?'

'Exactly. Freezing up there.' He pulled a face at the very thought of the cold. 'And out of business. Permanently. It's the cold that gets you on this job. My knees are almost shot to pieces now. But for them, I could probably work for P&Z and make three times the money I make repairing roofs.'

Eager to shut him up, I showed him my brass warrant disc, which in retrospect was a mistake as he formed the immediate impression that the missing ladders were being treated as theft by a police commissar, even though it was now obvious to us both that nothing at all had been stolen.

'No need for any law here,' he mumbled. 'The ladders are back. I wouldn't want to get anyone in trouble. Especially with yourself, sir. I'm sure they didn't mean nothing by it.'

'I understand that. But I need to get up onto the roof and look for something.'

Rolf Müller eyed the rifle slung over my shoulder uncertainly.

'Don't worry. I'm not planning to shoot anyone. Not today.'

'If you were, that'd be the rifle to do it with. The most successful bolt-action rifle ever made, the old G98. Saved my life on more than one occasion, that rifle.'

'And mine. The ladders?'

'Certainly. Always happy to help an officer of the law. I'm a good German, I am. You know, I almost became a policeman myself. But that was in Rosenheim many years ago. And I'm glad I didn't because of Mayor Gmelch. I never liked him much. Now, Hermann Göring, he's a different page in another book. He's from Rosenheim. We were in the same infantry regiment, you know. Me and him. Of course I was just a ranker, but—'

'The ladders,' I said. 'Could you finish tying them onto the tower so we can climb there and take a look?'

'I haven't repaired the roof yet. Nor the chimney pot. It was that fearful wind the other night that brought the old one down.'

'Just tie the ladders on, please,' insisted Kaspel. 'We're in a hurry.'

Ten minutes later we were up on the Villa Bechstein's rooftop, crawling carefully along a horizontal ladder that led up to the side of the dormer window on the eastern side of the house, where it had been secured earlier. A piece of old carpet was laid across several rungs near the end of the ladder and it was plain from the number of cigarette ends on the snow that the gunman had been lying there for a good while. I bagged a few just to impress Kaspel. And then I spotted another empty brass 8-mm cartridge. I bagged that, too.

Even without binoculars I could clearly make out the Berghof terrace. I brought the rifle up to my shoulder and put my eye behind the sights, and the crosshairs on the head of the SS man I'd used as a head model. I was never a great shot with a rifle, but with a sniper's scope on a G98 and five bullets in the stripper clip this was a shot even I could have made. It always gives me a strange feeling to get a bead on a man through a rifle scope. Couldn't pull the trigger on a fellow like that, myself. Even a Tommy. Too much like murder. I wasn't the only person who felt that way: snipers and flamethrower operators – in the trenches, they were always singled out for special treatment when they were captured.

'Did you warn everyone what's about to happen?' I asked Kaspel.

'Yes,' he said.

'Right, then.'

I opened the breech on the Mauser, thumbed the clip down the way I'd done a thousand times before, and pushed a live round up the spout. Then I pointed the rifle straight up at the Bavarian blue sky and pulled the trigger five times. The Mauser Gewehr 98 was a nice smooth weapon and an accurate one, too, but quiet it wasn't, especially with a whole mountain range to bounce the sound off. You might just as well have tried to ignore the crack of doom.

'Hard not to hear that,' said Kaspel.

'Exactly.'

We came back down the ladders with the optimistic aim of questioning Rolf Müller again and found him still talking, as if our previous conversation hadn't actually ended.

'Johann. Johann Lochner. That was his name. Been trying to remember it. He was shot through the lungs. This mate of mine in the trenches. With a Gewehr rifle. They say there's another war on the way but I reckon people would be a lot less keen on one if they saw what a rifle bullet that's moving at the speed of sound can do to a man. The mess it can make. They should have to see a man drowning in his own blood, the politicians, before they start another.'

It was hard to argue with that, so I nodded sadly and let him go on in this vein for another minute before I drew him back to the events of the day before.

'Why didn't you come yesterday?' I asked.

'I told Herr Winkelhof about that. In advance. It wasn't as if he didn't know. He did. You ask him.'

'Just answer the question, please,' said Kaspel.

'I had a doctor's appointment. I've got this back, you see. And these knees. That's a lifetime of building work for you. Anyway, I wanted the doctor to give me some painkillers. For the pain.'

'And who else did you tell that you weren't coming yesterday?'

'Herr Winkelhof. He knew I wasn't coming. I did tell him.'

'Yes,' I said, patiently. 'But who else? Your wife, perhaps?'

'Not married, sir. Never met the right woman. Or the wrong one, neither, depending on how you look at it.'

'Then you were in the beer house,' I said.

'Yes, sir. How did you know?'

'It was just a guess,' I said, eyeing his considerable belly. 'Which beer house was that, Herr Müller?'

'The Hofbräuhaus, sir. On Bräuhausstrasse. Nice place. Very friendly. You should try it while you're visiting down here. From wherever it is you're from.'

'Were there many people in there that night?'

'Oh yes, sir. Berchtesgadener beer is the best in Bavaria, sir. You ask anyone.'

'So someone could easily have overheard you saying that you weren't going to work the next day.'

'Easily, sir. And they wouldn't have to try too hard to hear me, neither. I'm not what you'd call a closemouthed man. Especially with a pot of beer in my hand. I like to talk.'

'I noticed that.'

I thought carefully about asking the next question, and then asked it anyway. Lesson one of Liebermann von Sonnenberg's famous book on how to be a detective is that you have to learn patience; at the very least you needed to be very patient to finish that book without throwing it at him. Certainly the Nazis thought so, which is why he was now serving, obscurely, in the Gestapo.

'Are any of those people handy with a rifle?'

'Everyone around here likes to hunt now and then. Ibex, chamois, red deer, roe deer, marmot, capercaillie, a few wild pigs

– there's lots to shoot for the pot around here. Not that we're allowed much, these days. Best shooting's up here.'

'And when it's not for the pot? Have any of them expressed an interest in shooting at men?'

Müller's eyes moved to the side like a guilty hound; he stared at the ground for a moment and shook his head silently. It was the silence that surprised me, not him denying that he knew anything.

'You know the sort of thing I'm talking about,' I said. 'I'd like to shoot that Fritz, or I wish someone would put a bullet in this fellow's head. The sort of thing that sounds like an idle threat over a few beers and that no one takes seriously until someone actually stops being idle and goes and does it.'

Müller shrugged and shook his head again. For a man who liked to talk, especially to himself – when you're a self-employed roofer, who else is going to answer? – and who'd already talked a great deal, his silence was the most eloquent thing he'd said all morning. This was the kind of detail that von Sonnenberg should have put in his book, the sort of thing detectives get a nose for. If he didn't know exactly who had taken a shot at Flex, then almost certainly he knew lots of people who'd like to have done so.

'All right,' I said. 'That's all. Thanks for your help, Herr Müller.'

'By the way,' said Kaspel, 'did the doctor sort you out? Your knees, or your back, or whatever it was that took you there?'

'Yes, sir. He's a good doctor, that Dr Brandt.'

I looked at Kaspel. Brandt wasn't exactly an uncommon name in Germany. Nevertheless I felt obliged to ask the obvious question. Sometimes they're the best ones.

'That wouldn't be Dr Karl Brandt, would it?'

'I don't know his first name, sir. Young fellow. Handsome, with it. Married to a champion swimmer, he is. Not that there's much swimming round here in the winter, mind. But there is in summer. The Königssee is a lovely place to swim. Cold though.

Even in August, it's cold. That's glacier water, you see. Like swimming in the ice age.'

'You mean the Dr Karl Brandt who's in the SS, don't you?' said Kaspel.

'That's right, sir. The Leader's doctor. When the Leader's not here Dr Brandt runs a clinic out of the local theatre in Antenberg. Keep his hand in, he says. Likes to give something back to the community for its hospitality. Very popular with local people, he is. They both are, him and the wife. Although they're not from round here. He's from Mulhouse, I believe, which is as good as being French, in my book. Not that I hold that against the doctor, since he is, quite obviously, thoroughly and completely German, through and through.'

Kaspel and I walked back to the front door of the Villa Bechstein.

'That's interesting,' he said. 'About Brandt, I mean.'

'I thought so, too. But I don't see him crawling around that rooftop in the snow. Do you?'

Leaving the rifle in the hallway, we returned to the car just as a gardener turned up and started to take some tools out of his van. I closed my eyes and put my ear into the cold air. All I could hear was nature's lingering mountain silence, a persistent and very audible hush, which felt more like the subaural gasp of thousands of tiny Alpine tumults and commotions.

'It's so very still in this place,' I said. 'So very quiet after Berlin, don't you think?' I shrugged. 'I guess I'm just a city boy through and through. Every so often I like to hear a tram bell and a taxi engine. Reminds me I'm actually alive. Up here on Hitler's mountain – well, you might easily forget something important like that.'

'You get used to it. But I guess that's why the Leader likes it so much.'

'Strange that it should be so quiet and yet no one heard five shots fired from a G98. I can't figure that at all.'

Meanwhile, the gardener had laid a big log onto a sawhorse near the bottom of the ladder and was now filling a chainsaw with petrol.

'You the gardener here?' I asked the man before he started the chainsaw.

'One of them. Head gardener is Herr Bühler.'

'Do you cut logs with that every morning?'

'Have to. They burn a lot of wood in that house. Maybe fifteen or twenty baskets a day.'

'That much?'

'At this time of year, I'm cutting logs almost every day.'

'And always with that?'

'The Festo? Absolutely. From my point of view this is the best thing a German ever invented. I'd be lost without this machine.'

'And here? On this same spot?'

He pointed at the pile of logs. 'This is where the wood is.'

'Rolf Müller, the roofer,' I said. 'How well do you know him?'

The gardener grinned sheepishly. 'Well enough to start this chainsaw when I see him coming. I'm not much for talking myself. But Rolf – he does like to talk. Only, it's a little hard to know about what, sometimes.'

'True. Have you ever seen anyone other than Rolf Müller up on that roof?'

'No, sir. Never.'

We watched the gardener start the chainsaw. It sounded exactly like the Alba 200 motorcycle I'd owned just after I got married. And was probably every bit as dangerous.

'Maybe there's the reason nobody heard anything, right there,' shouted Kaspel.

'Maybe,' I said, and took a deep breath. I felt as if I had a chainsaw revving impatiently in my chest. That was the methamphetamine. The dry mountain cold was easier to ignore.

CHAPTER 21

October 1956

After a poor night's sleep I awoke beside a silent guard of swaying poplars, unnourished, light-headed, and ravenously hungry. I was as cold and stiff as an English princess who believes she might be head-over-heels in love with someone other than herself. I tried a few shoulder stretches and succeeded only in making my half-strangled neck sore. I ought to have felt a little more hope for the day on seeing the sun rise above the misty fields of open countryside, I suppose, but I didn't. Instead, at that early waking hour I was one of the undead, the outlawed, the damned; but I had only myself to blame for that. I would surely have been in England by now if I'd gone along with Mielke's plan. So I started up the Citroën and drove on for about an hour until, in a little town called Tournus, I saw a café and a *tabac* that were opening up. I stopped the car beside a malodorous public lavatory, where I washed and shaved, and bought a couple of French newspapers and a packet of Camels before heading next door for a coffee and a croissant and a smoke. I was becoming more French than I might ever have believed possible. It was a sunny morning so nobody was paying much attention to me or my sunglasses, or my grimy shirt; this was provincial France after all, where grimy shirts are the prevailing style. But I'd already made page three of *France Dimanche*. I suppose there wasn't yet another breathless story they could print that week about Brigitte Bardot and Roger Vadim getting a divorce. God might have created woman. Monsieur Vadim had merely tried his best to make her happy. I could have told him not to bother. Gentlemen prefer blondes but blondes don't know what they prefer until they get a strong sense that they're not going to get it. The next best thing to Bardot and Vadim's matrimonial convulsions was a double murder on the Blue Train between Nice and Marseilles, and that was me. I had to hand it to Friedrich Korsch. It had been inspired of my former criminal assistant to kill the train guard *as well as* Gene Kelly. I hadn't seen that coming. Now the French police had an even better reason to look for me other than one dead German tourist called Holm Runge, which seemed to be the dead Stasi man's real name – the man I'd battered on the head. The French police prefer to investigate murder when it involves their own citizens; they like to take things personally. According to the paper, the police were anxious to speak to a man called Walter Wolf in connection with the murders. Formerly a hotel concierge on the Riviera, he was also known as Bertolt Gründgens, which was of course the name in my shiny new passport. The man was believed to be armed and dangerous, and German. The police would probably like that, too.

The police gave a pretty good description, including the dark glasses I was wearing. Of Bernie Gunther there was no mention; then again, Bernie Gunther didn't have any papers, so I was hardly likely to be using that name. The newspaper story didn't have my picture but it did print the number plate of my motor car, which meant that I would certainly have to ditch the Citroën, and soon. I thought that if I could drive as far as Dijon, which was another hundred kilometres to the north, then, in a proper city like that, I might get a bus or a train somewhere else heading northeast, perhaps even to Germany. At that hour I had good reason to hope that the police in that sleepy part of France might still be having a coffee and cigarette themselves. Even so, I thought it probably wiser to stay off the quicker N7 and so chose the more scenic D974 through Chagny and Beaune to take me into Dijon. This was the heart of France's Burgundy region, where some of the finest wines in the world are made, not to mention some of the most expensive ones. Erich Mielke had certainly appreciated them back at the Hotel Ruhl in Nice. I didn't intend to stop before Dijon but in Nuits-Saint-Georges, I saw a pharmacy and, because my eyes were hurting so much, I stopped to buy some collyrium. A bottle of red Burgundy might have done me a bit more good; at least it would have matched my eyes.

In the car, I used the eyewash and was about to drive away when I noticed the gendarme in my rear-view mirror; he was walking slowly towards my car and it was obvious he was going to speak to me. I paused. The worst thing to do would be to start the engine and drive away quickly. Cops don't like squealing tyres – it makes them think you've got something to hide – and the gun in the glovebox was not an option. So I sat there as coolly as I could manage, given that I was now a wanted man, and waited for him to reach my window. I wound it down and looked up as best as I was able as the cop bent down.

'You see that sign?'

'Er no, I had something in my eye and stopped so that I could get some eyewash in that pharmacy.' I showed him the bottle of collyrium to substantiate my story.

'If you'd read that sign, sir, you'd know that this street is less than ten metres wide. Which means that since your car has an odd-numbered number plate you can only park here on an odd-numbered date. Today's the eighteenth of October. That's an even date.'

As a policeman I'd been obliged to enforce some stupid, arbitrary laws in my time – in Germany it was strictly forbidden to deny a chimney sweep access to your house, and you could be arrested for tuning your piano at night – but this seemed like such an absurd system of parking that I almost laughed

in the flic's face. Instead I apologized in my best French accent
and explained that I was just about to move the car anyway.
And with that I was on my way once more, although now very
much aware that my French accent was not nearly as good as
I supposed, and that it would probably not be long before the
gendarme connected me and the sight of my sore eyes with the
fugitive German murderer from the famous Blue Train. When
it wants to be, the organization of the French police is superb;
after all, there are so many of them. Sometimes it seems that
there are more policemen in the French Republic than there are
nobles and hereditary titles. And I didn't underestimate their
capacity to catch a wanted German fugitive, only their capacity
to catch any wanted Vichy war criminals. Always supposing
that such men, and women, ever existed, of course. So I turned
the car around and, in full sight of the gendarme, drove south
out of Nuits-Saint-Georges, before finding another way to head
north again.

About ten kilometres further on, in Gevrey-Chambertin, I saw
a sign for the local railway station and finally abandoned the
car in a gentle grove of beech trees on the strangely named Rue
Aquatique. The road extended for at least a kilometre through a
very dry-looking vineyard and couldn't have looked less aquatic
if it had led through the Ténéré desert. I might have parked in
front of the station, but I didn't want to make it too easy for
the police to follow my trail. So, carrying my holdall and following the sign, I walked west, beyond another large vineyard.
It was an oddly depressing landscape. It was hard to believe that
such a place could give birth to so much liquid luxury. Gevrey-
Chambertin was just endless vineyards and an even more endless
expanse of clouds and blue sky punctuated by the occasional
black squiggle that was a bird; it didn't make me want to set up
an easel to paint a picture of my place in the world, just shoot
myself. No wonder Van Gogh cut his ear off, I thought; there's
nothing else to do in a place like this *but* cut your ear off.

The sun went behind some clouds and it began to rain gently. I bought a ticket for Dijon and sat on the empty platform. The station looked like it hadn't changed since the First Republic. Even the washing hanging limply on the line outside the kitchen door looked as if it had been there a while. At least the trains were moving. Several of them roared through the tiny station before finally one stopped and I boarded it. And only now did I perceive the enormous handicap that was my own appearance, whose reflection I'd started to examine critically in the carriage window. If there is one thing that nature abhors more than a vacuum it's a man wearing sunglasses indoors or when it's raining. If I kept the glasses on I looked like the invisible man, only a little less inconspicuous. If I took them off I looked like the creature from the black lagoon but only after he'd pulled a long night on the shorts. The other people on the train were already giving me those sideways glances reserved for the recently bereaved or men who belong in a Nuremberg courtroom dock alongside Hermann Göring. After a while I decided to take them off – maybe a little extra light would be good for the whites of my eyes; it couldn't do them any harm. I lit a cigarette and let the smoke gently soothe my fraying nerves. I think I even tried to smile at a stout woman with a snot-nosed child who was seated on the opposite side of the aisle. She didn't smile back, but then if I'd had a child who looked like hers I wouldn't have smiled much myself. They say your children are your real future; if that was so I didn't give much for her chances.

Trying to look on the bright side of things, I told myself that not driving the car anymore would give my neck and shoulders a much-needed break – that I might start to feel normal again and I'd be able to rest my eyes. I closed them, and for once they didn't hurt. I even managed to doze off in the thirty minutes it took for that little train to crawl into Dijon and I awoke feeling almost refreshed. At the very least it was the best I'd felt since jumping off the train in Saint-Raphaël. This feeling did not last, however. As soon as I got off the train and entered the main entrance hall I saw several policemen, more than seemed normal even in France, and I was very glad I'd removed my sunglasses which, under the shade of the dirty glass roof, would certainly have marked me out as someone suspicious. But they weren't interested in people arriving off the local trains; they seemed to be grouped near the platforms for trains arriving from Lyons and trains departing for Strasbourg. It was a good call and one I'd probably have made myself if I'd been with the French police: Strasbourg was just a couple of hours away, and only a few kilometres from the German border – given the impending Treaty of Rome, perhaps even closer than that – and probably where any sensible German fugitive now in Dijon would have headed.

It had stopped raining, so I went outside and sat in the park opposite the station while I tried to calculate my next step. A tramp was seated on a nearby bench and he served to remind me once more that if I was to move freely among law-abiding men I would have to look like one first, which meant I needed something to make my eyes appear to be the eyes of someone respectable. So I changed into my only clean shirt and walked south for a while on Rue Nodot until I came to an optician's shop. I thought for a moment and then went and found the tramp again, and offered him two hundred francs to help me out. Then I put my sunglasses on and returned to the shop on the Rue Nodot.

The optician was a smiling, benign sort of man, whose arms were too short for his otherwise neat, buttoned white cotton jacket. The glasses he was wearing on the end of his nose were rimless and almost invisible, quite the opposite effect from the one I was hoping to achieve. There was a light smell of antiseptic in the air, which the hyacinth on the marble mantelpiece was doing its drooping best to dispel.

'I've lost my glasses,' I explained. 'And I need a replacement pair as soon as possible. All I have are these prescription sunglasses without which I'd be quite short-sighted, I'm afraid. But I can't keep walking around with these on, and in this weather.' I smiled. 'Perhaps you could show me some frames.'

'Yes, of course. What kind of style were you looking for, monsieur?'

'I prefer a heavy frame. Much like these sunglasses of mine. Yes, I think I'd like to have tortoiseshell or black, if you have them.'

The optician – Monsieur Tilden – smiled back and opened several drawers that were full of dark-framed glasses. It was like looking into Groucho's bedside table.

'These are all heavier frames,' he said, selecting a pair, cleaning them quickly with a green cloth, and then handing them to me. 'Try these on.'

They were exactly like my own sunglasses, except that they were filled with plain glass, and hence perfect in every way for my present needs. I turned to the mirror and swapped them for my sunglasses, careful not to let Monsieur Tilden see my bloodshot eyes. The frames were perfect. Now all I had to do was steal them. It was at this point, right on cue, that my accomplice came lurching through the shop door.

'I think I need some spectacles,' he said biliously. 'My eyes are not what they were. Can't see straight. Leastways, not when I'm sober.' For a moment he studied the Snellen eye chart as if it were a language he could speak fluently, and then he belched quietly. A strong smell of cider and perhaps something worse filled the shop and even the hyacinth looked like it was about to admit defeat. 'I like to read the newspaper, you see. To keep myself informed about what is happening in this benighted world of ours.'

The tramp was not someone the poor optician considered to be a likely customer but in the time it took Monsieur Tilden to persuade the man to leave, I'd swapped the frames I'd selected for my own sunglasses, closed the drawer from which they came, apologized, and then left – as if driven away by the tramp's ripe smell. I walked back to the park, where several minutes later the tramp returned to receive the second half of his fee, and my thanks.

At another shop I bought a beret to help cover my head of thinning blond hair and, within just a few minutes, I managed to make myself look like a real Franzi. All I needed now was to neglect my personal hygiene, and to obtain a service medal for a war I hadn't fought in.

I walked back to the train station and, from a safe distance, kept a watchful eye on the Strasbourg train platform. The cops were checking everyone's identity and even with a beret and glasses it seemed unlikely I could slip through a cordon like that. I didn't doubt that the same level of security would be present in Strasbourg itself. But it took only a minute or two to figure out a way around the French police check: to my surprise there was no police check on trains leaving Dijon for Chaumont, which is about an hour further north. Why not go there? I thought. And then take another train on to Nancy, from where I might hitch a ride to the German border somewhere near Saarbrücken? I daresay that in 1940 it took Hitler not much longer than a minute or two to figure out that it was simply easier to go around the back of the Maginot Line than through the front of it. It seems obvious now. Frankly, it seemed obvious then. But that's the French for you. Adorable. I went to the ticket office and bought a ticket on the next local train bound for Chaumont.

CHAPTER 22

April 1939

'If the gardener was cutting wood with that chainsaw,' I said, 'and that was what covered up the sound of the shots, then would the shooter have risked him seeing the rifle when he came back down from the Villa Bechstein roof?'

Kaspel was driving us to the P-Barracks, at the Gartenauer Insel, in Unterau. He shook his head.

'It's not the sort of thing you could fail to notice,' admitted Kaspel. 'Equally, the gardener would surely have noticed someone other than Rolf Müller coming down from that roof. That's what he said. Unless they're in it together.'

'No. I can't believe that, either.'

'You sound very sure about that. Why?'

'You get a feel for these things, Hermann. Neither man was particularly nervous about answering our questions. Most of the witnesses I ever questioned, I knew within seconds if they were on the level or not. Didn't you?'

'You're the commissar, not me.'

'A man can go from being an innocent witness to being your number one suspect in the space of five seconds. Even Doctor Jekyll couldn't manage a transformation that fast.' I shook my head. 'I'd have left the rifle up on the roof. And just made my escape. For all we know he's across the border by now and hiding somewhere in Austria. Besides, you said the RSD searched almost everyone in the vicinity immediately after the shooting. If they had found someone with a rifle they'd have arrested him and I wouldn't be enjoying this mountain air.'

'But if he'd left the rifle up on the roof of the Villa Bechstein, we'd have found it. And we didn't. Just the shooter's used brass.'

'Then maybe he tossed it off the villa's roof, into the woods. And picked it up later. Or maybe it's buried in a snowdrift. Or – or, I don't know.'

'In which case we should probably organize a search of the Villa Bechstein's grounds. I'll sort it out the minute we come back from Unterau.' Kaspel paused. 'Why are we going to the P-Barracks anyway? The girls are all French and Italian. Not to mention the fact that they're whores. They're not going to tell us a damn thing.'

'Maybe. Maybe not. But let me and Heydrich's money do the talking. Besides, I like talking to whores. Most of them have the kind of degree that you can't get from the Humboldt University of Berlin.'

At the foot of the mountain we turned right towards the Austrian border and Salzburg, and drove north along a flat road that always stayed close to the course of the River Ache, meandering through a giant landscape designed by God to make a man – most men, anyway – feel small and insignificant. Maybe that's why men build churches; God must seem a little friendlier and more likely to listen to prayers in a nice warm church than on top of a cold jagged mountain. Besides, a church is a lot easier to get to on a winter's Sunday morning. Unless you're Hitler, of course. The air was a curious mixture of wood smoke and hops from the chimney of the Hofbräuhaus, which we soon passed on our left. A collection of large yellow buildings with green shutters and proud red-and-blue banners – none of them Nazi – it looked more like the headquarters of some rival political party than the local brewery, although in Germany beer is more than just politics, it's a religion. My kind of religion, anyway.

'Another thing. Rolf Müller. My guess is that he's heard people in that beer house wishing Bormann and some of his men dead on several occasions before. And he just didn't want to say who they were. Men who might also have overheard him mentioning his doctor's appointment.'

'Then it was lucky it was you who was questioning him and not Rattenhuber or Högl, otherwise right now they'd be trying to beat some names out of him in the cells underneath the Türken Inn.'

'That's the former hotel between Hitler's house and Bormann's – where the local RSD is garrisoned, right?'

'Right. I've got a desk there. But I prefer to stay as far away from Bormann as possible.'

'Would they really do that? I mean, beat some names out of him?'

'In the name of the Leader's security? They'd do anything.' He shrugged. 'Might save a bit of time if we leaned on him just a little. If Bruno Schenk does come up with some names of his own, we might have Müller look them over and see if we can't narrow it down. You never know.'

'I've never been one for the strong-arm stuff myself,' I said. 'Not even in the name of a good cause. Like the Leader's all-important safety.'

'You say that like you don't mean it.'

'Me? Whatever gave you that idea, Hermann? God bless and keep the Leader, that's what I say.' I smiled because for once I didn't add my usual under-the-voice coda to this thought, which was common enough in left-wing Berlin but best not uttered in Berchtesgaden: God bless and keep the Leader, far away from us.

'Look, Gunther, I may have lost some of my naïve optimism about the Nazis and what they're capable of, but I still believe in the new Germany. I want you to know that.'

'From what you were telling me, I somehow gathered the impression that the new Germany is just as corrupt as the old one.'

'With one important difference. No one kicks us around now. Especially not the French. Or the Tommies. Being German – it means something again.'

'Very soon it will mean we've started another European war. That's what it means. And Hitler knows that. My opinion is that he wants another war. That he needs one.'

Kaspel didn't answer, so I changed the subject. 'This must be on the way to St. Leonhard, right?'

'Yes. Why?'

'Because there's a guest house in St. Leonhard called the Schorn Ziegler where I'm supposed to meet Heydrich's man, Neumann, if I've got something interesting to tell him. So he can give the general a report on what's happening here without Martin Bormann knowing all about it.'

'I know the place. It's about seven or eight kilometres further up the road from Unterau. Family place. Good food.' He paused and then added, 'And what *are* you going to tell him?'

'That all depends on what kind of state I'm in.' I glanced at my wristwatch and sighed. 'It's thirty hours since I was in a bed. But I feel like my blood has been replaced by luminous plasma. When I take a leak I half-expect to see Saint Elmo's fire. By tonight I could be a nightmare walking and liable to say all kinds of things best not said in Germany. This meth stuff makes you kind of gabby, doesn't it? You have to watch out for that with a man like Heydrich, or his dark elves and dwarves. Like you said before, the greatest mystery on this magic mountain is how I'm going to break this case without getting myself broken permanently.'

A wide oxbow on the fast-moving Ache had created Gartenauer Island, which was mostly trees and a monastic, grey-granite building sitting immediately on the riverbank; west of the island was a deep forest reached by a small stone bridge. Across the bridge and several hundred metres along a narrow track, and almost completely hidden by the thick forest canopy, was a long, single-storey, dirty-white wooden hut with blue shutters. This was P-Barracks and in the snow it was perfectly camouflaged, which, I supposed, was the way Bormann preferred it. There were no painted girls on show, no signs, no music, not even a brightly coloured lightbulb – nothing to indicate what went on inside; it was probably the most anonymous brothel I'd ever seen. We pulled up in a small parking lot and stepped out of the car. We were just about to go inside when a small truck arrived in a spray of gravel and a group of four workers got out. Two of them were carrying thermos flasks, but from the smell of them they'd all been drinking something stronger than coffee.

'They're coming here now?' I said. 'Christ, it's not even lunchtime.'

'These men from P&Z end their shifts at all times of day. This lot have probably been working through the night.'

'Look, I want a few answers here, only I'm not about to wait in line behind some local Heinrich and his hard-on.' I took out my warrant disc and held it up. 'Police,' I said. 'Come back in an hour, boys. I need to ask these whores some questions. And I'd prefer not smelling your fish soup while I'm doing it.'

'I wouldn't do that if I were you,' said Kaspel. 'These lads have got their hearts set on some female company. Their pricks, too. What's more, in case you hadn't noticed, this place is deliberately remote. People have gone missing out here.'

It was good advice and in normal circumstances I'd have probably taken it, especially after my remarks about not being one for the strong-arm stuff. But the men who'd gotten out of the truck showed no inclination to get back in and leave; what's more, they regarded me and my beer token with contempt. I couldn't blame them for that. Another time I might have left and come back myself, but this wasn't one of those. The largest of the workers spat and then wiped his unshaven chin with the back of a powerful hand.

'We're not leaving,' he said. 'We just pulled a fifteen-hour shift and now we're going to have some fun with these ladies. Maybe you're the ones who should leave, copper. Just ask your boyfriend in black. Not even the SS gets between us and our pleasures.'

'I can understand that,' I said. 'And it's lucky for you I understand that the beer and schnapps are what's talking, not you. I speak it pretty good myself sometimes. Besides, this is the only friend I need when I'm yakking to you, Fritz.' I unholstered my Walther, thumbed back the hammer, and fired the round that was already in the breech. The automatic pistol jumped in my hand like a living thing. Who needs a dog when you have a Walther PPK? 'So get back in your truck and wait your turn before you find an extra hole in your head. And don't think I wouldn't do it. I haven't slept since yesterday morning and my judgment is worse than the Kaiser's right now. It's been six months since I shot anyone. But I really don't think I'm going to miss any sleep about shooting you.'

The workers turned away, grumbling but quiet, and climbed back in their truck. One of them lit his pipe, which is always a good sign when you're a copper. It's a deliberate, thoughtful sort of man who smokes a pipe; I don't think I've ever exchanged blows with a man who had a briar in his mouth.

The warning shot I'd fired had summoned a couple of girls to the barracks' door. At least they looked like whores. One of them wasn't much more than twenty, wearing a grey astrakhan coat, high-heeled shoes, and very little else. The official German football team's black shorts she had on under the coat were an interesting touch; I expect she wanted to demonstrate a bit of loyalty to her adopted country. The other girl was older and dressed in an army Red Cross officer's greatcoat, but the blue stockings and garters, and enough crimson lipstick to supply the Moscow State Circus, persuaded me that she probably wasn't a doctor. Hardly able to contain his distaste, Kaspel pushed gently past these women and I stamped the snow off my boots and followed him inside.

The entrance area held a few battered leather armchairs and an upright piano, with a threadbare carpet on a linoleum floor, and a dilapidated sideboard with a choice of liquor bottles. There were also several showers for the customers, and shards of soap lay on the mildewed tile floor. The whole place smelled strongly of cigarettes and cheap perfume. A large wood-burning stove occupied a central place among the chairs. The hut was at least warm – warmer than the unwelcoming woman who ran the place. She wasn't anyone's idea of a madam but then her clients were rough untutored men who had no more idea of what passed for a proper house of love than the archbishop of Munich. Unlike the others, she wore a thick woollen dress, a white collarless shirt, a traditional green velvet gilet, and a warm beige shawl, but the main reason I knew she was in charge was the Tet biscuit tin under her arm that I supposed was full not of biscuits but of cash. She had quick, rapacious eyes and I knew the minute I saw them that she had the answers to all of my questions. But for a minute or two I left them all unasked. Sometimes, if you're wise, it's better to hear answers to the questions that you wouldn't ever have thought of asking. Maybe Plato wouldn't like that kind of dialogue, but it always worked at the Alex.

CHAPTER 23

April 1939

'What's your name, handsome?' she asked.

'My name's Gunther. Bernhard Gunther. And this is Captain Kaspel, from the RSD.'

'That's a relief. I thought it must be a cowboy. What was the shooting about, cowboy?'

'Martin Bormann sent me,' I said. 'Your clients were very impatient for your company and didn't seem to understand that I'm not accustomed to waiting in line. I felt it was all the explanation I owed them.' I shrugged. 'They're outside, in their truck. I told them to wait an hour.'

'Thoughtful of you, I'm sure.' She lit a cigarette and blew some of the smoke my way, which was generous. 'They've been a bit cranky since the local supply of Pervitin dried up. That's the local drug of choice. Poor man's cocaine, if you ask me.'

'So I hear.'

'If you're here from Martin Bormann, then I assume Flex must not be coming. Besides, he's usually here by now with the hand-out for his lordship's share.'

'Dr Flex won't be coming anymore on account of the fact that he's dead. Someone murdered him. Put a bullet in his head.'

'You're joking.'

'No. I've seen the body. And believe me, it's not funny at all. Half his head was gone. And his brains were piled on the floor.'

'I see.'

The woman said no more about Flex's death, and her expression gave away nothing. It seemed she wasn't going to miss him very much. I'd yet to meet anyone who was.

'Tall, aren't you? Almost as tall as Flex.'

'I was a lot shorter until I started working for the deputy chief of staff. Couple of weeks ago I was carrying a pickaxe, looking out for six brothers and answering to the name of Grumpy.'

'That happens a lot around here. But you're thinking of Doc, aren't you? Grumpy just scowled a lot and looked out for himself.'

'Like I said, Doc's dead. Besides, I'm not that clever. Just the one with the biggest nose and the worst temper.'

'I've seen worse. As you've already discovered, some of these local dwarves like to play rough. But I can usually take care of it.' She lifted her gilet a few centimetres and let me catch sight of a little automatic she was keeping warm under there. 'You see? I make an excellent wicked stepmother when the need arises.'

'I'll bet you do,' said Kaspel.

'He's not as nice as you,' she told me. 'I expect it's the uniform.'

I shrugged. 'Captain Kaspel? He always tells the truth, I'm afraid. Just like the slave of the magic mirror. So be careful what you ask him. You might not like the answer, your majesty.'

'Am I supposed to pay you from now on? Do tell.'

'I'm not here to discuss the new arrangements. Frau?'

'Lola,' she said. 'They call me naughty Lola. Like Marlene Dietrich, you know?'

But there the similarity ended. I nodded all the same, hardly wanting to earn her displeasure by laughing in her face, which looked like a wax orange, there was so much paint covering it. On the way to some information there was still room for a bit of common courtesy and good manners, especially after pulling a gun on her customers and making free with Bormann's name

like some pompous Party official. Surrounded by so much ruthless efficiency in the name of the Leader, it now fell to someone
like me to try to redress that balance. Perhaps. I shot Kaspel a
look, hoping to dampen his contempt. Maybe Lola wasn't the
fairest of them all but she was still the queen of the hut and I
needed her talking.

'Sure,' I said. 'I know. *The Blue Angel* is one of my favourites.'

'Then you're in the right place, Herr Gunther. Maybe I'll come
sit on your knee and sing you a nice song, if you're a good boy.'

I managed not to laugh at that one, too, but Kaspel was
finding it harder to keep a straight face. I needed to get rid of
him, and quickly, before he could upset her. Outside the grimy
window it had started snowing again. Undeterred, the four P&Z
workers were still awaiting our departure. A part of me was
already feeling sorry for all the girls who were trapped in this
awful love hut in the forest. At least Snow White never had to
sleep with the seven dwarves. Not in the version I'd read, anyway.

'Can we talk somewhere in private?' I asked her.

'You'd better come into my office.'

'Captain Kaspel,' I said, 'would you mind keeping an eye on
the car? I wouldn't put it past those bastards in the truck to do
something to our tyres.'

'They wouldn't dare.'

'Please.'

He frowned for a moment, probably considered arguing about
it, and then remembered the inflexible reputation of the man
who had sent me down to Berchtesgaden in the first place. 'All
right,' he said, and went outside.

Lola led me into a room with a bed, a shower, and a toilet,
and closed the door. There were some religious prints on the
walls and from these and from her accent I concluded that she
might be Italian. On the bedside table was a bowlful of Gummis
and I supposed she was not above handling a few clients herself,
when things were busier. I sat on the only chair; she sat on the

bed and finished her cigarette. The office part was probably the metal desk and the filing cabinet by the window. There was even an old candlestick phone. Meanwhile, Kaspel was walking back to the car.

'Sorry about him,' I said. 'Von Ribbentrop he's not.'

'If you mean he's no diplomat, I'd say that's true. But then Ribbentrop isn't much of a diplomat, either. You're different. Well, let's just say we could have used you down here back in September, when Chamberlain came to eat Hitler's shit. Maybe things would have turned out different. Then again, I'm Italian. We like everyone to be happy. That's why we have Mussolini. He at least seems to enjoy his fascism in a way you Germans don't.'

'You've been in Berchtesgaden for a while, then.'

'About a year. Seems a lot longer, especially when there's snow on the ground. We get to keep half of what we earn on our backs. Flex used to take the rest, for our room and board, he said. If that's what you can call this dump. I hope you're not here to renegotiate that rate.'

'No, I'm not here to renegotiate anything. Look, Lola, I haven't been entirely honest with you. I'm a police commissar from Berlin. A detective. I've come down here to investigate the murder of Dr Flex. And I was hoping you might be able to help me.'

'Beyond the fact that I'm glad he's dead, I don't know what to tell you, Herr Commissar. Karl Flex was a chiselling son of a bitch and deserved that bullet. I just hope he didn't suffer – for any length of time shorter than several hours.'

'Those are strong words, Lola. And, if you'll take my advice, perhaps best moderated, given who he worked for.'

'I don't care. I've had enough of this place. You can arrest me and throw me in a cell and I'll say the same thing. But of course you won't because nobody wants to hear what I've got to say. In the beginning, when Bormann ordered this place to be built, we were handing over only twenty-five per cent. But about three months ago, Flex told us it was now fifty. When I protested he told us to take it up with Bormann if we didn't like it. Not that we could. We can't even go into Berchtesgaden. Once we tried it and the locals almost stoned us. Of course, none of us are German, so that makes us easier to spot. And easier to control, too. Flex knew damn well that we didn't really have any choice but to do whatever he told us. And I do mean whatever he told us.'

'Meaning what – that he enjoyed the favours of some of these girls himself?'

'Just the one girl, actually. Renata Prodi.'

'I'd like to speak with her, if I can.'

'Well, you can't. She's gone. Sent home to Milan by the doctor. On account of the fact that Flex gave her gonorrhoea. I'd catch a train home myself if I had enough money. But I don't.'

'He gave it to her? Jelly?'

'Almost certainly.'

'When was this?'

'A few days ago. It almost closed us down. The doctor has got us all on silver proteinate.' She leaned forward and tugged open the bedside drawer to reveal the same Protargol that I'd seen before, on the list of Flex's personal effects – the drug thoughtfully removed by Karl Brandt. 'Not that there's any real need. Renata was the only one affected. And she used Gummis with all her clients. All except Flex. He insisted on not wearing a raincoat. But you couldn't argue with a man like that. He really was wicked, you know. Not like you.'

'I'm part of the same crummy football team.'

'But not in your heart. I can read men really quickly, you know, Commissar. There's a kindness in your eyes, which is why you keep them narrowed and well shaded by the brim of your hat, so that no one will notice that you're not like the rest of the dwarves. No, you're Humbert the Huntsman. I can tell. If the wicked queen told you to take Snow White into the woods and cut her heart out, you'd let her go and take a pig's heart home with you in a nice box with a ribbon on it. Flex's heart, probably. Assuming he had one.'

'Was it always Flex who came for the money?'

'No, once or twice it was another Fridolin. Fellow named Schenk. Cold bastard. Almost as bad as Flex. I expect he'll be the one who we have to deal with now. Something else I'm not looking forward to.'

'Who gets the money from this little house of silk? Bormann, I suppose?'

'I imagine. There's not much that happens around here his lordship doesn't know about. Or from which he doesn't take a nice fat cut. Based upon what the men who work building his hotels and his roads and his tunnels are telling me, he must be worth millions. But certainly he's hated every bit as much as Flex was. Strikes me you've got your work cut out for you, Herr Gunther.'

'That's what it feels like, for sure. I'd like to speak to your girls, if I could.'

'What? You think one of them might have shot him? That's inspired.'

'No, but they might have screwed the man who did. That's fair, isn't it?'

'I promise you, you'd be wasting your time. For one thing, they're not like me. Kids, mostly. And too afraid to say anything. Besides, there are only two girls who speak good German.'

'What? No German girls here at all?'

'No. Not one. There's a Sudeten Czech and an Austrian girl. Maria. Hitler would go mad if he even knew about this place, that's what I heard. But he'd be even angrier if any German women were ever found working here. It seems as if they're something holy.'

'Haven't you heard? Our women are supposed to be breeding a master race, not falling in love again, like Lola, or headlining the local cabaret in a top hat with stockings and garters.'

'So you did see the movie.'

'It's a favourite of mine.'

Lola nodded. 'Not that we haven't had some local girls turning up here looking to make a little pocket money. But I had to send them packing. Flex might not have noticed a few extra girls. But Dr Brandt would have. He's the one who examines all the girls for jelly. Once a week, regular as a Swiss watch.'

This was a name I hadn't expected to hear in the local brothel.

'Brandt? I thought it was some pill Jesus from Salzburg who looked after you all.'

'It was. But he decided this wasn't his cup of tea and stopped coming. So Brandt took over. Dr Infernal we call him. One time he came over and he was wearing the uniform under his white coat. Some of the girls found it quite sexy, I think.'

'Interesting.'

'Well, pin your ears back, Commissar, because he does a lot more than examine girls for a dose of jelly.'

'He likes a dish on the side, too?'

'No, not him. They'd probably kick him out of the SS for something human like that. No, what I mean is that he's carried out at least three midnight abortions since I've known him. For money, of course. None of these men do anything for nothing. Knows what he's about, though, I'll say that much for him. The rumour is that before he came down here he used to perform scrapes on women who were mentally handicapped, or because they were Jewesses who'd got themselves in trouble with a nice German boy. They say he's Hitler's own doctor. But I wonder what Hitler would say if he knew about all this kind of thing.'

'I wonder.' I sighed, not wondering very much. 'These abortions carried out by Dr Brandt. Can you remember who had one?'

'Yes, but I don't think I should tell you.'

'Was one of them Renata Prodi?'

'Now I come to think about it, yes, it was.'

'So it's quite possible that Karl Flex was the father.'

'It's possible, yes.'

I sighed, liking the case less and less. It's common enough for a detective to hate an investigation he's been tasked with, but it's less often the case – at least for me – that I dislike myself so thoroughly for investigating it. It made me want to do something good.

'Where are you from, Lola?'

'Milan. Do you know Milan?'

'No, I'm afraid I don't.'

'It's beautiful. Especially the cathedral. I miss that most of all.' She took out a handkerchief and wiped her eyes. 'I'd love to go back but I think I'm stuck in this misbegotten place, for the moment, anyway. All the money I've earned I sent home already. It'll be at least a month before I can save enough to make the trip. I should have gone back at Christmas, when I had the chance, but La Befana didn't come last year. She's the Italian version of Santa Claus. Still, that's hardly surprising in a place like this. We don't even have a proper chimney. At least, not one that Befana could come down.'

I thought about this for a moment, and we were both silent while my thoughts buzzed around my head and then flew out to the rooftop. I was glad to see them go. I hadn't been wasting my time as much as I'd feared. 'What will happen to the other girls if you leave?'

'They'll be all right. Aneta can take over. She's Czech, but speaks excellent German and is very capable. At the beginning of the summer they'll bring some new girls to replace the girls now working here. Besides, I'd like to leave before someone like Dr Infernal finds out the truth about me.'

'Don't tell me, Lola. Truth is not something to share with anyone in Germany these days. You wouldn't know it now, I used to like talking. But lately I've been struck dumb, like the angel Gabriel told me I was about to father a son called John. Life's safer that way.'

'I told you before. You have kind eyes. And don't let those pictures of the saints fool them. They're just for show. The fact is, I'm Jewish.'

'Then you should certainly leave while you can. How much would it take to get you home?'

'A hundred reichsmarks would probably cover it. Don't worry about me. I'll make it. I just hope I can do it before the war starts.'

'Pity' and all of its many soft synonyms was not a word in Reinhard Heydrich's devilish dictionary. I already knew he thought I was a sentimental fool. Maybe I was. But there and then I decided to live up to the general's low opinion of me and donate some of the money I'd persuaded him to let me have for information and bribes to Lola. And of course I was well aware that giving money to a Jewish whore was the absolute opposite of the way he would have preferred it spent. Which made what I was doing less an act of generosity and more a token act of resistance. Even as I handed her a hundred marks I was paying less attention to the real pleasure and relief that now crossed her clownish face and more to the look of outrage that I imagined would have been on Heydrich's horse-like features had he witnessed this scene.

'Here,' I said. 'With the compliments of the SD. And if anyone ever asks, I'm doing this because I loathe and despise Jews and want all of them safely out of the country as soon as possible.'

Lola smiled and put the money in a little pocket next to the automatic she was carrying.

'I knew I was right about you, Humbert. I'm only sorry I couldn't be more helpful.'

'On the contrary. You've been very helpful.'

'I don't see how.'

'No, but I think I do. Sometimes, seeing what's been right in front of my nose all along is what this job is all about.'

CHAPTER 24

April 1939

I climbed back up onto the roof of the Villa Bechstein to take another look around. It was an operatic skyline. I might have been facing the impregnable walls of Asgard; even the clouds were like Odin's beard. It was a sky for a man with an idea of his own destiny. Or perhaps a misleading vision of one. Rolf Müller came over and asked if he could help. But now it was my turn to be annoyingly cryptic.

'The chimney,' I said, pointing out the stack with the curious bell tower.

'What about it?'

'Plenty of room for Santa Claus and a whole sackful of presents, don't you think?'

'Santa Claus?'

'Don't tell me you don't believe in Santa Claus, Herr Müller.'

'It's April,' he said weakly. 'Too late for Santa Claus.'

'Better late than never, wouldn't you say?'

I smiled but actually I wasn't so very sure that I hadn't just seen Santa Claus zooming across the skies above Obersalzberg, with a full squadron of flying Valkyries drawing his sleigh. That was the methamphetamine. It was still like I'd been wired up to the main electricity supply, which felt good even though hallucinations are supposed to interfere with your powers of observation – at least they are according to the rules for being a good detective, as described by Bernhard Weiss. It's bad enough that you miss things you should have seen before; it's wholly inexcusable when you start seeing things that you know aren't there at all. Not that this ever stopped anyone at the Alex from stowing a lunch bottle in his desk drawer, and a couple of drinks certainly never slowed me down very much, but the arrival at the Villa Bechstein of a cortège of black limousines sporting stiff little Nazi flags persuaded me that I was now going to have to try a lot harder to pull myself together and behave like a real Nazi.

I came back down the ladder, fixed a stupid smile to my face, and saluted smartly, although not nearly as smartly as Hermann Kaspel; his was good enough for the both of us, at least I hoped it was. The deputy party leader had arrived with his Dalmatian dogs, and as soon as the heavy car doors opened, the two mutts went galloping off into the thickly timbered woods behind the house. Then Hess climbed out of the car, stretched a little, glanced up at the roof, and returned the salute absently with a motion of his swagger stick. He was an unprepossessing fellow. Most people I knew thought that Hitler kept him around to make himself seem a bit more normal; with his monobrow, *Phantom of the Opera* eyes, and Frankenstein skull, Rudolf Hess would have made Lon Chaney seem normal. I waited until he and his fawning entourage of brownshirts had gone inside and then went quietly up to the first bedroom shown to me by Winkelhof, the butler. I knelt down on the floor and tried to lift the chimney flap but it was still stuck – not with soot and rubble; it felt like something heavy was resting on top of the flap. I had a shrewd idea what it was, and as soon as Winkelhof had finished showing Hess to his apartments and had come to see if he could assist me in some way, I asked him to fetch me a sledgehammer.

'May I enquire what you plan to do with a sledgehammer, sir?' he asked with polite disapproval.

'Yes, I plan to remove this faulty fireplace as quickly as possible.'

'Are you feeling all right, sir?'

'Yes, I'm fine, thank you.'

He took off his glasses and began to polish them furiously, almost as if he were trying to erase me from his sight. 'Then may I remind you, sir, that the fireplace in your own room is working perfectly.'

'Yes, I know. But something is jammed on top of the flap in this fireplace, and I do believe that something is a rifle.'

Winkelhof looked pained. 'A rifle? Are you sure?'

'More or less. I think someone dropped it down the chimney before making his escape.'

'And if it's less? What I mean is, I don't think the deputy leader will like you hammering on the wall with a sledgehammer immediately below his apartments, sir. He's had a long and tiring journey and has just informed me that he intends to get some rest. That's rest as in peace and quiet, and he's not to be disturbed under any circumstances until dinnertime. Perhaps a chimney sweep might be summoned tomorrow—'

I tried not to smile at the prospect of ruining the deputy leader's beauty sleep but this proved to be impossible. That was the meth, too, I suppose. I was ready to face him down if necessary, at some risk to myself and all in the name of an investigation into the death of a man whom no one had liked. 'It can't be helped, I'm afraid. I need to clear this matter up as soon as possible. So I have my orders, Winkelhof. Bormann's orders.'

'And I have mine.'

'Look, I understand your quandary. You're trying to run this house, like a good butler should. But I'm trying to run a murder investigation. So I'll find some tools myself. And take full responsibility if the deputy leader tries to make my ears stiff because of it.' But I wondered about that; in a cocks-out size contest between Martin Bormann and Rudolf Hess, I had no idea which would reveal himself to be in possession of the largest bratwürst. I was, perhaps, about to find out.

Kaspel and Friedrich Korsch were waiting for me in the drawing room.

Korsch had my prints of the autopsy and the crime scene. 'You were right about that other photographer,' he told Kaspel. 'There was a local man called Johann Brandner. Only, he used to have his business premises up here, in Obersalzberg, not in Berchtesgaden. Guess where he is now. Dachau. Seems as if he kept writing to Hitler to ask if his little shop might be spared from compulsory purchase. Bormann got fed up with him and had him carted off for a barbed-wire holiday. I had the devil of a job getting anyone to admit they'd even heard of the poor bastard.'

'Put a call in to the Munich SD,' I told Hermann Kaspel. 'See if he's still there. And Friedrich. I'm going to need a sledgehammer. You might like to try some of those workers from P&Z we saw on the road. Maybe they'll lend you one.'

Then I went to my own room, lay down on the rock-hard mattress, closed my eyes, and breathed deeply through my nose in the hope that the voices I could hear would quickly disappear. Mostly they were telling me that I should borrow a car, drive across Austria and into Italy as soon as possible – Sesto was only two hundred kilometres away – find a nice girl, and forget about being a cop before the Nazis decided to throw me in a concentration camp, this time forever. It was probably good advice, only a little too loud and clear for my liking and hearing it made my skin crawl like I was in the way of an army of voracious soldier ants. Staying awake for a day and a half was, I now realized, as sure a way of receiving a personal message from the gods as anything described in the Holy Bible. Half an hour passed. I didn't sleep for a minute. My eyes shifted under their lids like excited puppies. The voices persisted: if I didn't leave Obersalzberg soon I was going to be tied up inside a sack with a gang of oversexed workers from P&Z and hurled off the top terrace of Hitler's tea house. I got up and went downstairs before I started talking back.

Friedrich Korsch didn't much resemble Thor, the thunder god; for one, his face was too crafty and the pimp moustache on his upper lip much too metropolitan, but the hammer he was carrying over his shoulder did make him look as if he meant to crush a mountain or two. He brandished the tool eagerly as if looking forward to the designated demolition work. I expect he'd have done what he was told if I'd ordered him to batter out the fireplace but, in the circumstances, I thought it best to do it myself; if anyone was going to incur the wrath of Rudolf Hess it seemed better that it should be me. So I took the hammer and climbed back up the stairs. Kaspel and Korsch followed, keen to witness the destruction I was about to inflict on Hitler's precious guest house. I took off my jacket, rolled up my shirtsleeves, spat on my hands, grasped the shaft of the hammer firmly, and prepared to do battle.

'Are you sure about this, boss?' said Korsch.

'No,' I said, 'I'm not sure of anything very much since I started taking the local magic potion.'

And while Kaspel explained to Korsch about Pervitin, I laid into the fireplace with the sledgehammer. That first blow felt as satisfying as if I'd struck Hess on his absurdly high forehead.

'But I am willing to bet five marks that the rifle is behind this wall.'

I hammered it again, smashing the tile surround and some of the bricks behind it. Korsch pulled a face and looked up at the ceiling as if he expected the deputy leader to reach down through his own floorboards and grab me by the throat.

'I'll take that bet,' said Kaspel, and lit a cigarette. 'I think it's just as likely the shooter chucked it into the woods from where he could retrieve it later on. In fact, I can't understand why you didn't let me organize a search of the grounds before you decided to turn this room into a rock pile.'

'Because the roofing contractor, Rolf Müller, doesn't smoke,' I said. 'And because right next to the chimney there was a

cigarette end and some footprints. And because it's too late for
Santa Claus. And because there are too many trees out there;
if he'd tossed the rifle it might have hit one and bounced back
onto the path and risked alerting that gardener. Dropping it
down the chimney was the safer thing to do. Because it's what
I'd have done myself if I'd had the guts to take a potshot at
someone on the Berghof terrace. And because there's something
sitting right on top of the flap in this chimney that's stopping
it from being used.'

I swung the sledgehammer a third time, and this time made
a fist-sized hole in the wall around the fireplace. But suddenly
Korsch and Kaspel stiffened as if the devil had put in an appearance.

'What the hell do you think you're doing, Commissar Gunther?'

I turned around to find Martin Bormann occupying the
doorway, with Zander, Högl, and Winkelhof standing immediately behind him. I glanced back at the fireplace. I decided that
another blow of the sledgehammer would probably do it and
that it was one of those uniquely German situations in which
actions speak louder than words. So I swung again, and this
time I altered the position of the fireplace itself. It now looked
possible to pull the thing out by hand. And I might have done
just that but for the Walther police pistol that had now appeared
in Bormann's chubby fist.

'If you wield that hammer again I will shoot you,' he said, and
worked the slide just to show that he meant business, before
pointing the PPK at my head.

I threw down the hammer, and taking the cigarette from
Kaspel's hand, started to smoke it myself with one eye on Bormann's face and the other on the gun. For the moment, however,
I said nothing. Nothing is always an easier answer to give when
there's a cigarette in your hand.

'Explain yourself,' insisted Bormann, and lowered the weapon
– although as far as I could see, the gun was still cocked and

ready for action. I had a good idea that if I'd picked up the sledgehammer again he wouldn't have hesitated to shoot me. 'What the hell do you mean by smashing the room up like this?'

'I mean to find the man who murdered Karl Flex,' I said. 'Correct me if I'm wrong, but that's what you told me to do. But to do that I need to find the murder weapon.'

'Are you suggesting he shot him from in here? From the Villa Bechstein?'

'Not from in here,' I said calmly. 'From the roof.'

'No! From the Villa Bechstein? Tell it to your grandmother. I don't fucking believe it. You mean he wasn't in the woods above the Berghof after all?'

'There's spent brass all over the roof,' I said. 'And I already measured the angles of trajectory from the terrace. The shooter was down here all right. It's my theory that having shot Flex, he dumped the rifle down the chimney before making his escape. This chimney. I noticed the flap on the fireplace wouldn't open earlier. And so I decided to check it out. Look, sir, when we spoke last night I gained the impression that a degree of urgency was going to be necessary with this inquiry. Not to mention a certain amount of discretion. I'm afraid I took you at your word, otherwise I'd have summoned a local chimney sweep and risked the whole town finding out what happened up here yesterday morning.'

'Well, is it there? The rifle?'

'I don't honestly know, sir. Really, I was just playing a hunch I had. I might pull that fireplace out right now and find out for sure but for the funny idea I have that you might put a hole in me with that police pistol in your hand.'

Bormann made the Walther safe and then slipped it back into his coat pocket. With the automatic he was a bigger thug than even I had supposed. 'There,' he said. 'You're quite safe for the moment.'

Meanwhile Rudolf Hess had appeared behind his shoulder

and regarded me with the kind of staring blue eyes that must sometimes have made even Hitler a bit nervous. The dark wave of hair on top of his square head was standing so high it looked as if it were concealing a pair of horns; either that or he'd been standing a little too close to the lightning conductor in Frankenstein's castle laboratory.

'What the hell is going on here?' he asked Bormann.

'It would seem that Criminal Commissar Gunther is about to search the chimney for a murder weapon,' said Bormann. 'Well, go on, then,' he told me. 'Get on with it. But you'd better be right, Gunther, or you'll be on the next train back to Berlin.'

'Murder weapon?' said Hess. 'Who's been murdered? What's this all about, Commissar?'

Bormann ignored him and it certainly wasn't up to me to say who was dead or why. Instead, I knelt down in front of the fireplace and, almost hoping that I could be on the first train back to Berlin, I tugged hard at the fireplace and dislodged an object that came tumbling onto the floor in a cloud of soot and gravel. Only it wasn't a rifle but a leather binoculars case, covered with soot. I laid the case on the bedspread, which did little to endear me to Winkelhof.

'That doesn't look like a rifle,' said Bormann.

'No, sir, but a pair of field glasses might help you to find your target. Assuming you actually cared who you were shooting at.'

With five shots fired at the Berghof terrace I still wasn't a hundred per cent sure that the shooter had only intended to hit Karl Flex. I knelt down again and pushed my arm up the chimney. A few moments later I was holding a rifle up for the inspection of everyone in the room. It was a Mannlicher M95, a short-barrelled carbine manufactured for the Austrian army with a telescopic sight mounted slightly to the left so the rifle could be fed by an en-bloc stripper clip.

'It would seem you know your business after all, Commissar,' said Bormann.

I worked the bolt and a spent brass cartridge popped out of the carbine's breech. I picked it up; it was the same as the others I'd found already.

'I apologize,' he added. 'But what the hell's that on the end of the barrel?' Bormann took a closer look. 'It would appear to be a Mahle oil filter.'

'It's a little trick I've seen here before,' explained Kaspel. 'The local poachers fit them to their rifles. You need to make a thread on the end of the barrel but it's something almost anyone with access to a workshop can do. An oil filter makes a very effective sound suppressor. Like the mute on a trumpet. Just the thing when you're stalking deer inside the Leader's Territory and you don't want to get caught by the RSD.'

Bormann frowned. 'What poachers? I thought that was all sorted when we erected the fucking fence.'

'There's no point in getting into that now,' I said. 'It would certainly explain why no one heard the shots.' Seeing Bormann's eyebrows sliding up his forehead, I added, 'That's right, sir. There was more than one shot fired. We found four bullets in the woodwork of the first-level balcony above the Berghof terrace.'

'Four?' said Bormann. 'Are you sure?'

'Yes. Of course, we still haven't found the fifth one – the one that killed Karl Flex. My guess is that it was lost forever when the Berghof terrace was cleaned up by your men, sir.'

'I demand that someone tell me what's going on,' said Hess. Clasping his hands in front of his belt buckle and then folding his arms again, as if nervous, he looked as if he was about to make his usual shrill, high priest's speech at the Berlin Sportpalast. 'Now, please.' He stamped his jackboots one after the other impatiently and for a moment I actually thought he was going to scream or even throw his Party tiepin on the floor.

Bormann turned to Hess and explained, reluctantly, what had happened to Karl Flex.

'But this is terrible,' said Hess. 'Does Hitler know?'

'No,' said Bormann. 'I don't think that would be a good idea. Not yet. Not until the culprit is in custody.'

'Why?'

Bormann grimaced; clearly he was not accustomed to being questioned like this, even by the man who was nominally his boss. I took another look at the carbine while they argued and tried to pretend that none of this was happening. But it seemed as if I was about to discover who was going to win the bratwürst contest.

'Because I think it would almost certainly interfere with his future enjoyment of the Berghof,' said Bormann. 'That's why.'

'I insist that he be told as soon as possible,' argued Hess. 'I'm certain he'd want to know. The Leader takes all such matters very seriously.'

'And you think I don't?' With a face as red as a pig's head in a pork-butcher's window, Bormann pointed at me. 'According to General Heydrich, this man Gunther is the top criminal commissar in the Berlin Murder Commission. I've no reason to doubt that. He's been sent here to clear up this matter as soon as possible. All that can be done right now is being done. Please take a minute to think about this, my dear Hess. Quite apart from the fact that it might spoil his birthday if you told him about Flex's death, Hitler might never come to Obersalzberg again. To this – his favourite place in the world. Surely you, as a Bavarian, could not wish such a thing ever to happen. Besides, it's not as if we've uncovered an attempt to kill Hitler himself. I'm quite sure that this was a matter entirely unrelated to the Leader. Wouldn't you agree, Commissar?'

'Yes, sir, I would. From what I've learned so far I'm confident that this has nothing to do with Hitler.'

I laid the carbine on the bedspread, next to the binoculars. It was also covered in soot and I thought it was unlikely that the firearm would yield any fingerprints. I was more interested in the serial number. And in the Mahle oil filter. Given what Kaspel had said, we were clearly looking for someone who owned or had access to a lathe. Quietly I asked Korsch to fetch my camera from my room, so that I might add some pictures of the carbine to my portfolio.

Hess's narrow mouth turned petulant, like a schoolboy who had been punished unjustly. 'With all due respect to the commissar, this is not a matter for Kripo, but for the Gestapo. It may be that there is some conspiracy here. After all, it's only a few months since that Swiss, Maurice Bavaud, came here with the express purpose of killing the Leader. It may be that this is connected with that earlier incident in some way. It could even be that the murderer mistakenly believed he was shooting at Hitler, in which case he may try again, when Hitler is actually here. At the very least the Leader's Territory should now be extended to the foot of Salzbergerstrasse, where it crosses the River Ache.'

'Nonsense,' said Bormann. 'I assure you, dear Hess, that nothing of the kind has happened here. Besides, we'll certainly have caught the culprit before the Leader's birthday. Isn't that so, Gunther?'

I hardly wanted to disagree with Bormann, especially as Hess was beginning to sound like a complete spinner. Already Bormann looked like the safer choice of top Nazi with whom to ally myself. 'Yes, sir,' I said.

But Hess wasn't about to let this matter go. His eagle-eyed devotion to Adolf Hitler was absolute and it seemed that he could not countenance the very idea of keeping the Leader in the dark about anything at all, and Bormann was obliged to accompany him to his apartments upstairs, where they continued their discussion, in private. But everyone in the Villa Bechstein could hear them talking.

That was just the way I liked it: two very important Nazis arguing loudly about their positions in the government's odious pecking order. It wasn't about to get any better than that on Hitler's mountain.

CHAPTER 25

October 1956

I changed trains in Chaumont and boarded another headed north for Nancy, which is over a hundred kilometres from the German border, although the realization had now dawned that I wasn't sure where exactly the border was, not anymore. I knew where the old French–German border was but not the new one, not since the war. After the defeat of Germany in 1945, France had treated the Saar as a French Protectorate and an important resource for economic exploitation. Then, in the referendum of October 1955, the dominantly German Sarrois had voted by an overwhelming majority to reject the idea of an independent Saarland – which would still have suited the French – a result that was generally interpreted as the region's rejection of France and an indication of its strong support for joining the Federal Republic of Germany. But I had no idea if the French recognized this result, which would mean they had finally ceded control of the Saar to the FRG. Knowing the French, and the historic significance our two countries had attached to this much-disputed territory, it seemed unlikely they would let it go so easily. Given the bitterness of the ongoing French–Algerian war, and France's obvious reluctance to leave North Africa to rule itself, I could hardly imagine the Franzis were just going to walk out of a region of even greater industrial importance such as the Saar. The fact was, even if I got as far as Saarbrücken, I had no idea if being there would really make me any safer from arrest. There would still be plenty of French policemen around to make my life as a fugitive hazardous. I had to hope that as a French-speaking German native, I might at least be a little more anonymous. Anonymous enough to get me to the true Federal Republic. But even Nancy began to seem like a long way off when, just as the train was pulling out of the picturesque town of Neufchâteau, about halfway to my chosen destination, some uniformed French police got on and started checking identity cards.

I walked slowly to the opposite end of the train, where I lit a Camel and considered my options. I thought I had just a few minutes before they would reach me, whereupon I would be arrested and probably taken back to a jail cell in Dijon. And there I would soon find myself at the mercy of some Stasi poisoner. Of course, the police might have been looking for someone else, but my detective's nose told me this was unlikely. There's nothing police like more than a nationwide manhunt. It gets everyone excited and gives the local cops an excuse to neglect their paperwork in order to try to put one over on the big-city boys. My only hope now seemed to be that the Nancy train would stop or slow down long enough for me to jump off. But even a glance out the window told me that while this was good country for growing grapes, it was a poor place to hide; there was very little cover and, along the bank of the River Meuse, everything looked as flat and featureless as the French economy. Things would have been easier in Germany where there is a more established tradition of hiking and wandering the country-side. But the French are not given to walking anywhere except to the local bakery and the *tabac*. With some dogs on my tail, the police would certainly catch me in a matter of hours. A few minutes of reflection persuaded me that my best chance – if I had the nerve for it – was to hide from the police in plain sight. It wasn't much of a plan but there are times when a poor plan looks like a better choice than a good one – when a crooked log makes a straight fire. We've got a word for that, but it's a very long one and most people run out of breath before they finish it. I was running out of breath myself.

So I waited until the train was about to enter a small copse of plane trees, reached up above my head, braced myself, and then pulled the emergency brake. As the train shuddered to a screeching halt I threw open a door in the carriage with a loud bang and then hid inside the nearest lavatory. I waited there for several minutes, like a real *Sitzpinkler,* until I heard some shouts down on the track outside that were enough to tell me that the police truly believed that a passenger had taken fright at their presence and jumped off the train. Then I left the lavatory and walked slowly back to those carriages where I had seen the police already conducting an identity check. None of the other passengers paid much attention to me; they were all too busy looking out of the windows at the police, who were running alongside the train or looking underneath it for a wanted felon. From time to time I stopped and looked outside myself and asked people what was happening. Someone told me that the police were looking for an Algerian terrorist from the FLN; someone else assured me that they were looking for a man who'd murdered his wife, and grinned when I pulled a face and asked if this still counted as a crime in France. Nobody mentioned the Blue Train murderer, which gave me hope that I might yet pass through this part of France undetected.

At the very end of the train I sat down and started to read the early edition of the *France-Soir* I'd bought in Chaumont. I hoped that in the time it would take the driver to reset the brake, and the police to conduct a search of the area surrounding the tracks, I might recover some of my nerve, but I found BLUE TRAIN MURDER occupying a whole column of page five, which did little for my confidence. Reading it, I could almost feel the noose tightening around my neck, especially since the memory of a noose around my neck was all too vivid. The suspect's

Citroën had been found in the town of Gevrey-Chambertin and he was believed to be on the run somewhere in Burgundy. My nerves were stretched to breaking, however, when two or three policemen got back on the train. It seemed the others were making their way back to Neufchâteau to collect a search party. To my relief, the policemen on the train had given up any thought of checking more identities. Instead, the train drove off at half speed with the cops looking out the windows, hoping to spot a man making a run for it across the open fields. After a while one of them even came and sat beside me and asked me for a match. I handed him a box and let him light his cigarette before I asked him what all the excitement was about. He told me they were hunting for the Blue Train murderer and that as soon as they were back in Nancy, they were going to organize the local police to conduct an extensive search of the area around Chaumont.

'How do you know he's in this area?' I asked coolly.

'We had a tip he was in Dijon after his car was found a short way south of there. And a man answering his description was seen near the station.

'He must have been on this train. It's obvious he saw us get on and decided to make a run for it. But we'll catch him soon enough. He's German, you see. There's no way a German can hide in France. Not since the war. Someone's bound to give him away sooner or later. Nobody likes Germans.'

I nodded firmly, as if such a thing were quite irrefutable.

In Nancy I marched swiftly away from the main railway station, confident only that I would not be taking any more French trains for a while. For no reason I could think of except that I was dog-tired and emotionally exhausted – I could certainly have used a tube of Pervitin now – I found my heart poking through the ribs of my chest: for the first time in a long time I thought of my late mother, which necessitated a brief halt in a telephone kiosk where I applied some more collyrium to my eyes. After that I walked a short distance east, through quiet streets to an impressively baroque church called Saint Sebastian, and there I was at last able to relax. I even managed to doze off for a while. Nobody looks at a man who's in a church with his eyes closed; not the faithful at prayer, nor the nuns cleaning the place, nor the priests taking confession; even God leaves you alone in a church. Perhaps God most of all.

I stayed in the church of Saint Sebastian for a full hour before I felt confident enough to venture outside again, by which time it was late afternoon. I'd thought about taking a bus but that seemed as potentially hazardous as a train, and I was merely putting off the moment when I would surely have to find a more private means of transport. Another car required too much paperwork and I was thinking about a small motorcycle or a scooter; but on Rue des 4 Églises I saw a shop full of second-hand bicycles. A bicycle was surely the least suspicious mode of transport available; after all, children, schoolteachers, and priests, even policemen, ride bicycles. A bicycle implied that you were not in a hurry, and there is nothing that arouses suspicion less than someone who is not in a hurry. So I purchased an old green Lapierre with good tyres, some lights, and a luggage rack, onto which I tied my bag. I couldn't remember the last time I'd ridden a bike – probably when I was a beat copper – and, in spite of the old saying that you never forget how, I almost did and nearly spilled myself into the path of a delivery van, which provided me with a very useful private lesson in the nicer points of the French language. I steadied myself beside the machine, mounted it a second time, and was just about to start pedalling away from Nancy for good when I saw the central covered market next door to the bicycle shop and had an idea how to render myself even more inconspicuous. I went inside and within just a few minutes I had also bought several strings of onions. The stall owner gave me a suspicious sort of look as if to say, *What could you want with so many?* and even in France, onion soup didn't seem to be much of an answer, so I offered no explanation, just my money, which, for the French, is usually all the explanation required, especially near the end of a long working day. And, with the strings hanging on my handlebars, I was soon cycling east, across the Meurthe River towards the open countryside of Moselle, like a real Onion Johnny. At the very least, if a cop did stop me I thought the onions might be used as a means of explaining my red eyes.

I cycled through the evening and into the night, but not very used to the effort of it, I managed only about fifteen kilometres an hour. Being a schoolboy with a bicycle never felt so strenuous; then again, Berlin is very flat and a perfect place to cycle anywhere, as long as it's near Berlin. Before the war you could go for kilometre after kilometre without encountering so much as a bump in the road.

At nine o'clock it was too dark to travel any further and, in a crummy little village called Château-Salins, I finally had to admit my exhaustion and stop to give my eyes and my backside a rest. I regarded the pink Hôtel de Ville next to the town hall on Rue de Nancy with longing, imagining the excellent dinner and the soft bed I might have enjoyed there, but I would have been required to show them an identity card or a passport and I was keen to avoid leaving any kind of a paper trail that the French police – and by extension the Stasi – could pick up. I wheeled the heavy Lapierre through the streets until, on the tattered edge of town, I saw a field covered with hay bales in the moonlight, and I learned that they had a soft bed free for the night that did not require me to show any identification at all. And there, in hay still warm from the heat of the day and with only a few insects for company, I ate the bread and cheese I'd bought in Chaumont – I even ate a raw onion, too – drank a bottle of beer, smoked my last Camel, and slept as well as any man ever slept who had no job, no home, no friends, no wife, nor any notion of a future. *Plus ça change, plus c'est la même chose.*

CHAPTER 26

April 1939

When I returned to the Berghof from the Villa Bechstein I discovered another loud argument in progress – this one between Arthur Kannenberg, the house manager, and a voice that Hermann Kaspel quickly identified as belonging to Hitler's local adjutant, Wilhelm Brückner. They were in the Great Hall at the time but the main door was open and from where we were standing, on the stairway immediately above, we could hear almost every bitter word. The Great Hall's double-height ceiling made certain of that. I daresay it was an excellent room for a piano recital or even a small opera by Wagner, assuming there is such a thing, but this was already quite a performance. It seemed that Brückner was a ladies' man, and Kannenberg, who was unprepossessing to say the least, suspected the handsome officer of making a pass at his wife, Freda, in the winter garden, which seemed unlikely to anyone who'd seen Freda, or for that matter the winter garden: it was freezing in there.

'You stay away from her, do you hear?'

'I don't know what you're talking about.'

'If you have a question about the running of this house, you come to me, not her. She's had enough of your filthy remarks.'

'Like what? What am I supposed to have said?'

'You know damn well, Brückner. How you're not getting enough in the bedroom department.'

'I don't have to answer your filthy accusations,' shouted Brückner. 'Besides, no one gets more out of this place than you, Kannenberg. Everyone knows that you're making a very nice kickback on all of the food and beverage that comes into this house.'

'That's a damn lie,' said Kannenberg.

'You're a lousy crook. Everyone knows *that*. Even the Leader. You think he doesn't notice? He knows all your little scams. How you charge some of his guests for late-night room service. Or a packet of sneaky cigarettes. Hitler just turns a blind eye for now. But it won't always be like that.'

'This is very rich coming from someone whose girlfriend had to be compensated by the Leader to the tune of forty thousand reichsmarks because you refused to marry her. And if that wasn't bad enough, everyone knows you put pressure on poor Sophie to give you half that money, to help pay your debts.'

'That money was for some hand-painted ceramics she did, which were a gift for Eva.'

'Forty thousand seems like a lot of money for a coffee service and some oven tiles.'

'To an uncultured oaf like you, perhaps. But those ceramics were a private commission from Adolf Hitler himself. Sophie did give me some money afterwards, but it was in repayment of an old debt incurred after the car accident when I paid all of her medical bills.'

'An accident that would never have happened if you hadn't been drunk. You can be sure the Leader knows that, too, Brückner.'

'I expect it was you who told him.'

'No, actually, I think it was Sophie Stork herself. She's none too fond of you since she found out you tried to screw the local mayor's sister. Not to mention the gamekeeper's wife, Mrs Geiger. And Mrs Högl. I bet that every woman on this mountain has an interesting tale about your wandering hands.'

'Every woman except your wife. That ought to tell you something, you fat little swine.'

'You know, I wouldn't be at all surprised if it turns out that the person who shot Karl Flex was really aiming at you, Brückner. He was standing right next to you, after all. There must be a lot of men in Berchtesgaden who would pay to see you dead. Me included.'

'But there's just one wife who'd like to see *you* dead, I expect, Kannenberg.'

'This is interesting,' observed Kaspel. 'And just when we thought we had a good motive, too.'

'The dead are usually better off than the poor bastards they leave behind,' I said. 'With any homicide it's not just the victim who gets killed. Plenty of reputations get murdered, too.'

'Just stay away from Freda,' shouted Kannenberg. 'If you know what's good for you.'

'That sounds like a threat,' said Brückner.

'It's our job, Hermann,' I added. 'To murder reputations. To turn everything upside down. And not to give a damn how much damage we cause so long as we catch the killer. It used to be that catching the killer was all that mattered. These days, most of the time, it really doesn't matter at all.'

'You go near her again, Brückner, and I'll tell your current girlfriend just what kind of movies it was you used to make when you were at film school in Munich.'

'You know, Hermann, I wish I had five marks for every time I've finished an investigation having come to the conclusion that the dead man had it coming and the murderer was actually a decent sort of fellow. And I expect that's what's going to happen here.'

'You're a swine,' said Brückner. 'I pity Freda, having to be married to a prick like you, Kannenberg. It's just as well you play the accordion because I don't see you amusing her in any useful husbandly way.'

'Your days as an adjutant are numbered on this mountain. You may have stood beside Hitler in the beginning—'

'That's right, Kannenberg. Since before the Munich putsch. Can you say the same? You should always remember the saying: "He who is close to the Leader cannot be a bad person."'

'Maybe so. But he now regards you as a liability. I'd be very surprised if you last another summer up here. It's not like we're about to run short of SS adjutants.'

'If I do go, you can be sure I'll take you down with me, Kannenberg. It might almost be worth it, just to see your ugly face when you fall.'

With this remark the argument ended, although it was unclear exactly why. Maybe they remembered the secret microphones. We heard footsteps in the entrance hall and quickly made ourselves scarce, although not before discovering that many others in the Berghof had also been shamelessly eavesdropping. Our excuse was better perhaps; cops are paid to be nosy. For everyone else it was just a bit of entertainment because there is nothing in life quite as entertaining as other people's pain.

We went into my first-floor-bedroom office and closed the door so that if either man came to look for us, we might pretend to have heard nothing. I fed some wood into the green-tiled stove and warmed my hands. I was feeling the chill after listening to Brückner and Kannenberg at each other's throats.

'No love lost there,' observed Kaspel.

'None. But I have the feeling it's that kind of house.'

I went back to the table and picked up one of two envelopes I'd found addressed to me, removing the sheet of paper inside and reading what was handwritten there.

'With five shots fired,' said Kaspel, 'and four that missed, maybe the killer *was* aiming for Wilhelm Brückner. I'm sure the oil filter on the end of the barrel can hardly have helped with the shooter's accuracy.'

'And if not Brückner then perhaps someone else, someone other than Flex. Why not, indeed? I certainly don't think that Bruno Schenk is about to win any popularity contests. For that matter, I doubt any of his colleagues are. You know, maybe it really didn't matter who he shot as long as he shot *someone* on that terrace. Have you thought about that? This is the list of names I asked Schenk to compile at breakfast. People that Bormann's cack-handed lackeys have managed to seriously upset since the great Leader made Obersalzberg his Alpine home away from home. There are over thirty names written here, along with the various reasons they might bear a grudge.' My eyes alighted on one particular name. 'Including Rolf Müller, our witless roofing contractor at the Villa Bechstein.'

'You're joking.'

I handed Kaspel the sheet of paper.

'I wish I was. It seems he had a small cottage behind what is now Göring's adjutant's house, and was none too happy when it was forcibly acquired for less than its market value. Even uttered a few half threats. Frankly, I'm a little surprised that Schenk could make sense of anything that man said.'

'Müller must have had plenty of opportunity,' said Kaspel. 'But somehow I don't see him as a killer.'

'Sometimes opportunity is all it takes to make a man into an assassin. Being in the right place at the right time, with a gun. Which is probably why Bormann forbids guns at the Berghof, at least when Hitler's here.'

The telephone rang and while Kaspel answered it I started to search the chintzy room. Behind the chintzy curtains, underneath the chintzy cushions and the chintzy chairs, even up on the wrought-iron chandelier with its chintzy lampshades. Everything about that room resembled the parlour of an old lady suffering from green colour blindness; it was like being inside a bottle of Chartreuse. It took only a minute or two to find but, having been warned by Heydrich and then Kaspel that the house was wired for sound, I knew what I was looking for. Behind a small drawing of Hitler on the chintzy wall was a dull metallic microphone. It was about the size of the mouthpiece in a telephone. I left the microphone in place, but it was easily disconnected from the power supply and rendered harmless. I looked for some more but found only the one and concluded that one per room was probably enough for any surveillance team to manage. Especially a team of eavesdroppers already deafened and blinded by all that chintz.

When after several minutes Kaspel finished his call, he said, 'I wish you hadn't done that. If a man knows always to check what he says, then he can't go wrong. But if we think we can speak freely in here, we might just do the same somewhere else, and then where will we be? I'll tell you where. In jail.'

'Sorry, but I can't do this any other way, Hermann. When our job is to look for the truth, it strikes me as odd that we daren't speak it in the very place where we're working. Who was on the phone?'

'The Munich Gestapo. The local photographer, Johann Brandner, the one who used to have a business up here on the mountain? The poor bastard who was sent to Dachau when he complained about the compulsory purchase of his premises? He was released a month ago and is now living in Salzburg. Coincidence, or what?'

'His name is also here.' I showed him Schenk's list.

Kaspel glanced over the contents and nodded. 'It seems he didn't always have an eye just for shooting a good picture. According to the Gestapo, before he was a photographer he was a Jäger with a Shützen battalion in the Bavarian Third Corps. A sharpshooter, no less.'

'I hate to say it, but we'd better have the Salzburg Gestapo check if he's still at his last known address. I think we just found our number one suspect, Hermann. I don't believe in coincidence very much.'

'Yes, boss.' He pointed at the first name on the list. 'Hey, wait a minute. Schuster-Winkelhof,' he said. 'Isn't that the name of the butler at the Villa Bechstein – Herr Winkelhof?'

'Yes, it is,' I said unhappily. 'Frankly, I'm a little surprised that your own name isn't on that list.'

'It does seem fairly comprehensive. I think thirty names is almost half of all the people in Obersalzberg who were dispossessed of their homes. Conducting interviews, checking out alibis – this is going to take us forever.'

'That's why we got the Pervitin. So it won't take as long as that. Or if it does, then perhaps we won't notice.' I shrugged. 'Maybe we'll get a break. With the serial number on that Mannlicher. Or those field glasses. Did you take a look at them? They're good ones. Ten by fifty. He probably used them to spot his target first. A good sniper always uses field glasses.'

'Any prints?'

'I already checked. There's nothing. He wore gloves. I'm sure of it. Wouldn't you? It's cold on the villa's rooftop.'

Kaspel opened the webbing case and took out the binoculars. 'Serial number 121519. Made by Friedrich Busch, of Rathenow.'

'It's a small town west of Berlin that's famous for its optical instruments. Anyway, Korsch is checking these and the carbine.'

'Can you trust him? In general. I mean, do you think he's a spy?'

'I trust him. As far as something like that goes. Friedrich is a good man. But tell me about the oil filter sound suppressor. You said you'd seen one before.'

'It was actually a fellow called Johannes Geiger who told me about it. Said he'd seen a rifle adapted like that once. In the forest underneath the Kehlstein. Abandoned next to the carcass of a dead deer. Must have been a poacher. But we never managed to find out who actually owned it.'

'Johannes Geiger,' I said.

'Yes, he's actually called the chief hunter, but everyone calls him the gamekeeper. Mostly he shoots the local cats. At least the ones that stray into the Leader's Territory. Hitler hates cats, on account of the fact that they hunt the local birds. Which he loves, of course.'

'Thus the ornithologist.'

'Yes.'

'Hmm.'

'Don't tell me Geiger's name is on that list, too.'

'No. But the initials JG are marked on the inside of the lid of that binoculars case.'

'So they are.'

'Didn't Arthur Kannenberg just accuse Brückner of trying to screw the gamekeeper's wife?'

'Yes, he did.' Kaspel shook his head and tried to stifle a yawn. 'I feel exhausted just thinking about all this. It's at times like these I realize I was never much of a detective. Not like you, Gunther. I didn't have the patience for it. I think I'm going to need some more magic potion.'

I tossed him my tube of Pervitin. He took two tablets, broke them into a fine white powder with the butt of his gun, and sucked it up with a rolled banknote into one nostril and then the other. As before he spent the next minute or two stalking noisily around the room, rubbing his nose and punching the air and blinking furiously.

'Christ, I can't believe we're here, in Hitler's own house,' Kaspel said. 'The fucking Berghof. That his study is just across the hall. I mean, Jesus Christ, Gunther. Talk about sacred ground. I mean, we should pull off our shoes or something.' It was almost as much of a performance as the one we'd overheard in the Great Hall.

'Being RSD I'd have thought you'd been in here before, Hermann.'

'What gave you that idea? No, it's only Rattenhuber or Högl who ever get to come into the Berghof. They're Bavarians, you see. It's only Bavarians that Hitler really trusts. Rattenhuber is from Munich. And Högl is from Dingolfing. I don't know where Brückner is from. But he was in a Bavarian infantry regiment. Hitler hates Berliners. Doesn't trust them. Thinks they're all reds, so it's just as well he's not going to meet you, Gunther. It's people like you who give us Berliners a bad name. No, this is the first time I've ever been through the front door of this house.'

'Help yourself to a souvenir, if you see one, Hermann. Take that crappy watercolour that was on the wall, if you like. I certainly shan't tell anyone.'

'Aren't you even a little bit impressed by the fact that you're here?'

'Sure.' I picked up the Leica and took his picture. 'If I were any more impressed with being in this place I'd take off like a hot air balloon and not land until they shot me down over Paris.'

'You're a sarcastic bastard, you know that?'

'I thought you knew that. I'm from Berlin.'

'Do you want me to take a picture of you?' he asked.

'No, thanks. I'm hoping to forget that I was ever here. It already seems like a bad dream. But then, so does everything else that's happened since we strolled into the Sudetenland.'

Kaspel wet his finger, wiped away the remains of the powdered Pervitin, and then licked it slowly.

'Do you always take it like that?' I asked him. 'Like a human Electrolux?'

'After a while you get a sort of tolerance of the magic potion when you take it orally. Takes a while to kick in. When you need the effect to be immediate, it's best you take it like snuff.'

There was a knock at the door. It was Arthur Kannenberg. His eyes were bulging a bit more than was usual for him; in that respect they reminded me of his stomach. Hitler might have been a vegetarian and a teetotaller but it was plain Kannenberg liked his sausage and his beer.

'How's it going?' he said affably.

'Good,' I said.

'Anything you need, Bernie?'

'Nothing, thanks.'

'I spoke on the telephone with Peter Hayer, the ornithologist.

Like you asked. He's there now, at the apiary. If you want to speak with him.'

'Peter Hayer? Sure. Thanks, Arthur.'

'I suppose you heard everything. That argument between myself and Brückner.'

'I don't think we were the only ones, Arthur. But then I suppose you were both aware of that. What's the big idea? That some of what you said might get back to the Leader without you having to tell him, I suppose. Only you'd better remember, that works two ways.'

Kannenberg looked sheepish for a moment. 'I suppose you know he's a murderer. Brückner. He served under Colonel Epp, during the Bavarian communist insurrection in 1919. They killed hundreds of people. In Munich and in Berlin. I've even heard it said that it was Brückner who commanded the Freikorps men who murdered Rosa Luxemburg and Karl Liebknecht. Which is one reason that he's especially close to Hitler, of course. I mean to say – what's one more murder for a man like that? I happen to know he has a rifle with a sniper scope at his house in Buchenhohe. You might care to see if it's still there.'

'Arthur,' I said patiently. 'You really can't have it both ways. You already told me that Flex was standing next to Brückner when he was shot on the terrace. Remember? Besides, what happened to Luxemburg and Liebknecht? In Berlin they might still think that was murder. But certainly not in any other part of Germany. Least of all this one.'

'No, I suppose not.' Kannenberg smiled sadly. 'But you know, Brückner and Karl Flex, they weren't exactly what you'd call friends. Brückner threatened to kill him once.'

'Oh? What did he say?'

'I don't remember the exact words. You should ask him about it. But I will say this: his best friend on the mountain used to be Karl Brandt. It was Dr Brandt who treated Brückner after his car accident. Which is also why Brückner recommended him to

Hitler. Brandt owes everything to Brückner. Everything. Not only that, but Brandt is a pretty good shot, by all accounts. His father was a copper with the Mühlhausen Police and showed him how to handle a gun when he was a kid.'

'They used to be friends, you said? Implying that they aren't any longer.'

'Brückner fell out with Dr Brandt, too. I'm not sure exactly why. But I think because Brandt was into something with Flex.'

I nodded patiently.

'Thanks, Arthur, I'll bear all that in mind.'

'Just thought I'd mention it.'

'Duly noted.'

Kannenberg smiled back at me and then left.

'What do you make of that, boss?' said Kaspel.

'Frankly, I'm not surprised, Hermann. In a place like this, where truth is always at a premium, we're going to hear plenty of good stories. I suppose Neville Chamberlain heard one about the Czechos and I suppose you have to believe what you want to believe. Therein lies the problem, you see; I worry that I'm going to think one of these people actually did it. Not because they did do it, but because I start thinking that someone must be telling the truth.'

I grabbed my coat and the binoculars and headed towards the door with Kaspel following. Halfway downstairs I stopped for a second to show him the list of names compiled by Bruno Schenk; the last name on the list belonged to the man we were going to see, the Landlerwald's ornithologist, Peter Hayer.

CHAPTER 27

April 1939

It was snowing lightly and there was a party of workers shovelling the stuff off the road along the western perimeter of the Leader's Territory. They looked pretty sullen about it, too, although I don't know that there's any other way to look when you're shovelling while it's still snowing.

'Slow down,' I said, realizing, too late, that I should have been driving: Kaspel had so much meth inside him I was afraid he might have some kind of seizure. I felt a bit high myself. The voices were gone for the moment but I was still buzzing, which seemed only appropriate given where we were going. 'I make a bad passenger at the best of times. But I don't want to get killed while I'm here. Heydrich would never forgive you.'

Kaspel slowed a little and drove us further up the mountain towards the Kehlstein, past the Türken Inn on our right, and then Bormann's house. He pointed out the sights as we went along, which did nothing to make me feel any safer. Meanwhile, I opened the second envelope that had been on my desk, which was from Major Högl, if only to avoid looking at the twisting road ahead.

'That's the kindergarten, the greenhouse – Hitler likes his fresh fruit and vegetables – the SS barracks. You can't see it, but Göring's house is down there to the left. Naturally it's the biggest. Then again, so is he.' He pulled up at a small crossroads. 'That's the post office. And next to it the chauffeurs' quarters, garages for all the official cars, and behind those the Platterhof Hotel, which is still being constructed, of course.'

'It's like a small town up here.'

'Christ only knows what they're doing underground. Sometimes you can feel the vibration of all the tunnelling that's going on in Obersalzberg and it's like the Nazis are inside your skull. Of course there are lots of government buildings down in Berchtesgaden as well. Only that tends to be the brother's territory. Albert Bormann. He's in charge of the Chancellery and a small group of adjutants who don't take their orders from brother Martin. There's even a theatre up here, but outside the Leader's Territory. They put on all sorts of things for the locals, to try and improve community relations. I heard our friend Schenk give a talk there once. Or was it Wilhelm Zander? Yes, Zander.' Kaspel laughed. 'He talked about *Tom Sawyer* and the American novel. You can imagine how that went down.'

'It's a great book.'

'Zander certainly thought so.'

'I suppose he's another Bavarian.'

'No. He's from Saarbrücken.'

The car slithered a bit as it accelerated again. In some parts the road was high up and narrow, and I didn't give much for our chances if we came off it. 'What's the story between Martin and Albert?'

'They hate each other. But I don't know why. Heydrich is always pushing me to find out, but I still have no idea what the reason is. Once I heard Martin Bormann refer to Albert as the man who holds the Leader's coat. Which says all you need to know.'

'Unless you're Heydrich.'

'Maybe you can find out something. In case you didn't know it, I think you're doing all right.'

'I wish I shared that opinion.'

He jerked his thumb behind him. 'Anyway, that's the Leader's Territory and strictly off-limits to everyone who's not anyone. But surrounding this three-kilometre area is another enormous fence measuring eleven kilometres long; it encloses almost the whole area around the Kehlstein, which is the game and bird sanctuary. That's where we're headed now. A couple of years ago, when Bormann was planning to have the whole area enclosed, Geiger, the gamekeeper, pointed out the disastrous consequences for the local wildlife. Much of that was already gone because of all the noise from construction work. Driven off like many of the people, I suppose. Mindful of Hitler's love of nature, Bormann created the Landlerwald Forest, just south of the Riemertiefe, and they've reintroduced chamois, fox, red deer, rabbits, you name it. Everything except a unicorn.'

'No wonder the poachers like it here.'

'They drive Bormann mad. And of course he's scared Hitler will find out and want to do something radical about it. I think Hitler cares more about little furry animals than he does about people.'

'Evidently,' I said.

'What are you reading?'

'It's from Major Högl. A list of all the fatalities sustained by the local workforce during the last couple of years. Ten workers killed in an avalanche on the Hochkalter. Eight killed when a tunnel collapsed under the Kehlstein. One worker who fell into the lift shaft. Five workers killed by a landslide below the Südwest tunnel. Three truck drivers killed when their vehicles went off the road. One worker stabbed to death by a co-worker at the Ofneralm camp, because he didn't want to pay off a bet. And this is odd: there's a P&Z worker listed as dead, cause unknown.'

'Nothing odd about that. People die for all kinds of reasons, don't they? If the work doesn't kill them, the magic potion will. I'm sure of it. I've got to lay off that stuff myself. My heart feels like a hungry hummingbird.'

'So lay off it. I won't mind if you want to get some shut-eye.'

'I'll be okay. Just tell me what's so odd about this dead worker.'

'Only the name, so far. R. Prodi.'

'And?'

'There was a snapper who went home from the P-Barracks because she had a dose of jelly. Her name was Prodi. Renata Prodi. She was the one favoured by Karl Flex.' I paused, and when Kaspel didn't say anything, I let a couple of thoughts loose in the car. 'But maybe she didn't go home after all. Maybe her being on this list is some kind of bureaucratic oversight. At the very least we ought to find out if she ever made it to Milan. And how she comes to end up on a list of dead workers put together by your boss.'

A few minutes later we drew up in front of a wooden chalet that was about twenty metres long and perhaps half as wide; there was a chimney on the sloping roof and about two hundred and fifty small square windows in the four walls. There was no glass in the windows because they weren't the kind of windows anyone was going to be looking through or even going near, not without a veil and a smoker. What I was looking at was the Adlon Hotel of beehives.

Inside the apiary door the first thing you saw was a little glass bee house where, if you were interested, you could see a hive of bees doing what bees do. They call it work but I'm not so sure that the bees would; I doubt they had a union. But it was only the one bee I was interested in – the one in my pocket, from the dead man's trouser turn-up. I wasn't especially curious about the rest of the bees, but the three men in the small apiary office were of great interest to me, not least because two of them had scoped rifles and one of them stood up and smiled as soon as he saw me and what I was holding.

'You found my field glasses,' he said simply.

'You must be Herr Geiger, the gamekeeper.'

'That's right.'

I let him have the binoculars and then shook his hand. 'They *are* yours, then?'

He unfastened the lid and pointed to what was written there. 'My initials: *JG*. Where did you find them?'

I wasn't ready to supply an explanation to that so I showed them my brass warrant disc. That usually deflects questions I don't want to answer. 'I'm here from the Police Praesidium in Berlin at the request of Government Deputy Chief of Staff Bormann to investigate the murder of Karl Flex.'

'Bad business,' said one of the other two.

'And you are?'

'Hayer. I'm the Landlerwald ornithologist.'

'Udo Ambros,' said the other, who was smoking a pipe. 'One of the assistant hunters. And I ain't ever been to Berlin. Nor likely to go, neither.'

'Did any of you know Dr Flex?'

'I've seen him around,' said Geiger.

'Me too,' said Ambros. 'But I didn't know he was a doctor.'

'He was a doctor of engineering,' I said. 'With P&Z.'

'That explains it, then,' said Ambros. 'They're not what you'd call popular around here, the folk from P&Z.'

'Still,' added Hayer, 'no one deserves that. To be murdered, I mean.'

I left that one alone. So far I'd not seen much to persuade me that Flex hadn't had it coming.

'It's quite the place you have here,' I said. 'I had no idea that bees could live so well in Germany.'

'These bees have better lives than a lot of Jews, I think,' said Geiger.

'Yes, but they're just as cliquey,' said Ambros.

'It's not only the bees who are well looked after in the Landlerwald,' said Geiger. 'There's another hut like this one just a few hundred metres away where the deer come and go for hay and grain. Especially in winter, when the grazing's harder.'

'Not to mention a sanctuary for predatory birds,' added Hayer. 'Eagles, owls. To protect our many breeding species.'

'Bigger windows, I suppose,' I said.

Nobody smiled. Things were a bit like that in Obersalzberg. Their own jokes were just fine; but there was nothing funny about a Kripo commissar from Berlin.

'We have about two thousand numbered breeding boxes for every variety of bird, some of which are quite rare,' said Hayer proudly. 'They're all over the Landlerwald.'

'But it's not a zoo,' insisted Geiger. 'There are no tame animals here. Our work here is governed by the rules of the Bavarian State Forest Administration.'

I took another look at the three men in the apiary office. They had durable outdoor faces and durable outdoor clothes. Thick tweed suits, with plus-four trousers, stout boots, cream woollen shirts, green woollen ties, and Bavarian-style felt hats with grey feathers. Even their thick eyebrows and moustaches looked like the warmest ones in the shop. Their German rifles were mounted with sniper scopes and well maintained; you could smell the gun oil. There were also a couple of shotguns on a rack behind the desk. It looked like a lot of firepower for killing a few cats.

'So why the rifles?' I asked.

'You're not much of a hunter without a rifle,' said Ambros. In his buttonhole was an enamel badge featuring a pickaxe and a mallet, and the words *Berchtesgaden Salt Mines* and *Good Luck*. It made a pleasant change from a Party badge with a swastika.

'Yes, but what do you shoot?'

'Squirrels and feral cats, rooks and pigeons. Meat for the Leader's table, when we're asked to supply it.'

'So it's not a reserve in the sense that the animals are protected.'

'The animals *are* protected. From everyone except us.' He crossed his legs and grinned; he was wearing the same Hanwag boots as me.

'We're not in the business of shooting men, if that's what you're driving at,' said Geiger.

'Someone was,' I said. 'And they used an Austrian-made Mannlicher carbine fitted with a telescopic sight to do it. Not to mention your field glasses, Herr Geiger. To answer your earlier question, I found them thrown down the chimney of the Villa Bechstein, as well as some spent brass on the rooftop – the spot the assassin fired his shots from.'

'And you think I might have had something to do with that? I lost these binoculars a couple of weeks ago. I've been looking for them ever since. They were my father's.'

'That's true, Herr Commissar,' said Hayer. 'He's been a real pain in the arse about them. Even looked for them myself.'

'And I would hardly have said I owned them if I'd had anything to do with shooting that man, now would I?'

'The Mannlicher carbine was down the same chimney. And it wasn't Santa Claus who left it there. A carbine fitted with a sound suppressor. A Mahle oil filter on the barrel.'

'Poacher's trick,' said Geiger. 'The locals come and go around here using the old salt mine tunnels. We found a couple last summer and blocked them up. But this whole mountain is riddled with gravel pits and salt mines. People have been mining salt here for hundreds of years.'

'What about poachers? Ever catch any?'

Geiger and Ambros shook their heads. 'About a year ago I found a rifle,' said Geiger. 'With a silencer on it. Same as what you described. But sadly not the man who used it.'

'What happened to the rifle?'

'I gave it to that Major Högl fellow. From the RSD. Poaching's a crime, you see. And all crime in Obersalzberg has to be reported to the RSD.'

'You wouldn't happen to know anyone who owns a Mannlicher carbine, would you?'

'Common enough gun in this part of the world,' said Ambros, puffing his pipe. 'I have a Mannlicher at home.'

'That's not missing, I hope.'

'I keep all my weapons in a gun cabinet, Herr Commissar. With a lock on it.'

'I myself only own a shotgun,' said Hayer. 'To shoot a few rooks now and then. So I do find myself wondering why Herr Kannenberg should have telephoned to say that it was me you wanted to speak to. That's right, isn't it, Herr Commissar? You did want to speak to me?'

'If you're the beekeeper, I do, yes.'

'I am.'

I showed him the bee I'd found in Flex's trouser cuff.

'It's a dead bee,' said Hayer.

This sounded like dumb insolence, but perhaps only because it was the kind of dumb insolence to which I was much given myself.

'A clue, is it?' asked Ambros. More dumb insolence.

'It was in the dead man's clothes. So perhaps it is, I don't know. What kind of bee is this, Herr Hayer?'

'A drone. A male honeybee that's the product of an unfertilized egg. Its primary function is to mate with a fertile queen. But very few drones are successful in this respect. Most of the drones live for about ninety days and all drones are driven out of the hive in the autumn. Of course, there's no telling how long this one has been dead. But even without honey to eat, some of them can survive long after they've been ejected from the hive.'

'I know the feeling,' said Kaspel.

'If it is a clue, it's not much of one. You'll find dead or dying drones almost everywhere around these parts in the autumn months. Behind the curtains. Usually somewhere warm.'

'I found two just the other day in my towel cupboard,' confessed Ambros. 'I reckon they'd been asleep in there for months.'

'Perfectly harmless, of course,' said Hayer. 'They can't actually sting you. Drones don't have a sting, just sexual organs. I'm sorry I can't be more help.'

'Actually, sir, you've been an enormous help.' I had the strong feeling that this was not what he wanted to hear, and I ladled it on a bit. 'Hasn't he, Hermann?'

'Yes, sir. An enormous help.'

Hayer smiled thinly. 'I don't see how.'

'Perhaps. But that's my job, isn't it?'

'If you say so.'

'Did you know Dr Flex, Herr Hayer? You didn't say.'

'I had some dealings with him, yes,' he answered stiffly.

'Might I ask what those dealings were?'

'They were in relation to the sale of my house to the deputy chief of staff.'

'Am I right in assuming that you didn't want to sell?'

'That is correct.'

'And what happened? Exactly.'

'They made me an offer and eventually I agreed to sell my house. That's all there is to it. If you don't mind, that's all I want to say about it, Commissar.'

'Come on, Herr Hayer, it's common knowledge that you weren't very happy about it. Did Karl Flex threaten you?'

Peter Hayer leaned back in his chair and silently regarded a shelf full of books on beekeeping. Next to them was an old print of some medieval beekeepers, their faces covered with what looked like basket-woven masks.

'At least that's what I've been told,' I said. 'From what I've heard he liked to throw his weight around. Pissed a lot of people off. Seems as if he had that bullet coming, by popular demand.' The ornithologist was looking at his fingernails, his face about as inscrutable as the three medieval beekeepers in the print on his wall. 'Look, Herr Hayer, I'm a city boy. I don't much like the mountains. And I don't much like Bavaria. All I care about is that I catch the man who pulled the trigger on Flex so that I can go home to Berlin. I'm not in the Gestapo and I'm not about to report people who talk out of turn. I say quite a lot that's out of turn myself. Isn't that so, Hermann?'

'He's not even in the Nazi Party,' Kaspel said.

'So let's just be straight here. Karl Flex was a bastard. One of several bastards employed to do Bormann's dirty work in Obersalzberg. Isn't that right?'

'He didn't just threaten me,' said Hayer. 'He ordered some men to remove my front and back doors. In the middle of winter. My wife was expecting at the time. So I had no choice but to sell. The house was worth twice what I was paid for it. Anyone will tell you that.'

Geiger and Ambros were murmuring their agreement.

'The house was demolished, immediately after I'd vacated it. My grandfather built that house. It was one of several that used to be where the local Theatre Hall is now. In Antenberg. The one they built to show films and other entertainment for the local workers. I sometimes go there just to be reminded of the view from my old house.' He glanced at his watch. 'As a matter of fact, we're all going there tonight.'

'Tell me what happened after you were obliged to sell,' I said.

'There's nothing much *to* tell. After that, Dr Flex put an advertisement in the *Berchtesgadener Anzeiger* informing readers about what had happened to me and announcing that anyone else who resisted appropriation would be treated as an enemy of the state and sent to Dachau.'

'When was this?'

'February 1936. So. As you can see, I've had three years to get used to the idea that I don't live up here anymore. No, now I live down in the town. In Berchtesgaden. If I had been going to shoot Flex, I think I would have done it back then, when my blood was hot about it.'

'It takes a cool head to make an accurate shot.'

'Then that lets me out. I never was much of a shot.'

'I can vouch for that, Commissar,' said Ambros. 'Peter's a terrible shot. He can barely hit a mountainside with the shotgun, let alone the rifle.'

'What about Johann Brandner? The local photographer who fell foul of Bormann. He's a good shot.'

'He's in Dachau,' said Ambros.

'Actually he was released a couple of weeks ago and is living in Salzburg.'

'Sensible of him,' said Geiger. 'To stay away from here. I expect people in Berchtesgaden would be too afraid to give him work now.'

'Anyone think he could have shot Flex?'

'No one's seen him,' said Hayer.

'He was a better shot than he was a photographer,' said Ambros. 'That's all I'll say.'

'You know, now I come to think of it, Herr Commissar,' said Geiger, 'I'm almost certain that the poacher's rifle I gave to Major Högl was a Mannlicher carbine. With a telescopic sight. Perhaps you should ask him about it. Or for that matter, ask him who shot Dr Flex.'

'You might even find that they were both sweet on the same whore from the P-Barracks,' added Ambros. 'Then again, be careful how you ask that question. Our Major Högl was in the Sixteenth Bavarian Infantry.'

'So? I wouldn't have thought that's so unusual around here.'

'He was a noncommissioned officer. A sergeant. And by all accounts his orderly in the Sixteenth was a man named Adolf Hitler.'

CHAPTER 28

April 1939

After leaving the Landlerwald we stopped in the village of Buchenhohe, outside the Leader's Territory, to search Flex's house. Like
everywhere else in Obersalzberg there was no one abroad or on
the streets that I could see. Possibly the people were all huddled
indoors keeping warm, listening to the BBC and holding their
breath while we waited to find out if there would be war. Nobody,
including me, could quite believe that the British and the French
might be prepared to fight for the Poles, whose Sanation government was no more democratic than the government of Germany.
All wars seem to start for all the wrong reasons and I didn't
suppose this one – nobody doubted that Hitler wasn't prepared
to call the British bluff – would be any different.

The house itself was made of wood and stone, and was sited
close to a curious little grey church that was nearly all sloping
roof and squat steeple; it looked like a Big Bertha – a forty-two-
centimetre heavy howitzer we'd used to destroy the Belgian forts
at Liège, Namur, and Antwerp. It was quite out of keeping with
the Bavarian quaintness of Buchenhohe. But the idea of firing
an eight-hundred-kilogram shell at the Berghof was not an unat-
tractive one, and well within a giant howitzer's twelve-kilometre
range. That really was a prayer to send up more than once a day.

'Most of the RSD officers employed at the Berghof live here
or at Klaushohe,' said Kaspel. 'Myself included. And quite a few

of the engineers from P&Z. With the major difference that the majority of these houses were purpose-built. No one here had their house bought by compulsory purchase. At least nobody that I know of.'

'How do you stand it here after Berlin?' I asked. 'It's like being trapped inside an endless Leni Riefenstahl movie.'

'You get used to it.'

Kaspel parked the car on a postage stamp of a driveway in front of a stone-arch doorway that was beneath a heavy black wooden balcony. Friedrich Korsch was there to greet us. Using a car borrowed from the Villa Bechstein, he'd driven the long way round to Buchenhohe, via the main road through Berchtesgaden, and was now peering in through the window. Hermann Kaspel had brought the house keys found in the dead man's pockets, but it quickly became apparent that we wouldn't need them.

'Someone's been here already, boss,' said Korsch. 'Unless the cleaner didn't come today and they had a wild party last night, it looks as if this place has been burgled.'

Kaspel opened the front door, which was no longer locked. I stopped to take note of a piece of string hanging out of the letterbox and then followed Kaspel inside. Flex's books and ornaments were strewn everywhere. There was even some house dust still floating in the air as if a gorilla had just finished shaking an outsized snow globe.

'I don't think they've been gone for very long,' I said, clearing my throat of dust.

'Maybe we should wait for the fingerprints people,' said Korsch.

'What's the point? On Hitler's mountain it's bound to be someone that Flex knew, whose fingerprints were already here before they turned the place over.'

On the floor was a silver salver, and on the table in the kitchen, a ten-mark note. 'It certainly wasn't money and valuables they were after,' I said. 'Whatever it was, I'm guessing they didn't find it.'

'Why's that?' asked Kaspel as we wandered from room to room.

'Because there's so much mess,' said Korsch. 'Usually when people find what they're looking for, they stop throwing things around.'

'Maybe it just took them a while to find it. Whatever *it* might be.'

'When you create this much havoc, it actually makes it more difficult to find something,' said Korsch. 'And there's always one room that's left untouched if they do find what they want. But here it looks like they were desperate. And short of time. And they probably went away empty-handed. Which is good for us. Because that means we might be more successful than they were.'

'How do you work that out?' asked Kaspel.

'Because we're the law and we don't mind if anyone sees us in here. And because we're not in a hurry.'

'There's something else,' I said. 'None of the drawers have been opened but the furniture has been moved around quite a bit. Things were knocked over and broken when the furniture was moved. And when the pictures were removed from the walls. It's as if they were looking for something larger. Something you might hide behind a sideboard or a picture.'

'A safe, perhaps?' Korsch picked up a polished rosewood humidor that was still full of Havana cigars.

'A safe, probably,' I said. 'The list of Flex's possessions included a set of house keys that we now have. And a key on a gold chain that was around his neck, and which we think Dr Brandt might have stolen. Might that have been the key to a safe? A safe someone knew of? Someone who knew not to bother with the house keys, perhaps because they already had another set. Or knew where one was. Which would explain the piece of string hanging out of the letterbox. There was probably a door key on the end of that. I don't suppose you noted a manufacturer's name on the missing key, did you, Hermann?'

'I didn't write one down,' said Kaspel. 'But I'm pretty sure it was an Abus.'

'Abus make padlocks,' I said. 'Not safes.'

'I didn't know that,' said Kaspel.

'I imagine our burglar didn't know it, either. But I'll still bet my pension it's a safe he was looking for. There isn't one wall in here that hasn't been exposed and examined. By the way, where does Dr Brandt live?'

'Here. In Buchenhohe. A couple of hundred metres away. Close to the Larosbach River.'

'So he'd have had plenty of opportunity, then.'

'He could easily have come straight here after the autopsy,' said Kaspel.

I went into the kitchen again. In the corner was a white metal cabinet – an Electrolux cold cabinet – and because I didn't know anyone who owned one, I opened it up to find several bottles of good Mosel, champagne, some butter, eggs, a litre of milk, and a large tin of beluga caviar.

'Flex liked expensive things, didn't he? All those gold trinkets in his pockets. Cigars. Caviar. Champagne.'

Meanwhile, Kaspel collected a bottle of bright yellow liquid off the dresser. 'Nothing expensive about this,' he said. 'It's neo-Ballistol.'

'Foot care and gun care,' I said. 'Because no one else will.'

'What's neo-Ballistol?' asked Korsch.

'It's an oil,' I said. 'In the trenches, we used Ballistol on our feet *and* on our guns. I'm not sure which of them it was better for.'

'Not just our feet,' said Kaspel. 'Lip balm, disinfectant, digestive problems, and a universal home remedy. Some people swear by this stuff. But it's been banned up here on the mountain since 1934 when Hitler was poisoned with Ballistol. No one knows if he took too much of his own volition, or someone else gave him too much in his tea. Which is what he likes to drink.'

'I'll remember that when I invite him round with the intention of poisoning him.'

'Either way, Brandt sent the Leader to hospital, and everyone in Obersalzberg was ordered by Bormann to get rid of their personal supply or risk imprisonment.'

'Everyone except Karl Flex,' said Korsch.

'How is it for heart palpitations?'

I swept some books off the sofa, sat down, and lit up a Turkish 8, which was my own universal panacea; tobacco and a spoonful of schnapps are two household substances that are almost impossible to abuse, at least in my own self-medicating experience. I glanced at my watch and calculated that it was now thirty-six hours since I'd slept in a bed. My hands were trembling like I had a palsy and my knee was bouncing up and down as if I were the subject of an amusing medical experiment by Luigi Galvani. I rubbed my hand across my face, waited in vain for the nicotine to calm my nerves, and then decided that what I really needed was a shave. I wandered into Flex's bathroom and looked in the cabinet mirror. The stubble on my chin was beginning to look like an engraving by Albrecht Dürer. I found a brush, some soap, and a good sharp Solingen razor made by Dovo, which I honed for a minute on a thick leather strop. Then I took off my coat and my jacket and started to lather up.

'You're going to shave?' asked Korsch. 'In here?'

'It's a bathroom, isn't it?'

'Now?'

'Sure. Carving my own face with a razor helps me to think. It's a chance to see things differently. Who knows? Maybe it will help me to stop my hand shaking.'

But while I shaved, I talked: 'So far what we've got is a tall man with half his brains blown out who nobody liked except Martin Bormann. Which isn't saying very much, since most of Bormann's affection is clearly reserved for Adolf Hitler and Frau Bormann. That lady probably thinks her husband shits ice cream but I'm not so sure she isn't being sold short. One way or another he's made a lot of enemies. Him and the minions he employed to do his dirty work. One of those minions was called Karl Flex and probably there were lots of people who wanted him dead. Because it was a lot safer to kill Flex than it was to kill Martin Bormann, someone who found out about yesterday's meeting at the Berghof decided to take advantage of Rolf Müller's trip to the doctor to take a shot at Flex from the roof of the Villa Bechstein. Maybe it was even Rolf Müller, although I doubt it. What's even clearer is that almost anyone else on the Berghof terrace might just as easily have satisfied the assassin as a target. Even if he'd missed Karl Flex – and we know he missed four times – he'd have hit *someone* hateful to folk around these parts.

'You know, I never much liked Bavarians until I came to Berchtesgaden and realized how many Bavarians there are who don't much like the Nazis, and for even better reasons than the familiar ones I have. What makes it so funny to an old social democrat like me is that security up here is supposed to be tighter than my hatband. But in fact it would seem the locals can come and go as they please in the Leader's Territory on account of how they know all the old salt mine tunnels better than they know their wives' gynaecology. And if some of them weren't mad enough already about Bormann taking their houses from them, they're even more ill-tempered since the supply of the magic potion dried up. Maybe they need that stuff to pull those twelve-hour shifts. Maybe that's why they shot someone from P&Z. Maybe it's a message from the construction workers' union.

'We also know that Flex was taking a cut from the girls in the P-Barracks in return for which he gave one of them, Renata Prodi, a dose of jelly, which required everyone there to take Protargol. Maybe that's how he afforded his lifestyle. Anyway, that girl is now missing, possibly dead. Also involved with the girls from P-Barracks was Dr Brandt, who seems to have made himself responsible for protecting Flex's posthumous reputation in that he's the chief suspect in the theft of a number of Flex's personal effects. Some Protargol. Some Pervitin. A key on a chain. A notebook with some names in it. Which would also make him the chief suspect in this burglary. You steal one thing, you'll steal another. Very possibly Dr Brandt also carried out an abortion on Renata Prodi, who may have been carrying Flex's child. This leaves me with an interesting investigative dilemma. Because it's going to be damn difficult to question Dr Brandt about any of this on account of the fact that Hitler and Göring were the principal guests at his wedding. If I so much as accuse him of not telling me the right time of day I'll be on the next bus to Dachau.

'We have one chief suspect: Johann Brandner. The local photographer who was sent to Dachau when he objected to having to sell his business premises to Martin Bormann. The evidence is only circumstantial, but the circumstances are these: Salzburg is just forty minutes away by car; he's a former sharpshooter with a Jäger battalion; he could have come down to Berchtesgaden, fired the shots, and gone home again without anyone even registering he was ever here. How about it, Friedrich? Any word from the Salzburg Gestapo?'

'Not yet, boss. They're also checking out the serial numbers on the carbine and the binoculars.'

'What do you want to do about the Mannlicher carbine that Geiger says he gave to Major Högl?' asked Kaspel.

'See if you can find out what happened to it. Maybe it's the same gun we found in the chimney.'

'And if he doesn't know?'

'Then that's another question I'm not looking forward to posing. Just the suggestion that Högl might at one time have been in possession of the murder weapon is going to make him look bad in front of Martin Bormann. So I guess I'll burn that bridge when I come to it.'

I swept the blade of the razor up my throat and then wiped it on Flex's Egyptian-cotton towel. Everything he'd owned or used seemed to have been of the best quality. Even his toilet paper was shiny. At home I just used the *Völkischer Beobachter*.

'Of course, Geiger might have been mistaken about that carbine. Or he might have been lying. None of those three men we just met in the apiary struck me as particularly helpful. And after what Arthur Kannenberg told me about Brückner at the Berghof, it would seem that everyone on this mountain wants to make soup for someone else to fall in. Right now the only person I'm absolutely sure didn't do it is Adolf Hitler. Which says a lot more about the state of modern Germany than it does about my forensic skills.'

I wiped my face clean and then searched the bathroom cabinet for some cologne. Of course Flex had the latest American stuff with a sailing ship on the bottle and I put some of that on. It felt like I should have been drinking it.

'Friedrich, I want you to stay here and see what you can find of interest. Don't ask me what that is because I sure as hell couldn't tell you. I'm assuming you won't find a safe but there's certainly no harm in having another look. But make sure that you leave all the lights on while you're doing it, please. I want Dr Brandt and anyone else with something to hide and who lives around here to think that we are going to persevere until we find out what that is. Maybe that will provoke something . . . something interesting, like someone trying to kill you, Friedrich. That would really help, I think. We need that kind of sacrifice if we're ever going to crack this damn case.'

'Thanks, sir, I'll see what I can do.'

'If you do find something interesting, telephone me at the Berghof. I need to try and shut my eyes. Hermann? I want you to go home for a couple of hours and do the same. Your eyes are starting to scare the hell out of me. It's like looking at Marguerite Schön in *Kriemhild's Revenge*. If my baby-blue oysters are anything like yours, I owe the ferryman a couple of marks.'

CHAPTER 29

April 1939

On the winding road back down the mountain to the Leader's Territory I saw a number of people walking along the road to Antenberg and decided to follow them on the assumption that they knew something I didn't. That wouldn't have been difficult. Curiosity might have killed the cat – especially in that neck of the woods – but even in Nazi Germany it's still a detective's main stock in trade, although these days it sometimes results in a similarly terminal outcome. Still, I saw little or no harm in this curiosity here and now, especially when it transpired that everyone was going to the Theatre Hall that had been built for the entertainment of the construction workers and people from the town of Berchtesgaden – the same hall that had occasioned the compulsory purchase of the ornithologist's house, among others. And it was easy to see why those houses had been acquired by the Nazis. The location was enviable and, if you like that kind of thing, it had fine views in almost every direction; personally, I can take or leave a fine view unless it's through a woman's bathroom window, or a keyhole in a girls' dormitory. I was never one for looking at beautiful scenery, and certainly not since 1933; it distracts from the more important and admittedly metropolitan business of keeping an eye out for the Gestapo, which, with my politics, is an ever-present dilemma.

The theatre was a very large wooden building about the size

of an airship with a tall banner featuring a Nazi eagle, to ensure people didn't miss the point. The hall was not well built, however, and already the high saddle roof seemed to be sagging a little under the weight of the snow piled on top of it, and leaking, too. Inside were several strategically placed buckets and almost a hundred people, including the three characters I'd met in the apiary. To my surprise, the people were all there to hear Martin Bormann's adjutant, Wilhelm Zander, talk about *Tom Sawyer* again. At least that's what I thought until I noticed that when he'd finished speaking, a movie – *Angels with Dirty Faces* – was to be screened. I'd seen it already and liked it a lot. I like any picture about gangsters because I hope that German people will see them and be reminded inexorably of the Nazis. In the end, the bad guy, Rocky Sullivan, goes to his own execution a coward, which is just how I always planned to do it myself – dying yellow with a lot of shouting and screaming makes it harder on the executioners' nerves. I should know. I've seen several last performances at Plötzensee that took away my appetite for days.

It was the first time I'd seen the locals en masse. Like any Berliner, I regarded Alpine-dwelling Bavarians with the same indifferent opinion I had for any kind of German wildlife. It didn't surprise me that they smelled a bit and looked slow and ill-fashioned in their traditional *Tracht* as much as the fact that I was surprised to see them at all. I'd seen so few people since arriving in the area that I had almost started to believe it was a town where real people no longer existed. A few of the locals were armed with a variety of hunting rifles and I spent several minutes casting my eye over these and their owners. Some of them were wearing ammunition belts and looked more like members of a Bolshevik workers' militia than conservative Bavarians. I certainly wouldn't have bothered looking if Flex hadn't been killed with a rifle. Not that I expected to find out anything very useful; in that part of the world, men carried rifles and skis the way they carried briefcases and rode bicycles back in Berlin. One man had even brought a brace of rabbits and I wondered what the nature-loving Hitler would have said if he'd seen these animals slung over his shoulder like a fur collar. Also present in the theatre were Bruno Schenk and Dr Brandt, who was offering a private surgery for anyone who wanted to see a doctor. He had a community clinic going in a room behind the stage and the line of people who were in need of medical attention extended into the auditorium. I've been sick myself in the past and it was my opinion that none of the people waiting to see Brandt looked particularly sick. They were chatting among themselves and by their complexions I'd have said most of them were a lot healthier than I was. Which wasn't saying very much. Ever since my arrival in Obersalzberg I'd had the feeling that I was suffering from some sort of terminal illness. At any moment I felt my life might suddenly end. Martin Bormann had that effect on you. And so did Reinhard Heydrich. I walked over and joined the line.

Bruno Schenk regarded my unannounced presence in the Theatre Hall as uncomfortably as if Antenberg had been hosting a fiftieth-birthday party for Josef Stalin. He probably wished me dead. Brandt was even less pleased to see me in the line of people waiting for him. Again he wore a white coat over his black uniform, and his expression was as sombre as a starless night sky. I'd been saving some questions for him and this was as good a time as any to ask them – for me, anyway. For him it was obviously inconvenient, which again, suited me very well. Making a nuisance of yourself is what being a policeman is all about and suspecting people who were completely above suspicion was about the only thing that made doing the job such fun in Nazi Germany.

'What are you doing here?' he asked suspiciously.

'Hoping to speak to you, Doctor.'

'Are you sick?'

'Ever since I arrived here I've thought I must be suffering from forensic amnesia. People keep treating me like I've forgotten how to be a policeman. But that's not why I wanted to see you. Actually I wanted to ask you about Renata Prodi.'

'Who's she?'

I smiled apologetically and looked at the people who were waiting to see the SS doctor. They were all watching me as carefully as if I were a dog that might bite. It wasn't a bad idea at that. 'I could tell you out here, but why take the risk? All these nice people, they really don't want to know about what's inside my dirty mind.' I lit a cigarette and smiled nonchalantly. 'That's the worst thing about being a cop, Doc. I have to think and then say things that most people just find plain offensive.'

'You'd better come into my office,' he said coldly.

I followed him and the first thing I saw was another brace of rabbits hanging on a peg behind the door. These were still bleeding. A few spots of blood had collected on the wooden floor like the scene of a tiny execution.

'Somehow I didn't think you were a hunter, too,' I said.

'I'm not. The people pay me any way they can. Rabbits, mostly. Pheasant. Some deer. I've even been given the carcass of a wild boar.'

'You must invite me to dinner sometime, Doctor. Although it had better be when the Leader's not around. I doubt he'd approve of all this meat. In fact, he wouldn't.'

Brandt smiled weakly, as if the idea of inviting me to his house was unimaginable. 'I can assure you that all of the game I am given by these people was sourced outside the Leader's Territory and the Landlerwald.'

'I'm sure you're right.' On the desk, beside a little cloth wallet of surgical instruments, was a packet of Pervitin. I picked it up, only to have him take it out of my hand, and while he was doing that I picked up an amber medicine bottle and glanced at the label. Brandt sighed as if he'd been dealing with an unruly child and snatched that away, too.

'What's this about?' he asked. 'I have real patients to see, so get to the point, will you?'

'That's the point.' I nodded at the tablets in his hand and then at a well-stocked medicine cabinet containing more of the same. 'Among other things. The Protargol. We both know it's for treating venereal disease. And seeing it here on your desk, as if you were expecting to prescribe it this evening, well, it makes me wonder if any of the locals have got a dose, too. I mean, like Karl Flex.'

'You wouldn't really expect a doctor to comment on any of his patients,' Brandt said stiffly. 'Especially something as sensitive as that.'

'Oh, I respect patient confidentiality, Doc. But I don't think it usually applies to someone who's dead. Especially when that someone has been murdered. And when he's the subject of a police autopsy. It's common practice for a doctor to tell the police about every little thing he can see that's wrong with a human body. And that means everything from a gaping hole in the head to a dose of jelly. Flex had the jelly, too, didn't he? But for some reason you chose not to mention it.'

'I suppose I just didn't think it was relevant to the cause of death,' said Brandt. 'Which was obvious. He had been shot in the head. Look, Commissar, Karl Flex was a friend of mine. He was a guest at my wedding. And in all honour I felt obliged to allow the man some privacy. It's what any decent German would have done.'

'Well, that's very nice of you, Doc. What is your SS motto? "Blood and honour," isn't it? That would seem to cover almost everything here, wouldn't it? But you can take my word for it, nothing private is ever permitted to a man after someone has blown his skull apart with a rifle bullet. The pieces of skull and brain tend to land all over the place. And when that place is the Berghof terrace, it tends to make his privacy entirely *irrelevant*. It might surprise you to learn that I'm no stranger to things like honour myself. But I don't rate Flex's blood and honour that highly. Not when he was little better than a common pimp for the girls at P-Barracks. Not when he gave the jelly to one of them.'

'Who told you that?'

'It doesn't matter.'

'I should have thought it much more likely that it was one of those damned whores who gave it to Karl.'

'Maybe. Either way, you're the one with the cure on his desk. And you're the one who's been looking out for the health of those damned whores. Isn't that right?'

Brandt said nothing, which I suspect was his normal response to anything in Obersalzberg. When your masters are Hitler and Bormann, saying yes or very little is always the hallmark of true loyalty.

'How about I ask you a straight question and you try to give me a straight answer, Doc? Are there many other people in this community infected with gonorrhoea?'

'Why do you ask?'

'That's not a straight answer. At which point I might normally brush some dandruff off your shoulders. How about you have another shot at answering before I ask the question again, only this time maybe I'll ask it so that everyone out there can hear me.'

'Look, Commissar, this is an extremely sensitive matter. I don't think you can have any idea how sensitive.'

'I get that. Nobody wants the Leader to find out about the P-Barracks. He'd be furious, of course. Venereal disease is spread by Jews, not by decent Aryan folk. How many?'

'Maybe fifteen or twenty,' said Brandt.

Reminding myself that this was a man at whose wedding Hitler and Göring had been the guests of honour, I asked my next questions with my heart in my mouth.

'Renata Prodi. She had it, too, right?'

'Unlike Karl Flex, she's alive, so I don't have to answer that.'

'Are you sure she's still alive? Only, someone told me she wasn't.'

'To the best of my knowledge.'

'That's not saying much on this mountain.'

'I beg your pardon?'

'I understand you also carried out a termination for her. An abortion. And that this was Karl Flex's child.'

'And this is based on what? The word of another whore? Against that of a German officer.'

'So you're denying it, then. Fair enough. I didn't expect you to admit it.'

'I fail to see what any of this has to do with the murder of Karl Flex, Commissar.'

'Frankly, so do I. But it won't always be that way, I can assure you. I will know everything soon. As a detective I am tenacious.'

'I can believe that.'

'I make no apology for this. It's my job to make myself a nuisance. Do you know that it's even been known for some people to wish me dead before I can solve a case.'

'I can believe that, too.'

'I've taken enough of your time, Doc. And theirs, too. We'll talk again, when I have more information at my fingertips. In fact, you can bet on it. Assuming betting's allowed on Hitler's mountain. I mean, it's bad enough that you can't smoke.'

'I don't think the Leader has any objections to gambling.'

'Good. So put a blue on me solving this case before the end of the week. That's money in the bank.'

I spoke to several of the locals on my way out. Most worked for the Obersalzberg Administration or the local brewery but, despite the Nazis having closed down access to the mountain, a few still managed to work their own private salt mines, which struck me as a better trade than digging gold since there was so much of the stuff to be found and, when it was, it fetched a high price among discerning cooks all over Europe.

As I passed by they asked who I was and where I was from and when I told them they looked as surprised as if I'd been Anita Berber pissing on their shoes, and I realized that in spite of all the Nazis had done to change it, they still regarded Berlin as a sink of iniquity and a place where corruption reigned. I certainly missed the iniquity but maybe they were right about the corruption. Quite what they thought of Zander's talk on *Tom Sawyer* I have no idea. I listened for a while, and then lit out ahead of the rest.

CHAPTER 30

April 1939

They'd cooled things down a bit at the Berghof when I arrived back there. Someone had thoughtfully left the big window in the Great Hall open and the place was chillier than the cold cabinet in Flex's kitchen. You couldn't sit in my room without keeping your coat on. I wondered if that was just the way Hitler liked it, if they were trying to save money on fuel, or if they figured that keeping the place freezing cold would have the useful effect of making people tremble in the Leader's presence. Maybe that was part of his diplomatic secret. Hermann Kaspel had told me Hitler didn't much like snow, or the sun, which was why he'd chosen a house on a north-facing slope. I guess the cold and damp air of the Berghof reminded him of the Viennese slum he'd lived in as a young man. Alone in my office opposite Hitler's study, I closed the door and filled the stove with as much wood as it could take, and placed a chair right up next to it. I was planning to read some more witness statements, which, I hoped, would send me to sleep. I thought about asking Arthur Kannenberg for some sausages and a bottle but reflected that I could do without the criminal allegations concerning Wilhelm Brückner that were certain to be added onto my supper tray. I lit a Turkish 8 absently, and then cursed when I remembered whose house it was and immediately threw the cigarette in the stove. Being there, at the Berghof, was like being in some mad

Swiss sanatorium where everyone was dying of tuberculosis and only the purest mountain air could be tolerated. I looked at the packet of Turkish 8, considered stepping onto the terrace to smoke one, and then grimaced; the thought of going outside in the freezing-cold night air of Obersalzberg to do something as harmless as smoking a cigarette seemed so absurd that I laughed out loud. What kind of crazy damn world was it when such ordinary human pleasures like cigarettes were so strictly controlled? And it struck me that perhaps, in Hitler's disapproval of tobacco, I'd discovered the true essence of Nazism. I might have gone down to the Villa Bechstein, but for the certainty that Rudolf Hess would find and question me in detail about what had happened at the Berghof. I'd no wish to interpose myself in some Alpine clash of Nazi Titans.

I had the room light low and was trying to make less noise than the wood in the stove, so my spirits fell a little when there was a knock at the door. It opened to reveal a tall woman in her thirties, elegant, but not pretty, not even good-looking, but somehow still attractive, in a horsey sort of way. She was dressed in a black suit and a black coat, with a matching black beret, and she was as slim as a used match.

'I thought there was someone in here.'

I stood up and pointed sheepishly at my boots.

'I was trying to creep around but I've got these new boots, you see? I'm still getting used to how big they are. Look, I'm sorry if I disturbed you. Next time I'll wear tennis shoes, hold my breath, and drape a towel across the bottom of the door.'

'Oh, I didn't say I heard anything. No, I caught the scent of your tobacco. You are aware of the fact that the Leader hates smoking, aren't you?'

'You know, it's a funny thing, but I think I did hear something about that, yes. And for about two seconds I forgot where I was and lit one. I suppose I'm going to have to face a firing squad for that cigarette in the morning.'

'Probably. I can fix it for you to be shot somewhere so that you can have a cigarette in your mouth when they do it, if you want.'

'I'd like that. But no blindfold, okay? Especially if you can also fix it for me to be wearing a bulletproof vest when they do it.'

'I'll see what I can do. My name is Gerdy Troost, by the way. Who are you?'

'Bernhard Gunther, a police commissar from Berlin Kripo.'

'You're the man who's here to investigate the murder of Karl Flex, I suppose.'

'Bad news travels fast, doesn't it?'

'That's almost right. Look, I was going somewhere for a cigarette myself. Perhaps you'd care to join me.'

'I guess it can't be any colder out there than it is in here.'

I stood up and followed her along the hush-carpeted corridor and down a staircase in the easternmost corner of the ogre's castle. I almost felt like we were creeping out of there with a bag of stolen gold coins.

'The panoramic window in the Great Hall is stuck,' she explained. 'The motor has stopped working. There are a couple of starter handles that they use to operate it manually, but no one can find them. It's the biggest piece of glass ever made. Eight and a half metres long by three and a half metres wide. Now, that really is bulletproof and it weighs a ton. I told him it was too much for one motor. Three windows would be better, I said. But sometimes he's too ambitious and lets his heart rule his head. When it works, it's something to see. But when it doesn't, well, you can certainly feel the disappointment in the air tonight.'

I shivered inside my coat collar and decided that perhaps this was a better reflection of the true essence of Nazism than a disapproval of smoking. At the foot of the back stairs we were in a hallway attached to the kitchens. Gerdy Troost led the way through the door and onto a narrow terrace behind the house and, sheltered from the wind by an almost vertical bank on top of which was a whole copse of trees, she opened the black leather handbag she'd been carrying under her arm and produced a packet of Turkish 8. The terrace was already littered with cigarette ends.

'I don't much like these,' she said, lighting me and then herself with a thin gold Dunhill. 'But I've learned to smoke them because they're the only cigarettes you can buy up here, and when everyone smokes the same brand that makes things a little easier for addicts like me. I started smoking after I had a bad car crash in 1926. I'm not sure what's been worse for my health. The accident or the smoking.'

When we were both alight she moved us in front of a metal grille in the embankment through which a current of warm air was moving like a heavenly zephyr. And seeing my surprise, she smiled.

'I guess I shouldn't be telling you this but you're a detective, and one is supposed to help the police, right? For everyone in the Berghof this is known as the smoking room. Because it's always the warmest spot at the Berghof. That's a local secret. But I figure you'll need a few cigarettes to help solve this case.'

'More than a few. It's what we detectives like to call a twenty-packet problem.'

'That many?'

'At least. It's not easy tiptoeing around the egos of so many important people.'

'Not people, *men*,' she insisted. 'Important men. Or at least men who think they're important. To my mind there's really only one man who's important around here. With very few exceptions everyone else is out for themselves.'

This seemed hardly worth disputing. 'I'm not immune to a bit of that myself. Only I call it survival.'

'A social Darwinist, eh?'

'Only I'm not particularly social. By the way, where's the warm air coming from? It's certainly not the house.'

'Underneath the Berghof is a whole network of tunnels and secret bunkers.'

'Bunkers? You make it sound like someone's expecting a war.'

'There's no harm in being prepared.'

'None at all, provided the preparations don't include the invasion of Poland.'

'You're a Prussian, aren't you? Don't you think we have a legitimate case?'

'Don't get me wrong, Frau Troost, the whole situation involving the Polish Corridor strikes me as nonsensical. There's nothing I'd like to see more than Danzig properly part of Germany again. I just think there's maybe a better time to do it. And a cheaper way of bringing it about than another European war.'

'And if negotiations fail?'

'Negotiations always fail. Then you negotiate some more. And if that fails you try again the next year. But people stay dead for even longer. This was my own experience during the last war. We should have talked a bit more at the beginning. And then the end might have been very different.'

'Maybe they should let you handle the negotiations.'

'Maybe.'

'And this case. Think you can handle it?'

'Someone thought so, otherwise they wouldn't have given me my bus fare from Berlin.'

'And who was that?'

'My superiors.'

'Himmler, I suppose.'

'He's one of them, last time I looked.'

'You don't have to play skat with me, Commissar. You want to find this killer, don't you?'

'Sure.'

'So if you're going to play Hans Castorp it might pay you to cultivate a few local allies up here on the magic mountain. Wouldn't you agree?'

I liked the fact that she thought I was bright enough to have heard of Hans Castorp.

'We can help each other, perhaps,' she added.

'All right. A cop can always use some new friends. Especially this cop. On the whole I rate pretty highly for a lack of people skills.'

'So do I. Most of the men in the Leader's intimate circle have learned to be very wary of me. I usually say exactly what I think.'

'That's not always healthy.'

'I'm not out for myself.'

'Makes you pretty unusual these days.'

Gerdy Troost shrugged impatiently.

'Anyway, please forgive me if I seemed a little guarded. Actually it was Generals Heydrich and Nebe who told me to come down here. You see, if I fail, it won't reflect badly on them. I'm expendable.'

'And how is that, do you think?'

'Well, it's like when you get invited to a wedding and the bride and groom really don't give a damn if you turn up or not.'

'I know what it means, Commissar Gunther. I was just wondering how anyone should think such an unkind thing about a man like you.'

'What it means is that Karl Flex's murder is Martin Bormann's problem. If I can solve it, then he'll be grateful to Heydrich and Nebe. And if I can't, then it's still Martin Bormann's problem, not theirs.'

'Yes, I do see your own problem. My late husband would have called that a fool's dilemma.'

'I'm not such a fool that I can say no to men like them. At least not so that they'd ever notice. It's one of the things that makes me such a good detective. Generally speaking I point the fold in my hat where they tell me and hope for the best. And somehow, so far, I've managed to stay on this side of the barbed wire.'

'There's a bottle of good schnapps down there, behind that drainpipe,' said Frau Troost. 'Some of the general staff keep it there so they can have a drink while they smoke.'

'One's often better with the other.'

'Hitler doesn't drink, either.'

I bent down to take a look and smiled; she was right; there was even a stack of clean glasses. I helped myself but she didn't want one herself. I toasted the general staff, silently. For once I had no complaints about their military preparations.

'One thing I don't mind being cold is schnapps,' I said. 'Your husband was Paul Troost, wasn't he? Hitler's architect, until he died a few years ago.'

'That's right.'

'And now his architect is Albert Speer.'

'He thinks he is. That man is always trying to ingratiate himself with Hitler. But in truth, I've been carrying on Paul's work since 1934. I may even be the only woman the Leader actually listens to. Except when it comes to windows. But I was right about that, too. Mostly I just offer my advice on building, art, and design. My studio is in Munich. And when I'm not there, I'm here. Lately I've been working on some new certificates and presentation boxes for military and civilian honours.'

'No shortage of those in Nazi Germany.'

'You sound like you disapprove.'

'No. Not even a little. I always did like a ribbon on my cake.'

'Maybe you'll get an honour after you've solved this case.'

'I certainly won't be looking for one. From what I've been told this is a matter requiring absolute discretion.' I poured myself another. 'You know when I said bad news travels fast, about Karl Flex being dead, you said I was almost right. Meaning you didn't think it was such bad news, after all.'

'Did I say that?'

'Now who's playing skat. I've been here for less than twenty-four hours but already it seems to me that quite a few people were happy to see Flex dead.'

'We can talk about that,' she said. 'But first I want a favour from you.'

CHAPTER 31

April 1939

'So ask it, Frau Troost. I have no idea why, but the schnapps has made me accommodating.'

The terrace at the back of the Berghof was less lethal than the one at the front; the most dangerous thing that happened here was smoking too much. Gerdy Troost shrugged and threw away her cigarette. Under the black beret her light brown hair was bushy and gathered behind her head, which seemed to accentuate the woman's ears; like her nose, these belonged properly to an elf. But she wasn't a small elf. I guessed she was probably a head taller than Martin Bormann. It was a shrewd, clever head, too, that much was obvious. Cleverer than Bormann. The voice was educated and accustomed to being listened to, the eyes dark and inquisitive, the chin pugnacious and determined, the mouth just a little petulant; you might almost have assumed she was Jewish but for the violent anti-Semitism of her infamous patron. It seemed safer to assume that she was a bluestocking, only this had nothing to do with the colour of her stockings, which were black.

'Gerdy. Short for Gerhardine. My parents christened me Sophie but I never took to the name.'

Looking at her, I figured there was quite a lot about being a girl she didn't take to, not just an old-fashioned name. You get a feeling for that kind of thing.

I toasted her with the glass in my hand. 'Pleased to meet you, Gerdy.'

'The fact is, I know who you are,' she said. 'More importantly, I know what you are. No, I don't mean that you're a policeman. I'm talking about your character. I believe you're a man of some courage and integrity.'

'No one's accused me of being that in a long time. Besides, if I really was what you say I am, then I'd be somewhere else.'

'Don't sell yourself short, Herr Gunther. One day soon this country is going to need a few good men.' She rubbed her chest and her face turned anxious as if she had a pain.

'You all right?'

'I get a little angina sometimes. When I'm under pressure. It'll pass.'

'Are you under pressure?'

'Everyone here is under pressure of one kind or another. Even Hitler. Everyone except Martin Bormann.'

'He's a busy man, isn't he?'

Gerdy smiled. 'Busy looking out for himself, almost certainly.'

'There's a lot of it about.'

'For some. Now listen, do you remember a man called Hugo Brückmann?'

I frowned as I recalled the name. Then I stared at the ground, noticing her largish feet and her black shoes, which had little straps across the ankles. 'Brückmann,' I said evasively. 'Let me see. No, I don't think so.'

'Then let me refresh your memory, Commissar. In 1932, Hugo Brückmann and his wife went to stay at Berlin's Adlon Hotel. He is a German publisher and was a great friend of my late husband's. Married to Princess Elsa Cantacuzene of Romania. Now do you remember?'

I hadn't forgotten either of them. Nor was I likely to. But like anyone else in Germany I was a little cautious about admitting to knowing someone who had deliberately thwarted the Nazis, especially to a member of Hitler's intimate circle. While Hugo Brückmann was a Nazi, he was a decent Nazi and a friend of Bernhard Weiss, the former head of Kripo and a Jew whom I and Lorenz Adlon had helped to hide from the Nazis in the last days of the Weimar Republic. But it had been Hugo Brückmann and his wife, Elsa, who had paid for Weiss and his wife, Lotte, to escape to London, where the former detective was now running a printing and stationery business.

'If they're friends of yours, then yes, I remember them both.'

'I want that man – the principled young detective from the Alex who helped Hugo Brückmann to help Bernhard Weiss escape from Germany – to help me find someone who's gone missing, in Munich.'

'I'm not saying I did help them. That wouldn't be healthy. But lots of people go missing these days. It's one of the challenges of life in modern Germany.'

'This man's a Jew, too.'

'For them most of all. But yes, I'll help. If I can. What's his name?'

'Wasserstein. Dr Karl Wasserstein. He's an ophthalmologist and a surgeon who treated my late husband. But he lost his position and his pension in 1935, and then his licence to practise medicine in 1938. I spoke to the Leader about his case last year and Dr Wasserstein's licence was restored, allowing him to continue in private practice. But when I went to see Wasserstein in Munich the other day, he had gone and no one seemed to know or even care where. He left no forwarding address and I was wondering if you might find him for me. I just want to know that he's all right and that he's not short of money. But I get the feeling I've already asked enough questions around here on his behalf. There's a limit to what even I can achieve on anyone's behalf. Especially when they're Jewish.'

'Maybe he's left Germany for good.'

'He just got his licence back. Why would he leave Germany?'

'The best people do. On the other hand, a lot of Jews have left Munich and Vienna to go and live in Berlin. They think that things are a bit easier for Jews there.'

'And are they?'

'A little, perhaps. Berliners have never made good Nazis. It's a metropolitan thing, I guess. People in big cities don't care much about race and religion. Most of them don't even believe in God. Not since that other German madman. They're a little cynical to be wholly enthusiastic acolytes.'

'I'm beginning to see why you're expendable.'

'But give me Wasserstein's last address and I'll see what I can find out.'

'Thanks. Commissar Gunther, I want you to know that I'm loyal to the Leader.'

'Isn't everyone?'

'You're not.'

'No, I'm not.'

'Look, it isn't him who's at fault. It's the people around him. People like Martin Bormann. He's so corrupt. He runs this whole mountain like it's his personal fiefdom. And Karl Flex was just one of his more loathsome creatures. Him and Zander, and that awful man Bruno Schenk. Those are the kind of people who give our movement a bad name. But if I'm going to help you I have to do it in my own way.'

'Sure. Whatever you say. And that's just the way I was going to handle it.'

'I don't want to hear any lectures about police procedure and withholding evidence.'

'All that stuff means nothing now, anyway.'

'So here's what I'm offering. I've been coming here for almost a decade and I'm often in this house. Sometimes on my own. Sometimes not on my own. I see things. And I hear things. More than I should, perhaps. By the way, there are listening devices all over the Berghof so be very careful what you say and where you say it.'

I nodded, hardly wanting to interrupt Gerdy Troost by telling her I already knew about the listening devices.

'That's another reason why this terrace – the smoking room – is so popular. It's safe to talk here.'

'So what have you got to tell me now?'

'Nothing that might reflect badly on Hitler,' she said carefully. 'He's a man of great vision. But if you ask me a question, I'll do what no one else on this mountain will do, Commissar Gunther, I'll try to give you a straight answer. You tell me what you think you know and, if I'm able to, I'll confirm it. Clear?'

'Clear enough. You're going to be my own oracle at Obersalzberg. And it will be up to me to make sense of what you tell me.'

She nodded. 'If you like.'

'How much of what Flex was doing did Bormann know about?'

'Everything that happens on this mountain happens because Martin Bormann wants it that way. Flex was merely carrying out his master's orders. Sure, he was an engineer with lots of letters after his name, but he was just a button that Bormann could press. Once for this and twice for that. Bormann's difficulty is that he desperately needs this man caught or the Leader will never come back; but in order for that man to be caught he risks the exposure of all his local rackets. Which means you're right about that police medal. You solve this case, you might not live to collect it.'

'I figured as much.' I lit another cigarette. 'Dr Brandt. Is he one of Bormann's buttons, too?'

'Brandt's in debt,' she said. 'A massive amount of debt. Because of his lavish lifestyle. He used to rent part of the Villa Bechstein but now he has a house in Buchenhohe. Not to mention an expensive apartment in Berlin, on Altonaerstrasse. All on a doctor's salary of three hundred and fifty reichsmarks a month. And because he's in debt he has to make ends meet by being part of Bormann's rackets. He might seem honourable. But he's not. Don't trust him.'

'Capable of covering up a murder, do you think?'

Gerdy nodded. 'Not just of covering one up. Capable of committing one, too. Tell me. You've lifted a few rocks already. And seen what slithered out. Why do you think Flex was killed?'

'Because someone bore him a grudge, because of a compulsory purchase – perhaps.'

'Maybe. But that's just fifty or sixty people. And quite a narrow sample of people on the Berg with a substantial grievance. You're going to need to cast your net much wider than that to get a proper idea of what's been going on here. You do that and you'll have a much better idea of who killed Karl Flex.'

'The P-Barracks. The brothel? Does Bormann get a cut of that as well?'

'Bormann gets a cut of everything. But I'm disappointed. You're still thinking like a policeman. The money generated by fifteen or twenty girls is tiny. No, there are much bigger rackets than that in Obersalzberg, and at Berchtesgaden. You need to expand your horizons, Commissar, to think on a more grandiose scale, to build your ideas of what one man can achieve if he has the resources of an entire country at his disposal.'

I thought for a moment. 'Construction,' I said. 'The Obersalzberg Administration. Polensky & Zöllner.'

'Now you're getting warmer.'

'Is Bormann getting a kickback from OA?'

Gerdy Troost stood a little closer to me and lowered her voice.

'On *every* contract. Roads, tunnels, the tea house, the Platterhof Hotel, you name it, Martin Bormann is getting a cut. Think of it. All those jobs. All those workers. All that money. More money than you could imagine. There's nothing that happens around here he doesn't take his cut from.

'It's going to take you a while to find out just what he's been getting away with. You're going to need to build a case, carefully.

And when you do you're going to need not just my help, but the help of someone close to the Leader who's as honest as I am.'

'And who might that be?'

'Martin Bormann's brother, Albert.'

'Where can I find him?'

'At the Reichs Chancellery building, in Berchtesgaden. Up here on the mountain might be Martin Bormann's territory, but down there, in the town, that definitely belongs to Albert. In case you didn't know, they hate each other.'

'Why?'

'You'll have to ask Albert.'

'Maybe I should go and see him.'

'He won't talk to you. Not yet. But he knows you're here, of course. And he'll see you when he's ready. Or when you've got something concrete on his brother. But you haven't got that yet. Have you?'

'No. Not yet. And I get the feeling I'm crazy even to try.'

'Perhaps.'

'You could speak to Albert Bormann. Tell him to see me now.'

'You'd be fishing. Wasting his time.'

'How will I know when I'm close to the truth? Will you tell me?'

'I probably won't have to. The closer to the truth you get, the more your own life is going to be in danger.'

'That's a comforting thought.'

'If you wanted comfort you'd have stayed at home.'

'You haven't seen my home.' I sighed. 'But from what you've told me, I'm going to be lucky if I ever see it again.'

CHAPTER 32

October 1956

Home was beginning to seem tantalizingly close. Germany – what I called Germany, which is to say the Saarland – was less than eighty kilometres away. With any luck I thought I might get there before dark.

There was an almost invisible stream on the edge of the field of stubble where I washed my hands and face and tried to make myself look as respectable as you can be after you've spent the night in a haystack. A light drizzle was falling and the sky was grey with the threat of something worse. I ate the rest of my food, mounted the bicycle uncomfortably, and cycled northwest, away from Château-Salins. A few dogs barked as I cycled past farm gates and cottage gardens but I was long gone before any locals could look out of their net-curtained windows and see a suspicious character like me. The road was straight and relatively flat, as if some Roman engineers had not long finished their lapidary endeavours. I was now in Lorraine, which had been annexed by another great empire following the war of 1871 and made a part of the German territory of Alsace-Lorraine. After Versailles, Lorraine had been given back to France, only for it to be annexed by Germany again during the Second World War. But it looked solidly French to me now, with French flags displayed in nearly every wart of a town or village, and it was hard to understand why Germany had ever wanted this dull, featureless region of France. What use was it? What did it matter which country owned one stinking field or another misshapen wood? Was it for this that so many men had died in 1871 and in 1914?

A few kilometres further up the road, in Baronville, I dismounted at an unremarkable café, ate some breakfast at the bar, bought some cigarettes, shaved quickly in the lavatory, searched for myself in the newspaper, and was relieved to see that there was nothing more than what had already been reported. But the polished wood radio in the café was switched on and in this way I gradually became aware that the French police believed they were now close to catching the Blue Train murderer; a man answering my description had been seen three times in Nancy before any police inquiries had begun, and all roads between there and the Saarland were now being watched. Perhaps I would have learned more but the *patron* started to retune the radio and, before I could check myself, I asked him – much too abruptly – to leave the radio station alone, which only served to draw attention to me. The *patron* did as he was asked but now regarded me with more interest than before so that I was obliged eventually to explain myself. He had a sharp nose and an even sharper eye, not to mention a boil on his scrawny bird's neck that was equal in size to any of the onions on my handlebars.

'It's just that I reckon I saw that German,' I said, improvising quickly. 'The fugitive the police are looking for. The Blue Train murderer.'

'Really?' The man wiped the marble counter with a cloth that belonged in an Omo commercial and then emptied the Ricard ashtray that was in front of me. 'Where was that, monsieur?'

'It was yesterday, in Nancy. But he wasn't headed for Germany; what the radio announcer said was wrong. He was buying a ticket for a train to Metz.'

'Killed his wife, did he? It happens.'

'No, I don't think so. Someone else. I'm not sure who. The guard on a train, I think.'

'Then they'll cut off his head,' said the *patron*. 'Kill your wife, you might stand a chance. But not a man in a uniform.'

I nodded but I considered I had worse to fear than an appointment with the French guillotine; at least that would be quick. Thallium poisoning sounded like a fate worse than death. And for the first time I wondered if I should somehow make an effort to warn Anne French that the Stasi were planning to poison her.

'Nancy, eh? You've come a fair way, monsieur.'

'Not so far. Forty or fifty kilometres. On a good day I can do seventy-five or eighty.'

'We don't see many onion sellers on these roads. Not since the war.'

'Usually I head for Luxembourg. Or Strasbourg. Plenty of money there. But that's too far for me now. The legs are not what they were.'

'So where *are* you headed?'

'Pirmasens.'

'Pirmasens? Seems like a lot of effort to sell a few onions.'

'A man has to make a living any way he can these days.'

'True.'

'Besides, my family seems to own the only field in Nancy that's no good for grapes. Usually I sell a lot in Pirmasens. The Germans like their onions and these days you've got to go where the market is.'

'Except that they're French now, aren't they? In the Saar.'

'That's what we're told. But it doesn't feel very French when you speak to people. It's German they speak. When they speak at all.'

'They spoke clearly enough in that referendum they had a while back.'

'That they did.'

'Well, good luck to them. And you.'

'Thanks. But if you would be kind enough to direct me, I reckon I'll stop at the police station in Baronville before I carry on my way. And report what I saw. It's what any good citizen would do, I think.'

The *patron* came outside and indicated the way, and I cycled off, wondering if he was in the least bit convinced by my improvised patter. In that part of the world I figured my French was probably accented just about right, but you never can tell with the Franzis. They're a suspicious lot and it's easy to see why the Nazis had such an easy job running the country; the French are just natural informers. Of course, I wasn't planning to go anywhere near the police station but almost as soon as I pedalled off I wondered if the café *patron* might see the gendarme later on in the day and mention me; and if he discovered I hadn't actually been there, then naturally his suspicions would be aroused. I wished I'd kept my mouth shut about behaving like a good citizen. Better still, I wished I hadn't told him not to retune his damned radio. So I cycled to the police station after all, leaned my bicycle against the wall, and was just about to pluck up my courage and report seeing myself to the local gendarmes when I caught sight of some medals in an antique shop and, thinking that a First World War French Cross pinned on my lapel might help to deflect a bit of suspicion, I went into the shop and bought the decoration for only a few francs. Heroism is always cheaper to buy than it ought to be. Especially in *la belle* France.

Inside the police station the gendarme behind the desk regarded my medal and listened to my story with barely concealed indifference. He took my false name and address and made a few notes with a stub of a pencil on a yellow pad; meanwhile, I added a few things to the fugitive German's description. He had a limp, I said, and a stick, as if he'd injured his left leg; and I explained I knew he was German because when I'd overheard him buying a ticket at the local railway station I was quite sure I'd heard him utter a curse in German when he saw that the platform for the train to Metz was being watched by police.

'Anything else?' The cop said it like he hoped there wasn't.

There was a strong smell of coffee in the station and I guessed he'd been about to drink some when I showed up.

'He had a small cardboard case with a Marseilles sticker on it. And there was something wrong with his left eye.'

'How do you know?'

'He had an eye patch.'

There were two roads from Baronville to the German border: the D910 was the shorter and more direct route; I took the D674 via Bérig-Vintrange to avoid any French roadblocks. Not that such a thing looked in the least bit likely, despite what the radio announcer had said. The road to the Saar couldn't have been more quiet if the locals had heard the Wehrmacht was on the way again. All the same I was pedalling hard now, as if my life really did depend on it. By midmorning I was seated on a bench in front of the Church of Saint Hippolyte in Bérig-Vintrange, smoking a cigarette, regarding the church, and reflecting on my own situation. I couldn't have felt more alone if I'd been cycling across Antarctica. The church looked like any other in that part of the world, which is to say quiet, even a little neglected with a small en suite cemetery, but it was not without a priest, who arrived on a bicycle not long after me, removed his bicycle clips, and offered me a good morning as he unlocked the front door.

'Have you come to see our ossuary?' he asked.

I said I hadn't, and that I was merely resting my own dry bones after a long time in the saddle.

'Welcome anyway.'

We shook hands. He was a big man with shoulders as wide as the cross strut on a working crucifix and he wore the cassock like it was a boxer's dressing gown.

'Would you like a glass of water, perhaps?'

'Thank you.'

He led the way into the vestry and presented me with some water.

'Is it famous then? Your ossuary?'

'Quite famous. Would you like to see it?'

Not wanting to appear rude I said I would and, still carrying his Bible, he led me down to a crypt, where he proudly showed off a neat heap of skulls and bones and, in an unguarded moment, I let out a profound sigh as I recalled my service with the SS and what I'd seen at places like Minsk and Katyn. A collection of dried death always awakens in me a perverse kind of homesickness. It's as if these things follow you around like ghosts. I would call it a conscience except that part of me had always taken second place to simple prudence.

'They look how I feel,' I said. This wasn't exactly Hamlet but then again I'd been riding hard for several hours.

'For you are dust and to dust you shall return,' said the priest.

'Amen.'

'Although it's hardly the end. No, not at all. We have to believe in the life everlasting, don't you think? That there is something after this.'

He didn't sound convinced, but I wasn't about to help him with any crisis of faith. I had my own crisis to manage.

'Not in here, you don't,' I said. 'This is about as final as it gets, I guess. And what's more, I think God probably likes it that way, to remind us that this is our true glory in Christ. That everything wears away and falls to pieces until all we're left with is this heap of bones, this accumulated testimony, this grey monument to where we've been and the futility of all our human endeavours. Here are the real facts of life, Father. We're going to die. And there's none of us that matters any more than those onions hanging on my handlebars.'

Momentarily the priest looked taken aback. 'You don't really believe that, do you?'

'No, I suppose not,' I lied. More than anyone, priests don't want your honesty; it's what makes them priests in the first place. You can't be a priest if you are devoted to any empirical truth, which is the only kind you can rely upon. 'But sometimes it's hard to have faith in very much.'

'Faith isn't supposed to make sense. If it was, then it couldn't be tested.' The priest's eyes narrowed. 'Where are you from, friend?'

'Nowhere. That's where we're all from, isn't it? It's certainly where we're all going. And that's just the scripture you mentioned earlier. Ecclesiastes, wasn't it?'

He nodded. 'I'll pray for you.'

'I wonder if that might work.'

'You know, anyone might think you're a man who doesn't believe in anything.'

'Whatever gives you that idea, Father? I believe the sun rises, and that it sets. I believe in kinetic energy and air resistance, and gravity and everything else that makes bicycling such fun. I believe in coffee and cigarettes and bread. I even believe in the Fourth Republic.' But of course, I didn't. No one did – no more than they believed in the Third Republic.

The priest smiled a gap-toothed smile and put down his Bible, almost as if he was going to slug me. 'Now I'm certain you're a nihilist.'

'Well, why not be a nihilist? A man has to believe in something.'

'No, that's what you are, all right.'

'If I knew what that was I might even agree with you. I used to believe in God and in trying to do the right thing. But now – now I don't believe in anything at all.'

'You're him, aren't you? That man the police are after.'

'What man is that, Father?'

'The Blue Train murderer. I've been following your case on the radio and in the newspapers.'

'Me? No. I'm not much on trains these days. Too expensive. But what makes you say a thing like that?'

'Well, for one thing, I used to be a policeman. So I notice

things. For example, those shoes you're wearing. No one selling onions would wear shoes like those. They were bought in a nice shop somewhere down south, and not because they were practical but because they looked smart. The first heavy rain shower and those shoes will end up badly water-stained. Boots would have been better. Boots like mine. That wristwatch is a Longines. Not the most expensive. But then again, not cheap, either. Next there are your hands, which are clean and soft. Strong, but still soft. And well manicured. Living around here you shake hands with all kinds of men who make a living from the soil. Yours aren't at all like theirs, which are like sandpaper. Another thing is that your teeth are good. Like you've seen a dentist in the last six months. Again, people who work the land don't see dentists unless they need to have a rotten tooth pulled out. And only then because they can't stand the pain anymore. The medal's good. A nice touch. I like that. But not the glasses. There's just glass in them, no actual lenses, like you're wearing them for a reason other than to improve your sight.'

I nodded sadly, appreciating his keen eyes in a moment of utter detachment. 'You should have stayed being a cop. I don't need lenses in my glasses to know you had a clearer vocation for that. You're the best French cop I've met since I came to France.'

The priest stiffened a little as he now realized where he was and who he was with. 'I suppose you're going to try and kill me now.'

I shrugged. 'Maybe.'

'I should be easy enough to kill.'

'Yes. I have a gun. And it seems to me that there's no one else in here who's going to raise any objections. But the day I start shooting priests is the day I probably shoot myself, too. Besides, what would be the point?'

'So it's like I thought. You're not really a murderer.'

'Best stick with being a priest. You make an even worse psychologist.'

'Meaning what? That you really did kill someone?'

'Sure, I've killed men. But not since the war. Just for the record, I didn't murder anyone on the Blue Train. I was framed.'

'I see. My, you're in a spot, aren't you?'

I pointed at the ossuary. 'It could be worse. I might be one of them.'

'We could pray together if you like.'

'There's even less point to that than there is in killing you. But I am going to have to make you swear on that Bible that you'll give me a head start. Twelve hours should see me comfortably across the old German border into the Saarland. Twelve hours before you call a cop and tell them I was here. That's all I ask, Father.'

'What makes you think I'm going to agree to that?'

I took out my gun.

'Because if you don't, I'll crack you on the head with this, tie you up, and leave you in here with your friends, the bones. Or maybe I'll just set fire to your church. I'm German, you see. In the war we did a lot of that. So one more church really won't make a difference to my eternal soul. Only I think you'd be more comfortable just doing what I said. Twelve hours doesn't seem much to ask.'

The priest looked at his watch. 'Twelve hours?'

'Twelve hours.'

I handed him the Bible and he made the oath as I directed. Then he shook my hand again and wished me luck and told me he'd pray for me.

'I'll take the luck,' I said. 'It always worked better for me than the prayer.'

I went out of the church, collected my bicycle, and rode off, but not before I had dumped all my onions in a grass verge. With a hard ride for Saar in front of me I could do without the extra weight. And it was only now that I perceived my stupidity; the priest had been right. My hands and shoes could have given the game away at any time. I thought I'd been so clever, when all the time I'd been courting disaster. But none of this was quite as stupid as what I'd just done. Never put your faith in a priest. There's not one of them who can be trusted within reach of a good Latin dictionary and a wealthy church donor.

CHAPTER 33

April 1939

I managed to sleep for several hours. Somehow the proximity of Hitler's study door did not interfere with that. I was ready to collapse and I think I could have slept through a night on Bald Mountain. I was awoken by the telephone ringing in my room. I glanced at my watch. It was long past midnight.

'Hey, boss,' said Friedrich Korsch. 'It's me.'

'Did you find something?'

'There was some paperwork in Flex's desk drawer. A lease agreement. It looks as if our friend was renting a garage in Berchtesgaden. On Maximilianstrasse. It's owned by a local Nazi businessman named Dr Waechter. A lawyer.'

'Pick me up outside the Berghof in ten minutes. We'll go and take a look at it. See if we can't find something there.'

'You're forgetting that I'm not cleared to enter the Leader's Territory.'

'Then go back to the Villa Bechstein. I'll meet you there. Did you call Hermann?'

'On his way down to Berchtesgaden now.'

I went out of my room and downstairs to the hallway. The house was even colder than before but one or two servants wearing overcoats were still around; Kannenberg had told me that they were practising being up at this late hour for when Hitler was there. All I wanted to do was find a bed and sleep. I resisted the temptation to pop a couple of Pervitin and hoped for the best.

It was a short walk from the Berghof to the Villa. The sloping road was made treacherous by snow and ice and I was glad of the Hanwag boots that I was wearing on my feet. In the guardhouse at the bottom of the road the SS man was so surprised to see someone on foot and coming down the hill from the Berghof that he fell off his stool. He must have thought I was Barbarossa awoken from his thousand-year sleep inside the mountain; either that or he'd been asleep himself.

I found Friedrich Korsch waiting in a car at the Villa and together we drove down the mountain into Berchtesgaden. Maximilianstrasse ran from the hill behind the outsized main railway station to a point just below the local castle, which was a nice shade of icing pink. The garage address on the receipt Korsch had found was opposite the Franciscan monastery and immediately next to Rothman's Silver, which appeared to have gone out of business. The monastery looked like it was doing fine. On the shop window was the faint outline of a yellow star that had been cleaned off but only – I imagined – after the departure of Herr Rothman and his family from Berchtesgaden. Small towns like Berchtesgaden were harder on Jews than big cities; in small towns everyone knew who and where the Jews were, but in a big city, Jews could disappear. I wondered if, like Gerdy Troost's friend Dr Wasserstein, Rothman had gone to live in Berlin or, perhaps, left Germany altogether. I knew what I would have done.

I still had Flex's door keys and after trying them out found one that fit the lock in the garage door. We opened it and switched on a bare lightbulb to reveal a bright red Maserati – the one with the side exhaust – and polished to absolute perfection. With a bonnet as long as a coffin, the car was a tight fit in the garage. The starter handle had been removed and the front of the Italian car was resting against a mattress laid out against the back wall, so that the car could be pressed right up against it without damaging the front, in order that the garage doors might be closed and locked.

'It certainly doesn't look as though anyone was here before us,' I observed. There was a whole set of mechanic's tools on the wall but nothing was missing from that. 'Then again, there's not much to search. Only the car.'

'But what a car,' said Korsch. 'This would explain the pictures at the house in Buchenhohe.'

I shook my head. 'I can't say I paid much attention to them.' I peered through a connecting door into the empty shop.

'They were all about motor racing.' He pointed to a picture of Rudolf Caracciola on the wall. 'Grand Prix posters. Drivers. It seems our friend Flex was an enthusiast. I bet this car was Flex's pride and joy.'

'If that was the case then why not keep it up at the house in Buchenhohe?'

'Are you kidding? There's no garage up there, that's why. The man wanted to keep the snow off this pristine beauty. And I don't blame him. Besides, this thing doesn't have a hood. Perfect for summer but perhaps not so good in winter.' Korsch walked around the car smoothing the bodywork with his hand. 'It's a 26M sport. Built in 1930. Two-point-five litre, straight eight, two hundred horsepower. Must have cost a few marks.'

'You know about cars?'

'I was a mechanic before I joined the force, boss. At the Mercedes garage in Berlin west.'

The Maserati was parked over an inspection pit, which Korsch quickly inspected and reported was empty of anything but sump oil. Meanwhile I opened the car's boot and then the glovebox. As well as two pairs of goggles, a couple of leather helmets, and some driving gauntlets, there were maps of Germany and Switzerland and a receipt for the Hotel Bad Horn on Lake Constance. I even unbuckled the straps on the bonnet and searched beside the engine and found nothing much there, either. The keys were still in the car and Korsch couldn't resist sitting in the driver's seat and gripping the steering wheel.

'I'd love to own a car like this,' he said.

'Well, if you stay here on Hitler's mountain and manage to figure out a nice lucrative racket for a man like Martin Bormann, then maybe you'll be able to afford one. But I don't know that this tells us very much. Except that he liked to drive to Switzerland.'

'It tells us that Flex had good taste in cars. It tells us that he was making serious money. It tells us what he spent his money on. It tells us that no one we've talked to so far has mentioned this car, so maybe he didn't drive it that often. Maybe not many people knew about it. Or even about this garage.' He turned the wooden wheel wistfully. 'Can I start it?'

'Be my guest,' I said. 'Drive it around the town for all I care.'

We pushed the car back from the mattress and retrieved the starter handle from the tiny boot. We were just about to turn over the engine when the mattress toppled onto the Maserati's sloping bonnet. I went to lift it up again.

'Wait a minute,' I told Korsch. 'I think there's something on the wall behind this mattress.'

We pushed the car further back along the stone floor until it was halfway out the door and onto the street, and tugged the mattress away to reveal an old York wall safe with a combination lock. It was a big one, too – at least as big as a car door. I tried the small round handle but the door remained firmly closed.

'Must have belonged to the shop,' said Korsch. 'A nice way of hiding it, too. With this car.'

'I wouldn't mind betting that this is what the person who searched Flex's house was looking for,' I said.

'I'll buy that,' said Korsch. 'I mean, who's looking for a safe after you see something as eye-catching as this?'

'Looks like we're going to need the previous owner, Jacob

Rothman,' I said. 'Or perhaps the man whom Flex was renting this place from. Dr Waechter. For the combination.'

'Waechter is at 29 Locksteinstrasse, Berchtesgaden. That's a couple of kilometres from here.'

'So let's go and wake him up.' I smiled, imagining some greedy fat Nazi lawyer who'd taken advantage of the Rothmans' situation. I was already imagining the pleasure I was going to take in that interview.

'We could take the Maserati.'

'Why not? That's bound to wake everyone up.' I smiled at that idea, too; there was something about the quiet complacency of Berchtesgaden that needed a disturbance of the kind that only an eight-cylinder Grand Prix Maserati could achieve.

We left a note for Hermann Kaspel on the garage door, telling him to wait there for our return. And a few seconds later we'd managed to start the car and Korsch was driving us through the streets of Berchtesgaden and up the hill north, towards the Katzmann and the Austrian border. In spite of the cold wind in our faces – the windscreens were the fold-down, hardly-worth-having type – Korsch was grinning from ear to ear.

'I love this car,' he shouted. 'Just listen to that engine. One plug per cylinder, twin overhead camshaft.'

For me the driving pleasure was entirely sadistic; in that little Bavarian town, Flex's car sounded as if a Messerschmitt had lost its way in the valley, like one of the drones from the Landlerwald apiary. At midday the car would have been loud enough; but at almost one a.m., a bass alphorn would have seemed quieter. When we got to Waechter's address, just around the corner from the local hospital in Locksteinstrasse, I told Korsch to rev the engine a bit, just to make sure his neighbours were awake.

'Why?' he asked.

'Because when Rothman and his family were obliged to leave town I doubt any of these people lost any sleep about it.'

'You're probably right,' said Korsch, and grinning again, he hit the accelerator several times before allowing the engine revs to drop. 'That's what I like about you, boss. You're such a bastard sometimes.'

Korsch switched off the engine and followed me up the path.

The house was a large wooden one with a wraparound wooden balcony and a covered stairway up the side; it was the kind of place where they grew leather shorts in window boxes. All it lacked was a couple of clockwork figures with beers in their hands. I knocked loudly on the front door but the lights had already come on thanks to the Maserati. The man who came to the door was fat and very white, although that was probably with rage at being woken up. He was wearing a red silk dressing gown and had neat grey hair and a little grey moustache that was bristling indignantly. It looked like a whole regiment of tiny soldiers getting ready to march off his face and onto mine to deliver me with a set of stiff ears. He started to bluster and yell about the noise like a tyrannical schoolmaster but soon piped down when I showed him my warrant disc although I'd much prefer to have slapped him with one of the skis on the wall.

'Police Commissar Gunther.' I pushed past him the way I'd seen the Gestapo often do and we stood in his hallway out of the cold, idly picking up photographs and opening a few drawers. I came straight to the point.

'Rothman's Silver on Maximilianstrasse,' I said curtly. 'You're the current owner, I believe.'

'That's correct. I acquired the property when the previous owners vacated it last November.'

He made it sound as if they'd done this willingly. But I recognized the significance of this date, of course. November 1938. Kristallnacht, the Night of Broken Glass, when Jewish businesses and synagogues all over Germany had been attacked, had been on the 9th of November. It went without question that Jacob Rothman would have been obliged to sell his property at a knock-down price, which is to say that when you've been knocked down in the street on a regular basis you begin to know you're not welcome.

'That would be Herr Jacob Rothman, right?'

'Couldn't this have waited until morning?'

'No, it couldn't,' I said coldly. 'The garage next door to the property. That's yours, too, isn't it?'

'Yes.'

'And you've been renting it to Dr Karl Flex.'

'That's correct. Twenty marks a month. In cash. At least until I find a new tenant for the shop.'

'There's a safe, in the back wall. It's my guess it was used by Rothman to store his silver. Do you have the combination?'

'No. It was on a piece of paper that I gave to Dr Flex, with the keys. I'm afraid I didn't make a copy. Look, surely he'd be the best person to ask about this, not me.'

'The fact that I'm asking you means I can't ask him.'

'Why?'

'What about Rothman himself?' I said, ignoring Waechter's question. 'Would you happen to know where he went after leaving Berchtesgaden? Munich, perhaps? Or somewhere else?'

'No, I don't.'

'He left no forwarding address?'

'No.'

'Pity.'

'What do you mean – a pity? He's a Jew. And even if he had left an address, I'm afraid I'm not in the business of forwarding mail to some greedy Jew. I've got much better things to do.'

'I thought as much. And yes, it is a pity. For me. You see, that Jew could have saved me a lot of time. Maybe even helped to solve a crime. That's the trouble with pogroms. One day you realize that the people you've been persecuting have something you urgently need. That I need. That Martin Bormann needs.'

'There was nothing in the safe when the Rothmans left. It was empty. I checked.'

'Oh, I bet you did. Well, it's locked now and no one seems to have the number.'

'Is there something important inside it?'

'It's a safe. There's usually something important inside a safe, especially when it's locked. Anyway, it seems that Dr Flex won't be paying you any more rent for the garage. I'd say your agreement is over. Permanently.'

'Oh? Why's that?'

'He's dead.'

'My God. The poor fellow.'

'Yes. Poor fellow. That's what everyone says.'

'What happened to him? How?'

'It was natural causes,' I said. Now that I'd drawn a blank on the combination with both Waechter and Rothman, the last thing I needed was for anyone to know that the safe in the garage even existed, and I was already thinking that it hadn't been the cleverest thing I'd done since arriving in Obersalzberg to drive around in a car that had been kept hidden in a garage that perhaps only a few people knew Flex was renting. Certainly I didn't want the same person who'd already burgled Flex's house trying the same with the garage. For all I knew, that person might even know the safe combination. There was only one thing for it. Much as I hated doing this, I needed to scare Waechter into silence about the garage, the safe, Flex's death, everything.

'You're a lawyer, aren't you?'

'Yes, I am.'

'Then you understand the need for confidentiality in a case like this.'

'Of course.'

'Under no circumstances are you to mention anything to anyone about Karl Flex, the garage you've been renting to him, or the fact that there's a safe in that building. Do you understand?'

'Yes, Herr Commissar. I can assure you I won't mention anything.'

'Good. Because if you do, then I should certainly have to mention it to Deputy Chief of Staff Martin Bormann, and he would take a very dim view of a matter like this. The dimmest view possible. Do I make myself clear, Dr Waechter?'

'Yes, Herr Commissar. Very clear indeed.'

'This is a matter of national security. So keep your mouth shut. People have ended up in Dachau for much less.'

As we walked back to the car, Korsch laughed.

'What's so funny?'

'Natural causes,' he said, shaking his head. 'That's a good one, boss.'

'It's how Bormann wants this thing played,' I said. 'Besides, they *were* natural causes. I don't know what else you could call it. When someone blows your brains out with a rifle then naturally you die.'

CHAPTER 34

April 1939

Back at Rothman's Silver in Maximilianstrasse there was no sign of Hermann Kaspel, and the note I'd left for him, threaded through the door handle like a scroll, remained untouched. If the cat in the doorway of the Franciscan monastery opposite knew what had happened to him, it didn't say; you can't trust cats, especially when they're with the Franciscans. Korsch returned the Maserati to the garage and, reluctantly, locked it up again. But his mind was still in the car.

I looked at my watch. 'Are you sure Kaspel had the right address?'

'Absolutely,' said Korsch. 'I heard him repeat it. Besides, it's not like you can get lost in a place like this.'

'Jacob Rothman did.' I stamped my feet against the cold. 'He should have been here by now. Something must have delayed him. If we go back to the Villa Bechstein via the road to Buchenhohe then maybe we'll see him. There won't be many cars on the road at this time of night. Perhaps he broke down.'

'Not in that car he was driving,' said Korsch.

'Why do you say so?'

'I was listening to that engine when you pulled up outside Flex's house yesterday evening. It's a 170 and it sounds as sweet as a nut. Anyway, all these cars from the Obersalzberg car pool – they're much too well looked after to break down. You know

what I think? I think he fell asleep again. One of the RSD ser-
geants was telling me that once that magic potion wears off, you
could sleep for a thousand years.'

'I guess maybe that's what happened to Barbarossa. He just
stopped taking the pills.' I yawned; all our talk of sleep and pills
was making me sleepy again.

We drove along the river in the direction of Unterau and the
P-Barracks before turning east onto Bergwerkstrasse and driving
up the mountain again. A group of workers from Polensky &
Zöllner were widening the road where it ran alongside the River
Ache in case anyone wanted to drive a tank up there; to me the
road already looked quite wide enough. I caught some of their
toothless peasant faces in the big headlights of the 170. They
looked like they were only a couple of pitchforks and firebrands
short of being a mob bent on lynching the monster in the
Berghof. Bormann must have figured a tank might stop them. I
hoped he was wrong about that.

'We have to get into that safe,' I said. 'We also need to keep
quiet about it. So maybe it wasn't very smart to drive around
in that car.'

'Fun though. For me, anyway.'

'It won't be fun if I don't find this shooter, and soon.'

'I suppose it's beyond a local locksmith.'

'It is unless his name is Houdini. No, I think we're going to
need a professional nutcracker.' I thought for a moment. 'Whatever happened to the Krauss brothers? Those boys could open
anything with a lock. Including the Police Museum.'

The Krauss brothers' burglary of the Police Praesidium on
Alexanderplatz – to recover their professional tools confiscated
by the police – was still the stuff of near legend and, at least until
the Nazis took control of the place, about the most embarrassing
thing that had ever happened to the Berlin police.

'The last I heard they were in the cement. Doing five years in
Stadelheim Prison.'

'Not like them to get caught.'

'I don't think they were caught, boss. From what I heard they moved from Berlin to Munich to escape their reputation as the best safecrackers in Germany, and were promptly arrested by the Bavarian Gestapo and thrown in prison on some trumped-up charge.' Korsch lit a cigarette and laughed. 'That's how the Nazis keep the crime rate down. They don't actually wait for anyone to commit a crime before they throw them in jail.'

'Then we need to have Heydrich get the brothers out so we can bring them down here to crack that safe.'

'Perhaps we only need one brother.'

'Forget it. Joseph doesn't unlock his own back door without the nod from Karl. And vice versa. Make that your next job, Friedrich. Go to Munich and get them out. I'll send Heydrich a telex to organize it. And then bring them both here. In secret. And by the way, while you're there I want you to ask the police if they have any address for a Jew called Wasserstein. Dr Karl Wasserstein. I'll give you the address before you go.'

'Who is he?'

'A friend of someone called Gerdy Troost. She's staying at the Berghof and she's anxious to find out what happened to him.'

I shifted down into a lower gear and steered the big Mercedes around the next corner. A few metres further up the road I saw two football-sized headlights and braked hard.

'Christ,' I said. 'Well, now we know.'

On a slope about ten metres above us was a black Mercedes 170. It looked as if it had swerved in front of a narrow stone bridge and careered down a steep hillside, flattening several small trees before finally it had overturned and then hit a large wedge-shaped rock, which appeared to have cut the front of the car in half, almost. It looked like a dead beetle. The headlights were still on but the wheels had long stopped turning and the dry air was thick with the smell of spilled petrol. Wisely, Friedrich Korsch retrieved the cigarette from his mouth and stubbed it out on his sole before dropping it safely into his coat pocket. I switched off the engine and we jumped out to look for Hermann Kaspel.

'Hermann,' I yelled. 'Where are you, Hermann? Hermann, are you okay?' But instinctively I knew he wasn't.

What struck me immediately was the deafening silence. There was just the sound of our anxious breath and our thick boots as we scrambled up the wintry slope towards the wrecked car, and the snow freezing hard on the hillside and a light breeze in the frigid trees. Everything in nature was holding its breath. Clouds shifted ominously in the moonlit sky as if something terrible was about to be revealed. There was a dull thud and I looked around to see a heap of snow slipping off a branch. My heart was in my mouth. I'd seen a few car accidents in my time with the Berlin police. Bad accidents. Nothing ever quite prepares you for the sight of what can happen to the human body when a car suddenly encounters a solid immovable object at high speed. But this was as bad as anything I'd seen since the trenches. The car looked as if the imaginary Big Bertha shell fired from the angular church in Buchenhohe had landed right in front of it. Metal never looked so mangled. The driver's door was hanging open like a farm gate. Kaspel wasn't in the car but it was easy enough to follow where he'd gone. For one thing there was a perfectly severed leg still wearing a riding boot and a piece of his trousers beside the door; from there Kaspel had crawled away on his stomach, leaving a wide trail of dark blood in the snow.

'Oh, Jesus Christ.' Korsch turned quickly away, knowing the brutal truth of what we saw, and walked back to the overturned car.

Hermann Kaspel must have known he was going to die. He'd managed to sit up and lean against the trunk of a tree and light a last cigarette with shaking hands – the ground was strewn with spent matches – before he'd bled to death. The butt was still in his mouth and cold to the touch, and his bluish hands were gripped around the neat stump of his left thigh – so neat it looked like a skilled surgeon had used a saw to amputate his leg – as if he'd tried in vain to stop the flow of blood. His skin was as cold as the snow he was seated on and I guessed he'd been dead for at least half an hour. The heart pumps several litres of blood a minute and when the femoral artery is cut like that you bleed out in less time than it takes to finish one cigarette. Unlike his leg, his pale semi-frozen face was completely unmarked. He stared straight ahead of him and over my shoulder, and if I'd spoken to him I thought he might almost have answered, so clear were his eyes. The glint in the irises was just a reflection of the headlights of course but all the same it was strange how alive he still looked. I don't know why, but I wiped some of the frost off his eyebrows and hair and then I sat with him and lit a cigarette myself. I'd often done something like that during the war, when you stayed with a man and waited patiently for him to die, sometimes holding his hand, or with an arm around his shoulders. We always figured the spirit hangs around the body for a while before it finally disappears. Mostly you put the cigarette in his mouth and let him mix a few puffs with his last breaths. A nail could cure everything, from a mild case of shell shock to a severed leg. Anyone who'd been in the war knew that. And even though you knew tobacco might be bad for you, you also knew that bullets and shrapnel were worse and that if you'd escaped them, then a few cigarettes really didn't count as any kind of risk worth taking seriously. There was much I wanted to tell Hermann Kaspel but mostly it was that I'd misjudged him and that he'd been a good comrade and that's the best you can say to a man when he's dead or going to die. Even if it's not true. The truth isn't all it's cracked up to be. Never was. But I had learned to like and admire Hermann Kaspel. I was also thinking of his poor wife, whom I'd never met, and wondering who was going to tell her, and I decided I couldn't trust Högl or Rattenhuber to make a decent job of it. Each of them was about as sensitive as Kaspel's severed leg and every bit as detached. I would have to tell her myself even though I could ill afford the time that would take. After a while I got up and walked back down to the upturned car and Friedrich Korsch.

'I told him to slow down,' I said, 'the last time I was driving with him. Frankly, he scared the shit out of me when he was behind the wheel of that car. It was the meth, I think. The magic potion. It made him drive too fast. He joked that it would kill him. And now it has.'

Korsch shook his head. 'It wasn't the meth that killed him, boss,' he said. 'I'm pretty sure of that. And it wasn't his lousy driving. It wasn't even black ice on the road, although that hardly helped. And those are winter tires, with a thicker tread than summer ones. Almost new, by the look of them. Like I said before, the RSD's cars are extremely well-looked after.'

'So what are you saying? He crashed his car, didn't he?'

'He crashed the car because his brakes had failed. And the brakes failed because someone deliberately cut the hydraulic hoses that feed the brakes. Someone who knew what they were doing.'

I hadn't heard of anyone ever doing such a thing, so I shook my head in slow disbelief. 'Are you sure?'

'I told you, I used to work for Mercedes-Benz. I know the leads and the hoses on this car like I know the veins on my own cock. But even I might not have noticed something wrong if the car hadn't overturned like this. The 170 has a four-wheel hydraulic-drum brake system, which relies on hydraulic fluid, right? Liquids aren't easily compressible, so when you start to brake you apply pressure on the fluid's chemical bonds. Without that fluid there's no braking force at all, which means the brakes fail. You can see from the oblique angle of the cut on this cable supplying fluid to the drums that it didn't break and it didn't detach; it's been neatly cut with a knife or a pair of wire cutters. There's no fluid left in them. The fact is, the poor bastard didn't stand a chance. This car weighs the best part of one thousand kilos. From here to Buchenhohe is maybe five kilometres of winding mountain road. I'm amazed he managed to keep the car on the road for as long as he did. Hermann Kaspel was murdered, boss. Someone must have cut the brakes while the car was parked outside his house. One of his neighbours, I expect. And here's another thing you might want to consider, Commissar. It looks like you've been a lot closer to solving who killed Karl Flex than perhaps you'd ever thought. Because whoever murdered poor Kaspel here almost certainly intended to murder you, too. They must have hoped you'd be in the car with him when it went off the road. You see, if they kill you and him, then this investigation is ended. Make no mistake, Bernie. Someone in Obersalzberg or Berchtesgaden wants you dead.'

CHAPTER 35

April 1939

We left the scene of the accident and drove up the winding mountain road to Hermann Kaspel's address in Buchenhohe, parking our own car a short distance away so that we wouldn't wake his widow. There were no lights burning in the house, for which I was grateful, otherwise I might have felt obliged to go in and give the poor woman the bad news then and there. She was obviously asleep and unaware of the terrible tragedy that had overtaken her, which was just as well. The bringer of bad news certainly doesn't look any better at four o'clock in the morning, especially when he looks like me. Besides, all I wanted to do now was take a look at the spot in front of the house where Kaspel's car had been parked, while the crime scene was still relatively fresh. And keeping our voices down, we inspected the space with our torches.

'You can still smell the glycol,' said Korsch, squatting down and touching the wet ground with his fingertips. 'Most brake fluid is just glycol ether-based. Especially in a cold climate like this one. You see where it's melted the snow when it poured onto the ground?'

'It's just like you said, Friedrich.'

'No question about it. Hermann Kaspel was murdered. Just as surely as if someone put a gun to his head and pulled the trigger.' Korsch stood up and lit a cigarette. 'You're lucky to be alive, boss. If you'd been in that car, you'd probably be dead, too.'

I glanced up at the cold sky. The veil of earlier clouds had lifted to reveal heaven's great black canopy and, as I frequently did, I remembered the trenches, Verdun, and the freezing nights on sentry duty when I must have looked at every star in the sky, steadily reflecting upon my own imminent mortality. I was never afraid of dying when I looked up at the heavens; from cosmic dust we had come and to cosmic dust we would all return. I don't know that I thought much about the moral law within me; perhaps it was, after all, an extravagance beyond the horizon of my vision. That and the fact that it was a pain in the neck to keep looking up that way, not to mention dangerous.

Korsch walked a few metres away from the house and collected a length of old green-gingham curtain material he'd seen lying on the side of the road. It was only lightly dusted with snow but the edge was stained with brake fluid. On a backstreet in Berlin it would hardly have been unusual but in such a scrupulously tidy place as Obersalzberg, where even the flowers in the window boxes were standing neatly to attention, it seemed worthy of note.

'My guess is that he used this to lie on,' said Korsch. 'While he was underneath Kaspel's car. Careless to leave it here like this.'

'Perhaps he had to,' I said. 'Perhaps he was disturbed.' There was a maker's mark on the curtain lining, which told us only that it had been made a long way away, at a branch of Horten's department store – the DeFaKa, in Dortmund. 'If we could find the pair to this, then we might be in business as far as identifying Hermann's murderer is concerned. But somehow I don't see anyone allowing us to search every house on Hitler's mountain to look for a length of old curtain. As I'm often reminded, some of these people are Hitler's friends.'

As we walked away from the house my boots kicked a piece of metal lying on the road, which caught my torch, and I bent down to pick it up. For a moment I thought I'd found the knife used to cut the brake lines, but I soon realized that the object in my fingers wouldn't have cut anything. Made of rounded metal, it was thin and smooth and curved, about twenty centimetres long and less than ten millimetres in diameter, and resembled a misshapen table utensil – a spatula or a longish spoon without a bowl, perhaps.

'Is it something that fell off the bottom of the car?' I asked, handing it to Friedrich Korsch and letting him examine the object for a moment.

'No. It doesn't look like anything I've seen before. This is stainless steel. And much too clean to have come off any car.'

As we returned to the car, I slipped the object into my jacket pocket and told myself that I'd ask someone about it later, although quite who I might ask I had no idea; it didn't look like the kind of object that could easily be identified.

Friedrich Korsch dropped me back at the Villa Bechstein and, almost immediately, left for Munich to spring the Krauss brothers from Stadelheim Prison. I helped myself to a large brandy in the drawing room, toasted Kaspel's memory, and then walked back up the hill towards the Berghof. The sentry was awake this time but just as surprised as before to see someone on foot at that time of night. According to all the newspapers and magazines, Hitler loved to walk all over Obersalzberg, but I saw little evidence that he or anyone else for that matter walked anywhere other than to the next armchair in the Great Hall or the Berghof terrace. I walked on, past the Berghof to the Türken Inn, where the local RSD was headquartered. Everything was quiet and it was hard to believe that on a frozen hillside only a few kilometres away was the body of a man who had been murdered. The Türken was another Alpine-chalet-style building made of white stone and black wood, except that it had its own parade ground with an absurdly tall flagpole flying an SS flag, and an excellent view of Bormann's house nearby. There

was a little stone sentry box out front that resembled a granite
sarcophagus and I had the guard escort me to the duty officer.
Almost mummified with cold, he was glad to move some blood
around his polished black helmet. By contrast the RSD duty
officer in the Türken was tucked up in an office heated by a
nice fire, a small cooking stove, and a heartwarming picture
in *Berliner Illustrated News* of Göring proudly holding his baby
daughter, Edda. I envied him that much, anyway. On the office
table was a dinner plate with a loaf of bread, some butter, and
a chunk of Velveeta, which reminded me I hadn't eaten since
breakfast, and it was fortunate that I'd recently lost my appetite.
There's nothing like seeing a man you know cut in half to stop
you feeling hungry; but seeing a coffeepot steaming on the stove,
I helped myself before coming to the point of my being in that
office. The coffee tasted good. It tasted even better with sugar.
There was always plenty of sugar on Hitler's mountain. If there
had been a bottle I might have helped myself to that, too. The
officer was an SS-Untersturmführer, which is to say a lieutenant
with just three pips on his collar and a pimple on his neck; he
was about twelve years old and as green as his shoulder straps
and, with his glasses and his pink cheeks, his membership in a
master race looked all too provisional. His name was Dietrich.

'Captain Kaspel has been killed in an accident,' I said. 'On the
road to Buchenhohe. It would seem that he lost control of the
car he was driving and went off the road.'

'You're not serious,' said Dietrich.

'Well, actually, what I said, it's not quite accurate. I'm more
or less certain Kaspel was murdered. Someone cut the brake
hoses on his car. I think they meant us both to be killed, but as
you can see, I escaped.'

'In Obersalzberg? Who would do such a thing?'

'Yes, it's hard to believe, isn't it? That someone here, on
Hitler's mountain, could even think of committing murder. It's
incredible.'

'Do you have an idea who this person is, Herr Commissar?'

I shook my head. 'Not yet. But I will find out. Look, you'll have to notify the appropriate services to recover the body and the car. An ambulance, I suppose. And a fire truck. It's a real mess, I'm afraid, and not for the squeamish. The car's a complete wreck. Maybe a doctor, I don't know. Not that he can help. And perhaps you'd better tell Major Högl. Although I'm not sure if he's the kind of officer that you can wake up with important news or if it's best to wait for the morning. Only you can say, sonny. But around here I get the feeling that bad news always waits until the morning.'

I glanced out the window. There was a light on the ground floor in Bormann's house and I wondered if he would want to know about Kaspel's death and if I dared disturb the deputy chief of staff at this time of night. Leave it to Högl, I told myself; you've got enough to do, Gunther. You won't be able to tell Bormann without also having to report on your progress, which has been disappointing, to say the least. The only good news you could tell a man like Martin Bormann was that you'd caught the murderer; everything else was an excuse for your own incompetence. Besides, there was always the danger I might talk out of turn. There's nothing like seeing a man you like cut in half to make you a little too free with your opinions. Things like that happened a lot in the trenches. It's how I lost my first set of sergeant's stripes – telling some fool of a lieutenant that he'd got a couple of good men killed.

'God in heaven, this is terrible news. Captain Kaspel was such a kind man. With such a nice wife.'

'You can leave the widow to me,' I said, and yawned. The warmth of the Türken's office was making me sleepy again. 'Make sure Högl knows that. I'll tell her first thing in the morning, just as soon as I've snatched a few hours' sleep and had some breakfast.'

I was on the point of leaving when I noticed the rifle rack:

they were all the standard German army rifle – the Mauser Karabiner 98 – but one with a scope caught my attention. This was a Mannlicher M95, the same kind of carbine that had been used to shoot Karl Flex. I lifted it out of the rack, worked the bolt, and inspected the magazine, which was full. The gun was well maintained, too, and in better condition than the carbine I'd found at the Villa Bechstein; for one, it wasn't covered in soot. I turned the carbine and inspected the barrel; it was dirtier than it looked on first inspection but whether that meant it had been fired recently was not something I could determine.

'What's this doing here?' I said.

'That's Major Högl's rifle, sir,' said Dietrich. 'He uses it to go hunting sometimes.'

'What does he shoot up here?'

'Nothing inside the Leader's Territory or the Landlerwald, you understand,' he insisted. 'Nothing except a few local cats. Everything else is forbidden.' The lieutenant smiled uncomfortably, as if he didn't approve. 'The Leader doesn't really like cats around the Berghof.'

'So I hear.'

'They kill the local birds.'

I nodded. The fact was, I'd always liked cats and even admired their independence; being shot by the Nazis for doing what comes naturally was the kind of existential dilemma with which I could easily sympathize.

'Is this the same rifle that Captain Kaspel gave to him? The one that belonged to a poacher?' But even as I asked I wondered how Kaspel could have failed to have noticed it there, on the Türken's rifle rack. Surely he would have mentioned it following our trip to the apiary.

'I don't know, sir. Would you like me to ask him?'

'No,' I said. 'I'll ask him myself.'

I walked quickly back down to the Berghof and discovered my room was chillier than before on account of the fact that someone had been in there and left the door wide open. I wrote a message for Heydrich, collected my notebook and, thinking I needed to be somewhere warm, returned immediately to the Villa Bechstein, where I told the two RSD duty officers to send the telex, and to awaken me at eight. Then I went upstairs. Someone had thoughtfully left a bottle of schnapps on my dressing table, next to the Leica. I guess it did make a nice picture at that; it's nice to have a few snaps of a favourite place you've been, even if that place is at the bottom of a glass.

CHAPTER 36

April 1939

I was surprised to be woken, rather roughly I thought, at seven, by two men with thick leather coats, igneous faces, and uncompromising cologne. They were from the Gestapo. Naturally I assumed they had come straight to Obersalzberg with some important news about the missing photographer, Johann Brandner, who was officially my number one suspect in the Flex shooting. But it was soon clear that this was not the case. One of them was already searching through my bag and my coat. He quickly found my gun, sniffed the barrel, and then dropped it into his pocket. The other had something under his arm and wore silver-wire glasses that resembled manacles, although that might just have been my imagination.

'Brandner? Never heard of him,' said the one with the glasses.

'Get dressed and come with us please,' said the other. 'Quickly.'

Now, under most normal circumstances, I'd have been very cooperative with government thugs like these, but working for Bormann and Heydrich I had the unreasonable idea that there were more important things for me to do than waste valuable time talking to the Gestapo, answering their stupid questions. Surely the RSD would come to my aid if I asked them.

'Tell me you're not dumb enough to try to arrest me here,' I said.

'Just shut up and get dressed.'

'Does Major Högl know about this? From the local RSD?'

'This is a Gestapo matter.'

'What about Captain Neumann?' I got out of bed because I could see that, like all Gestapo men, they were eager to hit someone and soon. I grabbed the Pervitin and popped one in my mouth. I was going to need all the help I could get.

'Never heard of him either.'

'Hans-Hendrik Neumann. He's General Heydrich's adjutant. And currently working from your own HQ, in Salzburg. I assume you've heard of General Heydrich. Head of the SD and the Gestapo? He's on page two of the German Police and Gestapo Yearbook. Himmler is on page one. Smallish man with glasses who looks a bit like a village schoolmaster? Believe me, there will be hell to pay if they find out I've been arrested by a couple of comrade shoelaces like you. Neither of them much likes anyone interfering with the smooth running of the Nazi machine. Especially in Obersalzberg.'

'We're not from Salzburg. And we have our orders.'

'Orders are orders.'

'That's true,' I said. 'And the kind of logic that you boys can take comfort in. But with respect, that won't work here. I'm not sure it works anywhere.'

I started to get dressed. Already I could see their patience with me was wearing as thin as Himmler's smile.

'If you're not from Salzburg, then where *are* you from?'

'Linz.'

'But that's more than a hundred kilometres away.'

'You must have read a book about geography. And we take our orders from the High SS and Police Leader for Donau.'

'Donau?'

I thought for a moment as I climbed into my trousers, and then I realized suddenly who it was that had sent them. Donau, near Vienna, was the primary division command of the General-SS in Austria. All this time I'd been trying not to come between those big beasts Heydrich and Bormann and unwittingly I had

stepped into an internecine war between Heydrich and Kaltenbrunner. I was in a lot more danger than I'd ever imagined. With
Heydrich wanting dirt on his Austrian SS rival, Martin Bormann,
it had never occurred to me that Kaltenbrunner might try to
put a spanner in Heydrich's works. We'd underestimated him,
enormously.

'You're Kaltenbrunner's men, aren't you?'

'Now you're getting it, *piefke*.'

'Are we going to Linz now? Is that the plan? Because if it is
you're in big trouble, my friend. And your redundant proposi-
tional logic won't help you when they're tying you to a stake in
front of an SS firing squad.'

'You'll find out where we're going soon enough. And any more
threats out of you and my fist will feel obliged to interfere with
your smart mouth.'

'Look, one more thing. We're on the same side, after all. I've
been sent to investigate a murder in the Leader's Territory. As a
professional courtesy you could at least tell me what this is about
and why you think your mission is more important than mine.'

'High treason. And that certainly trumps any case you're investigating down here, Gunther.'

'Treason?' I sat down on the bed. It was quicker than falling
over. I started to pull on my boots before they lost patience with
me. 'You boys have made a serious mistake. Or someone's misled
your boss. There's no treason here.'

'That's what they all say.'

'Yes, but it's not all of them who report directly to General
Heydrich. I do, and he's going to have your kidneys devilled
and on toast.'

And then I saw it. The man with the wire glasses was holding
my own notebook as if it was something important, like exhibit
number one in a criminal investigation. The same notebook I'd
fetched from my office at the Berghof just hours before and
which had been on my bedside table. And it now occurred to

me that there was something in that notebook I didn't know about. Something that had been written there by someone else, perhaps. Something incriminating that could put me under the falling axe. I guessed the one in Linz was probably just as sharp as the one in Berlin. And I'd seen enough men with their heads sniffing their own toes to know that I wouldn't like it. Thanks to the Nazis, modern justice was quicker than a Reichspost telegram, with little or no time for defence arguments. Once I was in Linz they might execute me within hours of my arrival. I'd been measured out for this like Plato's hypotenuse. The two sent to arrest me were beyond all reason; I doubted that Immanuel Kant would have made a dent in their capacity for pure ignorance and categorical disbelief. I could hardly blame them for this; Ernst Kaltenbrunner was probably just as frightening to them as Heydrich was to me. By all accounts he was certainly uglier.

'Okay.' I stood up and put on my suit jacket. 'Don't say I didn't warn you.'

The one who'd taken my gun produced a set of manacles with which he proposed to handcuff me. Instead I reached for the Leica on the dressing table.

'You boys don't mind if I bring my camera, do you? Only, I've never been to Linz. Hitler's hometown, isn't it? I've heard it's very pretty. After this misunderstanding has been cleared up perhaps we'll look at the pictures I take and laugh about it.'

'Put the fucking camera down and show me your hands in front of you or I'll thump you very hard, Gunther.'

'And you? Did anyone ever tell you that you've got the kind of face the camera just loves? No?'

I laid the camera on the dressing table but I didn't let it go. I was just trying to bring the irritated man with the glasses a step nearer so I could take his photograph. Not that I was much of a photographer. Somehow I never mastered the idea that you're meant to put the subject's face in the lens and not on it, violently and at speed. Made of die-cast steel, the Leica was a small camera that produces a small negative image except when it's banged hard, twice, against a man's nose, and then the negative it produces is much bigger and more colourful, although I think there was too much red with this picture. I felt his nose crush under the second blow as if it had been a hard-boiled egg. The Gestapo man howled with pain, cupped his bleeding nose, and sank down on the floor as if he'd been shot in the face. I had enough time to take half a step back, which was just as well, as the other man landed a blow on my chin that would have dropped me like an old chimney if it had connected properly. I grabbed his thick wrist and used the momentum of the man's own weight to haul him into the dressing table, and then banged the cheval mirror hard on top of his skull, several times, smashing the mirror to pieces, which was unluckier for him than for me, as this left me an opportunity to grab a shard of glass and jam it into his neck with my left hand. I cut my hand but it didn't seem to matter as much as winning the fight and as quickly as possible. In any fight, this is all that ever matters. I hadn't killed him; I hadn't even severed his jugular vein, but with a piece of jagged glass sticking out of his neck the man recognized he was beaten and sat trembling on the floor, holding his neck and the shard that was now at right angles to it like a wayward shirt collar. The other man was still wailing and clutching his nose and, for no good reason that I could think of except that I was scared by the idea of what they'd have done to me in some Austrian Gestapo cell, I gave him a fond pat on the head. I took a deep breath, fetched my gun from the pocket of the man I'd stabbed, and collected their weapons. I worked the slide on my own Walther and brushed the wailing man's ear.

'Any more trouble from you two and I'll shoot you myself.'

I grabbed a handkerchief, wound it around my hand, and then retrieved my notebook from the floor next to the man with the glass collar.

I hadn't made many notes since my arrival in Obersalzberg, so it was easy to find the cause for their concern: the caricature of Adolf Hitler was well rendered and commendably obscene. Hitler with an erect cock that would have made a herm statue proud. And if it had been anywhere except a notebook with my name on it – an old habit from my gymnasium – I might have thought it was funny. But rather less treasonable cartoons of the beloved Leader had sent better men than me to an early death. The *Völkischer Beobachter* frequently carried stories about Germans unwise enough to make jokes about Hitler. He might have looked like Charlie Chaplin but a transnational sense of humour was not included with the silly moustache, the comic manner, and the doleful eyes. I tore out the offending page, crushed it into a ball, and threw this on the embers of the fire. It seemed obvious that the person who had drawn the cartoon had probably also telephoned the Gestapo in Linz in the knowledge that Heydrich's adjutant, Neumann, was currently stationed in nearby Salzburg and awaiting my call; quite possibly this was the same person who had cut the brakes on Kaspel's car.

'You can sit there and wait for the undertaker,' I said. 'Or a doctor. It's your choice, Fritz. But I want to know who called this in to Linz.'

The man swallowed with difficulty and answered breathlessly. 'Orders came direct from Donau,' he said. 'From General Kalten-brunner himself. Told us he'd had an informer report that you'd been seen making a libellous drawing of the Leader and that we were to arrest you for high treason.'

'Did he name this informer?'

'No. And no arguments were to be allowed. The Linz Gestapo had been chosen to carry out this assignment because you had too many friends in Salzburg and Munich who were likely to brush the affair under the carpet.'

'And then what were you to do?'

'We were to get rid of you on the way back to Linz. Shoot you in the head and leave you in a ditch somewhere. Please. I need a doctor.'

'I think we both do, Fritz.'

I went to fetch the two RSD men who were at the Villa Bechstein to guard Rudolf Hess. They were playing chess in front of the fire in the drawing room and jumped up as soon as they saw the blood rolling down my hand.

'Those two men who came in a few minutes ago,' I said. 'I want them placed under arrest and locked up in the cells underneath the Türken. Right now they're upstairs bleeding in my room. You'd better fetch a doctor, too. I'm going to want some stitches in this hand.'

'What happened, sir?' asked one.

'I told you to arrest them,' I said loudly. 'Not ask me for a history lesson.' The magic potion had started to kick in again. It was odd how it made you feel impatient and intolerant and even a bit superhuman – like a Nazi, I suppose. 'Let me spell it out for you. These two clowns have tried to interfere with a police investigation and the authority of Martin Bormann. That's why I want them locked up.' I'd seen enough blood for one evening and it angered me that some of it was mine. 'Look, you'd better fetch Major Högl. It's time he did something around here other than comb his hair and polish his Party badge. And I'm going to need to send another telex to General Heydrich in Berlin.'

Winkelhof, the villa's butler, turned up to see what all the commotion was about. Calmly and without complaint, he took charge of everything – even the stitching of my hand. It turned out he'd been a medical orderly during the war – and I had to remind myself that he, too, was on the list of the disgruntled and dispossessed Obersalzberg locals that Karl Schenk had compiled on my orders. This case had it all, I told myself: absurdity, alienation, existential anxiety, and no shortage of likely and unlikely suspects. If I'd been a very clever German of the kind who knew the difference between the sons of Zeus, Reason and Chaos, I might have been dumb enough to think I could write a book about it.

CHAPTER 37

April 1939

I ate a tasteless breakfast at the Berghof. Alone. I was dreading seeing Anni Kaspel and telling the poor woman that her husband, Hermann, was dead, and I wondered why I had been foolish enough to tell the spotty young lieutenant at the Türken that I would volunteer for this onerous duty. It wasn't like I'd spent that much time with Kaspel. And it was only when Major Högl and the cold herring he called his personality joined me in the dining room that I suddenly remembered why I'd said I would do it at all. It was like having breakfast with Conrad Veidt. After a few tense moments Högl confessed, smugly, that he'd already been up to Kaspel's house in Buchenhohe to break the news to the widow. Hearing this I winced and tried to contain my irritation with him, which he was at least perceptive enough to notice.

'Look here, as Kaspel's senior officer it was my duty to give her bad news like that, not yours,' he said. 'Besides, it's obvious why you told Lieutenant Dietrich that you wanted to tell her yourself.'

'Is it?'

Högl's eel-like lips writhed across his long Bavarian undertaker's face until they were a sarcastic imitation of a smile. Now he really did look like Conrad Veidt in *The Man Who Laughs*.

'Anni Kaspel is a very attractive woman. It's generally accepted that she's the most beautiful woman in Obersalzberg. Doubtless you thought you might ingratiate yourself with the woman and provide her with a convenient shoulder to cry on. You Berliners are so unscrupulous, so sure of yourselves, aren't you?'

I let that one go and, for a moment, diverted my thoughts away from this egregious insult by asking myself who among those with access to the Berghof might also have been a secret artist talented enough to draw a well-rendered caricature of Hitler in my notebook. It seemed a more considered reaction to what Högl had just said than grabbing him by the neat dark hair on his El Greco head and banging his bony nose on the breakfast table. Although it might at least have helped summon the waiter to bring me another pot of coffee. But after injuring two Gestapo men, I was in no hurry to gain myself a reputation for violence, even if it was probably warranted.

'How did she take it?'

'How do you think? Not well. But I wouldn't flatter yourself that your telling her would have made any difference to how the poor woman feels about it now. Her husband is dead and there's no way of polishing that table.'

'No, I suppose not.'

Högl poured himself a cup of lukewarm coffee and stirred some milk into it with a monogrammed teaspoon. If it hadn't been for the fact I'd just drunk some myself I could have wished it was poisoned.

'Besides,' he said, 'we're quite a close community up here in Obersalzberg. We don't like outsiders very much and prefer to handle these things privately, among ourselves.'

'You mean like murdering Hermann Kaspel? Or informing the Linz Gestapo that I had supposedly libelled the Leader? Yes, I can see how close you all are.'

'I have to tell you, Commissar Gunther. This whole thing strikes me as fantastical. Cutting through someone's brakes? I never heard of such a thing. No, it's quite unthinkable.'

'And I suppose that Dr Flex was shot by accident.'

'Frankly, I'm still not convinced he wasn't. I've seen no hard evidence yet that he really was murdered. In my own humble opinion he was probably killed by a stray shot from a careless hunter. A poacher, most probably. In spite of our best efforts we still get a few of those around here.'

'What about the rifle found in the chimney at the Villa Bechstein? I suppose it was left there by Shockheaded Peter.'

'There's no telling how long it had been there. It was certainly very dusty. Besides, it's no proof of intent. A poacher might just as easily have wanted to hide a rifle quickly as an assassin. The punishments for poaching are severe.'

I was already regretting that I hadn't banged Högl's head on the breakfast table; it might have knocked some sense into it. The man had the forensic skills of a rubber plant.

'By the way, Major, I meant to ask. That rifle of yours at the Türken Inn. The Mannlicher carbine with the scope. Was that the same rifle Hermann Kaspel gave you? The one that was found in the Landlerwald.'

'I really couldn't say.' Högl shrugged. 'I suppose it might have been.'

'Hermann said he thought it was a poacher's rifle. Because it was fitted with an oil filter sound suppressor. Just like the one I found in the chimney at the Villa Bechstein.'

'I'm afraid I can't help you there. I don't remember there being an oil filter suppressor fitted to the rifle when Kaspel gave it to me. But why is that important?'

'Whoever fitted your rifle with a sound suppressor may well have done the same with the assassin's rifle. It could be important evidence.'

'If you say so.'

I smiled patiently. 'I know you were a cop, Major. With the Bavarian Police. It says so in your file. But I do wonder why you don't see that this could be important. Perhaps it's fortunate for the Leader that your master, Martin Bormann, thinks differently.'

'For now,' said Högl. 'I wouldn't bank on him thinking that way forever.'

'Anyone would think you've got something to hide, Major.'

'Perhaps you suspect me of shooting Flex, is that it? And doing whatever you say someone did to poor Hermann's brakes.'

It was then – rather too late, perhaps – that I remembered what Udo Ambros, the assistant hunter at the Landlerwald had told me: that Peter Högl had been in the Sixteenth Bavarian with Adolf Hitler. As Hitler's former NCO he was much more powerful than he seemed.

'No, of course I don't suspect you, sir,' I said, backtracking hopelessly. It was only too easy for me to picture him telling Hitler that he wanted me arrested and thrown in jail as quickly as possible, and Hitler agreeing with him. 'I'm sure that your primary concern, as is mine, is the Leader's safety. But the fact remains the brakes *were* cut. And a man died as a result. My assistant, Friedrich Korsch, used to be a mechanic. He'll confirm what I said.'

'I'm sure he would. You Berliners do like to stick together, don't you? But it seems rather more obvious to me that Kaspel simply lost control of his car. These roads can be treacherous. Which is why so much effort has gone in to widening them to improve safety. Not only that, but he was almost a methamphetamine addict. He was an accident waiting to happen.'

'It's not the roads that are treacherous, Major Högl. I'm afraid it's someone in this community. I wish that wasn't the case. But I can see no alternative.'

'Nonsense. I don't mind admitting to you, Gunther, that I place very little faith in the other half of your story, either. This idea that someone drew a cartoon of the Leader in your notebook. It's quite ridiculous.'

'And it was me who informed the Linz Gestapo that I was guilty of high treason? Is that what you mean?'

'Perhaps I might see this offensive drawing? And judge the matter for myself.'

'I burned it.'

'May I ask why?'

'I should have thought it was obvious. I'm not keen to be framed a second time.'

'By whom?'

'The Gestapo, of course. They have a habit of throwing a man out of a window first and asking questions later.'

'Without the evidence of the offending cartoon, it makes your story very hard to substantiate, doesn't it?'

'My story doesn't need substantiation, Major. I'm a senior police officer investigating a crime at the request of Martin Bormann. I flatter myself that I was asked here because he thought the services of a real detective were called for.'

I wanted to add, *And I'm beginning to see why,* but I managed to restrain myself. I kept walking away from Högl's insults and contempt but they always came after me to offer some more of the same.

'Yes, I'm glad you mentioned that, Commissar Gunther. Shall I tell you what I think?'

'I wish you would, sir,' I said patiently. 'Two heads are better than one, eh?'

'It occurs to me that this whole story has been concocted by you to deflect attention from your obvious failure to resolve this matter quickly.'

'I tell you what was concocted, Major. Evidence. Evidence that might have put me under a falling axe in Linz. The fact is, earlier tonight, while I was elsewhere, someone entered the room I've been using at the Berghof and made a libellous sketch of the Leader in my notebook. I would of course have locked the door to my room except for the fact there are no locks and no keys.'

'Why would anyone do such a thing?'

'Doubtless whoever made the drawing intended it as a backup plan in case I escaped the car accident that had killed Kaspel. Someone in Obersalzberg or Berchtesgaden wants me dead, and soon. Even if it requires the help of Kaltenbrunner and the Austrian Gestapo.'

Of course, for the secret artist I had no shortage of suspects: Zander, Brandt, Schenk, Rattenhuber, Arthur Kannenberg, Brückner, Peter Högl, of course, even Gerdy Troost, and more or less everyone else, including Martin Bormann. I didn't trust any of them although it was harder to see Gerdy Troost sliding under a car and cutting through some brake hoses, or even knowing what they were. Not with those shoes and stockings.

'You're really suggesting that someone with access to the Berghof – one of the Leader's intimate circle – that they would do such a thing?'

'That's exactly what I'm suggesting, yes. Ask Bormann about it. He used to run the National Socialist Automobile Corps, didn't he? I bet he knows a thing or two about cars.'

'You're just being paranoid, Commissar.'

'Who's paranoid?' said a third voice. 'Let's not have any talk like that. We're Germans, gentlemen. We don't use Jewish words like "paranoid".'

Joining us at the Berghof breakfast table and smelling strongly of tobacco was Johann Rattenhuber, an SS-Standartenführer and Högl's superior. About the same age as his junior officer, Rattenhuber was a thickset, jollier man with a beer-hall voice, a ruddy face, and an Oktoberfest manner. I didn't doubt his pork-butcher's fists had seen a lot of action on the Leader's behalf. He probably punched holes in cast-iron buckets to keep in shape. He, too, was a Bavarian policeman by profession but much more obviously so than Peter Högl; even on his own he constituted a formidable bodyguard and just looking at him, I figured he could probably have protected the Sabine women from a whole truckload of randy Roman soldiers with one arm tied behind his broad back.

'The commissar here was just about to explain why he thinks I might have shot Karl,' said Högl.

'Nonsense, of course he wasn't,' said Rattenhuber. 'Were you, Gunther?'

'Not really, sir, no. Not for a minute. The major and I were merely having a useful discussion about the case.'

And then, as if this were all that needed to be said on the matter, Rattenhuber moved straight on to the subject of Hermann Kaspel, for which I was grateful. Talking to Högl was like playing chess with a snake; at any moment I had the idea he might stretch across the board and swallow my knight.

'It's terrible news about Hermann's accident,' said Rattenhuber. 'He was an excellent officer.' He glanced at Högl. 'Does Anni know?'

'Yes, sir. I told her myself,' said Högl.

'Good. That must have been hard for you, Peter. It's hard for us all.'

'And it's a real loss to the RSD. I was very upset when I heard about it.'

'So was I,' I said. 'Especially when I discovered it wasn't an accident.'

I explained about the brake hoses and while I did so, Rattenhuber nodded his closely cropped steel-grey head. It looked like a medieval mace and was probably just as hard. It made a noise like emery paper when he scratched it thoughtfully.

'Another murder, you say. But this is terrible. Bormann will go crazy when I tell him.'

I waited for Högl to contradict me but, to my surprise, the major said nothing.

'Obviously someone wanted you dead, Commissar,' said Rattenhuber. 'And you, not Hermann Kaspel. He was very much liked here in Obersalzberg, and I hope you'll forgive me for saying so, but you are not, by virtue of who you are and what you are doing.'

'I'm used to it.'

'I'm sure you are. But look here, you must be getting close to finding the murderer. It can be the only possible explanation for why this has happened, don't you think? Of course, there's no question of telling the Leader about this. I mean, about what happened to poor Captain Kaspel. Not until the criminal has been safely apprehended. We wouldn't like Hitler to get the idea that his motor cars are as unsafe as the terrace. Don't you agree, Herr Commissar?'

'I think that would be wise, Colonel.'

'By the way, these are for you.'

Rattenhuber handed over several telegrams, which I pocketed for later. But Rattenhuber wasn't having any of it.

'Well, aren't you going to read those?' demanded Rattenhuber. 'Damn it, man, they're telegrams, not love letters. There can be no secrets among men for whom the Leader's safety and welfare is paramount. Especially when his arrival is now so close. There's no time to lose. He'll be here in less than five days.'

I wasn't inclined to argue with that, not with the head of the RSD. So I opened them up and read them, providing a description of each for the sake of good manners.

'This is from the Gestapo in Salzburg. Johann Brandner, my leading suspect, hasn't been seen at the address where he's been living since before Flex was murdered. He's a trained marksman and a local man with a grudge, so you can see why he's of interest to me. The Gestapo has no idea where he's gone. At least that's what they say. They don't seem inclined to help me look for him, either. Perhaps Kaltenbrunner—'

'Kurt Christmann is in charge of the Salzburg Gestapo,' said Rattenhuber. 'He's an old friend of mine. So to hell with Kaltenbrunner. I'll telephone him later this morning and explain the urgency of finding this man.'

I opened another telegram. 'My assistant, Friedrich Korsch, has traced the Krauss brothers to Dachau concentration camp.'

'The Krauss brothers. Who are they?'

'They are also suspects,' I lied. 'At least they were. Before

Dachau, it seems they were banged up in Stadelheim Prison and so they couldn't possibly have had anything to do with Flex's murder.' Quickly I opened another telegram and glanced over the contents. 'But this is better news. They've traced the serial number of the Mannlicher carbine that was used to shoot Flex. The one I found dropped down the chimney at the Villa Bechstein. It turns out that the rifle was sold to Herr Udo Ambros.'

'I know that name,' said Rattenhuber.

'The assistant hunter,' I said. 'At the Landlerwald.'

'Geiger's man. Yes, of course.'

'I interviewed him yesterday.' I was speaking carefully now. The last thing I wanted was Ambros arrested by the RSD and a confession beaten out of him in the cells below the Türken. People have a habit of saying anything when they're guests of the Gestapo. If I was going to pinch anyone, I wanted to be sure that the person arrested had actually shot and killed Karl Flex. Besides, I could hardly see how Ambros might have had the access to the Berghof he would have needed to have drawn the obscene cartoon of Hitler in my notebook. At the very least he had to have had an accomplice. Perhaps more than one. 'I think it's time I questioned him again.'

I opened the last of my telegrams and glanced over it quickly. Heydrich had ordered his own adjutant to join me on Hitler's mountain. To watch my back, he said; after the visit from the Linz Gestapo this ought to have sounded just fine to me.

'We'll come with you. Perhaps we can help.'

'I'd prefer you didn't, sir. Not yet anyway. We wouldn't want to scare him into confessing to something he might not actually have done. When the Leader gets here, I don't want there to be any doubt that we have the right man in custody.'

'But it's his rifle, isn't it?' said Rattenhuber.

'Yes, but all the same, I'd prefer to hear his story as to why the rifle is no longer in his possession before I arrest him. It might actually be that there's a reasonable explanation for that.'

I didn't really think this was likely but I wanted to handle Ambros by myself. Rattenhuber said his office at the Türken would provide me with the man's address. For a Bavarian and a Nazi, he wasn't a bad fellow. But he still looked a little peeved about staying behind.

'Very well, Herr Commissar.'

'By the way, sir. Since Captain Kaspel is dead and my own assistant is currently in Munich, Captain Neumann is going to join me here in Obersalzberg. General Heydrich feels his adjutant can help me with this investigation. Perhaps you would be good enough to inform Deputy Chief of Staff Bormann.'

'As you wish, Commissar. You're the detective.'

I nodded gratefully but the truth was I had my doubts about this. After what had happened during the night I felt as if every time I stopped moving a disembodied hand chalked just a bit more of a thick white line around my still twitching body, like a corpse discovered on the floor of the palace during Belshazzar's feast. Uncovering the secrets of Hitler's mountain, I wasn't much more than another murder waiting to happen. Someone had taken a considerable risk in trying to kill me, twice. Possibly they would try again. And it was unfortunate that the man Heydrich had sent to watch my back would, if his master ordered him to, put a hole in it without a moment's hesitation. The one thing about the Nazis you could always rely on was that they were not to be relied upon. None of them. Not ever.

CHAPTER 38

October 1956

Two hours later, in the nothing town of Puttelange-aux-Lacs, I perceived the full extent of my folly and the consequences of trusting a Catholic priest. The police were at the crossroads on the other side of a small bridge and it was fortunate for me I saw them first. The blue flashing lights helped; they might as well have erected a red neon sign. I had no choice but to wheel my bicycle off the Rue de Nancy, remove my holdall from the luggage rack, and drop the machine on the other side of a disused, rusted gate set between two redundant brick posts that stood on the edge of an empty field like the last teeth in some vagrant's carious mouth. Satisfied that the bicycle could not be seen from the road, I walked across an unfenced field in the opposite direction, chucking away my war medal, my glasses, and my beret while I did so, hoping to approach the main road to Sarreguemines and, immediately beyond that, the old German border, from a less observed direction. But I soon realized this would not be possible. The road running through the centre of town was full of police cars and it was clear to me that the priest of Saint Hippolyte had given me up when I saw him sitting in one of these cars with a cigarette in his face and enjoying a joke with the gendarmes. So much for his Bible oath, I thought, and concluded he must have been one of those casuistic Catholics for whom reason is a way of explaining the world for their own convenience rather than a simple capacity for making sense of things. Which is to say almost all of them, of course. He didn't see me turn around and walk southeast, in the opposite direction, towards Strasbourg, although I was almost tempted to go straight back to Bérig-Vintrange and burn down his church like a true SS man. Instead I reached the outskirts of town in a few minutes and concealed myself in the back of an old blue van without wheels that was abandoned in the overgrown drive of a large empty house. I'd wait for dusk, when I figured I had a better chance of travelling unnoticed. There was some strong-smelling straw on the floor and behind the van's closed doors I was able to relax a little. It would have been a simple matter for the police to have surrounded me, but oddly, I wasn't that worried by my situation. As long as I remained quiet and didn't smoke, no one but the mice would ever have known I was hiding there. I thought I could probably circumvent the police once it was dark – hopefully they were still looking for a man on a bicycle wearing a beret – and get on the road to the Saarland again. I estimated that it was about thirty kilometres to the old border. Of course, now that I was on foot it would take me longer to get there but sitting in the back of an old van made me wonder if perhaps I could find a place in another van, or a truck, one going northeast as far as Germany, perhaps. I resolved to try.

For two or three hours I actually managed to sleep and when I awoke, feeling cold and stiff as if I were already in my unmarked grave, I picked the straw carefully off my clothes, lit a cigarette to chase off my hunger pangs, pocketed my gun, and, leaving the holdall behind – it was only going to draw attention to the fact that I was travelling somewhere – I walked back into town, where I found fewer police around. I tramped very slowly along the main road, which was also the road to Freyming-Merlebach, another Alsatian border town, and considered the dwindling number of options that were now available to me. I was quickly running out of ideas on how to deflect attention from myself and, deciding that fugitives are seldom ever intoxicated, and that real drunks never seem to be in a hurry, I went into a wine shop opposite the local town hall and bought a bottle of cheap red Burgundy. Besides the appearance of having an open bottle in my hand, like a true *clochard*, the effect of the wine was good for my fraying nerves and after several mouthfuls I was almost able to see the comedy in my situation. It seems to me that people don't really drink to escape their existence but to see its funny side instead; mine was beginning to resemble one of those delightful films starring Jacques Tati. The idea that the Stasi – the true heirs to the Gestapo – were using the French police to do their dirty work struck me as history repeating itself in the Marxian sense, which is to say, first as tragedy and then as farce. So, wine bottle in hand, I kept walking vaguely north hoping that I might pick up my pace as soon as I was out of town. In front of the police station I pretended to stand there indecisively, as if I had no particular place to go and even toasted two of the gendarmes with cigarettes in their faces and who were keeping a keen eye out for nothing much except their own tobacco smoke and the odd pretty girl.

'What's all the fuss about?' I asked. In the dying light I hoped they couldn't see my red eyes.

'We're looking for an escaped murderer,' said one.

'There's a lot of them about,' I said. 'After the war we had you'd think there would be less murder, but it doesn't seem that way. Human life is cheap after what the Germans did.'

'It's a German we're looking for.'

I spat and then took a swig from my bottle. 'It figures. Most of the Nazis got away with it, you know.'

I walked on until I reached the corner of the next road where a young policeman wearing a rather strong cologne I recognized as Pino Silvestre was twirling a baton. He eyed me with complete indifference as I proceeded slowly up the road towards what looked like a public park, but at the last minute he let out a shout and I turned on my heel and faced him insolently before putting the bottle to my lips.

'You going to the park?' he asked.

'I was thinking about it.'

'Not with the bottle, you're not. There's no drinking allowed in the park.'

I nodded dully and walked back down towards the main road, as if I'd changed my mind about the park. As I passed the cop again, he said, 'You should know that if you live around here.'

I toasted him with the bottle as if being sarcastic but of course a real drunk would have argued with the cop and told him where to shove his baton; instead I said nothing and, much too meekly perhaps, carried on my meandering way.

'Where are you from anyway?' he asked. 'I don't think I've seen you around here before.'

'Bérig-Vintrange,' I said, and carried on walking. It wasn't a good place to have picked and if I could have remembered one I'd certainly have mentioned another of the other, closer villages I had cycled through on the way to Puttelange-aux-Lacs.

'You've missed the last bus,' he said.

'Story of my life.' I hiccupped without turning round.

'If I catch you sleeping on the street I'll arrest you,' he said.

'You won't,' I said. 'I shall walk home.'

'But it's twenty kilometres. Take you at least four hours.'

'Then I'll be home before midnight.'

Several seconds passed and just as I thought I might have got away with it, the young cop shouted again. I assumed he was going to ask for my identity card and I took off running. I was fitter than I'd been for a long time; the bicycling and the fresh air had been good for me and I was pleasantly surprised that I could run as fast as I did. Of course, that might have been the effect of the wine, which I now tossed over a fence into someone's garden as I sprinted down a narrow path, vaulted a wooden gate into a yard, and pounded along a cinder track like an escaped horse, before deviating sharply right and into the small cemetery at the back of the local church. I heard the cop shout again and I crouched down behind one of the larger head-stones for a moment to get my bearings and catch my breath. I could hear more shouting in the distance and a whistle and the sound of engines starting and I knew I was just minutes away from being caught. I ran up to Rue Mozart and then right onto the road to Sarreguemines, which suited me very well. In the distance I could see a large copse of trees and I thought that if only I could reach it in time, I might lie still in the shrubbery, like a smart fox, and let the hunt pass me by. After a minute's hard running I reached the trees and not a moment too soon since I could now hear the sound of approaching police sirens. To protect my face I backed quickly into a thick hedge and then dropped flat on my front to find cover, narrowly missing impaling myself on an old rusting draw harrow. Fortunately the ground was bone dry and, crawling through the undergrowth, I found an excellent place in which to conceal myself – an empty drainpipe behind a thick laurel bush. I might never have found it at all but for a rabbit that ran into the pipe when it saw me. I quickly lit a match to inspect my new hiding place. The pipe was about a metre high and half a metre wide and evidently someone had been in there before because lying on the ground were several old copies of *Clins d'Oeil de Paris,* a pornographic magazine that wasn't one with which I was familiar. I threw the match away and waited. A few minutes later I heard the sound of a man crashing through the undergrowth and caught the smell of Pino Silvestre. It was the same cop who had challenged me, of course. I heard the whine of brakes urgently applied and running footsteps on the road. Meanwhile the cop nearest to me yelled out that I might as well give myself up, as it was only a matter of time before I was caught and that things would go better for me if I handed myself in. But when he blundered straight past my hiding place I knew this wasn't true. I even saw his polished black boots as he walked by, cursing the bushes as he pushed his way through them. My hand tightened on the gun; I wasn't quite convinced I would use it in order to avoid arrest. It was one thing killing an East German policeman who had tried to hang me; it was something else to kill a young French cop wearing too much aftershave. He stood there for a while, less than half a metre from my hiding place, swore again, and lit a cigarette. The cigarette smelled good after the aftershave and you know things are getting desperate when you silently take a deep breath of air in the hope that some of the nicotine's calming effect will drift your way. I thought I could probably wait things out in my drainpipe for a while as long as the French police didn't bring dogs. I hoped they would not have dogs. If they had dogs with noses, I was finished. After a while the cop shouted to his colleagues who shouted something back and he walked off, but not before dropping the cigarette on the ground. I waited for several seconds before reaching for the butt and then smoking it myself. As perfect pleasures go, it's hard to beat smoking the cigarette of a very determined policeman you've just managed to elude.

Gradually the police search receded and after several minutes' silence I risked peering through the bush. The cop with the pungent aftershave had gone. I waited another couple of minutes with my heart in my mouth and then crept out of my hiding place so I could go to the edge of the copse and look up the road to Sarreguemines. I could just see some lights flashing helpfully in the distance but in the dark it would be easy for me to make my getaway before the police fetched some tracker dogs and returned in force to search the trees. I reckoned my best direction was west, along the road to Freyming-Merlebach, which was the opposite way from Sarreguemines. So, hugging the bushes for cover, I walked back into Puttelange-aux-Lacs and then picked up the D656 out of town. After walking a few hundred metres I saw a hotel restaurant called La Chaumière, where a number of people were having dinner in the floodlit garden. I watched them a little enviously for a minute or two, wishing I might have been doing something as ordinary as eating a meal in a nice restaurant. I watched the cars they'd left in the car park. One of these, a green Renault Frégate with beige upholstery, still had the keys in the ignition and I calculated that I might enjoy the safe use of it for at least an hour, and perhaps even longer, until dinner was ended – an hour before the police were informed and more roadblocks could be set up.

It was a nice little car, very modern, with a radio. I didn't listen to it; instead I drove slowly through Hoste and Cappel, before deviating north at Barst, and motoring through Marienthal and Petit Ebersviller. It took me less than thirty minutes to reach Freyming-Merlebach, where I steered off the main road and down a long neglected farm track before dumping the car carefully under the branches of a very large weeping willow. I was now just a few kilometres from the old German border and a sort of freedom. Freyming-Merlebach was mostly shops and little white bungalows with very few public buildings of any note; more important, however, the town of Karlsbrunn was indicated on a signpost and it couldn't have looked more welcome. I walked north, up Rue Saint-Nicolas with a smile on my face as if I'd just completed an Olympic marathon in the gold-medal position.

The Saar might have been a *département* of France but the people there were Germans. Just to be among my own countrymen again would feel like a kind of victory in itself. I'd been away from Germany for too long. There's nothing like living in France to make a German feel like he's a very long way from home. But about halfway up the street, I saw a group of four or five men in front of the big bay window of a brightly lit bar and there was something about them that made me pause in a doorway opposite and watch them for a couple of minutes before I could even think of walking on. They were military-sized, with military haircuts, and wearing cheap, mass-produced grey suits of the kind no self-respecting Frenchman would ever have worn. Their shoes were weapons-grade with thick soles made to stamp on East German faces. The ties they were wearing looked as if they were made of cardboard and the fists they squeezed experimentally on the end of their circus-strongman arms were as big as beer mugs. As I watched them, a man who was speaking on the telephone by the door finished his call and came out of the bar smoking a cigarette. He shouted something in German. So close to the old German border, this wasn't at all remarkable. There were probably many other Germans in Freyming-Merlebach. But it did seem remarkable that the man with the cigarette and the eye patch who was doing all the shouting was Friedrich Korsch.

CHAPTER 39

April 1939

Udo Ambros lived on Aschauerstrasse in Berchtesgaden, about half a kilometre further on from the home of Dr Waechter, the lawyer who owned the exiled Jew's garage containing the red Maserati. Ambros's isolated house enjoyed a spectacular view of the Watzmann and backed onto a thick forest but it wasn't much of a place – certainly nothing to compare with Dr Waechter's; just a largish, two-storey Alpine building that was little better than a poorly built barn, with a corrugated iron roof, a rusting wire fence, an abandoned water trailer, and a pile of near-fossilized wood stacked under a row of long icicles hanging from the black eaves like the teeth of some extinct mountain carnivore. A red DKW motorcycle stood on the snow-covered path along which were a series of footprints that contrasted strongly with my own; these others were reddish, even blood-coloured, which raised a question in my head as to exactly how they got that way. A piebald horse was watching me carefully from the top of a long sloping field and a crudely carved bear stood guard by the front door; from the angle of his head and the snarling, aggrieved expression on his face he looked as if he had taken a bullet to the neck. There were only two windows, both of them on the ground floor. I glanced in one but I might just as easily have been looking through a fog, the glass was so grimy. Not that the dirty net curtains helped much, either.

I knocked at the door and waited but no one answered. The relentless silence of the valley felt as if it had been ordained by the local gods and it was unnerving, as if the whole of nature was desperately afraid of waking Wotan while he was taking a well-deserved nap with Fricka on a nearby mountaintop. Living somewhere like this would, I knew, have driven me as mad as King Ludwig. Berliners like me were not meant for empty places like this. We like the sound of noise more than we care for the noise of silence, which is always a little too long and loud for our cynical metropolitan ears. The true hallmarks of civilization are clamour, hubbub, and commotion. Give me pandemonium every time. The air was heavy with the sweet smell of dung and wood smoke. The smell of coal suits me a lot better; my smoker's cough works better when there's some sulphur dioxide and heavy metals in the damp atmosphere.

I might have concluded that the assistant huntsman was not at home if it hadn't been for the motorcycle. The cylinder of the 500-cc engine was cold to the touch but rocking the bike revealed the fuel tank was almost full. I kick-started it in the hope that the sound might summon its owner and the engine roared into life at only the second time of asking, all of which implied that the machine was regularly ridden and most probably the preferred method of transport for Udo Ambros; but only the piebald came to the edge of the fence to see what was happening, fixing me with the kind of wary, black-eyed, who-the-hell-are-you kind of look I normally only get from single women in bars. After a minute or more I allowed the bike to stall, walked back to the front door, knocked a second time, and peered through the window again. I don't know what I expected to see in there. A man hiding from me? Some firelight, perhaps? A witch with a cauldron full of stolen children? I turned around and went to question the mare in the hope that she might give me a clue where Ambros was to be found; and without hesitating, she did. As soon as I reached the fence she turned away and following her with my eyes for a few seconds I saw a man's legs sticking out of a door at the side of the house.

'Herr Ambros,' I said. He didn't answer, so I picked up a length of wood and threw it near him just in case he was underneath a car or a tractor; but of course I knew he wasn't. If the man had been alive he would have been summoned by the noise of the DKW starting up. Reluctant to risk tearing my suit by climbing over the fence I went back to the door. It wasn't locked. With so little real theft in this part of Germany – except, of course, the kind that Bormann and his people were guilty of – few bothered locking their front doors.

Death doesn't always have a smell, but it often has a distinctive feel, as if the silent wraith that has just crept away with a man's soul brushes against the edge of your own, like an invisible man on a crowded U-Bahn train. It can be unnerving at times. It was like that here and I almost didn't go any further into the house out of a reluctance to witness what I might see. You would think a Murder Commission detective would be used to looking at terrible things. But the truth is, you never are. Every horrible murder is horrible in its own way and the pictures of these can never be erased from your mind; even at the best of times my own memories often resemble a series of uglier paintings by George Grosz and Otto Dix. I sometimes ask myself if my temperament might have been very different if I hadn't seen so many crime scenes.

I forced myself to walk through a house that looked as if it was already accustomed to violent death. A rabbit lay half-skinned on the kitchen table while the walls of the hallway and the sitting room were full of various animal trophies – deer, badgers, foxes; it might have been my imagination, but they were all looking quite pleased with the way things had turned out. The probable author of their collective misfortune was history. I knew that as soon as I walked into the house. Udo Ambros was lying on the stone floor of the kitchen with his feet through the open door, although to be honest I wasn't absolutely sure it was him. A shotgun blast to the head at close range has a capacity to make nonsense of things like a man's identity. I've seen decapitated men at Plötzensee who had more of a head to speak of than Udo Ambros. There's no such thing as a cry for help when the suicide involves a shotgun; the victim always means it. Pieces of skull and brain and gouts of blood had made such a mess of the kitchen that it resembled a direct hit on a trench at Verdun and, had I not been standing in the dead man's own kitchen, the only reason I could have recognized him at all would have been the *Good Luck from Berchtesgaden Salt Mines* badge he was wearing in the lapel of his bloodstained *Tracht* jacket. A whole piece of his face, including the eye, was sticking to the tiled wall above the stove like a piece of a mural by Picasso or the relief on a Roman fountain. I swallowed hard, as if to remind myself I had a neck to which a head was attached, but kept on looking all the same.

I lifted up the dead man's shirt and put my hand on his chest; the body was quite cold and I guessed he must have been dead for at least eight hours. He was still clutching the shotgun, which lay between his outstretched legs like the sword on a Templar's tomb. I wrested the gun from his dead fingers. It was a Merkel side-by-side with a Kersten bolting mechanism, one of the more desirable German shotguns. I broke it open to reveal two red Brenneke slugs in the barrels, only one of which had been discharged. Not that it would have needed two; an ordinary shotgun cartridge filled with buckshot would certainly have done the job, but a slug that could have brought down a charging wild boar was making absolutely sure of it, like using a three-kilo hammer to crack an egg. I'd seen these slugs before, but for the life of me I couldn't remember exactly where. I'd seen so much lately that I didn't know where I'd left my own arsehole. The only question was, why had he done it? The man I'd met the previous day hadn't looked as if he'd had much on his mind except the enjoyment of my own discomfort; then again, he must have known I'd trace the Mannlicher carbine to him eventually. And when I did, things would have gone very badly for Udo Ambros. Very badly indeed. The Gestapo would have made quite sure of that. I hadn't cared to think about what might happen to Karl Flex's murderer when I caught him but I knew the Nazis well enough to be sure it could so easily have been something worse than the falling axe.

After a while I looked around for a suicide note and found one inside an envelope on the mantelpiece above a wood fire that was still warm to the touch. It was about now I started to wonder why a man who was planning to blow his head off would bother to build a large fire and start skinning a rabbit and pour a full cup of coffee that was still on the table, and I hoped that the note would explain all that.

TO WHOM IT MAY CONCERN. I HAVE KILLED MYSELF BECAUSE IT'S ONLY A MATTER OF TIME BEFORE THAT BERLIN COPPER TRACES THE NUMBER ON THAT MANNLICHER CARBINE AND GETS ME FOR THE MURDER OF KARL FLEX AND I DON'T WANT TO DIE, STARVED TO DEATH IN DACHAU LIKE JOHANN BRANDNER. FLEX WAS A BASTARD AND EVERYONE KNOWS HE HAD IT COMING. I LEAVE MY GUNS AND MY MOTORCYCLE TO MY OLD FRIENDS AND FELLOW HUNTSMEN, JOHANNES GEIGER AND JOHANN DIESBACH, AND THE REST OF MY STUFF TO ANY OF THEM WHO WANTS IT. SIGNED UDO AMBROS.

But the suicide note asked as many questions as it answered. It was the first one I'd seen that was entirely written in neat capital letters, almost as if Ambros had been keen to make sure that everything was quite clear and understood by the proper authorities; but it also managed to obscure something very important: the true handwriting of the man who'd written the note, which might have enabled me to determine absolutely – with the opinion of the huntsman Johannes Geiger, perhaps

– that Ambros had indeed penned it. As it was, I had my doubts. Not least because there was a spot of blood on the corner of the paper about the size of a pinhead. Laboratory analysis might have proved that this was the rabbit's blood and not a man's, but the rabbit itself looked to have been properly drained and bled before the skinning had begun. I would have bet a small fortune that the blood had arrived on the notepaper from the head of Udo Ambros. Nothing unusual about that perhaps, except that the note had been inside an envelope. I wandered around the house opening creaky cupboards and smelly drawers and being generally nosy. Meanwhile I asked myself if Johann Brandner, my leading suspect, was dead after all – as the suicide note had alleged. It wouldn't have been the first time that the Gestapo and the SS had lied about a death in Dachau, even to the criminal police. Death in Dachau might have been a normal occurrence but it was often treated by the authorities as something secret, to be hidden not just from concerned families but from everyone else as well. The few people who knew exactly what went on in Dachau were, I knew, the subject of a so-called Leader Order; and the only reason I knew about this was because Heydrich had once told me about it before sending me to Dachau himself. He was thoughtful like that. On the other hand, it was quite possible that Johann Brandner had returned to Berchtesgaden in secret, killed Udo Ambros, and hoped to put me off the scent by mentioning that he was dead in the suicide note. Being dead is a pretty good alibi for anyone who's in trouble with the law, but in Nazi Germany it was an existential hazard.

Having seen a gun cupboard in the hallway behind the front door, I searched for keys and eventually found a set on a chain in the dead man's trouser pocket. Which was when I started to become convinced that Udo Ambros had been murdered. Inside the gun cupboard were a couple of rifles, another shotgun, a Luger pistol, some rifle ammunition, and several boxes of Rottweil shotgun cartridges. Rottweil was owned by a company called RWS and after searching the entire house and the out-buildings I discovered that these were the only cartridges I could find anywhere; the two Brenneke slugs used to kill Ambros were made by Sellier & Bellot and the only two I ever found were the two in the gun, which strongly suggested to me that the murderer had probably brought his own ammunition. Perhaps he'd looked for some cartridges belonging to Ambros, realized they were safely locked away in the gun cupboard, and then been obliged to use the ones in his own pocket or ammunition belt. Which strongly suggested that the murder had not been one carefully planned beforehand; quite possibly the two men had met quite amicably and argued about something before the killer had slipped the two slugs into the victim's gun and then shot him. Which also suggested that they were friends, or at least acquaintances. And given the contents of the suicide note, what else but my investigation and the provenance of the Mannlicher carbine would they have been arguing about?

There were no bloody footprints leading out of the kitchen and through the house, which made me wonder about the red-dish bootprints in the snow on the path outside the front door. How had they got there? It didn't seem at all likely that the killer would have gone out the back door and climbed over the fence. Besides, the only prints on the snow outside the kitchen door belonged to the horse. With every light switched on, I went carefully through the house, but there wasn't anything even resembling a footprint. I grabbed Ambros's coat and went outside. I was never a detective much given to getting down on my hands and knees. For one thing, I didn't have many suits and the ones I had weren't the kind to take any punishment. For another, it never seemed worth a fingertip search given that most murders these days were committed by the people I was working for. Even so I dropped the coat beside one of the size-forty-five bootprints and took a closer look. The prints looked like they were from a pair of Hanwag boots, just like the ones I was wearing on my own feet. And the prints weren't really red at all. They were pink. And it wasn't blood that had stained the snow. It was salt. The highest quality pink salt. The kind that gourmet cooks were fond of using.

CHAPTER 40

April 1939

At Rothman's garage in Berchtesgaden, the Maserati was parked on the street again and Friedrich Korsch was seated in the passenger seat surrounded by several small boys who had gathered around to admire the car. But the biggest small boy was probably Korsch himself. Puffing a cigarette happily, he looked like he'd just won the German Grand Prix. Next to the Maserati was a Paulaner beer truck that hadn't been there before. Paulaner was the biggest brand of beer in Bavaria. When he saw me, Korsch climbed out of the Maserati, threw away the cigarette – which was promptly acquired by one of his young admirers – and came to the window of my car.

'You fetched the Krauss brothers?' I said.

'In the back of the truck. I was lucky. They were about to be transferred to do hard labour in Flossenbürg.'

'Good work.'

'Not entirely. They say they'll only open the safe if we let them go at the Italian border.'

'What does Heydrich have to say about that?'

'He's fine with it. If they open the safe, they can walk. There's just one problem, boss.'

'What?'

'These two yids don't trust us to keep our word.'

'How about if we sign a letter, something on paper, a guarantee—?'

'They don't like that idea either.'

'That's a pity.'

'Can you blame them? This is Berchtesgaden. Remember? If the *Chancellor's* own word isn't worth shit—'

'Strictly speaking, that was Munich, but I know what you mean. It sets a bad example for the rest of us.'

'So what are we going to do?'

'We have to get into that safe. I've a good idea it's the key to everything, if that's not a contradiction in terms. Look, I'd better speak to the brothers myself. Maybe we can come to an arrangement. What sort of condition are they in?'

'A bit dirty. I fed them both on the road from Dachau. And they had some beers in the truck, which ought to have put them in a better mood by now. But considering where they were, not too bad, really.'

'Bring them into the garage, Friedrich. We'll talk there.'

The two brothers were Jews from the Scheunenviertel, a slum district in the centre of Berlin with a substantial Jewish population from Eastern Europe and, before the Nazis, one of the most feared neighbourhoods in the city, a place where few policemen ever dared to tread. To make an arrest, the cops from the Alex used to have to go in there in substantial numbers, and sometimes with an armoured car. That was how the brothers had been arrested the first time, after a series of burglaries carried out in Berlin's biggest and best hotels, including the Adlon. It was said that they'd even burgled Hitler's suite at the Kaiserhof just before he became chancellor of Germany, and stolen his gold pocket watch and some love letters, but it was probably just one of the many stories about the Krauss brothers that had helped to make them notorious. Where Adolf Hitler was concerned, truth was a concept that only a Cretan would have recognized, and I suspect even he'd long forgotten where he'd hidden it. After Franz and Erich Sass – two Berlin bank robbers from the 1920s whose careers had reportedly inspired them – the Krauss brothers had been the most famous career criminals in Germany, and their burglary of the police museum at the Alex to recover their own tools made them almost legendary. They were small and dark and immensely strong but after several months in Dachau the clothes they were wearing were at least two sizes too big. They'd changed in the back of the truck and their prison clothes, with green triangles signifying they were career criminals, were still in their hands as if they didn't know what to do with them or didn't dare to throw them away.

I had an idea they were originally from Poland, where their father had been a famous rabbi, but if they were still religious it wasn't obvious; they were tough-looking men whose skill was not unlocking the secrets of the Zohar and the Kabbalah, but other people's safes. It was said that they could open a gnat's arse with a paper clip and that the gnat wouldn't even notice.

'That's a York,' said Joseph Krauss, inspecting the safe. 'From Pennsylvania, America. You don't see many American nuts like that in Germany. Last one of these I saw was in a jeweler's shop on Unter den Linden. A better shop than this one, too. Of course, that was when we still stole from Jewish businesses, but we gave that up when you Nazi *momzers* started doing it, too. Now, it could be a three-number combination, or a four. But you have to hope it's a three, which will take less effort to puzzle. I could drill it, of course, but that will take a lot more time and besides you have to drill it in the right place, and to do that you need to have seen the other side of the door and studied the mechanics of the lock. Maybe you'll find some other *shmegegge to* drill it for you. But he might not know where to drill and leave it *ongepotchket* and then you might never get it open.' Joseph Krauss shook his head and looked sad. 'Not that you do have to drill it, like I say. But I tell you honestly, the talent needed to open this safe *by feel* is rare. There are maybe three people in the whole of Europe who could puzzle it to order and my brother Karl is one of them. All he needs is that rubber mallet on the wall, in case it needs a good *zetz*. But that's not your main problem, Commissar.'

I nodded. 'I know. Assistant Korsch told me. You don't trust us to let you go after you've cracked the nut.'

'S'right. No offence, Commissar. You're both from the same *Kiez* as us, I can tell. Berliners are not like Bavarians. These people are like mud. But you're not going to make *schlemiels* of us. What's to stop you from sending us straight back to Dachau when we've cracked it? I tell you honestly, Commissar, it's been driving the two of us crazy. What to do? It's a real *tsutcheppenish*. You need us enough to say you'll pay our price, but we don't trust you enough to pay it when we've done the job. How can we do business like this? Without trust? Impossible. Isn't that right, Karl?'

But Karl Krauss was already giving himself the safecracker's manicure – brushing the ends of his fingers on the sleeve of his ill-fitting suit. 'I'd love to help you gentlemen,' he said. 'I tell you honestly, I could use the practice. It's been a while since I cracked a nut. I've missed it, so I have. But my brother is right. There's no basis here for trust.' He pulled a sad face, as if a deal was still a long way off for us. 'What's in there, anyway? Maybe if you told us. You must figure something important, otherwise you'd never have brought us here. All this way. At such short notice. And with such important people oiling our way out of that horrible place. General Heydrich, no less. Piorkowski looked like he was going to shit when he heard that man's *geshaltn* name.'

'Alex Piorkowski is the camp commandant at Dachau,' explained Korsch. 'A real bastard, if you ask me.'

'The man's a golem,' said Joe Krauss. 'A monster.'

'Look,' I said, 'I'll tell you honestly, gentlemen, I have absolutely no idea what's inside the nut. But I'm hoping what's in there will help prove that a local Nazi official was corrupt. He's dead but there could be evidence in there that will take a few others down with him. Papers, documents, ledgers, that's what I'm hoping for. But if there's any money or jewellery in there, it's yours. To keep. All of it. That and the Maserati sports car parked in the street. You can drive it anywhere you like. And I give you my word that we won't come after you. Or prevent your exit. You can hear me make the call to the border police to let you through. If necessary I'll even drive you there myself.'

'I'm liking this more now.' Karl Krauss shrugged. 'That red Italian job? It's a nice car. But even in Italy it's just a *noodge*. Not a car for *gonifs* like us. We've never been the kind to flash the money around when we had it. That's how you get pinched. We *gay avek* in a car like that and the whole world sees, and hears, too, probably. A military brass band couldn't make more noise than that car. So if we do this job for you we'll take the beer truck. Who notices such a thing in this part of the world?'

'Then that's agreed. The truck is yours.'

'But suppose there's nothing in the safe. Which means you're disappointed. What then, Commissar? You'll still let us go? It's difficult, like my brother Joe says. To have all this trouble for nothing.'

'Give him the keys to the truck now,' I told Korsch. 'And the car. Take both, for all I care. Drive in opposite directions. But please open that safe. You can be halfway to Italy in the time it takes for me to get over my disappointment. Not that I pay much attention to things like that these days. To be disappointed you've got to believe in something in the first place, and I haven't believed in anything of late. And certainly very little since 1933. The only reason I'm still a cop is not because I believe in the law or a moral order but because the Nazis wanted it that way. They had me back because they need a glove puppet they can use to ask the wrong questions, at the right time. Which makes me as bad as them, probably.'

'Listen to the police commissar, Karl,' said Joe Krauss. 'And we're the ones who were sent to Dachau. Can you believe it?'

'He's a real contradiction, and no mistake.'

'Have you got guns?' asked Joe.

'We're coppers, not Boy Scouts.'

'Let's see them.'

Korsch and I each pulled out a Walther PPK and tried to hold them in a way that wouldn't intimidate the brothers.

'So if you hand over the magazines, then maybe we'll feel a bit more comfortable,' said Joe. 'For safekeeping, you might say. We'll feel safer that way. My brother doesn't like working when there are guns around. Especially when he doesn't have one himself.'

'All right.' I turned the Walther upside down, thumbed the release catch, and then worked the slide to drop the last round from the barrel. I pressed the spare round into the mag and then handed it to Joe Krauss. Korsch did the same.

'That's more *haymish*,' he said, and pocketed the magazines. 'All right. We'll do it. Not because we trust you, Commissar. But because you're an honest fool and it's lucky for you that you have an honest fool's face. Isn't that right, Karl?'

'You're right, Joe. Honestly, only a fool would work for the Nazis and think there's not a high price to be paid for mere survival. But I suspect you know this already.' He nodded firmly. 'So let's get on with it, shall we? All I need is a pencil and paper and that rubber mallet. But it's not to hit the safe. It's to hit my brother on the head and knock some sense into him when you betray us after all.'

Karl Krauss knelt down beside the York and took hold of the dial and pressed his face to the door. 'So,' he whispered, 'we start with the mark at the top of the dial in the twelve o'clock position. Now we keep turning to the right and going very slowly we feel for the drop. It doesn't matter what order we get them in yet, all we're doing now is just feeling for the drop, see? And there's one right away on zero. There usually is. Most people like zeroes. It reflects their own life expectations.

Of course, if we have got more than one zero, then this complicates matters.'

Joe wrote the number on Korsch's notepad and waited as his brother explored the feeling in the dial for the next number. I smiled. He looked like any German listening, illegally, to the BBC on the radio.

While the brothers worked on the safe I took Friedrich Korsch outside and explained how the Linz Gestapo had tried to arrest me, and what I'd recently discovered at the house of Udo Ambros.

'Udo Ambros couldn't be more dead if he was Hindenburg's great-grandfather. Most of his head is sticking to the wall like the kitchen clock. Someone tried hard to make it look like suicide by shotgun. Left a nice confession for us on the mantelpiece, which was so neatly written it looked like a telegram. Hardly the work of someone who was getting ready to blow his own head off. I've seen enough real suicides to know a murder when I smell one. And this one is Limburger cheese.'

'Hey, talking of suicide, that yid eye specialist you were asking about, Dr Karl Wasserstein? Threw himself into the Isar last Saturday morning wearing his Military Merit Cross and drowned. The Munich cops found a note on his surgery door, which they let me have. I think they had orders from on high not to tell your friend Frau Troost. But if you ask me, that's another suspicious suicide. Who the fuck ends his life on a Saturday morning? Monday morning I could understand. But not a Saturday.'

Korsch laughed bitterly and handed the note to me, and I put it in my pocket to give to Gerdy later on; maybe. In Germany, disappointment was contagious and often came with consequences. I certainly wasn't about to squander her willingness to help me in my inquiry with some premature candour regarding the fate of her friend.

'Anyway,' he continued, 'it seems that he may have got his doctor's licence back, but only for general practice. Not for ophthalmology.'

'So maybe it was a suicide note after all.'

'Maybe. Anyway, the poor bastard said he thought his life had lost its meaning. Because he couldn't look at people's eyes.'

'Nobody looks anyone in the eye these days. Not if they can help it.'

'It would be like you being prevented from being a cop anymore, I guess.'

'Try me, Friedrich. The day I can walk away from this bloody life, you won't find me heading for the nearest river to drown my sorrows. I'll be at the lakes with a bottle of spiritual ointment, drinking it up in a park in Pankow like a good *Bolle* boy.'

'Maybe I'll join you, boss. I was born near that park. Schönholzer Heide. Tschaikowskistrasse, 60.'

'Then that makes us practically related. I know that building. Grey building near the bus stop? I had a cousin who lived there.'

'Every apartment building in Berlin is grey and near a bus stop.'

'Small world, isn't it?'

'It is until you have to catch the bus.'

CHAPTER 41

April 1939

I almost couldn't believe it when Karl Krauss turned the little handle and opened a heavy steel door that creaked like a lock-up in the basement of the Alex.

'Didn't I tell you?' said Joe proudly. 'My brother Karl is an artist. That man could top the bill at the German Opera. Just look at that door, Commissar, and then remember what it means to crack a nut like this. Drilled or puzzled, this is difficult. You appreciate that now, don't you?'

Joe Krauss was right about the mechanism. The inside of the door looked like a complicated toy or maybe even the workings of my own coin-operated mind. Not that I was paying much attention to that or even to what he said. I was too busy looking at all the money stacked in the safe. Even the ledger I could see on the bottom shelf didn't distract me as much as the cash. I selected a thick wad of twenties and held it up to my nose and riffled it like a pack of playing cards. I shook my head and said, 'There must be a thousand reichsmarks in this little bundle alone.'

'You have a keen sense of smell,' said Karl Krauss.

His brother Joe was already counting up the other bundles.

'I make it twenty thousand marks,' he said. 'A tidy little sum.'

'It's not so little,' murmured his brother. 'With money like this a man could buy himself a new life. Several new lives. One after the other. And all of them good.'

I tossed the wad of cash I'd been sniffing like a cocaine addict to Korsch, grabbed the ledger from the safe, and began to turn the marbled pages as if the money were of no account. There were names, alphabetically listed, and there were addresses, and there were records of what looked like payments made over several years. A few names I even recognized; they belonged to people I'd met, which augured well. I guessed that the contents were the long form of the notebook Hermann Kaspel had listed among Flex's personal effects, and which had been stolen.

'And did you find what you were looking for, Commissar?' asked Joe Krauss.

'To be honest, I'm not sure yet.'

'Are you disappointed?'

'No, I don't think so.'

It wasn't the kind of evidence that provides a neat library finish to a good detective story. Even though I say so myself, it lacked drama – real evidence rarely looks at all significant – and it wasn't the sort of thing to fill a man with much professional pride, but still, what was in the ledger had the look of something important. Although not as important as the money. That's the thing about money, especially a large quantity of money: it commands not just respect but attention. The cash in the safe was on everyone's mind now. The Krauss brothers were looking at me suspiciously, each asking himself if I was going to keep my end of the bargain. Friedrich Korsch was thinking exactly the same thing. He took me by the elbow and led me to the opposite end of the garage, where he spoke in the sort of hushed tones that would only have made the brothers even more certain that they were going to be double-crossed by the police. And they didn't look as if they were going to take this quietly.

'When you told them they could keep any cash in the safe,' he said, 'I thought it might be a few hundred reichsmarks. A thousand at the most.'

'So did I.'

'But twenty thousand reichsmarks, boss. That's serious money.'

'I always thought so. It's just as well it's not mine to give away, otherwise I might be feeling seriously depressed now at the prospect.'

He lit us both a cigarette, handed me one, and smoked his own nervously.

'You're not seriously considering actually handing it over? To them?'

'I am, Friedrich. Don't you think they could use a fresh start? After Dachau? A good meal and new suits at the very least. Nice clothes cost money in Italy. To say nothing of new lives. I wouldn't mind one of those myself. Maybe I can persuade them to take me with them. I could use a nice holiday in Italy.'

'Be serious, boss. Have you considered the possibility that some of this cash – I don't know, maybe most of it – that it belongs to Martin Bormann? I mean, it stands to reason some of it might be Bormann's, doesn't it? If Karl Flex was his bagman? This might be the proceeds of some of his local rackets. In which case—'

'That's very true,' I said.

'Bormann's not going to be very pleased when he finds out that you gave this money to – to anyone, let alone a couple of heebs.'

'So we'd best not tell him. In my limited experience he's not the kind of man who takes bad news at all well.'

'All right. Well, then, please consider this, boss. If that ledger contains evidence of any corrupt payments, and Bormann finds out you have it, then he'll conclude that maybe you also have all the money. Money that's maybe recorded in there. He'll figure you kept it for yourself. That we kept it. You and me. We could get into a lot of trouble here. They send bent cops to Dachau these days. I've just been there and I'm not at all keen to go back.'

'Then we'd better make sure it stays a secret, hadn't we? Look, Friedrich, a deal's a deal in my book. Without these two heebs, we'd be picking our teeth. I don't care about Bormann's money. I almost hope he does ask me about it. I want to see his farmer's fat face if he does. Maybe I'll tough it out and tell him the safe was open when we got here. That someone else must have stolen it. That there was no money in here. And then what will he do? Torture me?'

'It's not you I mind being tortured. It's me.'

'Spoken like a true German. But with any luck this ledger will help us find the murderer and Martin Bormann will be so damned grateful he'll forget all about this money. Keep in mind that it's Hitler's birthday soon. And by the way, remind me to buy him a nice gift.'

Korsch sighed with exasperation and looked away for a moment. It was my turn to grab him by the arm.

'Look, Friedrich, twenty thousand is nothing beside what they already spent on that goddamn tea house. From what I heard from Hermann Kaspel, it was hundreds of millions. The place looks like a pocket version of Neuschwanstein Castle and is almost as crazy. If Hitler gets spooked about coming back here because of what happened on the Berghof terrace, then all those millions they spent on the tea house and new roads and underground tunnels and compulsory purchases were wasted. And Bormann's career as the Leader's number one Obersalzberg sycophant is over. Honestly? Twenty thousand is the riches of Croesus to you and me but to Bormann, it's yesterday's sauerkraut. So yes, I'm going to keep my word. It's about time someone did in Berchtesgaden.'

I went back to the Krauss brothers, who had collected the money into an old leather satchel and were anxiously awaiting the outcome of my discussion with Korsch. I expect they would have fought us to the death for all that cash; I know I would have done. That was another consideration I hadn't mentioned to Korsch. They might have been in Dachau but each brother was still as strong as a bull. With big money like that to be had and a getaway vehicle parked just outside, I didn't doubt that in a fight these two career criminals could easily beat two unarmed policemen. Maybe even kill us. With three other murders in Berchtesgaden and Obersalzberg, another two wouldn't look out of place. In a way, that would end up suiting everyone; they'd be arrested eventually, and all five murders would be pinned on them. A couple of Jewish criminals? In Nazi Germany they were tailor-made to take the rap for something like that. I almost felt like suggesting it.

'So,' said Karl. 'Do the Jews get screwed by the Nazis again? Or is the *handl* we made before still good?'

'The money's yours,' I said. 'And the beer truck.'

'We've talked it over,' said Joe, 'and we're going to leave behind two thousand reichsmarks. For the sake of appearances. We've decided we wouldn't like you to get into trouble. Of course, what you do with that cash is your own affair.'

I smiled at the insolence of what was being suggested. 'Just get the hell out of here before I change my mind. I hate to see so much cash walking out of here in such bad company.'

'We also want to give you this,' said Joe, and handed me a manila envelope. 'It was hidden behind the money.'

'What is it?'

'Two passbooks for a Swiss bank,' said Joe. 'We were going to keep them if you didn't let us have the money. But since you did, they're yours. I hope they help you find what you're looking for.'

I glanced inside the envelope and nodded. 'Thanks.'

'I won't say you're a good man, Commissar,' said Karl Krauss, 'but you're a man of your word. Who can say such a thing in Berchtesgaden these days? One word of advice. From one German to another. What you were saying earlier? About not believing in a moral order? Just remember this, Commissar Gunther. A righteous man falls down seven times, and gets up again. You persevere. That's Torah.'

CHAPTER 42

April 1939

Friedrich Korsch and I watched the Krauss brothers drive slowly away from Berchtesgaden in the Paulaner beer truck. It looked as if they were driving south towards the Austrian border with twenty thousand reichsmarks in their pockets, but looks can be deceptive.

'It was a clever idea,' I said. 'Bringing them down from Munich in that truck. With any luck, no one will ever know they were here.'

'That was Heydrich's idea. His office telephoned the Paulaner Brewery in Munich and ordered them to let me have a beer truck. I'm not sure if they're expecting to get it back or not. But when the SD tells you to hand over a beer truck, you do what you're told, right? Even if that means supplying one that's still full of beer.'

'It figures. Heydrich was Gestapo boss in Munich before he took charge of the SD. If he ever learned how to make friends, then maybe he still has some.'

'I'm not sure what I'm going to tell them now the truck has gone. And, more important, their beer.'

'Heydrich's problem. Not yours. He'll probably just tell them it was stolen. What can you expect of Jews? Something sensitive, like that.'

'You know, I almost envy those two kikes,' said Korsch. 'Going to Italy with all that money. Think of those lovely Italian women with big tits and huge arses. I can't think of a better way to spend twenty thousand marks.'

'Me neither. Of course, it's just a guess, but I wouldn't be at all surprised if they turn around and drive northwest. Back to Berlin. Maybe even dump the truck and make for the railway station here in Berchtesgaden. It's what I'd do if it was me. After all, would you trust the police to keep their word if you were two kikes with twenty thousand in cash in your coat pockets?'

'Since you put it like that, no, I would not.'

'Do the opposite thing from what's expected. That's the key to survival when you're on the run. Besides, they'd only stand out in Italy in a way they don't stand out in Germany. Even today. It's the last place anyone would think to look for them. Especially now that they know we're going to be telling everyone they went to Italy.'

'They'd stand out anywhere. Half the time I didn't even know what they were saying. They're the kind of Jews who make you glad you're a German.'

'All that Eastern European Yiddish crap? They were laying it on with a baker's chocolate knife. For their own amusement. No, really, they were twisting your cord, Friedrich. They're not like that at all. That's how they were successful burglars for so long. Because they can blend in when and where they want. Of course, in that respect they're like any other Jews in Germany, very easy to spot. Most heebs look like you and me.'

'Maybe so, but I still think Germany's finished for the Jews.'

'Let's just hope it's not finished for the Germans, too. But Berlin isn't Germany. That's why Hitler hates us so much. If you know the right people and have enough money, a man – even a Jew – can still disappear in Berlin. The Krauss brothers are smart. It's where I would go if I thought the police were coming after me and I had all that coal in my pockets. I certainly wouldn't go to Italy. Not anymore. Not since the Duce started blaming his troubles on the Jews, too.'

Korsch gave me a sideways look and I could tell what he was thinking. I pulled a face.

'They *are* smart,' I said. 'It's only in stupid little towns like Berchtesgaden that people believe in all that subhuman horse-shit that Julius Streicher peddles in *Der Stürmer*. You know that as well as I do. There was no one smarter than Bernhard Weiss. Best chief of Kripo we ever had. I learned more from that Jew than I did from my own mother. What irritates me most about the Nazis is not that I'm supposed to hate the Jews, Friedrich. And I don't. Hate them. No more than I hate anyone else these days. What I find a lot harder to deal with is that I'm supposed to love Germans and everything German. That's a tall order for any Berliner. Especially now that Hitler's in charge.'

We returned the red Maserati to the garage, locked up, and took the ledger and the bankbooks to the nearby Hofbräuhaus, where, at a quiet corner table under a gloomy picture of the Leader, we ordered tall beers and long sausage with mustard and sauerkraut and, after paying the homage that was due to a waitress with a low-cut Bavarian-style blouse and cleavage that looked like a celebrated geological feature, we settled down to our rather less compelling financial study. Most of the men in the beer house were smoking pipes and wearing smelly leather shorts and trying to pretend they weren't interested in the local geology; it was obvious that they were but they were as slow as ancient glaciers and had less chance with the waitress than a deaf kid with scabies. If I'd not been on a case myself I'd have given her some city-smart story about how she was special and how I was in love with her already and maybe she would have believed it, because that is usually all it takes these days. In Germany love is as rare as a Jew with a telephone. And Hitler wasn't the only man who could be cynical. Meanwhile, I discovered that the bankbooks contained a more plausible story that was much easier to understand and relate than what was in the ledger. I could almost see the silent movie that would have illustrated it.

'So,' I said, 'it would seem that as regular as shit, on the first Monday of every month, Karl Flex took that lovely red Maserati out of the Rothman garage and drove all the way from here to St. Gallen in Switzerland, where he paid lots of cash into two separate accounts at the Wegelin Bank & Co., which, according to this passbook, purports to be the oldest in the country. One of the passbooks is in Karl Flex's name and the other is in Martin Bormann's. And will you look at these amounts? Christ, I never felt so poor until I came to Berchtesgaden. Karl Flex had over two hundred thousand Swiss francs in his personal account. But Bormann's account has millions. Can you believe it? With this amount of money the Nazis really don't need to conquer Poland by force of German arms. They could buy all the damn living space Hitler says we need for half of what Bormann's got put aside for a rainy day. Frankly, I wish he would; then maybe the Poles wouldn't put up as much of a fight.'

I showed Korsch the bottom line in the second NSDAP passbook and he whistled quietly over the creamy head on his white beer. 'This explains the hotel bill we found in the car,' he said. 'Remember? The Hotel Bad Horn? On Lake Constance? Lake Constance isn't very far from St. Gallen. Maybe fifteen or twenty minutes according to that map we found in the Maserati.'

'Right. So after he paid the cash into the bank in St. Gallen, he must have driven to Lake Constance, checked into a suite, eaten an expensive dinner, and then driven back here to Germany the very next day. Maybe took that missing whore from P-Barracks and made a nice weekend of it. Who knows? Maybe he left her there. Meanwhile, the cash kept on rolling in. Did you ever think you were in the wrong job?'

'Sure. It's an occupational hazard for any cop. Things always look better for crooks who are making serious money.'

'Especially when the crooks are in government.'

'Well, who knew? When they were elected. That they were crooks, I mean.'

'Pretty much everyone who didn't vote for them, Friedrich. And I suspect quite a few of the stupid fools who did. Which only makes it worse.'

'Who's this second signatory on the Bormann account? Max Amann?'

'I think he's chairman of the Reich Media Chamber. Whatever that is.'

'Must be close to Bormann.'

'I guess so.'

'Just seeing these two passbooks scares the shit out of me,' said Korsch. 'I don't mind admitting it. You know, it's like I was saying before, boss. What happens when Bormann wants his passbook? To have access to his money.'

'According to Bormann's passbook, there are three passbooks for that account. This one, and two others. Presumably the others are in Bormann's possession. Which explains why he's not asked about this one yet. Who knows? Perhaps he never will.'

'That's a comforting thought. But either way, Bormann's got to worry that if you do find his bankbook you're going to give it to General Heydrich. And that Heydrich will use it against him. It's exactly the sort of thing Heydrich would do. He collects dirt like a schoolboy's fingernails.'

'Even Heydrich isn't mad enough to believe he could blackmail Martin Bormann. Especially now, with another war looming.'

Actually, I wasn't so sure about this; Heydrich had just enough nerve to blackmail the devil himself, and collect on his menaces, too. I told myself it was the only reason I was working for the general, and sometimes I even believed my own story – that I really was tired of being a cop in Nazi Germany and craved a quiet life in rural obscurity, as a village policeman, perhaps. Of course, the truth was very different. Mostly you just do what you're good at, even if the people you're doing it for are no good themselves. Sometimes you want to kill them but most of the time you know you're never going to do it. In Germany that's what we call a successful career. I opened the big leather ledger and began to turn the stiff pages. But beyond recognizing a few names and addresses, I had no real clue what it all amounted to, apart from a great deal of money.

'It would seem that the details of what Flex and his masters were up to are in *this* book. Although for the life of me I'm not sure what I'm looking at. I never was very good with figures that don't wear pretty lingerie and ask me to buy them a beer with some red syrup in it. It seems clear to me that a lot of people around here were handing over sums of money quite regularly to Karl Flex. But it's hard to say exactly why they did that. Not yet, anyway. A lot of these names are marked with the letters *P*, *Ag*, or *B*, which must have meant something to Flex but it means nothing to me. Flex was at the money end of some sort of local racket that wasn't anything to do with compulsory pur-chase orders. These are people paying smaller, regular sums to Flex, not the Obersalzberg Administration paying them for their cuckoo-clock houses.' I shrugged. 'You know, this sort of thing reminds me of the good old days when there were criminal rings who charged people protection. The trouble is, the only people you need protection from these days is the government. They're the biggest criminal ring in history.'

Korsch turned the ledger to look at it and nodded.

'So here's a thought,' he said after a while. 'Why don't we just pick someone out from all these names and go and ask them? That fat lawyer, for example. Dr Waechter. The one who bought Rothman's premises? I see his name is down here in the ledger with a *B* and an *Ag* in his column. Let's go back there and just ask the bastard, straight out. And if he doesn't tell us, we should drive him straight to Dachau and threaten to leave him there. I know the road now. And I bet that Captain Piorkowski would go along with it, too. He'd just assume that Heydrich wanted things that way. Believe me, that bastard lawyer will start talking the minute he smells the not-so-fresh air and sees the friendly motto on the gate.'

'You really didn't like him, did you, Friedrich? Waechter.'

'Did you?'

'No. But I'm prejudiced. I never met a German lawyer yet who I didn't want to defenestrate from the sixth floor of the Alex.'

'You scared him once. You could scare him again. We both could. With any luck he'll shit himself on Piorkowski's office floor.'

'Much as I would like to put the fear of Heydrich up Waechter's fat arse I'd prefer to have half an idea of what this ledger means first. One thing I've learned since coming back to work for Kripo is that it's never a good idea to ask questions in Nazi Germany until you know what some of the answers are. Especially after that case last November. Karl Maria Weisthor. All that work to catch a murderer who turned out to be Himmler's best friend. What a waste of time. Himmler hated me for solving that case. I told you he kicked me on the shin, didn't I?'

'Several times. I'd love to have seen that.'

'It wasn't so funny at the time. Although I think Heydrich and Arthur Nebe enjoyed it. Besides, Waechter might tell Bormann and we'd lose possession of our Bible. Which is what we have here, I suspect. That's our edge. Even if we don't know what these people were paying for. No, right now we need someone to help us to decode what's here in Flex's holy book. God's high priest, perhaps.'

'There's only one true God in Obersalzberg. And Bormann is his prophet.'

'Then if not a priest perhaps a high priestess to help us understand the holy writ. A local Cassandra.'

'Gerdy Troost.'

I nodded. 'Exactly. She's not going to be pleased when I tell her what's become of her medical friend. When she finds out he drowned himself in the Isar she might just be ready to tell me everything she knows – which, I suspect, is quite a lot.'

'What's this woman like, boss? Pretty?'

'No,' I said firmly. 'Not particularly.'

'Well, that never stopped you before, did it?'

'Listen, I'm glad about that. I'd hate to be tempted to do something indiscreet in Hitler's house. If he dislikes smoking and drinking it's hard to imagine what he'd make of two people at it like rabbits in the guest room. For all I know she's the Leader's girlfriend. Although it's hard to imagine what they might get up to that wouldn't include a two-hour speech at the Sportpalast instead of dinner at Horcher's.'

'You'd think he'd pick someone pretty,' said Korsch. 'I mean, he could have almost any woman in Germany.'

'Maybe he likes good conversation over his tea and cake.'

'I can put up with a clever girl as long as she's pretty.'

'I'll let them know. Me, I'm a man of simple tastes, Friedrich. I don't mind what they look like just as long as they look like Hedy Lamarr. This one. Frau Troost. She's a designer, she says. As if that's unusual in a woman. In my experience they've all got their designs. Most of them never tell you what those are until it's too late.' I was thinking of my last girlfriend as I spoke. I still wasn't sure what Hilde had wanted, only that it hadn't included me.

'What happened to her old man, then?'

'Paul Troost? All I know is that he's dead. And that he was much older. Which makes me wonder about their marriage. Gerdy – she's not like most women. I don't think she likes men very much. Just Hitler. And I'm not sure he even counts in the man department. He probably doesn't think so. Not on the evidence of the tea house on the Kehlstein. It's the kind of place where gods go to plan the conquest of this world and the next.'

Korsch nodded. 'Well, if your friend Gerdy is disposed to foretell the future, see if she can predict if there's going to be another war.'

'You don't need Cassandra for that, Friedrich. Even I can tell there's going to be another war. It's the only possible explanation for Adolf Hitler. He just wants it that way. He always did.'

CHAPTER 43

October 1956

Hugging the shadows of the shop doorway like a nervous cat, I watched Friedrich Korsch as he barked orders at his men in front of the brightly lit corner bar in Freyming-Merlebach. So close to the historic border nobody would have paid much attention to a group of men speaking German – including one particular man wearing leather shorts. The Saarland might have become an administrative part of France but, from what I had read in the papers, few people bothered to *parler Français* there. Even in Freyming-Merlebach there were signs for German beer and cigarettes on the steamy window of the bar and just to see these made me feel a little closer to home and safety; it was ages since I'd necked a Schloss Bräu or puffed on a Sultan or a Lasso. A long time had passed since Germany, and its old familiar habits, had felt so near to my heart.

Korsch was wearing a short, black belted leather coat that I felt sure he'd owned almost twenty years before, when he'd still been a young Kripo detective in Berlin. But the leather flat cap he was wearing looked to have been more recently acquired and added a proletarian, almost Leninish touch to his appearance, as if he was anxious to conform to the political realities of life in the new Germany, or at least in half of it. But it was his voice I recognized most: among Germans, the Berlin accent is considered one of the strongest and most abrasive in the language, and among

Berliners, the Kreuzberg accent is about as strong as Löwensenf mustard. Korsch's accent had been one of the things that had, perhaps, stopped him from making commissar under the Nazis. Senior Berlin detectives like Arthur Nebe – who was the son of a Berlin schoolteacher – and like Erich Lieberman von Sonnenberg, an aristocrat, and even Otto Trettin had always regarded Friedrich Korsch as a bit of a Mackie Knife, which wasn't helped by the fact that he always carried an eleven-centimetre switchblade in his pocket, as a backup for the broom-handle Mauser he favoured. Kreuzberg was the kind of place where even grandmothers carried a switchblade or at least a long hat pin. In truth, however, Korsch was a well-educated man with his *Abitur* who enjoyed music and the theatre, and collected stamps for a hobby. I wondered if he still owned the twenty-pfennig stamp of Beethoven that lacked a perforation and which he'd told me would one day be valuable. Were communists allowed to do something as bourgeois as make money from selling a rare stamp? Probably not. Profit was always going to be the ideological doorjamb on which communism stubbed its ugly toe.

I pressed myself back against the door as the Stasi man in the leather shorts walked towards me, lighting a French cigarette. In the dusk the cigarette lighter also lit up a boyish face with a deep scar that meandered off his forehead and down his cheek like a length of unruly hair; somehow it missed an eye that was as blue as an African lily and probably just as poisonous. Halfway across the street the man stopped and turned as Korsch finished what he was saying with the words 'damned idiots', spoken loudly and with real venom.

Then he said, 'That was the comrade-general I was speaking to on the telephone. He told me his contact in the French police reported that a man answering Gunther's description was spotted a few kilometres west of here, in a place called Puttelange-aux-Lacs, less than two hours ago. The French police lost him, of course. Idiots. They couldn't catch a fucking apple if it fell off a tree. And he may have stolen a car – a green Renault Frégate – to help make his escape. In which case he could well be here by now. And if he is here it's my guess he'll dump the Renault and try and make it into the Saar on foot. Through here or one of these other shitty little towns along what used to be the border.'

'That's a nice little car,' said another Stasi man, echoing my own opinion.

'But it looks like Mielke was right about this place,' Korsch continued. 'We're to keep an eye out in case he tries to cross over tonight. Which means constant vigilance. If I find one of you bastards sneaking in some shut-eye when you should be looking out for Gunther, I'll shoot you myself.'

The news that Mielke had a man – possibly more than one – in the French police didn't surprise me. The country was riddled with communists and it was less than a decade since the French Section of the Workers' International – the SFIO – had participated in the provisional government of the liberation. Stalin might have been dead but the French Communist Party – the PCF – led by Thorez and Duclos, remained doctrinaire, hard-line Stalinists and none of the red Franzis, even the ones in the police, would have had a second thought about collaboration with the Stasi. But it did surprise me that the information being provided was up-to-the-minute and accurate. In itself this was alarming. But that the Stasi were devoting more effort to my elimination than even I could have imagined was worse; Erich Mielke wasn't the kind of man to leave loose ends, and of course I was as loose an end as you could find outside of a string factory.

'And if we do find him, sir?'

Korsch considered this for less than a second. 'We kill him, of course. Make it look like a suicide. String him up in the woods and leave the body for the local cops. Then go home. So there's your incentive, boys. As soon as the bastard's dead we can all go and get ourselves drunk somewhere and then head back to Germany.'

I heard the hobnailed footsteps of someone walking up the dimly lit street and, a few seconds later, a man wearing a blue boiler jacket and carrying a large shopping bag with a baguette poking out of the top like a submarine's periscope hove slowly into view on the same side as the dark doorway I was standing in. Of course, even in the dwindling light he saw me immediately, paused for a moment, allowed his face to register some surprise, muttered a quiet '*Bonsoir*', and then carried on walking until he came abreast of the Stasi man wearing the shorts and the long woollen stockings. It wasn't unusual in this rural part of France for men to wear *lederhosen*. Leather shorts were popular with Alsatian farmers because they are comfortable, hardwearing, and don't show the dirt. The man with the shopping bag would probably have ignored the Stasi man in the shorts but for the fact that the German stepped into his way with the obvious intent of checking that this was not me attempting to make my escape. I couldn't blame him for that; the man in the blue jacket looked more like me than I did.

'Yes?' he said. 'What do you want, monsieur?'

The man in shorts fired up his lighter and held it in front of the other man's face like someone exploring a cave. 'Nothing, Grandad,' he said. 'I'm sorry, I mistook you for someone else. Relax. Here, have a cigarette.'

The old man took one from the offered packet and placed it in his mouth. The lighter flared again. If the old man mentioned having seen me in the doorway further down the street I was dead.

'Who is it you're looking for? Perhaps I can help you find him. I know everyone in Freyming-Merlebach. Even one or two Germans.'

'Never mind,' said the Stasi man sharply. 'Forget it. It's not important.'

'Are you sure? You and your friends seem to be all over this town tonight. Must be someone important.'

'Look, just mind your own business, right? Now fuck off before I lose patience with you.'

While this conversation was taking place I stepped quietly out of the doorway and started back down the street, intent on putting as much distance as possible between me and Mielke's men. Hoping the Stasi man would assume I had just come out of the door and ignore me, I walked quickly but calmly, like someone who was actually headed somewhere in particular. I even stopped to glance in the window of a *tabac* before continuing and I had reached the premises of the local funeral home at the bottom of the street when a light came on at a window immediately above me. It might as well have been a searchlight designed to defeat enemy nighttime manoeuvres and it marked me out like an actor on a stage. The next second there was a shout and then a pane of glass shattered near my head. I glanced around and saw the man in shorts levelling a pistol at me. I had been recognized. I didn't hear the second shot, which made me think he was using a silencer, but I certainly felt the bullet zip past my ear and, taking to my heels, I turned sharply left and ran for about twenty metres before, next to a hairdresser's shop, I spied a narrow patch of waste ground behind an overgrown metal fence. I climbed over it quickly, dropped into a tall bed of nettles, and ran as far as I could until I arrived at an old garage door. Fortunately it was not locked. I went inside, squeezed past a dusty motor car, closed the main door carefully behind me, kicked open the back door, which had been locked, and found myself in the concrete yard of someone's house. Some threadbare towels were drying on a washing line next to a small herb garden and these helped to screen my presence. A man was seated in a barely furnished parlour listening to a football match on the radio, which was loud enough to conceal the sound of me opening his own door and stepping quietly onto the brown

linoleum floor of his malodorous kitchen; this was easily refer-
able to a plate of half-eaten andouillettes that lay on the table.
If ever a sausage-loving German needed a good excuse to dislike
the French it was the pissy smell of an andouillette. It seemed to
me there was only one thing worse than that smell and it was the
stink of my own unwashed underwear. I paused for a moment
and then advanced slowly through the half-lit house, unnoticed
by the man still listening intently to the radio. I reached the
front door, opened it, glanced outside, and saw a man running
along the street. Guessing he must be Stasi, I shut the door and
tiptoed up the house stairs in the hope I might find somewhere
to hide. The main bedroom was easily identified and even more
stinky than the kitchen, but the spare one was clean and from
the look of it, rarely ever used. A picture of Philippe Pétain hung
on the wall; he was wearing a red kepi and a grey tunic and
seemed every inch the proud warrior; his moustache looked like
a prize chicken, which was also a very good description of the
French army he and Weygand had commanded in June 1940. I
went to the window and watched the street for ten or fifteen
minutes as a car drove slowly up and down; the occupants were
obviously looking for me. I could just make out Friedrich Korsch
wearing his eye patch in the front seat.

It was cold in the room, and I wrapped myself in a red blanket
I found on top of the wardrobe. After a while I slid underneath
the bed with only a chamber pot and a few toenails for company. I told myself I was probably better off where I was, at least
for a couple of hours. Gradually my heart slowed and eventually I closed my eyes and even slept a little. Not surprisingly I
dreamed I was being chased by a pack of slavering wolves who
were almost as ravenously hungry as I was. For some reason I
was dressed as Little Red Riding Hood. If only I'd listened to my
Grandmother Mielke and stayed strictly on the path.

When I awoke the radio was off and the whole house was in
darkness. I slid out from under the bed, used the chamber pot,

went to the window, and checked the street. There was no sign of my pursuers but that didn't mean they weren't around. I took the blanket and crept downstairs. A wall clock was ticking loudly in the tiny dining room. It sounded like someone chopping firewood. The smell persisted; the andouillettes were still on the kitchen table and overcoming my very real disgust I ate them, almost gagging as inevitably they reminded me of that chamber pot, and then helped myself to some bread to strangle the taste in my mouth. I drank a cup of cold instant coffee for the caffeine, which was almost as bad as the sausages, took a sharp knife from the drawer, slid it inside the leg of my sock, and then left the house.

The town was still in darkness and as deserted as if a Gestapo curfew had been in force. I would have to move carefully, like one of those French resistance fighters who were now the stuff of popular fiction. And probably always had been. Anyone moving around at this time of night would raise suspicion. I knew the old border was at the top of the hill but not much more. Somehow I had to find it and then some rough country where, for a while, I might go to ground like a hunted fox. Moving from one little doorway to another as if I were delivering letters, I made my way stealthily up the streets of Freyming-Merlebach and through the town. Finally I saw a long line of conifer trees and knew instinctively that this was Holy Germany and sanctuary. I was just about to run across the road when I caught the strong smell of a French cigarette and paused long enough to see the man in the leather shorts seated in a bus shelter. I knew I would be fortunate to avoid being shot this time. Stasi men were always excellent marksmen, and with his silencer this one was probably an experienced assassin. Korsch would have taken a strip off him for missing me with any shots he fired. Maybe even put another scar on his face with that switchblade. I'd been lucky twice and I didn't think I'd ever be that lucky again. Somehow I was going to have to get past this man, but I couldn't see how.

CHAPTER 44

April 1939

Heydrich's tall, smooth-faced adjutant, Hans-Hendrik Neumann, was waiting for us up at the Villa Bechstein. In his hand was a book about Karl Ferdinand Braun and the invention of the cathode ray tube, which served to remind me that Heydrich had a habit of picking clever people from a variety of different backgrounds to work for him. Maybe this included me. Neumann had driven down from Salzburg with an order from Heydrich that had absolutely nothing to do with finding Karl Flex's assassin and, in the wake of Kaltenbrunner's clumsy attempt to have me arrested, everything to do with imposing his absolute authority on the Security Service.

'These two comedians from Linz,' said Neumann. 'Where are they now?'

'In the jail cells beneath the Hotel Türken,' I said. 'I stabbed one of them with a piece of glass.'

'I'm afraid his situation is not about to improve very much. Heydrich has some important questions he wants put to them. Before we shoot them and send the bodies back to Linz.'

I shouldn't have been surprised at this news, but I was, and while I disliked the Gestapo intensely I didn't appreciate being the reason why two men were going to be shot. 'You're going to shoot them?'

'Not me. The local RSD can do it. That's what they're for.'

Neumann looked at Friedrich Korsch. 'You. Criminal Assistant Korsch, isn't it? Go and find the duty officer from the RSD and tell him to organize a firing squad for tomorrow morning.'

Korsch glanced back at me, and I nodded. Now wasn't the right time to speak up for the two men from Linz. He got up and went off to find the RSD duty officer.

'The general wants these men to be made an example,' said Neumann. 'Interfering with a police commissar from Kripo HQ carrying out Heydrich's express orders – that's you, in case you didn't recognize yourself – is treasonable. And of course Kaltenbrunner will get the message this sends. But first, we have to interrogate them and make sure that they have told us absolutely everything.'

'I don't think you'll get much more out of them than I did.'

'Nevertheless those are the general's orders. I'm to make them talk if I can. And then to shoot them both.'

'Be my guest. But I think they already told me all there is to know. Kaltenbrunner sent them. Surely it's all that's important here.'

From his trouser pocket Neumann took out an English punch and slipped it over his knuckles. Suddenly he looked like he meant business and I had a much clearer idea of why Heydrich kept him on as his adjutant. It wasn't just his brain. Sometimes buttons needed to be pressed and faces rearranged. He grinned cruelly. 'The general calls me his circuit breaker. On account of my background in electronics.'

Maybe it was a better joke when Heydrich made it but I doubted it. On the whole I didn't share the same sense of humour as Himmler's number two. And while I knew there was a streak of cruelty in me somewhere – it was impossible to have survived the trenches and not have one – on the whole I considered it was nearly always and very properly suppressed. But the Nazis seemed to revel in their cruelty.

'You'd probably call me all sorts of unpleasant names if I told you how very persuasive I can be,' said Neumann.

'No, not even if I thought so. But you tell me what the general wants to know and I'll tell you what I think.'

He frowned. 'These men would certainly have killed you, Gunther. I'd have thought you'd be quite glad to watch them receive a good beating.'

'I'm not the squeamish type, Captain. I've no love for either man. It's you I'm thinking of. Besides, when you've questioned as many suspects as I have you learn never to trust what a man spits out of his mouth when you've beaten it from him. Mostly it's just teeth and very little truth. There's all that and the fact that there's so much more happening here than the general ever dreamed of. Take my word for it. This business with Kalten-brunner is a sideshow. There's enough going on in Obersalzberg to put Martin Bormann in Heydrich's pocket for the next thousand years. I can promise you he won't be disappointed.'

Neumann shrugged and put away the brass knuckles. 'All right. I'm listening. But I'm afraid there's nothing you can say that's going to save these men from a firing squad. By the way, I think you ought to be there when we shoot them. It won't look right if you're not present.'

Rudolf Hess was down in Berchtesgaden having a meeting with Party officials at the local Reichs Chancellery, which meant we had the villa to ourselves. So we went and sat in front of the fire in the villa's drawing room. Wearing his shiny black boots and immaculate SS uniform, Neumann resembled something that had already been consumed by the flames, something heretical, something cured and apostate, like some modern Templar knight. With the SS, you always had the feeling that there was no limit to their zeal – that there was nothing they wouldn't do in the service of Adolf Hitler. With a war looking imminent, this was an alarming prospect. I threw a few logs onto the fire and drew my chair a bit closer to the pyre. It wasn't that

I was very cold, I just thought there was less chance of there being a listening device hidden in a blazing fireplace. Then, over coffee drawn from the urn on the refectory table underneath the window, I told Hans-Hendrik Neumann everything I had found out since coming to Berchtesgaden and Obersalzberg, and quite a bit more that I was still guessing at. He listened patiently, making notes in a little Siemens leather notebook. He stopped writing when I described the P-Barracks in Unterau.

Neumann grinned. 'You mean Martin Bormann is actually running a brothel down here?'

'Effectively, yes. Bormann ordered it to be set up for the exclusive benefit of the local workers from P&Z. The weekly administration was being handled by Karl Flex, Schenk, and Brandt, like all the other moneymaking schemes he has running down here. But on a day-to-day basis I believe the place is now being run by a German-speaking Czech girl called Aneta.'

'Now, that is interesting.' Neumann started writing again.

'Is it?'

'Aneta what?'

'Her surname? I have no idea.'

'It doesn't matter. I should like to meet this whore. As soon as possible. Perhaps you could drive me down there now.'

'I'm supposed to be running an investigation here, Captain. That's why Heydrich sent me. To find the killer so that Hitler can come here and celebrate his birthday in total confidence that he's safe. Remember?'

'Oh, surely. But I don't think this need take up too much of your valuable time, Gunther.' Neumann closed his notebook and stood up. 'Shall we?'

CHAPTER 45

April 1939

At the P-Barracks, on Gartenauer Insel in Unterau, the business was brisk and Captain Neumann and I had to wait until Aneta had finished satisfying one of her rock-faced clients before she was able to meet with us in the car. She was wearing a strong perfume but you could still smell the sweat of the man who'd been with her, and probably much else from him besides that I didn't care to think about. I had no idea what was on Neumann's mind until he opened his tight mouth and started to speak. Aneta sat in the backseat of the Mercedes with her hands in her lap, clutching a small handkerchief as if she was about to start crying. She was a slight but pretty girl, probably in her mid-twenties, blond, and green-eyed, with a cute dimple in her trembling chin; she was scared, of course. Terrified actually, but I couldn't blame her for that. It's not every day a black angel asks you to step into his car, and to his credit Neumann did his best to try to reassure her. He gave her a cigarette, ten marks, his limp hand – no wonder he needed the English punch – and his most winning smile. It was a charming side to the man I hadn't seen before.

'It's all right, my dear,' he said, lighting her cigarette with a silver Dunhill. 'You're not in any trouble. But there's something I'd like you to do for me. An important service.' He frowned, and then solicitously moved a strand of yellow hair from her recently

– and perhaps, hurriedly – lipsticked mouth. 'Don't worry. I'm not interested in you in that way, Aneta, I can assure you. I'm a happily married man with three children. Isn't that right, Commissar?'

'If you say so.'

'Well, I am. Now then, Aneta. I'm sorry – what's your surname?'

'Husák.'

'Your German is very good. Where did you learn it?'

'Mostly here, sir. In Berchtesgaden.'

'Really? By the way – do you have your papers with you?'

'Yes, sir.'

Aneta opened her bag and handed over a grey German State Visitors Pass. Neumann inspected the pass and then handed it to me.

'Keep that for now,' he said.

I opened the pass and looked at it. Aneta Husák was twenty-three years old. She looked younger in her picture. I put the pass in my pocket. I still had no idea what Neumann was planning.

'Have you ever done any photographic work? Any acting?'

'Acting? Yes. I was in a film once. A couple of years ago.'

'Excellent. What kind of film was it?'

'A Minette movie. In Vienna.'

A Minette movie was one featuring naked girls. I never minded looking at naked girls but the ones in Minette movies were always a little too uninhibited for my taste. A little inhibition is good for a man's psychology; it makes him think the girl might not do what she's doing with everyone.

'Even better,' said Neumann. 'Perhaps you can remember the film's title.'

'It was called *Saucy Secretary*. Please, sir, what's all this about?'

'Aneta, if you do this favour for me, you will be paid, handsomely, in cash, and you will get some nice new clothes. Whatever you want. A whole new wardrobe of beautiful clothes. All I require from you is that you come with me now and do exactly what I tell you. An acting job. I want you to pretend to be someone else. A lady. Can you do that?'

'I think so.'

'It shouldn't take more than a day – perhaps a day and a half. But you must ask no questions. Just do what you're told. Is that understood?'

'Yes, sir. May I ask, how much will I be paid, sir?'

'Good question. How does five hundred reichsmarks sound to you, Aneta?'

'It sounds wonderful, sir.'

'If you do this job well, there may be more. You could even be asked to Berlin, where you will get to stay in a nice expensive hotel and have whatever you want. Champagne. Delicious meals. You are Czech, aren't you? From Carlsbad.'

'Yes, sir. Do you know Carlsbad?'

Neumann started the car's engine.

'As a matter of fact I do,' he said. 'Only I think, now that Czechoslovakia is part of the Greater German Reich – since last year – we must learn to start calling that part of the world Bohemia, wouldn't you agree?'

'Yes, sir.'

'I like Bohemia better, don't you? It sounds so much more romantic than Czechoslovakia.'

'Yes it does,' she agreed. 'Like something from an old novel.'

'So do you like being part of the new Germany?'

'Yes, sir.'

'Good. I went to the spa there once. And stayed at the Grand-hotel Pupp. Marvellous place. Do you know it?'

'Everyone in Carlsbad knows the Pupp, sir. My mother worked there as a waitress for many years.'

'Then perhaps she and I met once.' Neumann smiled kindly. 'It's a small world, isn't it, Aneta?'

From the P-Barracks we drove southwest, to a quiet address in north Berchtesgaden where we parked outside a neat three-storey,

Alpine-style villa. Some SS men were waiting on the front lawn and saluted smartly as Neumann walked up the snow-covered path, followed by me and then Aneta. On the elaborate wooden porch Neumann produced a set of shiny, new-looking keys and let himself in through the front door. As well as a large portrait of Adolf Hitler, the whitewashed walls in the hallway were home to several sets of duelling sabres and photographs of a *Burschenschaft* – a student society dedicated to the strange business of scarring the faces of young German men. As someone who'd spent most of the war avoiding injury, duelling was something I had never really understood; the only scar I had on my face was a small patch where a mosquito had bitten me. Inside the house, everything was of the best quality, expensive and heavy, as you might have expected in that part of the world and in a house that size. Evidently it was owned by someone important, which is to say, a Nazi. Nazis like to buy furniture by the ton.

In the split-level drawing room I picked up a framed photograph of a very tall, scar-faced senior SS officer – one of several placed on the grand piano – which explained the duelling sabres. I didn't recognize him but I did recognize the two uniformed men he was standing behind; one was Heinrich Himmler, the other was Kurt Daluege, the chief of the HA-Orpo – the security police. In another photograph, the same scar-faced officer was pictured with the Reich governor of Bavaria, Franz Ritter von Epp. And in another, he was shaking hands with Adolf Hitler. The man with the scars on his face was obviously very well connected.

'Whose house is this, anyway?' I asked Neumann.

'I thought you were supposed to be a detective, Gunther.'

'That used to be true. Now I'm just a spanner like you. Someone for your master to use to twist a few stubborn nuts and bolts.'

'It's Ernst Kaltenbrunner's country house,' said Neumann.

'I take it he doesn't know we're here.'

'He'll find out soon enough.'

'Which makes me wonder how you obtained the keys to the front door.'

'There's not much that Heydrich can't get hold of when he puts his mind to it. We had someone borrow them a while ago so that we could make copies.' Neumann looked at Aneta. 'Why don't you go upstairs and make yourself comfortable, my dear. In fact, why don't you take a nice hot shower?'

'A shower?'

'Yes, you must be feeling a little grimy after – after, you know. I'm sorry, my dear, I don't mean to embarrass you. Merely to make you feel as comfortable as possible. You're going to be here for a while, Aneta. Meanwhile, I will find some of those lovely clothes I was talking about. There are dresses here by Schiaparelli. I think they'll be your size. You're a thirty-eight, aren't you? I take it you do know about Elsa Schiaparelli.'

'Every woman in Europe knows Schiaparelli,' said Aneta. 'And yes, I'm a thirty-eight.' She smiled happily at the prospect of wearing these expensive clothes.

'Splendid. You'll find clean towels, soap, and lots of perfume in the bathroom. I'll bring the dresses up to you in a minute and you can pick one that you like. As well as a change of under-clothes, stockings.'

'Five hundred reichsmarks, you say?'

'Five hundred.' Neumann took out his wallet and showed her a good centimetre of banknotes.

Aneta went upstairs meekly, as asked, leaving me alone with Captain Neumann.

'I think I'm beginning to see what you're up to,' I said. 'A few pictures of the girl here, in Kaltenbrunner's country house, holding his framed photograph fondly. A signed statement that she was having an affair with him, perhaps. After which Heydrich has him on a tight leash. Behave and keep in line or Hitler will see the evidence of your egregious adultery. It's what you people are good at, isn't it? Blackmail.'

'Something like that,' said Neumann. 'Didn't you know? I thought we told you in Berlin. Ernst Kaltenbrunner is a happily married man. It's true, his wife, Elisabeth, knows everything about his affairs. That's probably why he's happily married. He has several mistresses. One of them is the Baroness von Westarp. Those dresses I was talking about belong to her. They're in a closet upstairs. But it will be a surprise to both wife and mistress to learn of his fondness for the local whores. Not just that but the lowest kind of whores who work in a brothel frequented by construction workers. And it will be a surprise to Hitler, of course. The fact that Kaltenbrunner was having sex with a Slav prostitute will be especially offensive to the Leader. And the fact that she came from a local brothel run by Martin Bormann should make things even more interesting.'

Neumann lit a cigarette and then sniffed at a decanter on the sideboard. His hand was shaking a little, which surprised me. Perhaps his skills as a blackmailer weren't quite as innate as I had imagined. 'Would you care for a brandy? I'm going to have one. Kaltenbrunner likes very good brandy, I hear. Which this is. And which probably explains why he drinks so much of the stuff.'

'Sure. Why not?'

He poured us each a large one and then drained his glass in one, which persuaded me he must have needed it. Forgetting he had a cigarette burning in the ashtray, Neumann lit another. I tried to catch his eye in an attempt to fathom what was bothering him but he turned his back on me so I decided to leave him to it, whatever it was. I didn't need to be present when the photographs were taken.

'If you don't mind,' I said, 'I've got work to do. I'll leave you to your work.'

Neumann pulled a face. 'I have my orders. Just like you, Gunther. So don't go all holy on me. Perhaps you forget that Kaltenbrunner planned to have you murdered. Whatever we have in the back of the shop for him I can assure you that bastard has got it coming. You can call it blackmail, if you like. I'd prefer to call it politics.'

'Politics?' I grinned.

'The use of power by one person to affect the behaviour of another? I don't know what else to call it. Anyway, none of this is your concern. Wait here a moment and then I'll give you a lift back to the Villa Bechstein.'

I sipped my brandy – it was indeed excellent – and waited patiently while Neumann went upstairs. I had seldom met a more contradictory human being; in some ways he seemed courteous and kind while in others he was wholly without principle. Undoubtedly clever, he had hitched his wagon to Heydrich and was determined to serve him in every way he could, even if it meant running someone over and of course thereby gaining his own advancement. Sometimes that was all it took to be a real Nazi; the absolute and unscrupulous desire for preferment and promotion. Which was why I was never going to thrive in the new Germany. I just didn't care enough about success to do it by standing on someone else's face. I didn't care about anything very much anymore. Except maybe the quaint idea that somehow doing my job and being a good cop – solving the occasional murder – might inspire others to have respect for the rule of law.

I was jolted from this naïve reverie by the sound of two gunshots on the floor above. I put down my glass and ran into the hall just as the captain was coming down the stairs. In his hand was a smoking Walther P38. His long face was tight with nerves, and there was blood on his cheek but otherwise he looked almost nonchalant, which, given the stopping power of the Walther was hardly a surprise; it's a brave man who will argue with a still-cocked P38. A 9-mm bullet will put a good-size hole in your beer barrel. I barged past him as I ran upstairs and into the lavishly appointed bathroom. But I already knew what I was going to find.

Aneta Husák lay naked in a pool of her own blood on the marble floor. She'd been shot in the head; her blood was still rolling down the white shower curtain as her leg twitched spasmodically, and suddenly everything was clear to me in a way it hadn't been before. Blackmail was so much more serious when a dead girl was involved, especially one who was naked. This way – just as soon as those SS photographers had done their job, and perhaps the local police were called in – Heydrich could keep Kaltenbrunner under his cold, thin thumb forever. And I had helped him to do it. But for me informing Hans-Hendrik Neumann of the existence of the P-Barracks, poor Aneta Husák might still have been alive. But what shocked me almost as much was how kind and solicitous Neumann had seemed when he'd been talking to the girl. Putting the poor creature at her ease, no doubt. It was the Nazi way to catch people unawares – to lie to them and gain their trust and then to betray them, ruthlessly. And after all, she was just a Czech, a Slav, which counted for nothing in Hitler's Germany. Certainly not since Munich.

I went back downstairs and found Neumann with the two SS men. He was pointing his pistol at me. I took out Aneta's visitor's pass and held it up like an exhibit in a courtroom. Not that there was any chance that this murder would ever get near a courtroom.

'She was just a kid,' I said. 'Twenty-three years old. And you murdered her.'

'She was a whore,' said Neumann. 'A common grasshopper for whom violent death is always an occupational hazard. You of all people should know that. Men have been murdering prostitutes in Berlin since time immemorial.'

'Blood and honour,' I said. 'Now I know what that SS belt buckle means. I guess it's supposed to be ironic, after all.' I threw the girl's visitor's pass at him. 'Here. You'll need this for the local police when they pretend to investigate her murder.'

'Please,' said Neumann. 'No recriminations, Gunther. I'm not in the mood for your breathtaking hypocrisy. As you said a few minutes ago, we're both like tools. Only I'm more of a hammer than a spanner.'

I went for him but before I got halfway to his throat someone hit me from behind, a third SS man I hadn't seen before who must have been standing behind the drawing-room door. The blow connected with the side of my head and knocked me across the room. I ended up near the sideboard where I'd left my brandy. And when at last I'd picked myself off the floor, my ear was singing like a kettle and my jaw felt like a bag of builder's rubble; I collected the brandy and knocked it back in one, which helped to take my mind off the pain in my cheek.

'I think you'd best leave, Commissar,' said Neumann. 'Before you get seriously hurt. There's four of us.'

'But that's still not enough guts to make one real man.'

I walked out the door before I was tempted to draw my own gun and shoot someone.

CHAPTER 46

April 1939

I walked into Berchtesgaden and back up the road to Obersalz-berg. Halfway up the mountain I stopped and looked back at the little Alpine town in the dying light of the late afternoon and reflected that it was hard to believe such an idyllic-looking place could have been the scene of two brutal murders in less than twenty-four hours. Then again, perhaps it wasn't that hard to believe, given the Nazi flags that were flying over the railway station and the local Reichs Chancellery. I carried on walking. It was a long climb made even longer by the feeling that my efforts were not just pointless but also a kind of subtle punish-ment; that nothing I did was ever going to make a difference to the way things were, and it was sheer hubris on my part to think they would.

By the time I reached the Villa Bechstein, I had calmed down a little. But that didn't last long. As soon as I arrived, Friedrich Korsch told me that the Gestapo had arrested someone for the murder of Karl Flex.

'Who is it?' I asked as I warmed myself by the fire and lit a cigarette to catch my breath.

'Johann Brandner. The photographer.'

'Where did they find him?'

'At a hospital in Nuremberg. Apparently he'd been a patient there for several days.'

'Pretty good alibi.'

'The local boys picked him up yesterday morning and brought him straight here.'

'Where is Brandner now?'

'Rattenhuber and Högl are interrogating him in the cells underneath the Türken.'

'Jesus. That's all I need. How did you find out about it?'

'The RSD duty officer. SS-Untersturmführer Dietrich told me when I asked him to organize that firing squad. Boss? Is Neumann serious about that? They're really going to shoot those two thugs from Linz?'

'The SS are always serious about shooting people. That's why they have a little death's head on their hats. To remind people that they're not playing games. Look, we'd better get along to the Türken before they shoot Brandner as well.'

'Sure, boss, sure. By the way. What happened to your face?'

I shifted my jaw painfully. It felt like a couple of spare panels from the Pergamon Altar. 'Someone hit me.'

'Captain Neumann?'

'I wish. Then I could have killed him. But no, it was someone else.'

'Here,' he said. 'Take a bite of this.'

Korsch handed me his own hip flask and I took a sip of the Gold Water he was so fond of drinking. The stuff contained tiny flakes of gold that went straight through your body unchanged and, according to Korsch, turned your piss to gold. Which, given the sheer weight of lead, is the best kind of alchemy there is.

'You should get that jaw seen to. Who's that SS doctor I've seen around Obersalzberg? The one with the hop pole up his arse.'

'Brandt? Knowing him, he'd probably poison me. Get away with it, too, knowing him.'

'All the same, boss, it looks to me as if your jaw might be broken.'

'That can only help,' I said through my teeth.

'How?'

'To keep my big mouth shut.'

I walked along to the Türken Inn where, in the officers' mess, I found Rattenhuber and Högl drinking champagne and looking very pleased with themselves. SS-Untersturmführer Dietrich – the young duty officer I'd met before – was there, as was a muscular RSD sergeant.

'Congratulations, Gunther,' said Rattenhuber, pouring me a glass. 'Have some champagne. We're celebrating. He's been arrested. Your very own number one suspect. Johann Brandner. We've got him in a cell downstairs.'

He handed me the glass but I didn't drink it.

'So I hear. Only he's no longer my number one suspect. I hate to spoil your party, Colonel, but I'm more or less sure it was someone else who killed Karl Flex.'

'Nonsense,' said Högl. 'He's already admitted it. We have his signed confession to everything.'

'Everything? Then it's a pity he's not Polish, too, and we'd have a good reason to invade Poland.'

Rattenhuber thought that was funny. 'Very good,' he said.

But Högl's face remained as straight as the seams on his black tunic pockets.

'All right,' I said, 'tell me everything he's admitted to and then I'll tell you if he's just talking to save his skin.'

'He did it all right,' insisted Högl. 'He even told us why.'

'Surprise me.' I sipped the champagne through gritted teeth and then put the glass down again. I wasn't in the mood to drink for any reason other than the anaesthetic effect it might have on my jaw.

'The same reason he was sent to Dachau. He blamed Dr Flex for the compulsory purchase order. For the loss of his photographic business here in Obersalzberg.'

'Maybe he did. But that's not exactly front-page news. Not up here. And to be quite frank with you, I doubt he killed anyone.'

'Look, Gunther,' said Rattenhuber. 'I can see why you might be sore with us. This was your case after all. And perhaps we should have waited for you before we interrogated him. But, as I'm sure I don't need to remind you, time is of the essence here. As of now, the Leader can come to the Berghof and enjoy his fiftieth birthday in total safety. Bormann will be delighted when he hears a man has signed a confession. That the status quo has been returned. And surely that's all that matters.'

'You can call me old-fashioned, sir, but I prefer to believe that what matters most is finding the real culprit. Especially in this case where the Leader's security is concerned. And it's not me who's sore. I don't imagine Brandner told you any of this voluntarily. My guess is that you had this orangutan smack him around a bit. Which is a poor way to solve any crime, in my experience.'

The sergeant bristled a bit at hearing this description but that was all right. I was sort of hoping he might take a swing at me so I could hit someone. After what had happened to Aneta Husák, I was desperate to hit someone, even an orangutan.

'Be careful, Gunther,' said Högl, grinning unpleasantly. 'It looks as though someone already hit you today.'

'I slipped. On the ice. There's a lot of it about up here. But if I do want someone to hit me, then I figure I'm in the right place for it. Which makes me think his confession is about as reliable as an Italian army. Nuremberg is three hundred kilometres away. It's just about possible Johann Brandner murdered Karl Flex but I don't think there's any way he could have murdered Captain Kaspel and got back there in time to be arrested yesterday. Or, for that matter, that he could have killed Udo Ambros, either.'

'Ambros – he's the assistant hunter, isn't he?' said Rattenhuber. 'At the Landlerwald.'

'He was,' I said, 'until someone removed his head with a shotgun. I discovered his body earlier today when I went to speak to him at his house in Berchtesgaden. I suspect Ambros had a shrewd idea of who really murdered Karl Flex. Not least because he owned the Mannlicher rifle that was used to shoot him. So someone else tried to make it look like a suicide. But it was murder. Suicides don't normally write neat legible letters that answer all of your questions except perhaps the meaning of life.'

'Maybe it was suicide,' said Högl. 'Maybe you're wrong. Like any Murder Commission detective, it seems to me that you've got murder on the brain.'

'Well, at least I've got a brain,' I said pointedly. 'Unlike Udo Ambros.'

'And I still don't believe that Captain Kaspel's death was anything but an accident.'

'Then there's the small matter of an alibi,' I continued, ignoring Högl's objections. 'From what I hear, Johann Brandner was in hospital when he was arrested. In which case I expect that there are lots of people – some of them doctors, German doctors – who might be prepared to say that Brandner was never out of bed. So unless he was hospitalized for persistent sleepwalking, I can't say that I think much of your confession, gentlemen.'

'Nevertheless he did sign a full confession,' said Högl. 'And in spite of what you might believe, it was all done with an absolute minimum of force. It's true. The sergeant was going to hit him at one stage. But the fact is he fell down the stairs.'

'I've certainly not heard that one before. Can I read this confession?'

Rattenhuber handed me a typed sheet of paper on which was an almost illegible scrawl of a signature.

'What the major says is absolutely true,' he said, while I glanced over Brandner's confession. 'He fell. But when we did question him, frankly, the threat of returning him to a concentration camp was more than enough to persuade him to volunteer the truth. He claims he's been suffering from malnutrition ever since Dachau.'

'That ought to be an easy claim to substantiate,' I said handing back the confession, which made no mention of Kaspel or

Ambros, not that I had really expected it would. 'I'd like to see him, if I may. Speak to the man myself. Look, Colonel, maybe he did kill Karl Flex. I don't know. Nothing would give me more pleasure than going straight back to Berlin right now, knowing that the Leader was safe. But I do have a number of questions I need to satisfy myself about before I can rubber-stamp this confession and turn it over to General Heydrich at Gestapo headquarters.'

I could see that this mention of Heydrich troubled them both, which was of course why I'd invoked his name; nobody in Germany wanted to incur his displeasure, least of all Rattenhuber.

'Yes, of course,' he said. 'We wouldn't want the general to think we've swept anything under the carpet here. Would we, Peter?'

But it was immediately clear that Högl felt his association with Hitler as old comrades from the Sixteenth Bavarian could trump my association with Heydrich; it was a reasonable assumption. I could almost see the Leader with his hand on his former NCO's shoulder. *This is my beloved son in whom I am well pleased; listen to him; he's a real fucking Nazi.*

'There's no question of that, sir,' he said. 'But to me it's beginning to seem very much as if the famous Commissar Gunther from the Berlin Murder Commission is much more interested in satisfying himself and rescuing his professional reputation than in apprehending the culprit. We have a confession from a local man with a proven grudge who knows the area and is a trained marksman. Frankly it seems like an open-and-shut case to me.'

'Then the Leader should be counted as fortunate that Reichs Leader Bormann and Heydrich put me in charge of this investigation, Major, not you.'

'It was Gunther who identified Brandner as the number one suspect,' said Rattenhuber. 'You have to hand it to him, Peter. Until he got here we were all half-inclined to believe that the shooting might have been an accident. A poacher's stray shot, perhaps. I think we owe the commissar a great deal.'

'If the commissar insists on interviewing this man again, I have no objection of course,' said Högl. 'That's his prerogative. I just don't want us to find ourselves in a position where Johann Brandner retracts what he has said so that the commissar here can indulge himself in some stupid fantasy about a whole series of murders here in Obersalzberg and Berchtesgaden.'

'You're not going to ask him to retract his confession, are you?' said Rattenhuber.

'I wouldn't dream of it,' I said. 'Not in this place.'

'What the hell does that mean?' asked Högl.

'It means that in the Türken Inn it's you and the colonel who are in charge, not me. And he's your prisoner. Not mine.'

'There you are, Peter,' said Rattenhuber. 'There's no question of the commissar persuading Johann Brandner to withdraw his confession. He just wants to check the umlauts are in place over the right letters. Isn't that so, Gunther?'

'That's right, sir. I'm just doing my job.'

CHAPTER 47

April 1939

A few minutes later, SS-Untersturmführer Dietrich ushered Friedrich Korsch and me to the top of a precipitous circular stone staircase that looked like the back door into the lowest part of hell.

'Did the prisoner really fall down these stairs?' I asked.

Dietrich hesitated.

'I won't tell you told me. But I really need to know if this confession is on the level. For the sake of the Leader. You see, if Johann Brandner didn't kill Dr Flex, then the real murderer is still running around Berchtesgaden. Just imagine if he decided to shoot someone else. That could really blow out Hitler's candles.'

'He was pushed. By Major Högl.'

'Good lad. I thought as much.'

'Sir. Can I ask you something?'

'Anything you like. But you'll probably have to listen hard to understand the answer with this jaw. I'd make a lousy ventriloquist.'

'Major Högl says the other two prisoners we have down here are to be shot. On Captain Neumann's orders. And that I'm to command the firing squad. I don't know what to say to them. I'd rather not do it, really. I've never commanded a firing squad and I'm not quite sure what to do.'

'I wouldn't worry about it too much, Lieutenant. I imagine

the orders will have to be checked with Berlin. Which could take some time.'

'They already were. Colonel Rattenhuber sent a telex asking Prinz Albrechtstrasse for confirmation and General Heydrich said we're to shoot them first thing tomorrow morning and then send the bodies back to Austria.'

'Then I shall want to send a telex myself,' I said. 'To ask the general if he'll change his mind. Can you help me do that?'

'Willingly. It's not that I'm questioning my orders, you understand. It's just that it doesn't seem right somehow, to shoot our own men.'

'Just for the record, Lieutenant, we've been shooting our own men and worse, since 1933.'

Thirty or forty metres down into the bowels of the earth was a low square corridor that led to a couple of damp, wooden-floored cells, and an empty kennel for a guard dog, which was where we found Johann Brandner, naked and in a bad way; he was thinner than a pipe cleaner and just as white, with a couple of large bruises on his face, one under each eye, and a broken nose that was still encrusted with blood. But I didn't need to speak to him. It was immediately plain that Brandner was weak from lack of food and clearly belonged in hospital. He could hardly stand, which wasn't made any easier by the height of the kennel. We fetched him out and helped him to drink some water.

'Please,' he whispered. 'I've told you everything.'

'Look, I'm going to get you out of here. Just be patient.'

Brandner looked at me fearfully, as if he suspected this was a trick and I would hit him if he now confirmed that his previous confession had been false. I fed a cigarette into his mouth and one into my own. Smoking is easy with a suspected broken jaw; it's all in the lips.

'No, no,' he said. 'I really did kill Flex. I shot him on the terrace of the Berghof, with a rifle.'

I nodded. 'Remind me how many shots you fired. One or two?'

'I only needed to fire once. I used to be a marksman in the army, you see. And it wasn't a difficult shot, from a window in the Villa Bechstein. That's right, isn't it?'

'What kind of a rifle did you use?'

'A bolt-action Mauser.'

'The Karabiner 98? With a three-power Voigtländer sight?'

'That's right. Good rifle, that.'

'All right,' I said. 'I believe you. By the way, why were you in hospital?'

'I went there after I was released from Dachau. I was suffering from malnutrition.' He took a drag of the cigarette and smiled weakly. 'Please don't send me back there.'

'I won't.' It was an evasive, cowardly answer, I knew, but I had no desire to add to Brandner's woes.

'What is going to happen to me, sir?'

'I have no idea,' I said, even though I had a good idea. It wasn't so long since the Gestapo in Stuttgart had arrested Helmut Hirsch for his part in a plot intended to destabilize the Reich that, perhaps, had included shooting some low-level Nazi bureaucrat – someone like Karl Flex. There had been very little evidence against Hirsch other than his own confession, but that certainly didn't stop the Nazis from proceeding with his prosecution. Soon after his arrest he'd been transferred to Plötzensee Prison in Berlin. And I could easily see how Brandner's confession might become the basis of a larger conspiracy that could justify a few more arrests and, eventually, executions, too. The Nazis had a morbid taste for the guillotine that was the equal of the revolutionary tribunal during the French Reign of Terror.

I sneezed, which was agony as far as my face was concerned, and for a minute I closed my eyes until I had processed the pain. My own head felt like someone had tried to cut it off with a butter knife.

'It wasn't us that did that, was it?' asked a voice. 'Smacked you on the head?' The two cells underneath the Türken were occupied by the Gestapo men from Linz who'd both come to the barred windows to listen to my conversation with Brandner. But given what I now knew about the fate that was planned for them, I hardly wanted to speak to either man.

'Someone else,' I said. 'It's been that kind of day.'

'Looks like your jaw might be broken,' said one. 'Best thing you can do? Take off that cheap Raxon around your neck and use it like a bandage, under your trap and over the top of your head. You'll look like a prick, of course, but you should be used to that, and it won't hurt quite as much. If you see a pill Jesus, he won't do much more than bandage it up anyway and give you some painkillers. I know what I'm talking about. This won't surprise you but I've broken a few jaws in my time. Fixed a few, too. Before I joined the Gestapo I was a corner man for Max Schmeling. And the quicker you do it, and the tighter you do it, the better.'

It sounded like he was having me on but I took off my tie and tied a nice bow on top of my head and a few minutes later my head looked like the last Christmas present in the orphanage. I put my hat back on, which made me look a little less ridiculous, perhaps, but only just. And he was right; it did feel a little better.

'Thanks,' I said through my teeth.

'Hey, Commissar Gunther,' said the other man – the one I'd stabbed with the piece of glass. 'What's going to happen to *us*? You can't keep us here. Kaltenbrunner isn't going to appreciate that if he finds out. But if you let us go now we won't tell him. We'll drive quietly back to Linz and it'll be like this never happened. We'll tell him we had a car accident or something.'

'It's not up to me,' I said. 'It's General Heydrich's decision. And they're none too fond of each other.' I gave each of them a cigarette and lit them both.

'No one told us you were working for him.'

'I think I did, but that hardly matters now, does it?'

'Look, it was nothing personal. We were only obeying orders.

You know that. You're a cop, just like us. You do what you're told, right? That's the job. Kaltenbrunner says jump, you say, how high? Sounds to me like the three of us got caught in the middle of a feud between your boss and ours. To hell with them both, that's what I say.'

'We can agree about their destination anyway,' I said. 'If not much else.'

'What *is* going to happen to us?' said the other. 'Seems to me like you're sidestepping the question.'

I was. So I told them what Neumann had in mind. And not because I wanted to give them grief but because I'd ducked the truth one too many times that day already. It was easily done in Germany and a bad habit I was quickly developing. But how else was I going to stay alive?

'I think they mean to put you in front of a firing squad.'

'They can't do that. Not without a court-martial.'

'I'm afraid they can. They can do anything they like. Especially here on Hitler's mountain. But I don't think it will come to that. I'm going to ask General Heydrich to change his mind. Not because I like you, either. But because – well, let's just say that I don't want anyone to be shot on my account. One way or the other, I've seen a bit too much killing of late. And I'd rather not see any more.'

'Thanks, Gunther. You're all right. For a Berliner.'

I went back to the stairs and started to go up, but I could just as easily have gone the other way. The stairs continued down as well as up. Far below my feet I could hear and feel the sound of men working with drills and the cold, damp air was thick with masonry dust.

'What's down there?' I asked Dietrich. 'More cells? Torture chambers? Secret weapons? The seven dwarves?'

'Bunkers. Tunnels. Power generators. Storage rooms. This whole mountain would look like a rabbit warren if you were to see it in cross-section. From Göring's house you can walk all the way to the Platterhof Hotel without seeing the light of day.'

'I guess that's the way these people like it. The Nazis always were a bit too nocturnal for my taste.'

'Sir, please. I've been a Party member myself since 1933.'

'You don't look old enough. But did you ever ask yourself what all these bunkers are for? Maybe someone knows something we don't. About our real chances for keeping that peace treaty we signed with the Franzis and the Tommies at Munich.'

Back in the officers' mess upstairs, Rattenhuber and Högl were waiting for me. Rattenhuber put down his champagne and stood up, a little unsteadily; Högl carried on reading a copy of the *Völkischer Beobachter* as if my opinion of the suspect's guilt or innocence mattered not at all.

'Well?' asked Rattenhuber. 'What do you think?'

'Johann Brandner couldn't possibly have murdered Karl Flex.' I was looking at Högl as I continued with my answer. 'In case you're interested.'

'You see?' Högl was speaking to Rattenhuber from behind the newspaper. 'I told you he'd make trouble, sir. In my opinion, the commissar wants all the glory for himself.'

'Why do you say this, Gunther?' Rattenhuber sounded exasperated. 'You said yourself he was suspect number one. Johann Brandner has the right background. A substantial and previously documented motive. The local knowledge. Everything. When the Gestapo arrested him in Nuremberg he even had a rifle at home. And we have a confession. Why would he confess to something he didn't do?'

'All sorts of reasons. But mostly there's only one that counts these days. Fear. Fear of what you people might do to him if he said he didn't kill Karl Flex. Look, nothing of what he just told me agrees with any of the forensic evidence I found up at the Berghof or the Villa Bechstein and that's what counts here.'

'Perhaps he was trying to mislead you,' said Rattenhuber. 'By contradicting his previous statement he hopes to muddy the investigative waters, so to speak.'

'Look, Colonel, if you and the major here care to take the trouble, you'll easily see that the man is innocent. If you want to inform Bormann that he's your murderer, then go right ahead. That's fine by me. I haven't asked him to retract his confession and I'm not going to. But I don't believe a word of it and I'm going to keep on hunting for the real killer until the Reichs Leader or General Heydrich tells me to stop.'

Högl put down his newspaper and stood up as if I had finally said something important enough to get his attention.

'Very well,' said Högl. He pointed out the window across the parade ground at the enormous four-storey house that sat at the top of the snow-covered field above the Türken Inn; with the Untersberg mountains behind, it looked more like a luxury Alpine hotel than the home of one man. 'Let's go and ask the Boss what he thinks. He's there now. I can see the light on in his office. I'll telephone Martin Bormann this very minute and ask if we can walk up there and speak to him. We'll let him decide on the guilt of this man, shall we?'

'You must really want to be rid of me, Major,' I said. 'But I wonder why you want to be rid of me so badly.'

CHAPTER 48

April 1939

We were ushered into Bormann's ground-floor study to await the arrival of the Reichs leader. The house smelled strongly of rosemary, as if someone was roasting lamb, and suddenly I was hungry. The whitewashed room we were in had a vaulted ceiling with a brass chandelier and a large red marble fireplace that was a smaller version of the one I'd seen up at the tea house. The blond oak doors had huge strap hinges that made you think you were back in church and, in truth, the three of us were just as quiet as if we were sitting in a row of pews instead of some richly upholstered armchairs, but the rest of the house was noisy with children, as if the huge building also housed a kindergarten. The Nazis liked big families; they gave mothers with lots of children medals for producing more Nazis. Mrs Bormann probably had an Iron Cross First Class.

Under the window was a set of shelves with lots of books that seemed like they'd been bought for how they looked and not how they read, several silver beer tankards, and various pictures of Hitler in his rare unguarded moments. In one of these he was seated in a deck chair on a hillside in a forest; over his left shoulder was a black dog that might have been his familiar. The wooden floor was covered with a thick red Persian rug and on the walls were a couple of broadswords, some choice tapestries, and several oil paintings of a dark-haired woman I assumed was

Bormann's fecund wife, Gerda. None of the paintings did her any favours; she looked tired. Then again, having six children to look after all day would tire the Pied Piper of Hamelin.

The refectory table-desk was home to an equestrian bronze, a small swing-arm lamp, a thick leather blotter, and another photograph of Hitler. But the room was dominated not by the hive-like ceramic stove, nor by a statue of Adolf Hitler, nor even by a suit of armour, but by a piece of electrical equipment from Telefunken the likes of which I'd never seen before. The centre of the machine was dominated by a piece of curved grey glass about the size of a dinner plate. And I was still looking at it, and trying to work out what it was, when Bormann bustled into the room. He was wearing a brown Party tunic and this helped me to form an impression of what a clean-shaven Hitler might look like if he'd not been a vegetarian. Bormann halted in the doorway for a moment, and shouted back over his shoulder: 'And tell the crown prince to get on with his homework.'

I smiled, assuming 'the crown prince' was what Martin Bormann called his eldest son; it's what anyone would have called his eldest son if he was a man as important as the Lord of Obersalzberg. I don't know why I smiled because this gave me a good idea of just how long the Nazis planned on remaining in power. Clearly the crown prince was destined for higher things in the new Germany.

'Well, hurry up,' said Bormann. 'I haven't got all night. I have to read an important speech the Leader's planning to make to the Reichstag. It's his response to Roosevelt's Jew-inspired demand for assurances that Germany has no intention of invading a whole shopping list of other countries, including America.'

I nodded as if taking this seriously, although everyone in Germany knew that following a fire at the real Reichstag in 1933, the Nazis had disposed of its powers, and moved all so-called parliamentary sessions to Berlin's Kroll Opera House. Parliamentary consent was not required for anything the Nazis did. Which must have been convenient when you were preparing such an important speech.

Bormann sat down on an inadequate-looking chair and, as he leaned back, he smiled a grotesque, gap-toothed smile as if he'd had a recent sight of his Swiss bankbook. He reminded me of Lon Chaney in *London After Midnight*. This wasn't so surprising, perhaps; all the top Nazis reminded me of someone in a horror movie.

'What happened to your face?' he asked. 'I don't remember you being quite so ugly before, Gunther.' He laughed out loud at his own good humour, which prompted Rattenhuber and Högl to laugh as well.

'I slipped and fell down a flight of stairs,' I said, staring hard at Högl. 'Hurt my jaw. Maybe it's broken, I don't know. It's less painful if I keep my jaw tied up.'

Bormann nodded. 'I get that. But still, I prefer the people who come and see me to be smart, to wear a tie. That's just good manners, see? Respect.' He opened his desk drawer and took out a mud-brown NSDAP tie. 'Here. You can wear this one.'

I put on the tie and adjusted my shirt collar.

'Actually, now I come to think of it, the last person to wear that tie was Adolf Hitler. He wore that tie when Chamberlain came to visit him. So actually you're very honoured, Gunther. He gave it to me, personally, but I can always get another.'

'Thank you, sir.' I tried a smile, not that anyone would have recognized it as one. The idea of wearing Hitler's own Nazi Party necktie was grotesque to me. A noose would have been more comfortable and, knowing Bormann, that could probably have been arranged just as readily.

'You should really see a doctor. I'll tell Brandt to come and have a look at you.'

'I don't have time to see a doctor, sir. Not while I'm still actively looking for the man who shot Karl Flex.'

The grin vanished and Martin Bormann stared at Högl with

narrowing eyes. 'Damn it, Högl, I thought you said you had some good news about that.'

'I do, sir,' said Högl. 'The fact is that we have a man in custody at the Türken Inn who has confessed to the murder of Karl Flex and signed a witnessed statement to that effect.'

'That *is* good news.'

'Yes, it might be but for the fact that the commissar here is too clever for something as simple as this. He seems to disagree with the colonel and me that the man we have in custody is the assassin. He believes that his collection of carefully gathered clues trump this man's admission of guilt.'

'Who is this man you have now?' said Bormann. He helped himself from a cigarette box on the table, lit one quickly, and dragged a large brass ashtray towards him. 'Tell me more about him.'

'The assassin's name is Johann Brandner and we've had some trouble from him before. He's a local man. Knows the area very well. He was sent to Dachau concentration camp after he persisted in writing letters to the Leader when his business here in Obersalzberg was closed down for security reasons.'

'Yes, that's right. I remember now. The photographer fellow. We made an example of him to discourage all the others from airing their grievances to the Leader. We even put an announcement in the local newspaper to this effect.'

'Johann Brandner was also a decorated marksman during the war,' added Högl.

I'd kept quiet through Högl's pre-emptive explanation, hoping he'd trip himself up with a factual error, and now he did.

'When Brandner was arrested he was also in possession of a rifle with a sniper scope, of the kind that was used to shoot Flex.'

'I see.' Bormann frowned at me. 'So what's the damn problem, Gunther? You've got an excellent motive. A rifle. A confession. What more do you need?'

'Evidence has been the bedrock of German jurisprudence for

longer than I've been carrying a warrant disc. And the plain fact of the matter is that there is none here. Johann Brandner confessed only because he was afraid of being tortured. Afraid of being sent back to Dachau. Frankly, the evidence against him is purely circumstantial. Which is to say, the present circumstances seem to dictate that when it comes to arresting someone for Flex's murder, simply anyone will do.'

'Explain,' said Bormann.

'For example, the Mauser rifle he was found with could hardly be the Mannlicher carbine that was used to kill Flex. Sir, you saw me find the murder weapon, in the Villa Bechstein's chimney. Just because he had a rifle when he was arrested or the fact that he's a marksman doesn't mean he shot Flex. There are plenty of other men living in Berchtesgaden who are pretty useful with a rifle. More than likely it was one of them who shot Flex. Moreover, I don't see how Brandner could have killed Captain Kaspel and the assistant hunter from the Landlerwald, Udo Ambros, when he was three hundred kilometres away from here, in a Nuremberg hospital where he'd been since his release from Dachau.'

'There's been another murder?' said Bormann. 'Why wasn't I told?'

'Because Ambros left a suicide note,' said Högl. 'It's mere conjecture on the part of the commissar that he was actually murdered. And the captain's death was more likely a simple car accident. Kaspel was addicted to methamphetamine, sir. He lost control of the car he was in because he was driving too fast. He always drove too fast.'

'His brakes were tampered with,' I said. 'Only, for some reason the major here seems to have set his face against any evidence I've managed to gather. I really don't know why. Even a German jury used to be equal to the task of understanding evidence when it's as clear and simple as this.'

'What *is* simple,' insisted Högl, 'is that we have a man in custody who's confessed to the murder of Karl Flex. Which is really all we need to put the Leader's mind at rest, should he ever need to be told about this unfortunate occurrence.'

It was only now that I understood that Högl didn't really care who killed Flex. And nor, it seemed, did Bormann.

'The major makes a very good point,' Bormann told me. 'Whatever happens, we are going to need someone to blame for this before the Leader's birthday. I should have thought of this before. And not even the Berlin Kripo can argue with a full confession.'

'On the contrary, sir. It's my opinion that it's always a detective's job to think the unthinkable, ask the unaskable, and accuse those who are totally above suspicion. The number of innocent people who turn out to be guilty is truly remarkable, even in this day and age. Go to any jail in Germany, sir, and you'll find that the cells are full of men who tell you they didn't do it. Conversely, it's my impression that this man's confession is wholly unreliable. And that the Leader won't be safe until the real assassin is in custody.'

'What do you think, Johann?'

Colonel Rattenhuber twisted his broad face into a semblance of deep thought. It looked painful, like one of those sixty-four canonical grimaces recorded in marble and bronze by Franz Messerschmidt, and almost as uncomfortable as my own face. But when it finally came, his answer was the most perfect example of Nazi justice that I'd ever heard outside of a novel by Franz Kafka:

'Back in the day, when I was a young copper in Munich, we used to say you'll find out that everyone's guilty if you hit him hard enough. In my book, a confession is never, ever to be doubted. Once you've got that, it's up to the damn lawyers. You let them sort it out. It's what they're paid for. Perhaps Brandner didn't do it. Perhaps what happened to Brandner seems coercive and amoral to someone like the commissar. That's not our problem here. The point is that he *could* have shot Flex. He certainly fits the profile that the commissar described himself. And that's what surely counts. So I say we keep him in the bag for now and let Commissar Gunther carry on his investigation for a while longer. To see if he can't find someone who's a better fit, the way he says. And if he doesn't, well then we can all say we have done our duty and we have someone in custody who deserves to be there. Because make no mistake, this fellow is guilty of something, otherwise we wouldn't have sent him to Dachau in the first place. Frankly, I think perhaps the commissar is in danger of losing sight of the main picture. In a perfect world it would be nice to catch the culprit and be absolutely one hundred per cent sure about that. But as I'm sure he will agree, such a thing rarely ever happens in police work. And in the real world we sometimes have to do what is pragmatic. I believe it's more important that the Leader is completely reassured than that we are completely satisfied that Brandner is our man.'

I was beginning to see how Rattenhuber had made colonel. And Bormann seemed to appreciate this argument. He was nodding.

'I like your thinking, Johann,' he said. 'I knew there was a reason why you were in charge of the RSD. Because you think the right way. The practical way. Hitler's way. So that's decided. We'll keep this man Brandner on ice but meanwhile we'll let the commissar carry on working diligently towards a different outcome, if that's possible. But given the circumstances we ought to have some sort of time limit on his detective work. Yes, I think that would be best. You have twenty-four hours to find a better candidate than the one we have now. Is that clear, Commissar? After that we'll have to assume it was Brandner who shot Flex and act accordingly.'

'Yes, sir. This is your mountain. And I'm under your orders. But back in Berlin? Well, let's just say I'm not sure what I'll be able to say if Himmler and Heydrich ever ask me about this particular case. And the fact is that you're too smart not to know that Karl

Flex was shot because he worked for you. I'm sorry to say this to you, sir, but it's my impression that around these parts you're hated even more than he was. Which means that next time the assassin – *the real assassin* – might be more ambitious in his choice of targets. The next time he might take a potshot at you.'

Bormann stood up slowly and came round the desk to face me and instinctively I stood. His whole head was beginning to turn red with anger, which must have pleased Högl. He was a powerful-looking man with pink hands that were quickly becoming white fists.

'Will you listen to this bastard?' he asked Rattenhuber and Högl. 'Talking to me like I was just some Fritz who'd walked off the street and into the Alex for help. Me. You should have sewed up your fucking mouth, Gunther, when you tied up your jaw like a Christmas pudding.'

The National leader took hold of my tie – the one around my neck – and pulled me to his level until I was close enough to smell the cigarette on his breath. That would have been bad enough, but he now produced a Mauser automatic from the pocket of his tunic and pressed it hard against my swollen cheek.

'You'll say what I fucking well tell you to say, Gunther. Is *that* clear? I have Adolf Hitler's ear, which means I own the fucking police in this country. So you'd best forget any noble ideas you might have about German jurisprudence. Adolf Hitler's the law now; and I'm his judge and jury. You got that? And if I hear you've so much as hinted to that slippery Jew bastard Heydrich that things are any different from what I've said, then I'll have you in a fucking concentration camp so quick you'll think you were the last yid in Berlin. I'll break your jaw into ten pieces, make you swallow them, and then hang you with that necktie. You take your orders from me, you fucking pig hound.'

I was alarmed to hear myself answer back. There was just half a chance in a hundred that this wasn't a mistake. And anyway, I was so tired I'd stopped caring very much about what happened to me. I needed some more magic potion, and fast. But only if I stayed alive.

'In my experience most people want to know when someone's out to kill them,' I said, swallowing my fear. 'But I guess you're just braver than most people. Maybe that's not such a surprise. With the RSD and the SS to protect you, sir, you must be the second-best-protected man in Germany. And the terrace in front of the Berghof must be the most secure place in the whole German Reich. At least it was before Karl Flex was shot dead. They say lightning doesn't strike the same place twice, but I say, why take a chance?'

For a moment I thought Bormann was going to hit me. But then he stepped back, smiled, relaxed his grip on my tie, and even started to straighten it for me, as if he now remembered who the tie had belonged to. I'd seen psychopaths behave in similar fashion and it was plain to see why Hitler kept him around; Bormann was fascism incarnate, carrot and stick on the same black lanyard. He could just as easily have been a crime boss as a senior member of the German government, although, in my estimation, there was little difference between the two. Germany was in the grip of a gang just as ruthless as Al Capone's Chicago Outfit. Bormann even looked like Capone.

'I hear what you say,' he said, pocketing the Mauser again. 'Maybe the real assassin *is* still out there. Maybe Flex *was* shot because he was working for me. Hey, I know I'm not liked up here. These fucking Bavarians are not as smart as us Prussians, Gunther. They have no idea what's necessary and what isn't.' He paused. 'You know, it took a lot of guts to say that to my face, Gunther. I'm beginning to see why that horse-faced Jew Heydrich keeps you on his key chain. Maybe you're even as good as he says you are and you really can find the Fritz who shot Karl Flex. But until then we're keeping Brandner in the cells. For the Leader's peace of mind, like Colonel Rattenhuber here says. And you know what? If he is innocent, then he's relying on you every bit as much as the Leader is. Because if you don't find someone else to put on a charge sheet, I'm going to have him shot. Just like those other two clowns from Linz. And not because Heydrich said so. But because I don't like anyone who thinks they can come up here to the Leader's Territory without my permission and arrest people who are working for me. So you can forget that fucking telex you wanted to send to Heydrich, Gunther. There's to be no mercy for them. They'll be shot first thing in the morning as soon as I've had my breakfast and there's the end of it. I want you there to see it, too. As for Kaltenbrunner, I can promise you and Heydrich that he will get the sharp edge of my tongue when next I see him. Don't you worry about that.'

'I'm sure the general will be very relieved to hear that, sir.'

What was the point of truth in a world dominated by cruelty and the arbitrary exercise of power? What had become of me now that I was so reduced? I was nodding away like a googly-eyed doll but all the time I was thinking I was a madman among the very mad, and how hateful I was. Everywhere I looked, I found my own life-preserving compromises staring back at me like friends I'd shamefully betrayed. If only Hitler could have hated himself as much as I now hated my own self. Perhaps nothing in life is more unpleasant to a man than to take the road that leads to himself. Perhaps I would only be free of these monstrous people on the day I went to hell. That's the trouble with being an eyewitness to history; sometimes history is like an avalanche that sweeps you down off the face of the mountain and into the oblivion of some hidden black crevasse. But for now I was going back to the Berghof, to seek out Gerdy Troost in the hope I might get some answers to the many cryptic mysteries of Flex's secret ledger.

CHAPTER 49

October 1956

There probably wasn't a bus for hours but the man in the leather shorts waiting at the stop didn't mind. He wasn't waiting for a bus. To reach the bus stop and deal with him, I would have to cross the road, and to cross the road probably meant being seen. The road was about ten metres wide and without any sign of traffic, and so quiet you could have heard a mouse cough. I could have shot him, of course, but the sound would certainly have brought other Stasi men to the scene and I'd have had a gun battle on my hands. One I was certain to lose. It had rained while I was sleeping and the cobbles glistened in the moonlight like the skin of an enormous alligator. There wasn't a breath of wind and the treetops were as still as if they'd been tied onto the sky. Somewhere in the thick forest behind the bus stop an owl was hooting, like Mother Nature's own alarm, as though to warn other animals that a man with a gun was close by. Probably I'd seen one too many films from Walt Disney's Wonderful World of Colour. But to me the trees couldn't have looked more like the real Germany if they'd been painted black, red, and gold. Whatever the French intended for the Saarland, it certainly looked like home to me. To get there, I needed to distract the Stasi man, and I knew I would only get one chance. If there was one thing the East German police were good at, it was guarding borders; since the creation of the GDR in 1949, 'flight from the Republic' was a specific and serious crime, and hundreds, perhaps thousands, of people were killed every year by the Grenzpo. Those who were caught were often executed and, at the very least, imprisoned.

I glanced around the other terraced doorways for an object I could toss over the roof of the corrugated iron bus stop to distract him – an old wine bottle or perhaps a piece of wood. There was nothing. The little town of Freyming-Merlebach wasn't the kind of place where anyone threw very much away. I squatted down on haunches tight from walking and cycling and watched and waited, hoping he might get up and stretch his long legs and leave the bus stop, but all he did was finish one cigarette and fire up another. They smelled good, too. In my book there's nothing that smells better than a French cigarette, except perhaps a Frenchwoman. In the yellow flame of his lighter I caught a brief glimpse of his scarred face and the gun in his hand, and I knew I would not be so lucky with this man a second time. From time to time he levelled the silenced barrel of the automatic at one of the windows opposite the bus stop, almost as if he was keen to shoot at something, anything, if only to alleviate the boredom of his all-night stakeout. I'd been there myself. Doubtless Korsch – and by extension, Erich Mielke – had impressed on his men the absolute necessity of killing me. For all I knew they were even offering a cash bonus on my head. I'd heard it said that Grenzpos could earn themselves a full weekend's leave with extra food and alcohol vouchers if they shot a *republikflüchtiger*.

I stared at my dirty shoes for a while and considered just how far they'd come since I'd left Cap Ferrat. Almost a thousand kilometres, probably. Just the thought of this distance made me feel a combination of victory and despair: victory that I had eluded capture for so long; despair at the loss of my old and comparatively comfortable life. And all because I was squeamish about killing some mendacious Englishwoman who wouldn't have cared if I was alive or dead. I wondered what she was doing now. Making tea? I had no idea. I didn't even like the English.

In fact, I probably hated the Tommies now even more than I hated the French, which was saying a lot. But for them and the Stasi, I might still be in my old job behind the front desk at the Grand Hôtel. I leaned back against the door and pondered what to do next. The cold andouillette I'd eaten kept repeating on me and every time it did my mouth seemed to turn to piss. Just like my life.

A black cat appeared at my side, stepped sinuously between my legs, wrapped its tail around my knee, and let me fold its pointy ears for a moment or two. I'm not sure I always liked cats, but this one was so friendly that I couldn't help but warm to it. When I was growing up in Germany my mother used to say that if a black cat crossed your path from left to right it was a sign of good luck; I couldn't tell if this cat was from the left but it was so long since anything or anyone had come near me by choice that I picked the animal up and stroked it fondly. I needed all the friends I could get, even furry ones. Perhaps he saw in me a kindred spirit, a solitary creature of the night without ties or obligations. After a while the cat blinked an apology at me with large green eyes and explained that it had one or two things to be getting on with and, having pushed its face into mine for a second to cement our new friendship, trotted across the road. In the moonlight the black cat cast a much larger shadow so that it seemed bigger than it was; but no one could have mistaken it for anything *but* a cat. Which made it all the more shocking when the man in the leather shorts leaned out of the bus shelter and took a shot at it with his silenced automatic. The cat sprang forward into the bushes and disappeared. I suppose that this was the moment I started to hate the Stasi man in the bus shelter. It was one thing him planning to shoot me but it felt like something else him taking a shot at a harmless animal. For me, friends were rare and to see one of mine having to dodge a bullet for something I'd done provoked in me a strong feeling of outrage. I felt like strangling this Fritz. In my book cruelty to animals is always a sign that cruelty to human beings is not far off. It's a well-known fact that many of Weimar Germany's worst lust murderers began their murderous careers by torturing and killing cats and dogs.

'You cruel fucking bastard,' I whispered.

It was now that I made out a few loose cobblestones about a metre in front of me. I crept forward, tugged one out of the road, and backed into the doorway again. I hefted the stone cube in my hand. It was about the size of a doughnut and seemed ideal for what I still had in mind. After seeing the Stasi man take a potshot at the cat, I think I would have preferred to have thrown the cobblestone straight at his head. Instead, I glanced both ways along the street to check there were no cars or other Stasi men on patrol and, seeing that it remained all but deserted, I stepped forward and hurled the stone over the bus stop and into the trees, where it bounced off a trunk and then landed with a thud on the ground.

The man in the shorts jumped to his feet, flicked away his cigarette, and stepped out of the bus shelter. I saw that he was wearing a grey woollen *Tracht* jacket now that made him look exactly like a grown-up Hansel who was looking for his Gretel, except that Hansel was never so dangerous. With his silenced gun close to his waist he advanced carefully into the trees, leaving me plenty of time to tiptoe across the slippery road behind him. I knelt by the bus stop and paused. A moment later, I almost cried out as I felt a searing pain in my knee, and it was a second or two before I realized that it was resting on the Stasi man's hot cigarette end. I cursed silently, brushed it quickly off my trousers, and then stepped into the bushes. I couldn't see him. I couldn't even hear him and I hardly wanted to move again until I was quite sure where he was. And then I heard the man a few metres ahead, coming slowly in my direction with one thing on his mind: to find and kill me. In truth, I might have stayed there a while longer and later on walked through the forest and into the Saarland, perhaps without very much hindrance. It was then that I saw it. The black cat. I reached out to stroke it and snatched back my hand when I found its fur was wet and sticky. Suddenly I realized that the Stasi man's bullet hadn't missed the cat after all. The animal had been shot as it crossed the road and had limped into the bushes where it collapsed and died. Tears welled up in my eyes – I was tired but I felt sick for my newfound friend, sick and angry now. Angry for the cat and angry that my life had been turned upside down by Erich Mielke and the Stasi, angry enough and perhaps tired enough to want to exact some kind of revenge. So, holding my breath, I crouched down behind a thick tree trunk, drew the carving knife from my sock, and waited for the man in shorts to come close enough for me to cut his throat. While I waited I caught sight of the burn hole in the knee of my trousers. I also had the beginning of a hole in the sole of my shoe and I wasn't far off looking like a genuine *clochard*, so the last thing I needed was a large bloodstain on the sleeve of my jacket, because it's impossible to kill a man with a cold blade and not end up resembling a character in a tragedy by Shakespeare. There's nothing like blood on your clothes to attract attention. And the thing most murderers usually forget is just how much blood there is in a human body. A human being isn't much more than a soft-sided jerry can full of liquid. Even as I was crouching there I remembered a bookmaker called Alfred Hau; he stabbed a man to death in an apartment in Hoppegarten – a man who'd weighed close to one hundred and fifty kilos – and the cops reckoned almost eight litres of blood came gushing out of his fat torso, so much that it leaked through the bare floorboards and onto the kitchen ceiling of a Kripo detective who lived in the apartment below. It was probably the easiest arrest the Berlin Murder Commission ever made. The more I thought about it, the more I realized that using my knife was out of the question.

I stabbed the knife into the ground from where I might

retrieve it, if needed. Then I whipped off my silk scarf, quickly tied a couple of knots along the length of it, wrapped an end tight around each of my wrists, and held it taut between my hands like an Ismaili assassin. Slowly, with my back pressed against the trunk, I stood up, and taking a silent, deep breath, tried to steady my already twisted nerves. I'd seen the bodies of men who had been strangled – it's probably the most common form of murder a cop ever sees – and I knew what to do: when there are two or more firm knots in the scarf or the rope, homicide is almost certain, but of course actually doing it was a very different proposition. In my limited experience, killing a man in cold blood usually involves killing a significant part of yourself. It's a fact that many men of my own acquaintance belonging to the SS *Einsatzgruppen* had often needed to get drunk in order to murder Jews, and even in the higher ranks, nervous breakdowns were common. I didn't consider myself like any of those but the thought of the dead cat and then the cruel way the Stasi had half-hanged me in Villefranche turned what was left of my heart to stone. I make no excuses for that. It was bastards like the man in the leather shorts who'd put me in this situation in the first place. It was him or me, and I hoped it would be him.

He paused next to the tree behind which I was standing but I waited in a state of suspended animation, the way a hungry tiger waits patiently until it is absolutely sure of a successful attack. I was close enough to smell my quarry now. The soap he'd used to wash himself with the previous day. The Old Spice on his face. The Brylcreem in his yellow hair – he looked like Lutz Moik, the German film actor. The smoke of the Gauloises he'd smoked that was sticking to his quaint clothes. The Mentos he was sucking. I could even smell the leather dressing on his stupid shorts. I almost wondered if he could smell me. I know I could. I was hoping he'd see the dead cat and bend down to inspect his cruel handiwork. It was easy enough to see the little pile of fur that lay in the moonlight like a fairy's black velvet cushion and the red ruby of blood in its dead centre.

'Hey, kitty, kitty. Did someone put the cat out?' And then the bastard laughed a high-pitched girlish laugh and shot the cat again, just for the hell of it. The silenced gun in his hand sounded not much louder than an old-fashioned mousetrap springing into action but no less lethal for that. And now I felt real hatred for him and the new Germany – another new Germany no one wanted – that he represented. Shooting the cat again was a sign that he had relaxed a little, that and the fact that he slipped a packet of cigarettes from a pocket in his leather bib, and pulled one out with his lips. Then he reached into his pocket for the lighter.

Which was when I attacked.

Hooking the silk scarf around his scrawny neck, I pushed him forward onto the damp ground and as he fell, I shoved a knee hard into the small of his back and then knelt on him while I tightened my ligature mercilessly, one knot up against his larynx and the other against his carotid arteries. His face was buried in the cat's dead body, which seemed appropriate but he was as strong as a bull, much stronger than I'd expected, and even as I set about trying to subdue him I was cursing myself for not just stabbing him in the neck as I'd originally planned. He twisted one way and then the other like a man whose whole body was convulsed with a large current of electricity. The thing about strangling a man is to remember that most such deaths are accidental, that it takes less time to kill someone like this than might be imagined – or so the forensic pathologists had always told me. Most victims of strangling are women – housewives strangled by drunken husbands who don't know what they're doing until it's too late. It's one thing strangling a woman after a night out on the beer; but it's another strangling a wiry, powerful man who was perhaps half my age. What gave me extra strength was the certainty that the German wearing the shorts would have killed me with no more thought than he'd given to shooting the cat.

The first ten or fifteen seconds were the worst for us both; he kicked and bucked like an angry rodeo horse desperate to unseat its rider and it took every bit of my strength just to lie on top of him and keep him pinned down, pulling with all my might on both ends of the silk scarf to maintain the pressure. After I'd obstructed the blood flow to his brain for at least twenty or more seconds he was clawing at my hands, which is when his legs started to slow down at last; and after more than a minute I was certain I was lying on top of the body of a dead man. I knew this with even greater certainty when I detected the strong smell of his bowels in his shorts; the unpleasant fact is that when you have all your weight compressing a man's dying body, it's like squeezing a tube of toothpaste. Something has to give. But still I stayed there a while longer, tightening the scarf one last time until every drop of blood was gone from his brain, every millilitre of air was gone from his lungs, and, it seemed to my wrinkling nostrils, every bit of shit was squeezed out of his arse.

CHAPTER 50

April 1939

Gerdy Troost was reading Hitler's book in her comfortable upstairs rooms at the Berghof when I turned up.

'My, but you're a sight, aren't you?'

'Didn't I tell you? I'm practising to be a ventriloquist. This is the best way to learn, according to the instruction manual.'

'I think you've been reading the one for the dummy.'

I smiled and regretted it immediately.

'What happened, anyway? And don't tell me you slipped on the ice. Nobody slips around here unless they're meant to.'

'Someone hit me.'

'Now, why would they do that?'

'The usual reason.'

'Is there just the one?'

'There is where I'm concerned.'

The room was dimly lit and now she switched on another lamp to take a closer look at me, which was when I noticed the German shepherd lying in the corner. The dog growled as Frau Troost touched my face solicitously. Her fingers were cool and gentle and caring and her fingernails were unvarnished, as if she wasn't much interested in that kind of thing. Maybe Hitler didn't like women who looked too much like women.

'Does it hurt?'

'Only when I laugh, so really not at all.'

The dog kept on growling but this time it stood up.

'Quiet, Harras,' she said. 'Just ignore him, Commissar. He's jealous. But he certainly wouldn't do anything about it. Which is more than can be said for whoever clobbered you. They caught you a good one, didn't they?'

'Being hit is an occupational hazard for someone like me. I've got that kind of a face, I think. People just seem to want to punch it. Nazis, mostly.'

'Well, that certainly narrows it down. It's probably too late to put something cold on it, but I could do that, if you like. It might still help to take the swelling down.'

'I'll be okay.'

'I hope you're right. Because Obersalzberg has no shortage of Nazis. Me included, in case you'd forgotten.'

'I hadn't; not in this house. But you'll forgive me if I say that you don't look like the kind of Nazi who hits people in the face. Not without a very good reason.'

'Don't be too sure, Gunther. I can get pretty worked up about a lot of things.'

'You don't have to worry about me upsetting you, Professor. My opinion on design and architecture counts for absolutely nothing. I don't know a pediment from a pedicure. And when it comes to art, I'm a complete philistine.'

'Then it seems to me you're a lot nearer to being a Nazi than you might think, Gunther.'

'You know, you certainly don't sound like the Leader's girl-friend.'

'Whatever gave you the idea I was?'

'You, maybe.'

'I like him. I like him a lot. But not like that. Besides, he already has a girlfriend. Her name is Eva Braun.'

'Does she know much about art?'

Gerdy smiled. 'Eva doesn't know much about anything. Which is the way the Leader seems to like it. Except for me and the

Leader, this whole administration is run by complete philistines.'

'If you say so. You see? I'm not disposed to disagree with you about anything very much. But if you do feel like hitting me, then maybe you'd be kind enough to ask the dog to bite me instead. I can probably spare a leg more than my face right now. And not because it's so handsome but because my face has my mouth in it. I figure I'm going to need that if I am going to solve this case in the allotted time.'

'Like that, is it?'

I said it was.

'Bormann putting on the pressure?'

I nodded again. 'Like I was the prime minister of Czechoslovakia.'

'He's good at that.' She picked up the telephone. 'Still, I think you'd better eat *something*. Keep your strength up. I was about to request dinner service. I suggest you have some scrambled eggs. You'll have no problem with that. And a Moselle to take the edge off the pain. And what about a hot banana cooked in cream and sugar? The Leader's very fond of that himself.'

'Did someone smack him, too?'

While Professor Troost gave my dinner order to someone in the Berghof kitchens I walked around her rooms looking at the paintings, the architectural models, and the bronze sculptures. I don't have much of an eye for art, but I can usually recognize a good picture when I see one. Mostly it's the frame that gives it away and helps to distinguish it from what's happening on the wallpaper. After she had replaced the cream-coloured receiver in its cradle she came and stood beside me in front of a rather nicely rendered watercolour of mad King Ludwig's famous castle in Bavaria. After all the cheap cologne I'd been smelling, her own Chanel No. 5 was a breath of fresh air.

'Recognize it?'

'Of course. It's Neuschwanstein. I've got one just like it tattooed on my chest.'

'Adolf Hitler painted that.'

'I knew he painted houses,' I said, 'but I didn't know he did whole castles, too.'

'How do you like it?' she asked, ignoring both my attempts at humour.

'I like it,' I said, nodding appreciatively and thinking better of making another joke. Besides, I had to admit, it was a good painting. A little predictable for some, perhaps, but there's nothing wrong with that kind of thing in my book; I like a proper madman's castle to look like a madman's castle, not just a chaotic collection of cubes.

'He painted this in 1914.'

'It certainly doesn't look like something anyone would have painted in 1918.' I shrugged. 'But it's nice. You see? As I already told you, I'm a philistine. Was it a gift?'

'No. Actually I bought it from Hitler's old frame maker in Vienna. Cost me quite a bit, too. I'm planning to give it to him for his fiftieth birthday. The dog *is* a gift from Hitler. He and I are hoping that eventually his own dog Blondi and Harras will mate and have puppies. But right now, they don't seem to like each other very much.'

I nodded and tried to look sympathetic to their plight but I was thinking that if Hitler's dog was the one I'd seen sitting behind him in the photograph on Bormann's bookshelves, then I could easily understand Harras's problem. I'd seen friendlier dogs with rabies.

'Like I always say, you can lead a horse to water but you can't make it have sex with a mare against her will. There are laws prohibiting that sort of thing. Even in Germany. Especially when the mare turns out to be a different breed.'

'Oh, they're the same breed, all right. They just don't get along.'

'Sure, I get it. Like me and the Nazis.'

The dog seemed to realize it was being discussed and, sitting down, it raised its right paw in the air.

'That's another problem,' she explained. 'Harras sits down and gives a paw when people give the Hitler salute. It's like – it's like he's saluting back. It looks disrespectful.'

I tried it and when the dog gave me a stiff right arm, I grinned. 'Clever dog. I like him better already.'

Gerdy Troost smiled an awkward smile.

'Are you always this outspoken?'

'Only when I think I can get away with it.'

'And you think you can get away with it with me, is that it?'

'I think so.'

'If I were you I wouldn't be too sure about that. I've been a loyal Party member since 1932. I may not hit you in the face. But I probably know a man who will.'

'I don't doubt it. But isn't that why you agreed to help me? Because there's been a bit too much of that on Hitler's mountain? Because Bormann is a bully and corrupt? Because he's been getting away with murder?'

Gerdy Troost was silent for a minute.

'That's right, isn't it? You did agree to help me. Not to volunteer anything. Just to answer a few specific questions? Me telling you what I know, and then you confirming it, if it's true. Just like my own Ouija board. Right?'

Professor Troost sat down and clasped her hands tight.

'You know, I've been thinking a lot about what I told you the last time we spoke and I realize I feel very awkward about this. So I've decided I don't want to say any more, okay? I think you're an honest man just trying to do his duty but—' She shrugged. 'I don't know, I can't see how it's a very good idea for me to help you. I'm sorry.'

I nodded. 'I understand. It must be very difficult for you to talk about this at all.'

'It is. Especially now. So close to Hitler's birthday. He's done so much for me and for this country. I wouldn't ever do anything to harm the Leader.'

'Of course not,' I said patiently. 'No one would. He's a great man.'

'You don't believe that.'

'Listen, any leader needs good advice. It's just some of these people around him are not what they should be. Isn't that right?'

'It's getting worse, too.'

'Mmm hmm.'

'The fact remains that I can't see how you could bring down Martin Bormann without damaging the Leader. So it's probably best I say nothing at all.'

I took out a cigarette, remembered where I was, and returned it unsmoked to the pack. 'Can you tell me anything, Professor? Anything at all. I've got a ledger here in my briefcase that was in Karl Flex's possession, which might be evidence that Martin Bormann is corrupt but I'm not sure. Perhaps I could show it to you.'

She stayed silent. But she was twisting the ring on her finger uncomfortably, as if what it signified might be troubling her at last.

'I could show the ledger to Albert Bormann, perhaps. Well, maybe he would talk to me if you won't.'

Gerdy Troost stared silently at the gold signet ring on her bony finger as if trying to remind herself of where her true allegiance lay, which was hardly surprising as the ring bore some Nazi Party insignia. In her white two-piece suit she looked like Hitler's reluctant bride. It was probably him or Frankenstein's monster.

'But I don't want you to feel in a difficult position,' I said.

'And I don't want to say any more, okay?'

'I guess I'll just have to take my chances with Albert Bormann.'

'You'll be wasting your time,' she said. 'He might agree to see you but he won't trust you. Not with this. Not without a word from me.'

'Still, I have to try, I think. Someone has to try and save the life of Johann Brandner.'

'Who's he?'

'Local man. Used to be a photographer in Obersalzberg until Martin Bormann forced him to leave the mountain. They're planning to pin Flex's murder on the man and have him in front of a firing squad before the Leader's birthday if I don't find the real killer.'

'I don't believe that. They wouldn't do that. Surely.' She shook her head firmly. 'Why would they do such a thing?'

'To reassure the Leader. Someone has to pay the price for this, even if it's the wrong man. For appearances' sake.'

'No, that can't be. They wouldn't shoot an innocent man.'

'They would and they do. And much more often than you think.'

I let that nail go in before I spoke again.

'Look, maybe I should leave now.' But I stayed seated. It was time I played my highest card. The ace I'd been saving for just such a moment. It was dealt off the bottom of the deck, perhaps, but I was tired of trying to play fair with these damned people. The Nazis didn't ever play by the rules, and by her own admission Gerdy Troost was a Nazi, so what did I care if I upset her? My cruelty was nothing beside the cruelty that had been visited on German Jews. That kind of institutional cruelty didn't seem to count for anything. I hardened my heart and prepared to inflict some mental anguish on Adolf Hitler's houseguest.

'Hey, I nearly forgot. Which is no disrespect to you or to your friend, only I have a million things in my mind at present. Maybe that's the real reason for the swelling on the side of my head. It's all the stuff I'm trying to keep in there. Anyway, look, I've got some bad news for you, Professor.'

'About what?'

'About Dr Wasserstein. You asked me if I could find out what happened to him? I'm afraid he's dead.'

'Dead? Oh my goodness. How?'

'The poor man committed suicide. I guess someone was

determined to stop Dr Wasserstein from practising medicine after all. Look, I know you tried to help him get his licence back. It was a nice gesture. Everyone's pet Jew, right? I get that. So there's no reason for you to feel in the least bit responsible for what others did. It's really not your fault he dead-ended. Not a bit.'

'What happened?'

'He Hermann Storked off Maximilian's Bridge in Munich and drowned in the Isar River. He was wearing his best suit and his Military Merit Cross at the time. I'm afraid it's not uncommon for Jews to do something like that when they want to emphasize their German identity. When they want to make people feel guilty. It doesn't make me feel guilty. But then, I never knew this Fritz. Not like you, Professor.'

'Did he explain why?'

'Yes, he did. He left a suicide note on the desk in his empty surgery. It's not young Werther but still, I thought you might like to see a copy that was provided for me by the Munich police. Most Jews who kill themselves these days write longish notes in the hope of making their situation public. They've read too much Goethe, probably. I think they rather imagine that the authorities will be more shocked than they ever are.' I shrugged. 'They never are. The fact is, nobody gives a damn about this kind of thing. At least not the people who are in authority.'

I handed her the evidence envelope from the Munich police that Friedrich Korsch had given me and watched as she fetched her handbag and found some reading glasses. She read the doctor's letter once, to herself, and then she read it again, only this time she read it aloud. Perhaps she thought it appropriate that a dead Jew's voice should be heard in that particular house and in this I think she was right. It was a hell of a letter.

To the 'German' police who may or who may not – as seems more likely – investigate the circumstances of my death.

I have decided to kill myself and if you're reading this then I'm very probably dead. I certainly hope so. I had planned to kill myself with pills but today I went to my local pharmacy and was told that as a Jew I could no longer write myself the prescription that would enable me to take my own life quietly at home. So I have decided to drown myself in the Isar River, which is nicely in spate at the present moment. I am not and never have been a praying man but I do ask almighty God that I succeed in killing myself and that someone who knows me will perhaps write to my family to tell them I am dead, and to ask them to forgive and condone what I felt obliged to do, but still to think of me with love nevertheless. I greet them and at the same time I say farewell to them forever, with all the love that any father ever had for his children. For fifty years I have been a loyal, hardworking German citizen. First as a soldier in the Prussian Army and then as a dedicated eye specialist in Berlin and Munich, treating Aryans and non-Aryans alike. The Military Merit Cross I am wearing on my jacket today I wear with as much pride as I did the day I received it, in 1916. It was the greatest moment of my life when the Kaiser himself pinned it to my tunic. In spite of everything that has happened I still believe in Germany and in the goodness of ordinary Germans. But I have stopped believing in any kind of a future for myself. I fear for all Jews in Germany and strongly suspect that for them at least the future will be even worse than the present, although that seems hardly possible. For fifteen years I was married to a non-Aryan who died not long after our last child was born. Since then I have had little or no contact with other Jews, brought my children up in the Aryan way, and exercised no Jewish influence on them. It really didn't seem that important. I even brought my children up in the Protestant faith. But none of this counts for anything these days and because the present Nazi government and its anti-Jewish laws class them as Jewish I sent them away to

England several years ago, for which I now thank God and the kind English family who took them in. I myself stayed on in Germany because I have only ever wanted to serve my country and my patients. Some good German friends were able to help me keep my licence to practise medicine but this was overtaken by recent events I now suspect were stage-managed by others determined to prevent this from ever happening. The fact is that I am informed by the police that one of my patients now accuses me of having libelled the Leader for which I have been ordered to appear at the local police station next week. It's a put-up job of course and I imagine the chances of my receiving a fair hearing are almost nil and that I am facing deportation or worse. But I don't want to live without a profession, a Fatherland, a people, without citizenship, while being outlawed and defamed. I don't want to carry the name Israel, only the name my dear parents gave me. Even the worst murderer gets to keep his own name in this country, but not, it seems, a Jew. I am so weary of life in Germany and have been through so much that I cannot now dissuade myself from this present course of action. I am the fourth person in my extended family who has killed themselves in as many years. But only when I am dead will I feel truly safe.

Karl Wasserstein, Doctor of Medicine, Munich, March 1939

When she'd finished reading, Gerdy Troost bowed her head as if she couldn't bear to meet my cold blue eyes. I let her take my hand and that was all right; I didn't have a drink or a smoke so I wasn't using it. Her grip was surprisingly strong. I didn't say anything. After a letter like that, what could I say except that the Nazis were bastards, and for obvious reasons I didn't want to say that. I still wanted her help. She was an intelligent woman, a lot smarter than me and she probably knew what I was thinking. It was time for Gunther to give his silver tongue a rest and let the silence turn to gold, perhaps. All the same I twisted the ring on her finger for good measure, as if tightening the bolt on a nut, trying to remind her that she was part of a vicious tyranny that persuaded German Jews to kill themselves, and perhaps threatened the fragile peace of Europe.

It was Gerdy who broke the silence.

'What do you want to know?' she asked tearfully.

CHAPTER 51

April 1939

After a light supper, Gerdy Troost looked at the ledger I'd taken from Karl Flex's safe. Mary Astor she wasn't, but Gerdy was better-looking than I'd led Friedrich Korsch to believe. A little thin to my taste, but well tailored and elegant with the kind of good manners you would have expected of an educated woman from Stuttgart. It's the kind of town where people say hello when you walk into a bar, as opposed to Berlin, where they try their best to ignore you. Her mouth wasn't much more than a slit; at least until she smiled, when she revealed a set of small, uneven but very white teeth that reminded me of the perforation on a stamp. She turned the pages of the ledger slowly, and with great concentration, while sipping at a glass of Moselle. After a while she said, 'You know, a lot of the names in this ledger are listed as employees of the Obersalzberg Administration. Polensky & Zöllner. Sager & Woerner. It strikes me that you'd be better off asking the state engineer August Michahelles about them. Or perhaps Professor Fich.'

'He's in Munich.'

'Then perhaps Ludwig Gross? Otto Staub? Bruno Schenk? Hans Haupner? I'll bet they could tell you about some of these names in minutes. They have files on almost everything.'

'So far, none of these officials have proved to be very helpful. It's my guess that they've been told to keep quiet about whatever the hell is going on here. And I'm forced to conclude that perhaps they have the same misgivings about helping the police with their inquiries that you did. But that's hardly a surprise. Law enforcement has ceased to mean very much to anyone these days. I had to get quite rough with the first administrator, Bruno Schenk, and polish my damn warrant disc with his nose before he would even give me the time of day.'

'Nevertheless, that's where your answers are to be found, I think. At the Obersalzberg Administration building in Berchtesgaden. But Schenk's not your man. Whenever I go there he's somewhere else. And even when he is there his nose is ten metres up in the air. You want someone like Staub or Haupner, someone who's in the office a lot and has regular access to the personnel files.'

'How often are you there?'

'Several times a week. Thanks to the Leader I have my own little office at OA where I do most of my design work when I'm here in Obersalzberg. Whereas Albert Speer has a whole architectural studio near his house. He never designs anything of interest but he's kissed the Leader's backside so often that Hitler imagines he has talent. Mostly he's just copying a simple, very German style perfected by my late husband, Paul. The Leader offered me a house and a studio of my own but I don't need much more than a desk and a chair for my own designs, so I declined.'

'Those all-important medals and decorations you've been designing for Hitler.'

'Exactly. I sometimes work down there in the evening when no one else is around and I can concentrate. I'm also asked my opinion on all sorts of local construction issues.'

She was beginning to sound self-important but then that was hardly surprising given where we were. Even the dogs in Obersalzberg seemed to have dynastic plans.

'Professor Bleeker wanted my opinion on almost all his ideas for the tea house. And I'm always on the telephone to Fritz Todt. He's the director of the Head Office for Engineering, you know.'

I didn't, but that was hardly a surprise, either; the Nazis had so many jobs for their boys, it was hard to keep abreast of the full extent of the NSDAP's nepotism. They had more 'nephews' than the Roman Catholic Church.

'I'd be glad to take you down there in the morning, if you like.'

'The last thing I need now is more Nazi bureaucrats closing ranks against me. A line of SA men with their arms linked couldn't have provided a more solid cordon to my inquiry than they've done. Besides, I see better at night. What's wrong with taking me there right now?'

Gerdy Troost glanced at her watch. 'I'm not sure the state engineer would approve of you being there. And I happen to know there are some architectural plans on the drawing board in the meeting room that might be confidential. Really, I should ask Dr Michahelles's permission first before taking you there.'

'Frankly I'd prefer it if you didn't. Not until I have half an idea of what I'm really looking for.'

'It doesn't seem right, somehow. I don't know.'

I let her waver like this for a while and then took out the last of the categorical imperative I was still carrying in my pockets. It was a long time since I'd read Kant but I still knew how to play a few of his angles. Any cop does. 'Sure you do. But if you've forgotten, then you'll probably find the reason on page two of Dr Wasserstein's prescription on how to be a decent German.'

'Is that what it was? I thought it was a suicide note.'

'It amounts to the same thing. And you know that helping me is the right thing to do, so why even argue about it?'

'What are you expecting to find?'

'Would you believe me if I said I don't think I will know for sure until I find it? Gathering evidence is like finding truffles. The pig has to stick its nose to the ground and sniff around for quite a while before it ever digs up anything interesting. And even then it's sometimes hard to distinguish a piece of fungus that's worth anything from a bit of shit.'

'You've made your point. But you don't act like a pig. And believe me, I should know. Martin Bormann is the biggest pig on the pork farm. You're more of a hound, I think. A Weimaraner. A grey ghost from Weimar. Yes, that's you.'

'The ghost sounds about right. My feet are sore, and ever since I got here my heart feels like a clenched fist and I think I will be grey by the time I finish investigating this case. So you'll take me there? To Obersalzberg Administration's offices?'

'All right. Only, do you mind if we go there in my car? I like to drive but I prefer not to when Hitler's here at the Berghof. He doesn't approve of women drivers. I'm not sure he approves of women doing anything very much except having babies and frying some Fridolin's schnitzel. He often says that a woman who drives is a woman who dies.'

'I guess that counts double if you're smoking at the wheel.'

'Probably.'

Professor Troost telephoned the Berghof duty officer and asked him to have her car brought around to the front. A few minutes later we were seated in a nice blue Auto Union Wanderer and heading down the mountain at the sort of speed that made me think Hitler was probably right about women drivers. By the time we reached Berchtesgaden I had him down as a pretty sensible sort of fellow who put a high value on his life. The dog, Harras, seemed to enjoy the ride, however; he sat behind us with a big stupid grin on his muzzle, pawing the air uselessly.

The offices of Obersalzberg Administration were ten minutes from the centre, on Gebirgsjägerstrasse in Berchtesgaden-Strub, a short distance past the Adolf Hitler Youth Hostel and the local army barracks, which was home, Gerdy told me, to a whole regiment of mountain infantry, just in case the RSD up in Obersalzberg proved insufficient for Hitler's defence. The office, part of a complex of impressive new buildings, was dominated by an enormous floodlit stone lion, which made a change from an eagle, I suppose; even so, the lion looked like it was doing something unspeakable to a ball finial, which was the same unspeakable thing the Nazis were doing to Germany. Gerdy Troost drew up in front of the OA building in a squeal of tyres and stepped out of the Wanderer. There were no lights in the office.

'Good,' she said. 'There's no one here.'

She unlocked the front door with a large black key, switched on a light, threw aside her fur stole, and ushered me inside, where everything was white walls, shiny brass locks, blond oak, and grey stone floors. Everything smelled of recently planed wood and new carpets; even the telephones were the very latest combination-rotary-dial models from Siemens. On the walls were lots of framed plans and drawings, photographs of Hitler, portraits of long-forgotten Germans, and, on the largest wall, a big print of Leonardo da Vinci's *Vitruvian Man*, which is beloved of fascists everywhere, as it shows the blend of art and science and proportion, although to me it always looked like a naked policeman trying to direct traffic around Potsdamer Platz. Under a coffered ceiling, double-sized windows ensured there was plenty of light during the day, and copies of *The Architectural Digest* lay on almost every table in the public areas. The dog ran ahead and disappeared upstairs to practise its salute. Gerdy showed me her office and what was on the drawing board, but by now I was less interested in her work than in the grey filing cabinets that were grouped in a large room on the ground floor and, in particular, those cabinets that housed the personnel files. I tugged at the drawer of one; it was locked, but that wasn't going to deter me now.

'I don't have the keys to those, I'm afraid,' said Gerdy. 'So we'll have to wait until we can speak to Hans Haupner in the morning.'

I grunted, but the Boker knife I carried was already in my hand. That and the slim piece of smooth, curved spatula-like metal I'd found on the ground where Hermann Kaspel's car had been parked in Buchenhohe; it made a very useful jimmy. With these simple tools I set about breaking into the drawer.

'You can't do that,' said Gerdy fearfully, even as I was able to prise open the cabinet with my makeshift jimmy and slide the lock catch to the side with the knife. My breaking and entering wasn't quite up to the standard of the Krauss brothers but it was good enough.

'It looks like I already did,' I said, hauling open the drawer.

'So that's why you wanted to come here. To get into these filing cabinets.'

I laid my tools on top of the cabinet. She picked these up and looked at them as I started to riffle through the files.

'Do you always go equipped for burglary?'

'Listen, when Roger Ackroyd gets murdered, someone's supposed to do something about it. Even if Roger Ackroyd was scum, someone is supposed to do something about it. That's one of the more important ways you know that you're living in a civilized society. At least it used to be. Hercule Poirot is supposed to make sure that Roger Ackroyd's killer doesn't get away with it. Well, right now, that Hercule Poirot's me until someone else says different. People lie to me, people try to kill me, people punch me in the face, people tell me I shouldn't ask questions about things that are none of my business, and me and my broken jaw just have to find a way around all that in the best way I can. Sometimes that includes a gun and a hat, and sometimes a knife and a piece of scrap metal. I never much was one for a magnifying glass and a briar pipe. But any day now I expect the Murder Commission to close up shop and for me to be made redundant and for General Heydrich – he's my boss – to say, "Hey Gunther, don't bother doing that shit anymore. It's not important who killed Roger Ackroyd because we killed him, see? And we'd rather our fellow Germans didn't know about this, if you don't mind." And that will be all right, too, because at least then I'll know I'm no longer living in a civilized society, so it won't matter. Because we will be living in a state of barbarism, and nothing much will matter anymore. I'll be able to go home and tend my window box and lead the kind of quiet, respectable life I always wanted to enjoy. If I sound cynical and bitter it's because I am. Trying to be an honest cop in Germany is like playing croquet in no-man's-land.'

'That's a nice speech. Sounds like you've given it before.'

'Only in front of my bathroom mirror. That's the only audience I trust these days.'

Gerdy Troost put the knife down but kept hold of the spatula, weighing it in her hand as if she enjoyed the feel of it and smiling a wry sort of smile. 'But this tells me that you're selling yourself short, Gunther. I doubt you could ever be as respectable as you like to make out. No one truly respectable would keep something like this in his top pocket.'

'You mean you know what that is?'

'Yes. Most women would. Most women and probably most doctors, too. But even for them it's hardly done to keep this next to your favourite fountain pen and Grandpa's old cigarette case.'

'It's a medical instrument?'

'You really don't know?'

'I keep away from doctors if I can.' I smiled. 'And I don't know anything about women.'

'Well, it's hardly scrap metal. It's a dilator. It's used to widen and lengthen a woman's private parts during an examination.'

'And here was me thinking that was done with forefinger and thumb. I don't mean to sound excited. Only the contents of my pockets don't usually come with such a fascinating history.'

'I seriously doubt that.'

'Used by who? What kind of doctor?' I knew the answer to this, but I just wanted to have it confirmed by someone else. I was already thinking about Dr Karl Brandt's previous existence, sterilizing women considered racially or intellectually inferior – to say nothing of his more recent work terminating pregnancies for the unfortunate women of P-Barracks, when he wasn't devoting himself to the Leader's health.

'A gynaecologist. An obstetrician.'

'Where would that kind of doctor normally keep such an instrument?'

'It's been a while since I, er – but in a little wallet or cloth wrap of medical instruments, probably. Somewhere cleaner than your inside pocket, I hope.'

'And might that wallet include something sharp? Like a curette?'

'Almost certainly.'

I had a vague memory of seeing just such a cloth wallet on the desk in Brandt's makeshift surgery at the theatre in Antenberg. And now that she'd explained what it was, the scene was easily pictured: Karl Brandt had got underneath Hermann Kaspel's car, taken out his medical instruments, used a curette to cut the car's brakes – probably the same curette he'd used to cut open Karl Flex's corpse – and the dilator had slipped out of the wallet in the dark. He probably didn't even know it was gone until long after I'd found it lying in a pool of hydraulic fluid outside Kaspel's house in Buchenhohe. Of course, it was one thing knowing this; it was quite another accusing an SS doctor of murder when Adolf Hitler had been the guest of honour at his wedding. That wasn't ever going to happen, and my nice speech about the murder of Roger Ackroyd sounded even more hollow now than it had before. They'd certainly shoot me long before they ever allowed Karl Brandt to go to the guillotine. It was for this reason I kept my new discovery to myself; the last thing I wanted was for Gerdy Troost to air an accusation like that over the tea table at the Kehlstein.*

---

* Three years later, in May 1942, I would have sight of a confidential medical report that raised the possibility that, on Himmler's orders, Brandt had poisoned Heydrich, who was recovering from wounds sustained during an attack by Czech partisans.

'Seriously, though,' she said. 'Where did you get this?'

'I found it. On the floor of the room at the local hospital where we took Karl Flex's body for the autopsy.'

'You sure about that?'

'Sure I'm sure.' I glanced around. 'Are we allowed to smoke in here? Only, my answers are always much more convincing when I have a nail in my face.'

Gerdy found her own cigarettes and poked one in my mouth and then one in hers. They were the good, solidly packed cigarettes with the best Turkish tobacco the Nazis kept for themselves, at least when Hitler wasn't around to sniff the air in the corridors and check for nicotine on their thumbnails. He'd have made a good detective, maybe. He seemed to have a nose for people breaking the rules. Takes one to know one. I let her light me, too. I realized I liked the idea of that. It made me feel as though we were almost fellow conspirators, two of life's problem children locked inside Hitler's morbid sanatorium, rebels seeking a cure from the stiflingly pure atmosphere of the magic mountain.

'You worry me, Gunther. And I just know I'm going to regret helping you.'

'You're the one pushing the cigarette in my mouth, lady. The Leader wouldn't like you corrupting me in this way. I was in the choir when I was at school. I had a lovely voice.'

'And you're the one breaking into confidential filing cabinets with vaginal dilators.'

'I love the way you say "filing cabinets". Which reminds me.' I handed her the ledger. 'Read out some of those names, will you? We've got work to do.'

CHAPTER 52

April 1939

In a civilization ruled by cruelty and blind obedience, ignorance and bigotry, intelligence shines out like the Lindau Lighthouse, casting its beam for miles in all directions. The famous old Lindau Lighthouse, situated on the northeastern shore of Lake Constance, is perhaps unusual in that it also boasts a massive clock that can easily be viewed from the city. Thus it was with Gerdy Troost. Not only was she extremely bright, she was also perceptive and informative and I seriously doubt I would have made any real progress with my investigation without her help. It was easy to see why Adolf Hitler had made this elfin-faced woman a professor and kept her around the Berghof; it wasn't only for her ideas on architecture. Famously, she had designed and supervised the construction of the Leader's new buildings on Munich's Königsplatz. Gerdy Troost was ferociously smart and from what she herself had said to me, I gathered that she was probably able to tell him a few home truths where no one else would have dared. When the most wicked and mendacious are in charge, truth is the one commodity that is the most valuable of all. To that extent, Gerdy Troost reminded me of me. But which of us would remain alive for longer in Nazi Germany remained to be seen. Truth nearly always outstays its welcome.

After reading aloud almost fifty names from Karl Flex's ledger, she and I had discovered only that none of them related to a specific personnel file that was in the OA filing cabinets for Polensky & Zöllner, or for Sager & Woerner. The names appearing in the ledger were in a single file on one master list of all OA employees – this amounted to more than four thousand men – but that was all. For none of Flex's B-list names did we find any individual personnel files with the kind of cross referencing of numbers for employment identification books, identity cards, labour service passbooks, craftsman's guild certificate numbers, NSDAP personal identity documents, racial declarations, family books, Aryan family tree records, and paybooks that appeared on the files of those employees who were not on the ledger's B list and which were entirely typical of the bureaucratically minded Nazis.

And as I closed one drawer and opened another, Gerdy said: 'I have a question. A fundamental question.'

'Go ahead and ask it.'

'You seem to have a great deal of faith that this ledger provides solid evidence of criminality. But why would someone record and keep evidence that could put him in prison? Or worse. You'd think he would want to keep this kind of thing a secret.'

'It's a good question. For one thing, Bormann doesn't trust anyone. Certainly not these people he uses for his dirty work – Flex and Schenk and Zander. They're criminals. I'm quite convinced of that. But they're also bureaucrats. Record-keeping is second nature to men like this. It's almost as if the keeping of detailed records makes what they're doing less criminal. They can even convince themselves that they were only doing what they were told. Besides, the ledger *was* a secret. I had to break into a hidden safe in order to find it.'

'Maybe so. But I'm looking at it now, and there's nothing in these OA files that corroborates any actual evidence of criminality. Either Karl Flex wasn't doing anything wrong in the first place, or the people running Obersalzberg Administration are just plain incompetent.'

'Did they previously strike you as incompetent? Careless?'

'Not in the least. If anything they're meticulous in OA. I happened to catch sight of the interior decorating expenses for the tea house the other day. Everything was noted. And I mean everything. The tablecloths from Deisz, the deck chairs from Julius Mosler, and the Savonnerie rug from Kurt Goebel.'

'As a matter of interest, how much does one of those rugs cost anyway?' I shrugged. 'I've been thinking of redecorating my apartment in Berlin.'

'Forty-eight thousand reichsmarks.'

'For a rug? That's more than my whole building cost.'

Gerdy looked sheepish. 'Everything used by the Leader is of the very best quality.'

'You don't say. By the way, and not that it's any of my business – I'm just a taxpayer – but how much in total has been spent on this vitally important project?'

'I can't tell you that. This is a very sensitive subject.'

'Tea houses usually are.'

'This one certainly is.'

'Come on. Who am I going to tell? The newspapers? The International Tea Association? The Emperor of Japan? Humour me.'

I opened another drawer to look for a file in the name of someone on Flex's list; but there was nothing. Gerdy let out a sigh and folded her arms, defensively.

'All right. And the numbers are, I admit, inherently unbelievable. But all this had to be done in time for Hitler's fiftieth birthday. So I think Polensky & Zöllner's costs are something in the region of fifteen million. Sager's, maybe half that. The fact of the matter is that the tea house on the Kehlstein has cost at least thirty million reichsmarks.'

I whistled. 'That's a lot of money for a cup of tea and a nice view. It might have been cheaper to buy Ceylon. It makes you wonder what the Berghof cost. And the rest of the houses here in Asgard. Not to mention all the roads and tunnels, the railway station, the Platterhof, the local Reichs Chancellery, the theatre, the youth hostel, and the Landlerwald.' I whistled some more. A figure like thirty million reichsmarks is worth a good deal of whistling. 'How much do you think Bormann makes in kick-backs on a figure like that?'

'It's only a guess, mind – but at least ten per cent. Not that you could ever prove it.'

'And Hitler? What about his end? Or is Bormann taking care of the Leader out of his share?'

'Hitler's not interested in money. That's one of the things that makes him different.'

'Look, I hate to sound penny-pinching regarding the Leader's comfort and relaxation but doesn't any of this strike you as just a little bit insane?'

'I can only say this,' she said. 'That Hitler is no ordinary man.'

'That much is obvious. There's nothing very ordinary about a man who owns a rug that costs fifty thousand reichsmarks. But this is the only thing that's obvious right now. This and the fact that Flex was clearly taking money from people listed in his ledger as employed by P&Z and Sager, who don't actually seem to have been employed by P&Z and Sager. At least none who can show any normal employment record. And the trouble with this is that when someone has a job that doesn't exist it's only a racket if they're being paid for that job. According to these files they're not. I hate to say this but on the face of things, you're right. There's no obvious sign of criminality in these records. Clearly we're missing something. But I don't know what it is.'

'Let's take a break,' said Gerdy. 'I'm tired. I don't have the stamina for this that you do. I'm just a designer, not a cop. I think you need an accountant.'

I followed her into the kitchen, where she filled a glass Silex with coffee and water and put it on the big gas stove. On the wall was a print of one of those awful fruit and vegetable portraits that make apples and grapes look like grotesque, erupting skin conditions. This one made me believe it was quite possible I had a marrow for a head and a tomato for a brain. But none of it looked any more ridiculous than having your jaw tied up with a necktie. I was a natural for a picture by one of those artists.

'You're hoping I'm wrong about all this,' I said. 'I can understand that.'

'Look, are you absolutely sure that Johann Brandner is innocent?'

'You have my word on it. When Karl Flex was shot, Brandner was three hundred kilometres away, in a hospital in Nuremberg. He went there suffering from the effects of malnutrition after spending six months in Dachau. Courtesy of Martin Bormann for obstructing the sale of his business premises in Obersalzberg to OA.'

'I remember him,' she said sadly. 'When I first came here, I tried to support some of the local businesses by giving them work. He printed some films for me. Pictures my late husband, Paul, took that had never been processed. He certainly didn't strike me back then as a man capable of murder.'

'I don't know that he's capable of anything now that the RSD have knocked him around. They made him sign a confession.'

'Who did that?'

'Rattenhuber. Högl.'

'Yes, they would.' Gerdy Troost frowned. 'Look, there is one thing that might be relevant. I don't know.'

'What?'

'Something Wilhelm Brückner once told me. Something he was a bit angry about – that Martin Bormann had arranged a while back. I'm afraid I've only just remembered it.'

'Which was?'

'Brückner's the kind of man who believes in the army as an idea. Serving in the army and then the Freikorps was the best thing that ever happened to him until he met Hitler. You've got to remember that during the war he served in the Bavarian Army with great distinction.'

'And?'

'Well, about a year ago Brückner heard that any kind of work for the Obersalzberg Administration was to be classed as a reserved occupation. It was Bormann's idea to make sure that all of the OA works proceeded as quickly as possible. It's what he calls a Leader Priority. In other words, if you work for P&Z, or Sager, or Danneberg, or any of these other local construction companies, this work is classed as being as important as being a coal miner or a worker in a factory making aeroplanes, and you don't have to serve in the army. At least for as long as you're employed by the OA. Of course, Brückner thought that was outrageous and unpatriotic. That it was the duty of every good German to serve his country in the army, and not with a pick and shovel.'

'Tell that to the German Labour Front.'

'Not that he ever said any of this to Martin Bormann. Or Hitler, for that matter. I mean, he couldn't. Wilhelm may be an SS general and the chief adjutant at the Berghof, but that's still not enough cauliflower on his lapel to take on Bormann. Besides, ever since his car accident and the affair with Sophie Stork, things haven't been going that well for poor Wilhelm. Bormann is just looking for an excuse to persuade Hitler to get rid of him. Crossing his lordship is simply not an option. Which reminds me, Gunther. If anything does come of your investigation, would you please make sure that you leave my name out of this? If Hitler finds out that I was behind the fall of his most trusted servant, I'll be on the first train back to Munich.'

'That isn't going to be much of a problem. Right now my investigation seems to be turning up absolutely nothing. I feel like the dumbest Fritz in the regiment. When I was in the army that was always the chaplain. In the trenches only the chaplain was dumb enough to believe in the existence of God. Today, well, I suppose it would be anyone who believes there isn't going to be a war. I sometimes wonder what's going to happen to all those naïve young men who put on an army uniform with such alacrity. I fear they're in for a very rude shock. I did my bit, but you know, things were different then. Back in 1914, I think Germany was probably no worse than the Tommies or the Franzis. Now, if there is going to be another war there won't be any doubt who started it. Not this time.'

'Maybe you're not as dumb as you look,' she said, tugging playfully at the tie underneath my chin.

'That's always possible. But I'm feeling a lot dumber than I expected to feel. I was quite sure that I'd have some answers by now. It's beginning to look as though poor Johann Brandner is doomed to become a lead paperweight after all.'

'Bernie, you can't allow that to happen.'

'I'm trying my best but I can't see how even Bormann can take a cut from people for a job they're not actually paid for.'

'Maybe the pay for the job isn't the point.'

'That's what I always tell myself when the Ministry of the Interior sends me my wages every month, but people won't pay out for what they haven't had. Even to Nazis.'

'Maybe they will. If there's something else they're getting instead of money.'

'Like what? A cup of tea with Hitler once a year?'

'Listen, Gunther, this might sound crazy—'

'Here, in Berchtesgaden? Nothing sounds crazy in a place where they spend thirty million on a lousy tea house. Nietzsche and Mad King Ludwig would feel right at home in this town.'

'You don't suppose it's possible that Karl Flex decided to take advantage of this reserved occupation status for OA employees, do you? On Bormann's instructions, perhaps? To offer young men and their parents a way of avoiding military service in return for money. Could the B next to all these names stand for *befreit*? Exempt?'

I thought about this for a moment and smoked another cigarette while she made the coffee. Surely it would have been courting disaster to operate such a scheme. Because it wasn't just Wilhelm Brückner who regarded being in the army as something almost holy, it was Adolf Hitler, too. He was always running off at the mouth about how the German army had shaped his life and destiny.

'It could,' I said. 'But Bormann would be running a hell of a risk, wouldn't he? If Hitler found out about it.'

Gerdy shook her head. 'Hitler isn't the Lord of Obersalzberg, that's Martin Bormann. Bormann's like Cardinal Richelieu, Bernie. And Hitler is like King Louis XIII. The Leader isn't a man who's at all interested in details. He's quite happy to leave everything like that to Bormann. Administration bores him. And Bormann takes advantage of that. The man has a genius for administration. Hitler appreciates that. In which case Bormann might easily feel sufficiently omnipotent on Hitler's mountain that he could get away with a scheme like this, especially when it's operated at arm's length.'

'And even if Hitler did ever complain about it, then he could blame everything on Flex and the other men running these schemes at one remove.' The more I thought about Gerdy's idea, the more I realized it wasn't just possible, it was probable. 'Yes, that might work. In fact, that might work very well.'

'You think so?'

'Yes, this is what I call a proper racket,' I said. 'Let's face it. Only the most fanatical Nazi actually wants to go and fight in Poland. Not with the possibility of the Soviet Union and the French coming in on the Polish side. That would put us right back to 1914. A war on two fronts. Stay out of the army, stay alive – you don't have to be Leibniz to understand that kind of equation.'

I sipped the coffee and nodded. Now that she'd mentioned it, the racket seemed blindingly obvious. Who wouldn't want to pay money to keep their eldest son or a beloved nephew out of the army?

'Clever girl.' I grinned at her. 'You know, I really think you've put your finger on it, Professor. There are hundreds of names on Karl Flex's list. And not just here in Berchtesgaden, but also in every town between here and Munich. This racket is being operated right across Bavaria.'

'Almost fifteen hundred,' said Gerdy. 'I counted them.'

'Given the strong possibility of a war in Europe this year, a racket like this one would be worth a lot of money. According to the ledger, each of them is paying the equivalent of almost a hundred reichsmarks a year, so that's a hundred and fifty thousand reichsmarks. And all of it going into the accounts of Martin Bormann and his collectors.'

'But what's the point of it if you can just charge a new Savonnerie carpet to the government?'

'Because at any moment the whole gravy train might just come off the rails. Even the Lord of Obersalzberg has to prepare for a rainy day. To have some cash salted away for his possible exile. And on the basis of these numbers, there's plenty of cash to be made from this particular cow.'

'If it's true, then you should certainly take this to Albert Bormann,' said Gerdy.

'If it's true? It has to be true.'

'I suppose so.'

'There's no other possible explanation. You don't think it is true?'

'It certainly looks that way, yes, but – look, you've got a persuasive argument. But proof needs more than that. It needs real evidence. Hard evidence.'

'You're right. It's been so long since we bothered with that kind of thing in the police that I'd almost forgotten how it works. To prove this to Albert Bormann's satisfaction I need to lean on someone who will go on the record. A witness. One of the names on Flex's *B* list.' I ran my forefinger down the names in the ledger. 'This fellow, for example. Hubert Waechter, from Maximilian-strasse, here in Berchtesgaden. There's a local Nazi lawyer with the same surname at this address. I imagine it means that the father has paid to keep his son out of the army. Very sensible of him. And rather loathsome. I had dealings with him on another matter. But I'd still like to find out what these other lists mean. The *P* list and the *Ag* list. What are those rackets about?

'One of these names appears on all three lists in this ledger. The *B* list, the *P* list, and the *Ag* list. What's more, it's a name I've come across before. On a bogus suicide note. Something in my bones makes me fancy him for the murder of Karl Flex. I don't think the *B* list gives me a clear motive for murder. But maybe the *P* list and the *Ag* list will provide me with one. Who knows? It's just possible that I might hit two rabbits with one bullet. That I can nail Flex's murderer and Martin Bormann at the same time.'

I finished my coffee and rubbed my hands.

'So let's go and see if we can persuade this particular Fritz to spill his guts.'

'How are you going to do that?'

'I told you. I'll lean on him. Bormann's not the only man who can throw his weight around the trench.'

'In which case you really don't need me, Gunther. I'm not so heavy around this time of night. Not in these shoes.'

I took her little hand and explored it for a moment before I fetched it to my lips. Gerdy blushed a little but didn't snatch her hand away. She just let me kiss it, fondly, as if she knew how much I appreciated her help and knew what it was costing her to help me like this. Maybe she wasn't the kind of woman I thought she was. Women never are what you think they are. It's one of the things that makes them interesting. Either way, I liked her. Admired her, even. I wasn't about to do anything about that, though. With so many Nazis on the scene, courting her would have been courting disaster. Like wooing a nun in the Sistine Chapel. Besides, Gerdy Troost was in love with someone else, that much was clear. I was just mad enough to think I stood a quarter of a chance of bringing down Martin Bormann, but not mad enough to think I could compete with Adolf Hitler in the affections of a woman who still clearly believed he was a demigod.

She smiled. 'I'll drive you back to the Villa Bechstein, where you can pick up your friend Korsch and your car. But when you're ready to speak to Albert, come and fetch me. Any time. I'll only be reading, probably.'

For a moment I pictured her reading Hitler's book again, and winced.

'I don't sleep much when I'm here in Obersalzberg,' she added. 'No one does. Only Barbarossa.'

'Maybe I should speak to him, too.'

'You can try.'

'Take him for a drive in your car. That should wake him up a bit. In fact, I'd be surprised if he ever slept again.'

CHAPTER 53

April 1939

I was always a keen reader and learned at my mother's knee. My favourite book was Alfred Döblin's *Berlin Alexanderplatz*. I had a copy at home in Berlin in a locked drawer because it was a forbidden book, of course. The Nazis had burned a great many of Döblin's books in 1933 but every so often I'd get out my own signed copy of his most famous work and read bits aloud, to remind myself of the good old Weimar Republic. But the fact is, I'll read anything. Anything at all. I've read everything from Johann Wolfgang von Goethe to Karl May. Several years ago I even read Adolf Hitler's book *My Struggle*. I found it predictably combative but here and there I also thought it was perceptive, although only about the war. A critic I'm not, but in my humble opinion there's no book that's so bad that you can't get something from it, even that one. For example, Hitler said that words build bridges into unexplored regions. As it happens, a detective does much the same thing, only sometimes he can end up wishing he'd left those regions alone. Hitler also said that great liars are great magicians. A good detective is also a kind of magician, one who is sometimes capable of making those suspects he has assembled theatrically in the library utter a collective gasp as he works his revelatory magic. But that wasn't about to happen here, more's the pity. Another thing Hitler said was that it's not truth that matters, but victory. Now, I know there are plenty of cops who feel the same way but usually the truth is the best victory I can think of. I could go on in this vein but it boils down to just this: as Friedrich Korsch drove us to Johann Diesbach's address in Kuchl, I was thinking a lot about Gerdy Troost reading that damn book in her rooms at the Berghof, and I couldn't help but reflect that since arriving in Berchtesgaden I'd had quite a struggle myself. Most murder investigations are a struggle but this one had been especially so because it's rare, even in Germany, that someone tries to kill you during the course of your inquiry. I hadn't yet worked out what I was going to do about Dr Brandt but I wasn't about to let him get away with the murder of Hermann Kaspel. Not if I could help it. There had to be something I could do. Now, that really was going to be a struggle. And I said as much to Korsch as the car laboured up the mountain road. He listened carefully and said, 'You want my opinion, boss?'

'Probably not. But we're friends, so you might as well give it to me.'

'You should take your own advice a bit more often.'

'Remind me.'

'How can you possibly nail Hitler's doctor for a murder? What the hell does it matter if they execute Brandner for Flex's murder? Who cares if Martin Bormann is a crook? The Nazis are just like every king we ever had in Holy Germany. From Charles V to Kaiser Wilhelm II. They all think that their best arguments come from the barrel of a gun. So. While we can still walk away from here, before one of those guns shoots you, or even worse, shoots me, we should quit now.'

'I can't do that, Friedrich.'

'I know. But look, I had to say it. Your trouble is that you're the worst kind of detective there is. A German detective. No, it's worse than that; you're a Prussian detective. You don't just believe in your own competence and efficiency, you make a damn fetish out of it. You think your devotion to the job is a virtue, but it's not. With you it's a vice. You can't help yourself. It's something that runs through your character like the black stripe on the old Prussian flag. That's your problem, boss. If you investigate a case you have to do it scrupulously and to the very best of your ability. Realism and common sense are powerless against your pigheaded devotion to doing the job as efficiently as it's possible to do it. And this takes away all your better judgment about the wisdom of what you're doing. You just don't know when it's in your own interest to stop. That's why Heydrich uses you. Because you always stay the course. You're like Schmeling; you keep getting up even though the fight is lost. To that extent you're the most Prussian man I've ever met. I admire you, Bernie. I also can't help but think that there's a real danger you're always destined to be your own life's saboteur.'

'I'm glad I asked. It's kind of refreshing to have the truth, even if it does feel like a slap in the face.'

'It's fortunate for you I'm driving, boss. Otherwise that's what you'd get right now. Commissar or not.'

'I had no idea you had such a keen understanding of me. Or indeed were such a keen philosopher.'

'I think I know you pretty well. And only because there's a part of me that's just like you. I'm a Prussian, too, remember? And I can usually figure out what your next move is going to be. It's usually the one I wouldn't have the nerve to make myself.'

Kuchl was a picturesque Austrian village on the other side of the Kehlstein and the Göll massif, which formed the border with Germany and, according to a large sign on the road, had been JEW-FREE SINCE 1938. The village was one of those very neat Catholic places that resembles a scene from a book of fairy tales with lots of pastel-coloured houses, a largish church, and a smaller one that was a useful spare, grotesque wood carvings that demonstrated the village's facility for carving wood grotesquely, and a *Gasthof* with painted window frames and an ornate wrought-iron sign that looked like a medieval gibbet.

On almost every building was a Nazi banner or mural, which must have baffled the life-sized Jesus nailed onto the crucifix in the main square; in the cold, bright moonlight that painted figure seemed less like the Christ and more like the poor Jew, Süss Oppenheimer, who gets hanged in a near blizzard by the good citizens of Württemberg at the end of Veit Harlan's notorious film. In the main square we asked a young man leaving the *Gasthof* on a bicycle for the way to Oberweissenbachstrasse and Diesbach's Boardinghouse and were misdirected, politely, to another Jew-free village, called Luegwinkl. It was only after we'd asked for directions again, almost an hour later, that we finally made our way across a bridge over the Salzach River, to the edge of a tree-covered hillside, where we found Diesbach's Boardinghouse – a three-storey wooden chalet with a wraparound wooden balcony and a working waterwheel. Under the eaves of the house was a wooden stag's head and, by the front door, a park-style wooden bench, underneath which were enough dirty boots to keep a shoe-shine in business for a day or two. The upper-floor lights were on and there was a strong smell of wood smoke from the chimney.

'We're only a few kilometres from Germany,' said Korsch as we stood outside the front door. 'And yet I feel we just went several centuries back in time. I wonder why that is. Something in the air perhaps? A slight taste of aspic jelly.'

'I wonder why that young bastard sent us in the wrong direction,' I said. 'We were only five minutes away from this place when we asked him for directions.'

'Your accent? Perhaps he didn't like you.'

'Maybe. But more likely it was this car. It looks official. At this time of night we look like we're police. Who else would be arriving here at ten p.m.?'

'These people are too respectable to try and fuck with the law.'

'They may be old-fashioned, but they're not stupid. That boy had more than enough time to cycle over here and warn Johann

Diesbach we were coming. Perhaps Diesbach has been expecting us.'

I got out of the car and walked across the snow-covered path to a dry rectangle on the driveway where a car or perhaps a small truck had been parked until a short while ago. On the ground a few metres away, next to an old light blue Wanderer on bricks, was a used Mahle oil filter of the kind that had functioned as a makeshift sound suppressor on the barrel of the Mannlicher carbine used to shoot Karl Flex. But it was the pink footsteps in the snow that interested me the most; they were the same pink footprints I'd seen outside the house of Udo Ambros. I picked up one of the boots from under the bench and inspected the lugged sole; it was the same pattern as the one I'd seen before. The sole was encrusted with tiny crystals of pink salt.

'There was a car parked here until it stopped snowing about an hour ago. I'll bet my pension Diesbach isn't here.'

'Someone's in,' said Korsch, looking up. 'I just saw someone at the window.'

'Look, when we're inside, keep whoever's there talking while I take a leak and have a snoop around.'

I knocked on the door and a window upstairs opened.

'We're closed for the winter,' she said.

'We're not looking for rooms.'

'What are you looking for?'

'Open the door and we'll tell you.'

'I should think not. Look, what do you mean by knocking on someone's door at this time of night? I've a good mind to report you both to the police.'

'We *are* the police,' said Korsch, and then grinned at me. He never tired of saying that kind of thing. 'This is Commissar Gunther, and I'm Criminal Assistant Korsch.'

'Well, what do you want?'

'We're looking for Johann Diesbach.'

'He's not here.'

'Can you open the door please, missus? We need to ask you some questions. About your husband.'

'Such as?'

'Such as, "Where is he?"'

'I have no idea. Look, he went out this morning and he's not come home yet.'

'Then we'll come in and wait for him.'

'Couldn't you come back here in the morning?'

'It won't be my colleague and I who are back here in the morning. It will be the Gestapo.'

'The Gestapo? What would the Gestapo want from us?'

'The same thing they want from everyone. Answers. I just hope you have them, Frau Diesbach. They're not as patient as us.'

The woman who switched on the hall light and answered the door was wearing a low-cut blouse, a red velvet waistcoat, and a white pinafore, and was carrying more in front than a busy waitress at Oktoberfest. She was very tall with short dark hair, dry thick lips, and a neck like Nefertiti's Zulu cousin. Attractive, I suppose, in an Amazonian sort of way, as if Diana the huntress had possessed an older and more obviously lethal sister. Her green eyes flicked sharply across our faces but the hand at the side of her red cotton dress was trembling as if she was terrified of something; us, probably, but there was nothing in her voice that betrayed her fear: she spoke clearly and confidently.

'May I see some identification, please?'

I already had my beer token in my hand, which was right under her substantial breasts. Maybe that's why she didn't see it.

'Here.'

'That's it? This little piece of metal?'

'That's a warrant disc, lady,' I said, 'and I don't have the time.'

I pushed past the twin Gordian knots that were her bosom and went into the house.

CHAPTER 54

April 1939

'What's all this about?' Frau Diesbach closed the front door behind us and wiped her large hands on the white apron she was wearing. She was taller than Friedrich Korsch by more than a head.

'Are you alone?'

'Yes. Quite alone.'

We were in a hallway with a flagstone floor, a dark oak sideboard, and, on the whitewashed wall, an old photograph of the even older Austrian emperor Franz Joseph I, who looked a lot like the wiliest animal in the Vienna woods, and another of Crown Prince Rupprecht of Bavaria. There were several other pictures of a heavily moustached Johann Diesbach in uniform that seemed to indicate he'd been part of the German Sixth Army and a veteran of the Battle of Lorraine, which was one of the very first engagements of the war and generally held to have been so inconclusive that it had helped to create the stalemate of trench warfare that persisted for another four costly years. On his chest was an Iron Cross First Class. Several hunting rifles and shotguns were on a rack beside a woodcut print of a hermit ticking off a group of medieval horsemen for some undisclosed offence: waking him up, probably. Everything smelled strongly of pipe tobacco and since the lady of the house didn't strike me as an obvious pipe smoker herself, I concluded a man had been there very recently.

'What does your husband do, Frau Diesbach?' I asked.

'We own a small salt mine,' she explained. 'In Berchtesgaden. We refine our own high-quality table salt. Which he sells direct to restaurants throughout Germany and Austria.'

'Sounds like a lot of digging,' said Korsch.

'There's not much digging involved,' she explained. 'We use a brine extraction process. Freshwater is fed into the mountain and the nonsoluble components of the rock sink to the bottom. It's all about pumps and pipelines now, and very scientific.'

'Is he at the mine now?'

'No, he's away selling gourmet-quality salt to our big customers in Munich, so he could be home very late.'

'Which customers would they be?'

'The head chef at the Kaiserhof.'

I walked into the drawing room and switched on a lamp that appeared to be made of a large rose-coloured crystal. On the table next to it were several jars of pink salt. I picked one up. It was full of smaller versions of the table lamp and was the same salt that I'd seen in the lugs of the boot outside.

'I told you, my husband's not here,' she insisted irritably, and tugged nervously at a piece of dry skin on her lower lip.

'Is this it? Your gourmet-quality salt?'

'That's what it says on the label.'

'He's in Munich, you say.'

'Yes. Of course, it's possible he might stay overnight. If he's had too much to drink. Having dinner with clients, he often does, I'm afraid. It's an occupational hazard when you're offering hospitality.' She lit a cigarette from a silver box with nervous fingers. By now the cleavage between her breasts was shifting like the San Andreas Fault.

'The head chef at the Kaiserhof, Konrad Held,' I lied. 'I know him well. I could telephone him if you like and find out if your husband's still there.'

'It might not be the head chef he's seeing,' she allowed,

tugging at the skin on her lip some more. 'But someone else in the hotel kitchen.'

I smiled patiently. You get to know when someone is lying to you. Especially with tits as eloquent as hers. After that it's just a question of judging the right moment to let them hear that. No one likes being called a liar to his or her face. Least of all in their own home and by the police. I almost felt sorry for the woman; if it hadn't been for that earlier bit of sarcasm I might have been polite, but as things stood I was more inclined to bully her now, just to hurry things along. An innocent man's life was at stake, after all. There was a fretted shelf running the length of the drawing room at just above head height and my eyes were already sorting through the books, looking for something to help bring some extra pressure to bear on her, to overcome any more resistance to our questions. Mostly the books were to do with geology, but I'd already seen a couple of titles that might serve my purpose. But for now I ignored them and walked across the drawing room to the wide, red-brick fireplace. Behind a wrought-iron screen, the log fire was still burning quietly; the log was hardly a size you'd have chosen if you'd been on your own. Whoever had built that fire from scratch had done it for a cosy evening made for two. Next to the fire was an armchair and on the chair was a copy of that day's *Völkischer Beobachter*. I picked it up, sat down, and laid the paper on the hearth next to an ashtray and a tin of Von Eicken with the lid left off; in the ashtray was a pipe. After a while I picked that up as well and found the cherrywood bowl was still warm – warmer than the fire. It was all too easy to picture the man who had been seated there in front of the fire not half an hour before, puffing his tobacco like a Danube boat captain.

'It's a nice house you have here,' said Korsch, opening a drawer in the bureau.

Frau Diesbach folded her arms defensively. Probably it helped prevent her from hitting Korsch over the head with the table lamp. 'Make yourself at home, why don't you?'

'Is there much money in table salt then?' he asked, ignoring her remark. Sometimes police work contains the very opposite of a Socratic dialogue: you say one thing, I pretend I didn't hear it and say another.

'Like anything else, there is if you work hard.'

'I wish that was true,' said Korsch. 'There's certainly not much money in being a policeman. Isn't that right, boss?'

'Is that what you're looking for? Money? I assumed you were here to investigate a crime, not commit one.'

Korsch laughed harshly. 'She's a sour one. Must be all that salt, eh, boss?'

'Sounds like it.'

'You should try refining sugar, instead, missus.'

'Are you going to tell me what this is about?'

'I told you,' said Korsch, pulling open another drawer provocatively. 'We're looking for your husband.'

'And I told you. He's not here. And he's certainly not in that bureau.'

'Lots of people start out trying to be clever with us,' said Korsch. 'But it never lasts for very long. The last laugh is usually ours. Isn't that right, boss?'

I grunted. I didn't feel much like laughing. Not with my jaw tied up. And certainly not after seeing poor Aneta Husák murdered in cold blood. I wasn't about to forget that in a hurry. On top of a baby grand piano were some photographs and it wasn't long before I started to believe that one of these was of the same scholarly looking young man who had sent us on the wild-goose chase to Luegwinkl. After a while I got up, collected the picture off the polished piano lid, looked at it for a while, and showed it to Korsch who nodded back at me. It was him all right.

'That explains a lot,' he said.

'Who's this?' I asked Frau Diesbach.

'My son Benno.'

'Good-looking boy, isn't he?' Korsch was being sarcastic. With his thick glasses, receding chin, and coy expression, Benno Dies-bach looked like a real wet paper bag and just the type of sensitive, weedy boy an anxious, doting mother would have wanted kept out of something as rough as the army. My mother had probably felt the same way about me when I was about twelve, assuming she ever felt anything at all.

'Where is he now?' I asked.

'I thought you said it was my husband you were looking for.'

'Just answer the question, missus,' said Korsch.

'He went out. For a beer with some friends.'

'He doesn't look old enough.'

'He's twenty. And he's got nothing to do with this.'

'To do with what?' asked Korsch.

'To do with anything. Look, why are you looking for him at all?'

'Who?'

'My husband. He hasn't broken the law.'

'No?' From among several books on geology on the shelves I fetched a copy of Alfred Döblin's famous novel and another one by Erich Maria Remarque for good measure. They were the same cheap editions I had at home. 'Someone has. Are these his books or yours?'

'They must belong to – look, does it matter? My God, they're just some old books.'

I felt sure she'd been about to confess that the books belonged to her son, Benno. He certainly looked like anyone's idea of a keen reader.

'These are not just books,' I said, 'they're *forbidden* books.' There were times when it was necessary for me to sound like a real Nazi. Times when I hated myself more than was usual, even by my debased standards. I already had the strong sense not only that Johann Diesbach had just escaped us but also that his escape was *prima facie* evidence of his guilt. There was that and the pink salt in the soles of the boots outside. I was pretty sure that the man who had worn those had murdered Udo Ambros.

But with each minute that his wife managed to delay us, the better were the man's chances of evading capture and the worse were Johann Brandner's chances of escaping a firing squad or the falling axe at Plötzensee. 'Since 1933 these authors have been banned because of their Jewish descent or because of their communist or pacifist sympathies.'

'I had no idea. Says who?'

'The Ministry of Truth and Propaganda, that's who. Don't you see the newsreels in the cinema theatres? For the last six years we've been burning books we don't like.'

'We don't go to the cinema very much.'

'Me, I couldn't care less what you read but ignorance of the law is no excuse, Frau Diesbach. Ownership of these books can result in deportation, imprisonment, or even death. Yes, seriously. So I advise you to cooperate with us and tell us exactly where your husband is, Frau Diesbach, otherwise it won't just be him that's in trouble, it will be you, too.' I wondered exactly how much she knew of what her husband had done.

'Your husband is suspected of being involved in the commission of two murders.'

'Two?' She looked surprised at the number so I guessed that maybe she'd known about Flex, but not about Udo Ambros.

'Didn't I say we'd have the last laugh?' said Korsch.

'I've already told you both,' she said dully. 'Johann's in Munich.'

'With clients, yes,' said Korsch. 'Yes. You said that. We didn't believe it the first time you said it.'

The woman sat down heavily in a cloud of Guerlain and despair, and lit another cigarette. I helped myself to the one she was still smoking and which was lying in a large salt-crystal ashtray, puffed it thoughtfully, and smiled a painful smile.

'May I use your lavatory, Frau Diesbach?' I asked. 'While you think things over, perhaps. And I strongly recommend that you do.'

'Yes, I suppose so. It's at the top of the stairs.'

'What time will your son be back?' Korsch asked her.

'I really don't know. Why?'

'When are you going to understand that we ask the questions, Frau Diesbach?'

While Korsch kept her talking I went up the narrow stairs and took a look around. The house was like a smaller version of the Berghof, only without the resident dwarf Alberich. The hallway was lined with several historic maps of the old Bavarian Rhenish Palatinate, an area of southwestern Germany that bordered the Saarland, and framed photographs of cave formations and what looked like salt mines and interesting geological formations. Opening a couple of the plain wooden doors I found small, comfortable rooms with the mattresses rolled up like pastry, and several prints of Alpine hikers. It was probably a nice, clean place to stay in the summer; any happy wanderer would have slept well and after a good German breakfast prepared by Frau Diesbach they'd think they'd done well choosing it – especially if they managed to catch a glimpse or two of her ample bosom.

I opened a closet and on a shelf behind some blankets I found several boxes of the same red Brenneke slugs that had been used to kill Udo Ambros. Leaning against a thickly papered wall in a corner of the chilly master bedroom was a Walloon sword as long as a ski pole, which almost made me glad we'd not got there earlier. A white cat was lying on the brass bed and he stared at me with bright blue eyes that were as sharp as the sword and full of a cat's questions, which meant the answers were no more important than the time of day, the taste of fresh snow, or the shape of a cloud formation above the Kehlstein. There are times when I think it would be good to be a cat, even in that part of the world, at least as long as you stayed away from Hitler and the Landlerwald. Some of the drawers in the bedroom chest were empty and still open and, lying on the carpet, were a cuff-link, a collar stud, and a 7.62-mm Parabellum cartridge; clearly someone with a Luger pistol had left in quite a hurry.

On the bedside table was a piece of paper and on this was

a long list of customer names and train times for Munich and Frankfurt, which was unremarkable except for the fact that whoever had written it preferred using the same neat, semi-literate capital letters that had appeared on Udo Ambros's 'suicide' note. I folded the paper and pocketed it. More pictures among the ivory-handled hairbrushes and combs on the Biedermeier dressing table showed several of Benno, the much-loved young man who'd misdirected us earlier, clearly to allow him enough time to cycle home and warn his father, Johann – who appeared in another photograph with Udo Ambros when he'd still been in possession of a head, and before someone blew it off with a shotgun – that the police were now hot on his trail. Ambros was a tough-looking man, but Diesbach looked tougher and altogether more dislikeable, not least because the moustache had been trimmed and now looked exactly like Adolf Hitler's. I removed the pictures from their frames, put them in my coat pocket, and went into the next room. I stared at the man in the bathroom mirror, retied the Raxon keeping my jaw tight, and growled back at him:

'No wonder the cat was looking strangely at you, Gunther. You look like someone's idea of toothache.'

The bath was full of cold water, as if Frau Diesbach had been on the point of having a bath when her heroic son had arrived home and announced my imminent arrival; her stockings and underwear lay on a white basket chair behind the door. In another place I might have picked them up and sniffed them; it had been a while since I'd enjoyed the intimate smell of an attractive woman and I was beginning to experience withdrawal symptoms. Instead I picked up her brassiere and for a moment or two admired its sheer size. It looked like a slingshot that had once belonged to Goliath and one that might have substantially improved his slim chances against the shepherd boy David. That and a decent boulder or two. I'd always felt sorry for Goliath. But Bavarian mountain air does strange things to a Berlin Fritz like me.

There was a chromium-plated electric radiator on the tiled wall, a set of false teeth in a glass on the windowsill, and a large bathroom cabinet above the basin. I opened it and immediately saw the answers to questions the white cat might have cared more about if he'd known exactly how they were going to affect him. The plain fact of the matter is that you can't get a plate of fish and a saucer of milk if your owners are locked up in a concentration camp, or worse. But of professional satisfaction at my having suddenly grasped the full extent of what was going on here in the Diesbach home, there was none. Besides, I doubted that it was the kind of elegant drawing-room solution to a crime you'd have found in the work of any respectable detective story-teller like Agatha Christie or Dorothy L. Sayers; it wasn't the kind of police evidence that made you feel anything but ashamed to have discovered it. And I felt sick to my stomach at what I was now obliged to go downstairs and say to Frau Diesbach's face, because in the circumstances I didn't know that I'd have done anything different from what Johann Diesbach had done – except perhaps not shoot Udo Ambros. Nobody deserved to have their face become the startled facsimile of a painting by Picasso. In the bathroom cabinet was a bottle of Protargol. And it was about then I remembered that Protargol was silver nitrate and that the symbol for silver on the periodic table was Ag. Which probably explained the Ag list in Flex's loathsome ledger. There was some Pervitin, too – P for Pervitin? – but that hardly seemed important beside the standard medical treatment for a venereal disease. The question was, which of them was afflicted with the dose of jelly? Johann Diesbach, his wife, or both? Benno Diesbach didn't even come into my thinking here; from the look of him he was a long way off that first moment of joy when a boy becomes a very startled man. I'd seen more obvious-looking virgins on a Berlin street corner. I pocketed both types of pill and ran downstairs with more evidence for my present theories than Archimedes wearing just a bath towel.

CHAPTER 55

April 1939

'There's no way to say this that sounds kind or polite, Frau Dies-bach, so I'm just going to say it and then, if you're sensible and you tell me where he's gone, I'll try to help you. Your husband, I can't help. But there's no need for you to go the same way. I will catch him and when I do it would look better for you if I could tell my superiors that you cooperated. Even if you didn't. If you start throwing things at me now and affecting pious outrage, then I tell you frankly I won't like that at all. Or you. I'm telling you straight that if you don't cooperate, you're going to jail. Tonight. The way I see it is that your husband, Johann Diesbach, who was probably full of methamphetamine at the time, shot and killed Karl Flex because Flex gave you a venereal disease.' I placed the Protargol and the Pervitin on the table next to the salt. 'Exhibits one and two. Flex had decided he wasn't satisfied with your husband paying him money to pretend that your son Benno was working for the Obersalzberg Administration in order that he be kept out of the army. He liked you, too, and decided he wanted something other than money. He decided he wanted you in his bed. In return for giving you what you wanted. Unfortunately he also gave you a venereal disease.'

I paused as the tall, handsome woman who'd been about to have a bath sat down heavily and fumbled in her sleeve for a handkerchief. 'Good, I'm glad you're not arguing with this.

Because my jaw hurts, as you can probably see, and I really don't have the energy to argue back. Karl Flex wanted you in his bed and you agreed, because you love your son and getting him into a reserved occupation for a hundred marks a year seemed like the best means of keeping him out of harm's way. I only met him briefly and he seemed like a good boy. Loyal and, yes, brave, but maybe a little wet behind the ears, and you were right to try to get him deferred from the army because in wartime it's those young men with the sweetest faces who are usually the first to buy it because they're always trying to prove that they're not so wet after all. You agreed to sleep with Flex and he gave you a dose of jelly. And when you complained he referred you to Dr Brandt, who agreed to help find you a cure, because he's in on the same mountaintop racket as Flex. But by then you'd given the dose of jelly to your husband, and so he decided to put an end to it all. The whole rotten business. This is why Johann shot him. And good for him. That's what I say. Karl Flex had it coming with a nice telegram from the Kaiser. If I was married to you, I'd have probably shot him myself. Maybe I wouldn't have used my friend Udo's rifle to do it, mind. That was unkind because it left Udo in the frame for Flex's murder. Although not as unkind as what happened when Udo guessed he'd been measured up for it by his old friend. What did he do? Threaten to tell the police? He must have done, otherwise Johann wouldn't have gone to poor Udo's house and shot him, too. You didn't know about that? It doesn't matter. Take it from me, suicide it certainly was not. My jaw may be broken, but there's nothing wrong with my brain. There's a box of the same ammunition used to blow Udo's head off in a closet upstairs, as well as a sample of the same hand that wrote the so-called suicide note. As a case of murder it's a more open-and-shut case than my office door at the Murder Commission in Berlin. You see, I've done this kind of thing before, Frau Diesbach. People – not just you, people who should know better because they run the government – they will persist in believing that I don't know when I'm being lied to. But I do. I'm pretty good at it, too. Lately I've had a lot of practice.

'Then, when Criminal Assistant Korsch and I came here tonight, who should we meet on the road but young Benno himself. I recognized him from the photograph on your piano. It was dumb to leave that out for us to see. But you probably didn't have time to hide it, what with your husband having to say his good-byes in five minutes flat. It was Benno who misdirected us in order to give him enough time to cycle back here and warn his father that the police were on the way, wasn't it? I figure Johann's got a good ninety minutes' start on us now. The question is, which way did he go? Further into Austria? Or to Germany? Or Italy, perhaps? I want some answers and you'd better make them good ones or it won't just be you who goes to jail, Frau Diesbach. I figure that when we catch up with him it will be Benno, too. Wasting police time in Germany was always a serious offence, but now we're obliged to take it personally.'

Frau Diesbach wiped her eyes and then lit another cigarette. I lit one, too, and so did Korsch because we both knew of old that any story sounds better when it's accompanied with a good smoke. Of course, a lot of the stories that cops hear are all smoke but this one was true; I could tell that straightaway because I could feel a strong twinge in my jaw when she talked. Besides, she was crying in a way that usually accompanies the truth and that you can't fake unless you're Zarah Leander and even she prefers not to do the type of crying that involves a lot of heavy nose-blowing; for a woman it's just not flattering, especially on camera.

'Benno is a good boy but he's not the army type. Unlike my husband. Who is. Johann's much tougher than Benno will ever be. And he's our only son now. You see, Commissar, Benno's older brother, Dietrich, was in the German navy, and was killed in Spain, during the civil war. Killed in 1937, at the Battle of Malaga, when the *Deutschland* was attacked by Republican planes.

At least, that's what we were told. I can't lose another son. Do I have your word that Benno won't get into trouble?'

'You do. So far it's only me and my assistant here who know he tried to sell us something from the toy catalogue. We can easily forget he even exists.'

She nodded and inhaled fiercely, as if she'd been trying to kill something inside her and when she pulled the cigarette from her lip the dry piece of skin on her lower lip came partly away with it and hung there off her mouth like a tiny cheroot. From time to time she wiped her cheeks clean of tears but after a while there were what looked like two dry riverbeds on her pale face.

'Take a moment,' I said kindly. 'Pull yourself together and try to tell us everything.'

Korsch fetched a schooner of something sticky from a bottle on the sideboard and handed it to her. She sucked it down like a hungry cormorant and then handed him the glass, as if soliciting a refill. I nodded at him. Alcohol can be a cop's best friend in more ways than one; it consoles even when it doesn't loosen tongues.

'You're almost right, Commissar Gunther. Karl Flex did sleep with me. Several times. But it wasn't at all like you said. Karl had taken money from me, not Johann, to keep Benno out of the army. That much is true. Benno is a very sensitive boy and frankly the army would kill him. I make no apology for that. Johann and I disagreed about it, of course. He was furious when he found out about it. He thought the army would make Benno a man. I thought it would make him – dead. After all, everyone suspects a war is coming. With Poland. And if it's with Poland, it will be with the Russians, too. And then where will we be? But Karl didn't force me to sleep with him, and it certainly wasn't conditional on him keeping Benno out of the army. You see, I found a letter from my husband's mistress, Pony, in his coat pocket. Yes, that's her name. Don't ask me how you get a name like Pony. Anyway, Johann was riding her on his business trips to Munich. So I slept with Karl out of revenge, I suppose. One weekend, when Johann was in Munich with Pony, we went to the Hotel Bad Horn on Lake Constance in Karl's lovely Italian sports car. But what I didn't know was that it wasn't just a sweet love letter that Pony had given to Johann, but also a venereal disease. Subsequently he gave it to me. And before I knew it, I'd given it to Karl. We had a big argument about it and in spite of his own indiscretions, Johann got very jealous and swore he would kill Karl. Only I never thought he would actually do it. But you are right about the methamphetamine. Like half of the men on the mountain, Johann is addicted to the stuff. It makes them kind of insane, I think. But the men who work for OA need it just to keep up with Martin Bormann's insatiable timetable. Only recently the supply of Pervitin ground to a halt. They're keeping the Pervitin for the army apparently. But then Karl and Brandt started selling it to anyone who had the cash. Which is just the way things work around here these days. I don't say that Bormann knows about it. But he ought to know about it.'

Korsch handed her another glass. His eyes asked me if I wanted one myself but I shook my head. I needed to keep a clear head if I was going to speak to Albert Bormann and then, perhaps, his brother, Martin. Johann Brandner's life probably depended on a careful use of German grammar and some thoughtful advocacy on my part.

'Of course as soon as I heard that Karl had been murdered I knew it was Johann who'd done it. Our salt mine is in Rennweg. The entrance is between the River Ache and Obersalzberg. That part is well known to me. But where it goes inside the mountain is anyone's guess. Well, anyone except my husband. There are old tunnels that go hundreds of metres straight under Obersalzberg. I confronted him about it, and he admitted it, more or less. Apparently there's an old salt mine tunnel that comes out of the mountain in the forest very close to the Villa Bechstein. You could walk straight past it and not even know it was there. Udo must have guessed that, too. Anyway, he and my husband were always borrowing rifles and things from each other. They were in the army together. The Second Bavarian Corps. Johann was a Jäger marksman and, like lots of local men, the best shot in his battalion. Udo was the same. Some of these men grow up with a rifle in their hands. The day before Karl was shot, I saw Johann putting a rifle with a scope in the boot of his car and while I'm not an expert, I'm pretty sure it wasn't a gun I'd seen before. And there was something stuck on the end of it. Like a can of something. Odd really. I even asked Udo about it the last time I saw him, and he didn't say anything. Which worried me as well.'

'Does your husband have a workshop?' I asked. 'With a working lathe?'

'Yes. He often has to bring pipes back from the mine for repair. How did you know?'

'It's not important. You were saying. About Udo Ambros?'

'I didn't know Johann had shot Udo, too. It's unthinkable, really. Udo would never have turned Johann in. Not without giving him plenty of good warning first.' She shrugged. 'So maybe that's what happened. Johann must have shot him when Udo said he was going to have to tell the police that Johann had borrowed his rifle. And used it to shoot Karl.'

Frau Diesbach sipped the second glass of spirits, winced as if she really didn't like the stuff, and let out a deep sigh.

'It's all my fault, really. If I hadn't paid Karl to get Benno on that list of OA workers none of this would have happened.'

'All right,' I said. 'No point in tiptoeing around that saucer of milk. Where's he gone?'

'I honestly don't know,' she said. 'He didn't say. I asked him, of course. And he said it was probably better I didn't know. That way I couldn't tell anyone.'

'Have a guess,' said Korsch. 'You knew him better than anyone. Pony included.'

She shrugged. 'In many ways Johann was a secretive man. A

lot of the time I didn't know where he was. And he was on the road a great deal. Selling our salt. He has friends in Salzburg, Munich, and as far afield as Frankfurt and Berlin. He could have gone almost anywhere. He has lots of friends in the local area, of course.'

'What about his car?' I asked.

'The car is a new one. A 1939 black four-door Auto Union Wanderer. I don't know the number plate off the top of my head. But I could find out, I suppose.'

'Does he have much money on him? Passport?'

'There was plenty of money in his wallet when I saw it earlier today. He gave me twenty reichsmarks for housekeeping. But there must have been two hundred more in there. And he has a German passport. That more or less lived in the car, for obvious reasons.'

'Come on, missus,' said Korsch. 'We're going to need more than that if we're going to help you and your son. Where is Benno, by the way?'

'He went to stay with some friends. Until the coast was clear, so to speak. I'm not sure who they are. But he was on his bicycle so he can't have gone very far. You won't arrest him, will you? You promised me my son.'

'It's your husband we're interested in, not your son,' said Korsch. 'But whatever Johann's excuses for doing it were, he's a murderer. So don't even think of protecting him. It's not just his neck, see? It's ours, too, if we don't catch him soon.'

'He's right,' I said. 'It's the Leader's birthday on the twentieth. And Martin Bormann wants the murderer of Karl Flex safely in custody before Hitler turns up at the Berghof to unwrap his presents. If only your husband had thought to shoot him somewhere else, Frau Diesbach, this whole thing might have been brushed under the rug. But as it is we're under a great deal of pressure to close this case before the candles on the cake can be lit. The party's cancelled unless we find the culprit.'

'I think it was probably quite deliberate that he shot him where he did,' said Frau Diesbach. 'On the terrace at the Berghof, I mean. I hope I won't get into any more trouble for saying this, Commissar, but Martin Bormann is hated on this mountain. With him gone, a lot of people think a lot of things would be better around here. Johann blamed Martin Bormann for employing people like Karl Flex, Brandt, Zander, the whole rotten bunch of them. He wanted to embarrass Bormann. Leave him looking like a fool in Hitler's eyes. Enough maybe for Hitler to get rid of him. Lots of people who know Johann would be inclined to help him escape, for that reason alone.'

'Where's he gone, missus?' said Korsch. 'I'm running out of patience here.'

'I can't tell you what I don't know, can I?'

'I suppose you think we're stupid, missus.'

'I don't suppose that,' she said in a way that made me think she was about to make another smart remark.

'Don't get clever with us, missus,' said Korsch. 'We don't like people who get clever with us. It reminds us that we're due a lot of overtime and expenses we won't ever get. And what kind of man doesn't tell his wife where he's headed when he's going on the run from the police?'

'The clever kind, obviously.'

'I'd tell my wife if it was me.'

'Yes, but would she care?'

That was when Friedrich Korsch slapped her face, twice. Hard. Hard enough to knock her off the chair she was sitting on. A good forehand and then a backhand, like his name was Gottfried von Cramm. Each slap sounded like a firecracker going off and he couldn't have slapped her better if he'd been auditioning for a job with the Gestapo.

'You need to tell us where he's gone,' shouted Korsch.

I'm not one for hitting people, normally. Most suspects who agree to tell the police everything figure that we won't notice when they try to hold just one thing back. And it always shocks them when they realize that isn't going to work. Me, I'd probably have questioned her for a while longer, but we were short of time, Korsch was right about that. Brandner's only chance of avoiding a short haircut was us catching Karl Flex's killer and soon. I picked her up off the floor and sat her down, which was a good way of making sure I was in the way of Korsch hitting her again. She looked shocked, as well she might. And while I disapproved of what Korsch had done I thought it was too late to complain about it.

'Sorry about that.' I took out my handkerchief, knelt down at the woman's feet, and wiped her mouth. 'Only, my friend here is the crusading type. You see, there's an innocent man in a prison cell in Obersalzberg who could go to his death for Flex's murder and that makes Korsch a bit physical. I don't think he'll do it again, but if you have any idea of where your husband's gone, you'd best tell us now. Before he starts to feel a sense of real injustice.'

'French Lorraine,' she said dully, holding her cheeks like she was a young *grisette* who'd been abandoned with a small child and an unfortunate complexion. 'He was stationed there during the war. With the Second Bavarian Corps. He always liked it there, in Lorraine. Was always talking about it. He speaks good French, you see. Loves the French. Loves the food. And the women, knowing Johann. That's where he said he'd go. I'm not sure precisely where. I've never been there myself. But once he's across the French border, he'll be somewhere in Lorraine.'

What she was saying seemed to fit with the framed maps I'd already seen on the walls, and the pictures of Diesbach in army uniform. It's odd how one feels about a place that saw so much death; I myself had always wanted to go back to northeastern France and the towns near the Meuse where, in 1916, the Battle of Verdun had been fought. But Korsch wasn't having any of that.

'You might as well have said Bermuda, missus,' he complained.

'It's seven hundred kilometres from here to the French border. And he won't have long enough to get that far. When we ask where's he gone, we mean where is he now, and not where would he like to go on vacation if he won the state lottery.'

He was going to slap her again but this time I stayed his hand because I knew exactly how Frau Diesbach was feeling. Both of us had been slapped enough for one day.

CHAPTER 56

October 1956

From the top of the skull-like hill all that could be seen was a black-and-white engraving of the inferno that was industrial capitalism.

In many ways the Saarland was just as horrifying as I remembered it from before the war: slag heaps as big as the Egyptian pyramids, a petrified forest of tall industrial chimneys belching so much grey smoke it looked as if the earth itself had caught fire, endless freight trains crawling along a venous system of rail tracks and sidings and double switches and signal boxes, pit wheels turning like the lazy cogs in a very dirty clock, gasometers and warehouses and factory buildings and rusting sheds, canals so black they looked as if they were filled with oil, not water, and all of this under a sky thick with coal dust and bruised by the incessant noise of metalworks and smelters and pile drivers and locomotive engines and end-of-shift whistles. With eyes that were prickling because of the sulphurous air, you could even taste the iron and steel on the back of your tongue and feel a low Morlock hum in the poisoned earth beneath your feet. As a testament to human industry it was not a very pleasing one from an aesthetic point of view. But it was more than merely ugly; it was as if a kind of original sin had been perpetrated against the very landscape, and I thought I might almost have been looking at Niflheim, the dark, misty home of dwarves, where treasure wasn't only hoarded, it was mined from the ground or forged in secret for the Burgundian kings. The French certainly thought so, which was why they had tried so hard to keep the Saar as a part of France and, like Siegfried, to steal its heavy industrial treasure. The dwarves of the Saarland, however, were as stubbornly German as their Wagnerian counterparts and, in a recent referendum that might have made the territory independent under the auspices of a European commissioner to be appointed by the Western European Union, they had voted no to Europe and the idea of remaining in economic union with France; any month now it was supposed that the so-called Saar Protectorate would finally become part of the Federal Republic of Germany. Every patriotic German certainly hoped so, and throughout the FRG the return of the Saar was generally viewed with enthusiasm, albeit of a more quiet sort than that which had greeted the reoccupation of the Rhineland in 1936. The major difference was that now there were no German troops involved and no treaties repudiated. It was perhaps the most peaceful change of flag in that region in almost a century, and the idea that Germany and France might go to war again about the Saarland already seemed as unthinkable as interplanetary space travel.

In the city of Saarbrücken things were more or less the same as they'd always been, too. Most of the serious damage inflicted by the US Army had been repaired and there was little sign that a world war had ever taken place. But this was never an attractive city and the rebuilding had left the place as hard on the eye as it had always been. Harder, maybe. The French were certainly not about to waste their money on urban planning or public architecture. Any new buildings were functional, not to say brutal; from what little I'd been able to see of the future, it seemed to be fashioned largely from concrete. Landwehrplatz, the main square in Saarbrücken, resembled a German prison yard from which the prisoners had all wisely escaped. Everything was as grey and solidly Germanic as the lead in a Faber-Castell pencil.

Up close, things were a little more ambiguous. All the newspapers and magazines in the kiosks were German, as were most of the street names. Even the names of the shops – Hoffmann, Schulz, Dettweiler, Rata, Schooner, Zum Löwen, Alfred Becker – made me think I might be back in Berlin, but the bunting and the flags and the cars – Peugeots and Citroëns, mostly – were all French, as were the records I heard in bars and restaurants: a lot of Charles Aznavour, Georges Brassens, and Lucienne Delyle. Quite a few of the Saarland police carried the word *Gendarmerie* on the shoulders of their dark blue uniforms, which provided a clear indication of who they took their orders from. I wasn't out of the woods yet; not by a long straw. Then there was the money: the official currency of Saarland was the franc, although thoughtfully the French called it the frank, and the denominations on the coins were stamped in German. And the big brands in the shops were mostly French or sometimes American. There were even a few French restaurants of the sort you could have found on the Left Bank in Paris. It was all very strange. With its German simplicity and French pretensions, the Saar resembled some ghastly transvestite – a very muscular man badly in need of a shave who was wearing lipstick and high heels in a hopeless attempt to pass himself off as a pretty coquette.

I bought twenty Pucks and some matches at the tobacconist, a copy of the *Saarbrücker Neueste Nachrichten*, and in Alfred Becker, a bottle of Côtes du Rhône, a loaf of bread, a box of Président Camembert portions, and a large bar of Kwatta chocolate. I didn't linger in the supermarket. I was acutely aware of the down-at-heel, beggarly figure I now presented. There was a hole in the knee of my trousers, my shoes were water-stained and ruined, I was badly in need of a shave, and I looked as if I had spent the night sleeping under a hedge, which I had. The people of the Saar might have been poor but unlike me they had washed recently, and their clothes, while not of the best quality, were clean; everyone looked gainfully employed and respectable. It takes a lot to make a hardworking German forget about his or her appearance.

On the road to Homburg, beside the only green space in Brebach, I sat down and ate a little of my bread and cheese and read the newspaper. I was relieved to see nothing about me in the paper, which was dominated by the Hungarian revolution, but even while I was enjoying a rare moment of peace and quiet, a cop on a motorcycle pulled up and gave me a look that was as hard as the passenger saddle on his R51. With his white shirt and dark tie, his long riding boots, his dark blue uniform, his Sam Browne belt, and his matching leather gauntlets he looked more like a pilot in the Luftwaffe than a moto rider. After a while he lifted the goggles onto his crash hat and summoned me with a jerk of his head. I got up off the ground and walked to the side of the bike. Fortunately I hadn't yet opened the bottle so there was no question of my being drunk. He was German, which was also in my favour.

'BMW,' I said as coolly as I could, given that I'd not long since strangled a man to death. Would Korsch and his men have found the body of the Stasi man in shorts yet? Perhaps. But I'd hidden him quite carefully. 'Best motorcycle in the world.'

'You German?'

'Berlin, born and bred.'

'You're a long way from home.'

'Tell me about it. Only that isn't going to change anytime soon. My home's in the east now. In the GDR. Behind the Iron Curtain. And so's my old job. At the Alex. I doubt I'll ever see either one of those again.'

'You were a cop?'

Every cop in Germany had heard of Berlin's Police Praesidium on Alexanderplatz. Saying you were from the Alex was like telling an English cop you were from Scotland Yard. In all the previous descriptions of me I'd read in the newspapers, my

past as a policeman was something the Stasi had left out of my
résumé. Chasing cops never played well with other cops, even
French ones. It gives them an itch.

'Twenty-five years in the uniform, give or take. When the war
ended I was a sergeant in the Order Police. By rights I should
have had a nice fat pension to go with my nice fat wife. But I
had to settle for getting away with my life.'

'Had it rough?'

'No worse than most people. When the Ivans showed up in
Berlin, cops like me were less than popular, as you can imagine.
Unlike my wife, if you receive my meaning. For a while there
she was very much in demand.'

'You mean?'

'I do mean. Twenty or thirty of the red bastards. One after
the other. Like they were using her for bayonet practice. I was
somewhere else at the time. Cowering in a shell hole, probably.
Anyway, she never got over it. Nor did I, if it comes to that.
Anyway, since I tossed away my beer token I've just drifted from
one job to the next.'

'What kind of work?'

'Odd jobs. The kind of not-very-talkative jobs an ex-cop can do
in his sleep. Which was just as well, as I usually was.'

'What's your name?'

'Korsch. Friedrich Korsch.'

'Where are you coming from now, Friedrich?'

'Brussels. My wife, Inge, was Belgian, you see. I was working
at the Royal Museum and then as a guard on the trains – the
Étoile du Nord – until I hit a bit of rough luck.'

'What kind of rough luck?'

I brandished my bottle of wine. 'The liquid kind. Hence, the
captain of industry you see before you now.'

'Where are you headed?'

I was looking at the road sign when I answered and I ought
to have known better than to trust the inspiration that the gods

provided for me at that particular moment. The only reason the gods get away with their own mistakes is by tricking us into committing mistakes of our own.

'Homburg. Thought I might look for a job at the Karlsberg Brewery.' I grinned. 'Just joking. My sister, Dora, works at the local brewery, so I thought I'd ask for her there. Figure I can probably get there sometime tomorrow. What is it? Thirty kilometres from here?'

'You fit a lot of descriptions,' he said.

'Not all of them, surely. There must be a couple of missing dogs and cats who don't look like me.'

The moto rider smiled. Making a traffic cop smile is no mean feat. I know. I used to wave cars around Potsdamer Platz. Breathing all that lead makes you grumpy. Which probably explains Berliners.

'Anyway, at the Alex we used to say that most police descriptions can fit absolutely anyone unless they're descriptions of the kind of people you could only see at a circus or a freak show.'

'That's true.'

'I'm not sure which one of those categories I fall into, myself. The latter, more than likely.'

He was still smiling and by now I knew I was more or less safe, at least for the time being; any minute he was going to tell me to be on my way, but I certainly didn't expect him to offer me a ride.

'Hop on,' he said. 'I'll take you to Homburg. My hometown, as a matter of fact.'

'That's very kind of you. Are you sure? I wouldn't want to put you to any trouble. Besides, I don't smell so good right now. It's been a day or two since I had a good wash. Or a decent manicure.'

'I was in the Panzer Corps,' said the moto rider. 'Tenth Panzer Grenadiers. Believe me, nothing could smell worse than five men living inside an F2 for a whole summer. Besides, on a bike you'll always be downwind of me.'

I climbed onto the passenger seat and found it surprisingly

comfortable. Minutes later we were speeding east along the road towards Kaiserlautern, and I was congratulating myself on the dexterity of my abilities as a liar. Lying effectively is a bit like one of those cards for a stereoscope: the card is two separate pictures, side by side, which only works if you end up seeing one clear central image, which perforce is an illusion, and is the picture of depth and clarity that you are meant to see, instead of what is actually there. It's the result of the left eye not knowing what the right is doing; the brain fills in the gap, which is a good way of understanding all kinds of deception. But the most important thing about lying to a cop is not to hesitate; he who hesitates gets arrested. And if all else fails, you punch the cop in the mouth and run for it.

It was nice to see the world go by from the back of the motorcycle, even if that world was the Saarland. A tractor towing a barge laden with coal along the canal; a cart hauled by a couple of heifers, which was followed by two women who were almost as sturdily bovine as their two beasts; a large family of Sinti camped colourfully in a field; an advertising hoarding from the previous October referendum still covered with posters advocating saying NO FOR GERMANY and others that read ONLY TRAITORS TO EUROPE SAY NO, SO SAY YES; a man on a street corner having his horse reshod by a farrier while a small boy held the animal's head steady; a huge German army bunker in a field that looked as though it had been broken in two by an earthquake; a white house dwarfed by a pile of black coal as high as a mountain. Life looked simple, basic, dull, commonplace, the way it always was for most people; I, for whom the path to heroism was now impossibly overgrown, who had lost any sense of enchantment with the world, would have given a lot for a life as ordinary as that.

Homburg was made up of nine villages, not that you'd notice; it's the kind of town that history forgot on its way to somewhere more interesting, which is nearly anywhere. Most people confuse it with the Bad Homburg that's north of Frankfurt, which is probably just wishful thinking. There's a ruined castle on top of a hill and an abbey and the tyre factory and the Karlsberg Brewery, of course – you can smell that all over the town – but the most interesting thing to do in Homburg is leave.

The moto rider dropped me near the brewery gate. Established in 1878, Karlsberg is one of the largest breweries in Germany and certainly looks like it. I'm not sure what they did about the big star of David on the cream-coloured concrete wall and on the bottle label back in the day when the Nazis were in power. This was blue and not yellow so maybe they just left it alone.

'Here we are.'

'Thanks. I appreciate it.'

'Don't mention it. And good luck to you, Friedrich. I hope you find your sister. What was her name again?'

I smiled at this copper's trick. He was making sure my story was consistent.

'Dora. Dora Brandt.'

It was odd how I'd fetched up in Homburg, and this begged all sorts of important and very German questions about fate. I'm not sure Nietzsche would have recognized in my being in Homburg again his concept of eternal recurrence, but sometimes it did seem as if the details of my life were destined to be repeated, over and over, for all eternity. Goethe might have said that I had an elective affinity for trouble, that I was chemically marked out for it. Either that or I was just doomed to wander the face of the earth, like Odin, seeking some kind of knowledge that might aid my own futile, twilight bid for immortality. Then again, maybe it was just the ancestral gods punishing my hubris for imagining that I had got away with murder, much as they usually did themselves. I might have stopped believing in God but I still needed the gods, if only to explain things to myself. You see, I'd been in Homburg before.

CHAPTER 57

April 1939

Friedrich Korsch dropped me back at the Villa Bechstein, because he was still forbidden to be in the Leader's Territory, and I walked up the hill, past the Berghof, and the Türken Inn where Johann Brandner now sat freezing in a prison cell, to Martin Bormann's hilltop house. Halfway there, I removed the tie from under my jaw; I needed to be taken seriously if I was going to save Brandner's life. It was well past midnight and I was relieved but not very surprised to see that a few lights were still burning behind the government leader's neat window boxes; Bormann had long ago adopted the habits of his near-nocturnal master and rarely went to bed before three in the morning, or so Hermann Kaspel had told me. But as I arrived at the house, I found a car waiting there with the straight-eight engine running and Bormann, plus several of his aides, coming out the front door. The top had been folded down and the back of the car was almost as tall as I was. Bormann was dressed in a fine black leather coat, a white shirt, a blue tie with white polka dots, and a misshapen brown felt hat. Seeing me, he waved me forward and then almost immediately held up his hand to stay my progress.

'Whoa, that's far enough. You look like you have the mumps.' Clearly he'd forgotten about my suspect broken jaw and before I could explain, he added, 'There are six children in this house, Gunther, so if you do have the mumps, you can fuck off now.'

'It's not the mumps, sir. I slipped on the ice and fell flat on my face.'

'Not the first time that's happened, I'll be bound. You know what's good for a swelling like that? Wrap a string of pork sausages around your neck, like a scarf. Takes the heat out. And also makes quite a conversation piece. Although you'd best not wear that around the Leader. He's a vegetarian and is liable to have anyone wearing a scarf made from a string of sausages shot. Or committed to a mental asylum. Which amounts to the same thing these days.' He laughed cruelly, as if this might actually be true.

'Are you going somewhere?' I asked, changing the subject. 'Back to Berlin perhaps?' Just saying that was enough to make me feel homesick.

'I'm going up the Kehlstein, to the tea house. Ride with me and, on the way there, you can tell me what else you've discovered about Karl Flex's murder. I assume you wouldn't have come here if you didn't have something important to tell me. I certainly hope so.' But then he shivered inside his coat, rubbed his hands furiously, and waved imperiously at the car. 'I've changed my mind about the top, boys. I think we'll have it up after all.' He looked at me and, a little to my surprise, explained himself. 'I've been stuck inside all day in meetings and I thought I wanted some fresh air, but now I realize it's much colder than I thought.'

I climbed into the back of the big 770K while Wilhelm Zander and Gotthard Farber – yet another of Bormann's aides I hadn't met before – set about lifting the hood. Meanwhile, I sat alongside Bormann and waited for him to tell me to speak. Instead, he lit a cigarette with a large gold ingot that doubled as a gaslighter and started to talk like a man who talked all the time and assumed that someone was always listening; but it was to me that most of this talk was directed now, and for that reason listening closely seemed only judicious.

'The Leader is a man of sudden fancies,' he said. 'He often

likes to do things on the spur of the moment. And since it's very possible that he will decide to visit his new tea house at any time of the day and night, especially in the beginning, it's imperative that I gauge the complete readiness of the Kehlstein staff and the building itself. A test flight, so to speak. Hence this visit. To satisfy myself that everything will meet his exacting standard.'

He glanced around impatiently as Zander and Farber struggled with the hood, which was obviously very heavy. It didn't help that Farber was only three cheeses high, which wasn't quite high enough to lift the hood all the way up on its steel frame.

'Hurry up, we haven't got all night. What's taking so long? Anyone would think I'd asked you to put up the big top in a fucking circus. This is a Mercedes limousine, not some Jew's jalopy.'

It took both his aides several minutes to secure the hood and by the time they climbed into the seat in front and we were ready to leave, they were severely out of breath, which would have made me smile if I hadn't been seated alongside the ersatz tyrant. My own breathing wasn't exactly easy. But at last the driver shifted the bus-sized gear lever, turned the huge steering wheel, and the giant enterprise of gleaming chrome and polished black enamel set off up the mountain road.

'The last time I went up there, Gunther, the cakes and the strudel were not quite to his taste. It's true he hasn't yet been to the tea house, but I know him well enough to say that there was too much fruit in the strudels and not enough cream in the cakes. And the tea they were serving was English tea, which Hitler despises. It certainly wasn't Hälssen & Lyon's decaffeinated tea. Hamburg tea. That's what he calls it. And that's the only one he'll drink. Of course, no one else but me would have noticed this. In many ways Hitler is a very austere, unworldly person with no real interest in his own comfort. Which is why I have to take care of these matters for him. I don't mind telling you, that's quite a responsibility. I have to think of everything. And he's grateful for it, too. You might find this hard to believe but Hitler really doesn't like telling people what to do. He much prefers people to work towards what he thinks.'

Bormann's lungs took a long tug on his cigarette and exhaled a generous mixture of smoke and alcohol, self-importance and hubris. Doubtless he was taking advantage of the Leader's absence to indulge his own vices. But as he talked I began to realize that he was drunk, and not just with power. From the smell of his breath, which now filled the backseat of the car like a smoke grenade, I guessed he'd consumed several brandies. I thought about lighting one myself and immediately rejected the idea. Bormann wasn't the kind of man with whom one could behave normally: him smoking a cigarette in an enclosed space was one thing; someone else doing it was probably a crime in the workplace and punishable with an improbably large fine.

'When I was last there I also noticed a slight problem with the Kehlstein's heating system,' he said. 'So now I have to make sure that the temperature up there is just right for a man who prefers the dark and doesn't like the sun very much. Not too hot and not too cold. You may have noticed that things are a little cool down at the Berghof. Did you? Yes, I thought so. That's because Hitler doesn't feel temperatures like ordinary men such as you or I, Gunther. Perhaps it's because he never takes his jacket off. Perhaps it's a legacy of his time in Landsberg Prison. I'm not sure, but that's my litmus test. The comfort of a man wearing a woollen jacket at all times.'

I decided not to distract Bormann by asking him about anything really trivial, such as the possibility of a German invasion of Poland that might spark off a second European war, and continued to await his pleasure. But after several minutes of talk about tea and cake and the correct room temperatures at the Kehlstein, I was becoming impatient of being seat meat and was on the point of broaching the subject of Johann Brandner's innocence, when suddenly Bormann yelled at the driver to stop.

For a moment I thought we'd run someone over except that Bormann would hardly have stopped for that. We'd just passed a group of construction workers standing under a forest of flood-lights by the side of the road and Bormann seemed infuriated by something they'd done, or, as it happened, not done.

'Open the fucking door,' he yelled at Farber, who was already fumbling with the handle before the enormous car had even halted. The minute Bormann got out of the car he threw away his cigarette and started kicking picks and shovels, punching workmen on the shoulders, and shouting at them like they were beasts of burden. 'What is this? A fucking trade union meeting? You're being paid treble time to work nonstop through the night. Not to stand around and lean on your fucking picks and shovels gossiping like a bunch of old women. Are you trying to give me an ulcer? This is intolerable. Call yourself German workmen? It's a joke, I tell you. Where's your foreman? Where is he? I want to speak to the gang master right now, or by God, I'll have you all sent to a concentration camp. Tonight!'

And then, when one cowering man came to the front of the others, cap in freezing hand, Bormann continued his ranting. They could probably have heard Bormann all the way down the mountain in Berchtesgaden. It was perhaps the most practical demonstration of National Socialism I'd ever heard and I realized with sudden clarity that Nazism was nothing more than the will of the Leader, and that Bormann was his bellowing mouthpiece.

'What's the meaning of this? Tell me, because I'd like to know. Yes, me, Martin Bormann, the man who pays your inflated wages. Because every time I drive past this bend in the road it's always the same thing I see out of the car window: you're standing around like a bowl of soft eggs and doing fuck all. And nothing ever seems to get done. The road is still a mess. So why aren't you working on it?'

'Sir,' said the foreman, 'there's been a problem with the steam-roller. We can't finish asphalt surfacing without the roller. You see, there's a fault in the smoke-box door. It won't close properly so we can't get up a good head of steam.'

'I never heard such rubbish,' said Bormann. 'It's just not good enough. You should have more than one steamroller. The Leader himself will be here in just a couple of days to celebrate his fiftieth birthday and it's imperative that this stretch of road is finished before then. I cannot have his visit to Obersalzberg disrupted in any way by local construction work. In any way at all. Now get these men back to work and finish this damned road before I have you shot, you communist bastard. Find another steamroller and get these men working again. If this road is not finished by tomorrow you'll wish none of you had ever been born.'

Still cursing loudly, Bormann climbed back into the Mercedes, exhaled loudly, wiped his low forehead, lit another cigarette, and then punched the quilted black leather door, not that this had the least effect on the car: the door was obviously reinforced with armour plating; I daresay the windows were bulletproof, too, just in case someone took a pickaxe handle to one as the limousine drove by. Riding in that 770K was like being driven around in a bank vault.

'Enemies I can deal with,' he muttered. 'But God preserve us from German workers.' He looked at me and his frown deepened, as if he hardly expected that I was about to improve his mood with my news. He leaned back on the seat and hammered on his not-inconsiderable gut with a fist. 'Better tell me something good, Gunther. Before I have a fit and start chewing the carpets in this damn hearse.'

'Yes, sir,' I said brightly. 'I believe I know the name of Karl Flex's murderer. I mean, his real murderer – not the innocent Fritz who's freezing his eggs off sitting in the prison cell underneath the Türken Inn.'

'And that name is?'

'His name is Johann Diesbach, sir. He's a local salt miner, from Kuchl, on the other side of the Hoher Göll. It seems Flex was involved with the man's wife. A fairly typical love triangle and, you'll be relieved to hear, nothing to do with you or the Leader.'

'Now, why does that particular name ring a bell?' asked Zander. 'Diesbach, you say.'

'Perhaps this will refresh your memory.' I handed Zander the photograph of Diesbach I'd taken from his home. Zander switched on the car's reading light and studied the photograph carefully.

'You're sure about this, Gunther?' asked Bormann. 'That Diesbach is your man?'

'Positive. I've just been to his house and found all the evidence I need to get him a first-class ticket straight to the guillotine.'

'Good work, Gunther.'

'Sir, I remember this man,' said Zander.

It was hard not to remember a man with a moustache like Hitler's.

'He came to one of my lectures on German literature, sir. At the local theatre in Antenberg. They were part of the outreach programme, to build bridges with the local community. We talked briefly afterwards.'

'That was the lecture on *Tom Sawyer*, perhaps,' I said. 'Read it myself once. Like almost every German schoolboy, I guess.'

'My God, no wonder these locals hate us,' said Bormann. '*Tom Sawyer*? What's wrong with some decent German writers, Wilhelm?'

'Nothing at all, sir. It was just that I wanted to talk about a book that had been important in my own life. Besides, it was the Wilhelm Grunow Leipzig edition of *Tom Sawyer*, in German.'

'I was joking, you idiot, as if I give a damn about a fucking book or your damned lecture.' Bormann let out a smoky guffaw. 'So where is this fellow Diesbach now, Gunther? Safely in custody, I hope. Better still, dead.'

'I'm afraid not. He guessed that we were on to him, and made his escape just before we could arrest him.'

'You mean he's still on the loose. Around here? In Obersalz-berg.'

'Yes, sir. But now that he knows I'm on his trail, I think he'll want to get out of Bavaria as quickly as possible.'

'Maybe so, but look, there's no time to lose. You simply have to find him. Before the twentieth. Without delay. I want him caught, do you hear? Before the twentieth of April.' Bormann was beginning to sound panicky. 'This is a matter of top priority. As soon as I get to the tea house I'll call Heydrich in Berlin. It's my order that you should mobilize the whole of Germany in the search for this assassin.'

'If you'll permit me to say so, I think it might be better if things proceeded on a more modest scale. By all means we should enlist the help of the police and the Gestapo in searching for him. But it's my understanding that this matter is still highly confidential. It might be hard to keep it that way if too many people are informed he's a fugitive. So let's put it out that he shot and killed a policeman. That way we can ensure the vigilance of all law enforcement agencies without revealing too much of why we're really hunting him.'

'Yes, of course.' Bormann stifled a belch but it did nothing for the atmosphere in the rear of the car. 'Good thinking.'

'Besides, I have a fair idea of where he might be heading.'

'Right. So what do you suggest, Gunther? I mean, you're the expert on this kind of thing. Fugitive criminals and wanted men.'

'That we close the German borders with French Lorraine. Temporarily. I happen to believe that's where he's heading.'

'Well, you've not been wrong before. But aren't you being just a little pessimistic? France is a long way from here. Surely he won't get that far. Not with the Gestapo looking for him.'

'Look, with any luck Diesbach will be arrested and soon. But I have a hunch he's going to prove a little more elusive than that.'

'What makes you say so?'

'In my opinion, the Gestapo are not nearly as omnipotent as

they would like people to believe. As for the uniformed police, well, Orpo has been losing its best men to the SS for a while now. The pay's better, you see. Most of the cops we have on the streets now are too old for the SS. They're too old for anything, probably. They're waiting for their pensions, most of them.'

'I bet you wouldn't say that to Himmler,' said Bormann.

'No, sir. But Himmler's not in charge in Obersalzberg. You are. Also, there's Diesbach himself.'

Bormann took the photograph from Zander and studied the face critically.

'He was a Jäger in the war,' I added. 'Stationed near the Meuse, with a top infantry detachment. A proper stormtrooper – not one of those beer-hall brownshirts that Ernst Röhm used to command. This man was probably trained in Hutier tactics. That means he's tough and resourceful. And a ruthless killer.'

'He does look tough, I must admit.'

'He's got plenty of money and a car, not to mention a lot of guts and a loaded Luger. My guess is that he's already on a train headed west.'

'All right. I'll speak to the Foreign Ministry. What else do you want?'

'I should like to go to the largest German town close to the Lorraine border – wherever that is – and assume temporary command of the local police and Gestapo myself.'

'That would be Saarbrücken,' said Zander. 'Which also happens to be my hometown.'

'Then you're to be pitied,' said Bormann bluntly. 'Did you know that in the 1935 referendum ten per cent of the Saarland electorate voted to remain part of France?'

'No, sir,' I said.

'That means ten per cent are not to be relied upon.'

'But ninety per cent voted to become part of Germany,' said Zander.

'That's hardly the point. In the heart of Germany's main

coal-producing state, ten per cent of the workforce are potential traitors. That's a serious matter. Anyway, you'd better go with the commissar, hadn't you, Wilhelm? To Saarbrücken.'

'Me, sir? I don't know what I can do.'

'A bit of local knowledge might come in useful, eh, Commissar?'

'I'm sure you're right. But perhaps your adjutant prefers not to be under my orders.'

'Nonsense. You'll be glad to assist the commissar in any way you can, won't you, Wilhelm?'

'Of course, if you think it's necessary, sir.'

'I do. And while you're there, make sure you ask the Gestapo if they're doing everything they can to root out those other traitors.'

'Yes, sir,' said Zander.

'Maybe now's the time to mention the innocent man who's still in custody at the Türken Inn,' I said. 'Johann Brandner. He should really be under medical supervision. Can I tell Major Högl to release him? And to have the man transferred back to the hospital in Nuremberg?'

'I think not. Nothing has really changed. You may have a name but you don't yet have your man. This fellow Brandner is our bird in the hand, so to speak. I might yet need a Fritz to blame for all this business, should you fail to make an arrest. If the Leader should happen to hear about the shooting on the Berghof terrace from someone jealous of my influence on him – and there are plenty of those, believe me – then I'm afraid I really can't look him in the eye and tell him that nobody has been arrested. That would be unthinkable. You understand? Until you have Diesbach under lock and key, I am forced to keep Brandner in custody.'

I nodded.

'But rest assured nothing will happen to Brandner so long as Zander here tells me that the search for this Diesbach fellow is still proceeding apace.'

'And the other two? The two Gestapo from Linz?'

'Heydrich wants them dead.'

'I'm the one asking.'

'All right. Them, too. Because I'm feeling generous.'

'Thank you, sir.'

'All the same, given its extreme sensitivity, we'd better have a code word or phrase for a successful conclusion to this operation. A short message that will indicate that Johann Diesbach has been arrested and that will allow me to order the immediate release of Brandner from the Türken Inn's cells. What do you say, Gunther?'

'I agree, sir.'

'So what would you suggest?'

I searched the felt-lined hood for inspiration as I tried to think of something, and then, rather desperately, I said: 'Well, now I come to think of it, there was another Johann Diesbach, Johann Jacob Diesbach, a Berlin paint maker who invented the colour Prussian blue, back in 1706. The whole Prussian army wore coats of Prussian blue until the Great War, when it moved over to field grey. At one time every Berlin schoolboy used to know the name of Johann Jacob Diesbach. So how about that, sir? How about Prussian blue?'

CHAPTER 58

April 1939

The Police Praesidium in Saarbrücken was on St. Johannerstrasse, a stone's throw north of the River Saar and conveniently close to the main railway station at which we had just arrived. Zander and I checked into the Rheinischer Hof on Adolf-Hitlerstrasse, consumed a very quick lunch at the *Ratskeller*, and then went straight to see Major Hans Geschke, the recently appointed Gestapo chief in the Saarland capital who was now coordinating the search for Johann Diesbach.

Made of concrete the colour of old dog shit, the Praesidium was a five-storey building of recent construction, with regular square windows, a cumbersome door that was clearly meant to remind people of how small they were in comparison with the state, and nothing to commend it architecturally. I could almost hear Gerdy Troost dismissing it as a typical Speer design, with no redeeming features and zero character, and that was exactly how I would have described Geschke, a baby-faced doctor of law from Frankfurt and probably not much more than thirty years of age. He was one of those smooth, clever types of Nazi for whom a career in the police was only a means to an end, that being executive power and its twin shadows, money and prestige. Pale-skinned, smiling, keen, bright-eyed: he reminded me of a sinister Pierrot who'd abandoned unworldly naïveté and the pursuit of Columbine for a leading role in *The Threepenny Opera*. But while

Geschke had been studying in Berlin, he'd read about one of my old cases, which he told me almost immediately I entered his office, and for several minutes I allowed myself to be flattered in the interests of congeniality and cooperation.* But I was glad it was him I was dealing with and not his predecessor, Anton Dunckern, now promoted to greater responsibility in Brunswick and known to many Berlin cops as a member of a notorious SS murder squad that had been very active in and around the city in the bloody summer of 1934. I had good reason to believe that Dunckern had murdered a good friend of mine, Erich Heinz, a prominent member of the SPD, whose body had been found near the town of Oranienburg, in July of that year. He'd been hacked to death with an axe.

'The border police have been alerted,' Geschke told us. 'And the transport police, of course. The local Gestapo are watching all of the local railway stations and I've been in touch with the French police, who, in spite of recent diplomatic tensions, are always extremely cooperative. If Germany ever rules France again you can be sure we'll have no problem with their police. Commissaire Schuman, who you might say is my opposite number, in Metz, has a German father and speaks the language fluently. Frankly, I think he has more in common with us than he does with that fool Édouard Daladier. It was Schuman who boarded the Berlin train to Paris last October and arrested the Swiss assassin Maurice Bavaud. By the way, is there any news of when Bavaud is to be tried?'

'I have no idea.' I thought it hardly worth mentioning that Bavaud hadn't actually killed anyone, but we both knew that the verdict in the man's trial was already a foregone conclusion.

Geschke nodded. 'Anyway,' he continued, 'the Lorraine border

---

* A couple of years later, at Heydrich's country house near Prague, in Bohemia, Geschke was to remind me of this acquaintance when he tried to strike up a friendship with me. But in 1939 I didn't know him.

is now as tight as the paint on a piece of Dresden china. But please, I'd welcome any suggestions as to what else we can do to assist the office of the deputy chief of staff, not to mention the Kripo detective who famously caught Gormann the strangler. We may be a small city by comparison with Berlin but we are keen to be useful. And we are very loyal. In the plebiscite of 1935, ninety per cent of Saarlanders voted to become a part of Germany. I'm glad to say that most of the opponents of National Socialism who took refuge here after 1933 are in prison or have fled to France.'

Wilhelm Zander, sitting in a chair by the windowsill, smiled thinly, as if he remembered what Bormann had said about the place. Roughly the same age, he and Geschke looked as if they'd come out of the same rat's nest and the only noticeable difference between the two was that unlike a great many of the people who'd risen to positions of power under the Nazis, Zander wasn't a lawyer, or, as far as I could see, a doctor of anything. Even after a longish train journey with Wilhelm Zander I knew very little about the man, but I had already come to the conclusion that I wasn't remotely interested in finding out more. For his part, he seemed totally uninterested in the fate of my mission and had spent most of the train journey reading a book about Italy where, he told me, he still had a number of business interests. I could hardly blame him; for anyone who came from Saarbrücken, Italy must have looked like Shangri-la. A house built on the slopes of Vesuvius would have seemed more attractive than the finest dwelling in Saarbrücken.

I didn't mind his disinterest in my job; in fact I welcomed it. The last thing I wanted was Martin Bormann's spy looking over my shoulder while I went through the motions of being a detective. And my only concern was that the Walther P38 he'd insisted on bringing from Obersalzberg would prove more lethal to him or me than to Johann Diesbach.

'Do you know how to use that thing?' I'd asked when first I'd seen the pistol in his luggage, on the train.

'I'm not an expert. But I know how to use a gun.'

'I hope so.'

'Look here, Commissar, I didn't want this job. And surely you don't expect me to help you look for a wanted fugitive without a weapon. Frankly, I'd have thought you'd be glad to have some backup firepower, given that your police colleague elected to remain in Berchtesgaden.'

'No, I told him to stay.'

'May I ask why?'

'Police business.'

'Such as?'

'I'm hoping he might obtain some more information out of Frau Diesbach. A last few crumbs, perhaps, concerning the exact whereabouts of her husband.'

'And exactly how will he do that? Thumbscrews? A dog whip?'

'Sure. And if all of that fails, then Korsch will light a fire under her feet. That always works. And one thing they're not short of in Berchtesgaden is a supply of slow-burning wood.'

I was joking about this but before I'd left I'd still felt obliged to tell Korsch very firmly that I didn't want Eva Diesbach slapped around. It was enough, I thought, that he'd already hit her; the possibility that he might do so again – not to mention the charges that might yet be levelled against her son Benno – was probably enough, eventually, to persuade her to yield up more information.

'We don't use methods like that in Kripo,' I told Zander. 'I leave that kind of thing to people like Major Högl.'

'I had no idea you were so particular, Commissar.'

'You start beating people up during an interrogation, it becomes a bad habit. In the long term the only person who comes out damaged is the cop who's prone to using his fists. And I don't mean the damage to the skin on his knuckles.'

After meeting Hans Geschke, we went back to our hotel and then to dinner at the Saar Terrace by the Luisen Bridge. Like the food, the weather was foul: wet and cold, and after the blue sky and snow of Berchtesgaden, Saarbrücken felt very dismal. Geschke had told us that if he heard any news he would fetch us immediately, but when we got back to the Rheinischer Hof, I found a message from Friedrich Korsch asking me to telephone him urgently on a Berchtesgaden number, which turned out to be the Schorn Ziegler, the guest house in St. Leonhard where Captain Neumann had been staying.

'I had to move out of the Villa Bechstein,' he explained. 'To make way for some Party bigwigs and their entourages who've turned up for the Leader's birthday. Apparently he's expected any minute now. Anyway, Captain Neumann said I could use his room here, in St. Leonhard, because he's not using it, on account of how he was going back to Berlin.'

'Yes, he's very thoughtful, is our Captain Neumann.'

I hadn't told Korsch about the murder of Aneta Husák; I wasn't sure there was much point in telling anyone about her. Murder – real murder, when someone innocent is killed by someone else – was becoming almost unimportant in Hitler's Germany. Unless it was designed to discredit someone in the eyes of the Leader.

'The latest we've heard from the Orpo is that Diesbach's Wanderer was found in front of the Frauentor, near the railway station in Nuremberg.'

'Nuremberg? I wonder why he went there.'

'Since 1935 Nuremberg's had the best rail connections in Germany. Because of all the Nazi Party rallies, of course. A man in the ticket office remembers a man answering Diesbach's description who bought three tickets: one to Berlin, one to Frankfurt, and one to Stuttgart. Trying to throw us off the scent, no doubt. Of course, Frankfurt and Stuttgart are a lot nearer French Lorraine. Assuming that's where he's gone.'

'How are you getting on with the Amazon lady?'

'I'm starting to quite like her, boss. She's got some dinner on her, hasn't she? Two lovely courses. I get hungry just looking at them.'

'Just keep your mind on the job and your mittens off her exhibits. She's a witness, always supposing that this Fritz ever goes to trial. More importantly, did you get anything else out of her?'

'Nothing. But young Benno showed up eventually and I could see why his mama wanted him kept out of uniform. He's much too warm for the army.'

'He's queer?'

'Like a talking gardenia. Anyway, after I crushed his silk scarf a bit – just a bit, mind, nothing serious, he can still wear it – he told me something interesting. He used to have an aunt in the Saarland. Apparently Papa Johann has or had an older sister in Homburg. Name of Berge, Paula Berge. I looked the place up on the map. Turns out Homburg is a small town about twenty kilometres east of Saarbrücken and just the sort of place you might hole up for a while before deciding it's safe to tiptoe across the French border. The Kaiser could be living there and no one would know. According to Benno, his dad and his aunt haven't spoken in a long while but Benno Diesbach reckons Frau Berge used to work as a secretary for the managing director at the local Karlsberg Brewery. For all he knows she might still be there. In Homburg. In which case—'

'Brother Johann and sister Paula might have patched things up.'

'Precisely.'

'What did Mama have to say to that?'

'Not much. But she certainly looked like she wanted to give Benno a good slap.'

'I can think of worse places to hide than a brewery, can't you?'

CHAPTER 59

April 1939

Early the next morning Zander and I borrowed a car from the police and drove out of town along the Kaiserslautern road, towards the little town of Homburg. I was behind the wheel of a very battered 260 convertible but Zander sat in the rear seat, as if I were his chauffeur. Not that I cared very much. I laughed when I realized this was how he proposed to make the journey to the Karlsberg Brewery.

'You really want to travel like this?'

'I don't drive. And I believe I might as well sit in the back as anywhere else.'

'It's not considered polite to treat a colleague like the hired help.'

'Since when did being polite worry you?'

'Now that you mention it, you're right. Maybe we should take the top down and some local dimwit will mistake you for the Archduke Ferdinand and put a hole in your big head.'

It was cold and we were both wearing overcoats but Zander was also dressed in his customary brown Party tunic, with the red leadership collar patches that signified something, I supposed, but I had little or no idea what this might be; all I knew was that the man from Saarbrücken looked as neat as a new pin and was just as prickly. Mostly he just smoked endless French cigarettes and stared sourly out the rear window as we left behind the grey streets and continued into the surrounding grey countryside. After a while, however, he spoke. I think it was me having to wait for a herd of red pied cattle to cross the road and the amount of dung they left behind that prompted him to open his slit of a mouth.

'Christ, I hate this damn place. The only good thing about being back here is the French cigarettes.'

'Anything in particular you hate?' I asked brightly. 'Or is it mainly yourself?'

In my rear-view mirror I saw him bite his lip before answering; I imagine he'd have preferred it had been my jugular vein. Clearly I'd touched a raw nerve.

'You wouldn't understand. The whole world looks different when you come from somewhere like Berlin.'

'I always thought so.'

I might have mentioned in evidence for this assertion the fact that the Nazis had never been that popular in Berlin, where no more than thirty-one per cent of people had ever voted for them in any election, but there seemed to be no point in antagonizing the little man, or in earning myself a trip to see the Gestapo. If Zander's red collar patches meant anything, they meant that he hadn't got where he was by ignoring even the smallest sign of disloyalty to the Party. He'd have denounced me as quickly as he could light another cigarette.

'Coming from Berlin you've probably never felt the need to escape from the place you came from to go somewhere else. Have you?'

'Not until very recently.'

'You're lucky,' he said. 'And you heard what Martin Bormann said about the Saarland, back in Obersalzberg. You're automatically suspect if you come from somewhere like this. Why else does the Leader surround himself with Bavarians? For the simple reason they were always there for him. From the very beginning. When Hitler was marching through the streets of Munich with

Ludendorff in 1923, I was growing up in a place that was ruled jointly by Britain and France under the Treaty of Versailles. I was a man without a country until 1935. What kind of a German does that make me in the Leader's eyes?' He sneered out the window. 'Of course I hate this place. Anyone would. Anyone who wants to get somewhere in the new Germany.'

After that he didn't say much about anything. But I now had a keener appreciation of why people became Nazis in the first place; perhaps it was like he said: that they wanted to get away from dead-end, no-account places like Saarbrücken, wanted to achieve some sort of status among their fellow men, wanted their shitty, insignificant lives to mean something, even if they could find that meaning only in being mean to others – Jews, mostly, but anyone who didn't agree with them would do.

We drove into Homburg and found it a place even less remarkable than Saarbrücken, which was saying something. The weather had closed in and rain lashed the windscreen so loudly it sounded as if someone was frying bacon. And Zander's depression was becoming infectious, like a bad spell. I followed the signs for the brewery, which was the sensible thing for any German to do, and the route led us up a hill in the same direction as the ruins of Karlsberg Castle.

'Is it an interesting castle?' I asked. 'Only I remember some of the lecture you gave at the theatre in Antenberg. You used to come here when you were a boy, didn't you?'

'There's very little of the castle left nowadays. It was one of the largest châteaus in Europe and the residence of the Duke of Zweibrücken until an ill-disciplined rabble of a French revolutionary army turned up and set fire to it in 1793. Most of the ruins are gone. Only the foundations remain, I think. The one building that still stands belongs to the brewery. Anyway, that was the last time anything interesting happened in Homburg. History has been sidestepping this place ever since.'

I pulled into a car park in front of the brewery, which was

itself as large as a decent-sized castle, much bigger and more modern than the one back in Berchtesgaden, and turned around to face my surly backseat passenger.

'You're not nearly as dull a travelling companion as I thought you'd be.'

He smiled a sarcastic, weary smile. 'I'll wait in the car,' he said, and sank further down into the collar of his greatcoat, like a grumpy Napoleon.

I opened the car door to a strong smell of roasting hops that made me wish I had a beer in my hand; then again, I already needed a beer after half an hour in the car with Zander.

I wasn't gone for very long. The director of the brewery, Richard Weber, was a big man in his seventies, with a pinstripe suit and a bow tie, an expensive-looking belly, puffy red eyes, a little grey beard, and a receding hairline. Like many affluent German men of a certain age, he reminded me a little of Emil Jannings, but mostly he reminded me of my own father. He even smelled like him: tobacco and mothballs. From the high point that was his office window I could see the town on the plain below and the hexagonal tower of the local church. It wasn't much of a view but it was probably the best one in Homburg.

Paula Berge, Richard Weber told me, had worked for his father, Christian Weber, who was almost a hundred years old now and retired. He provided me with her address from a detailed filing system that would have been the envy of Hans Geschke. She still lived in Homburg, in an apartment in Eisenbahnstrasse, on the corner of Markt Platz. Herr Weber assured me it was only a two-minute walk from his office. I rather doubted that; besides, it was still raining heavily and much as I would have preferred to leave Zander behind while I walked to the address, I hurried back outside and started the car again.

'Did you speak to her?' asked Zander, stirring inside his coat.

'No, but Herr Weber, the son of her old boss, gave me an address where we can find her. Diesbach, too, I hope.'

'Excellent.'

'Let's just hope she doesn't have a telephone.'

'Why would that matter?'

'In case Weber thought to call her up and warn her that the Gestapo are coming.'

'But you're not from the Gestapo.'

'There's not much difference when a man with a warrant disc knocks on your door. It's never good news.'

'But why would he? Call her, I mean.'

'Because he knew exactly who she was, and because he didn't have to look very hard to find her address. And because he only ever used her Christian name, like they were well acquainted. But mostly because the brewery switchboard is beside the reception desk and as I was on my way out of the door I heard one of the telephonists connecting Weber with a number he'd just asked her to get.'

'You should be a detective.'

'No, but calling her is what I would have done.'

'Calling Frau Berge to warn her of our arrival would hardly be the action of a good German.'

'Perhaps. But it might have been the action of a good friend.'

'Well, who knows who it was he called – it could have been anyone,' said Zander.

'We'll find out, won't we?'

The address on Markt Platz was a four-storey corner building next to a bookshop. On the opposite side of the square was a red-brick church – the same church I'd seen from Weber's office window. It looked like a maximum-security prison but then every building in Germany looks like a prison these days. The clock on the hexagonal tower said it was ten o'clock. It might as well have been another century. I parked the car and waited until the rain had stopped and then opened the door.

'You staying in the car again? Only, if she's in there, your uniform might help. No one likes to see a Nazi uniform like that first thing in the morning. Makes them feel guilty.'

'Why not? I could use some fresh air, or what passes for fresh air in this place. I swear, the backseat of this wretched car is covered in something sticky. I'm going to have to have this coat cleaned.'

'Probably blood. You'll usually find that the only clean seats in a police car are the ones in front, Wilhelm.'

'Why didn't you tell me?'

I frowned. 'I should care about a man who thinks I'm poor company.'

We got out of the car and approached Paula Berge's building. Ahead of us was a tall, blond woman carrying an umbrella. She was wearing black-and-white leather oxfords with two-inch heels and a grey tweed suit, and she walked directly into the bookshop. For several heart-stopping moments I thought I recognized her. Someone from my past. This was, I knew, unlikely to happen in a dump like Homburg. But before I had realized I had the wrong woman I'd ended up following her into the bookshop, where she quickly selected a copy of *Gone with the Wind* and took it to the desk. The clerk recorded the sale and then handed her a pay slip.

Six long months had passed since Hilde, the last woman to walk into my life, had walked just as smartly out of it. I didn't blame her for walking out, just the manner of her doing it. I don't know why, but a small part of me still hoped that one day she would see the error of her ways, just as a microscopic part of me hoped she would be happy with her SS major. Not that happiness meant anything anymore; it was just an idea for children, like God and birthday parties and Santa Claus. Life felt much too serious to be diverted by bagatelles like happiness. Meaning was what mattered, not that there was much of that around, either. Most of the time my life had less meaning than yesterday's crossword.

With eyes only for the woman in the bookshop – she was uncannily like the one I'd mistaken her for – I watched her hand over the pay slip at the cash till, pay for the book, and then leave, not far behind the shop's only other customer, a tallish man in a green loden coat who had somehow managed to forget his valise.

'Is that woman someone you know?' whispered Zander.

'No.'

'Good-looking, I suppose.'

'I thought so.'

'For Homburg.'

'For anywhere.'

Meanwhile, I'd picked up the valise and was about to call after the man when I noticed a neat little label on the leather side: it featured a pickaxe and a mallet, and the words *Berchtesgaden Salt Mines* and *Good Luck*. I'd seen that design before: on an enamel badge in Udo Ambros's buttonhole. Suddenly I realized who the man was and, still holding the valise, I ran out of the bookshop to see where he'd gone; but Markt Platz was deserted and Johann Diesbach – I was certain it had been him – had disappeared.

'Damn,' I said loudly.

Zander followed me out of the shop and lit a cigarette. 'She wasn't that special,' he said. 'Oh, I'll grant you, unusually good for these parts. But hardly worth losing your head over.'

'No, you idiot, the man who left this valise – it was Diesbach.'

'What?' Zander looked one way and then the other, but of Diesbach there remained no sign. 'You're kidding.' He frowned. 'That man at the brewery. He must have tipped the sister off, just as you supposed. You should go back and arrest him.'

'There's no time for that. Besides, I only told him I was looking for Paula Berge, not her brother. So he really doesn't deserve to be arrested.'

'But why did Diesbach leave his case?'

'Nerves got the better of him, I suppose. Here's what I want you to do, Wilhelm.' I handed him Diesbach's valise. 'Go and stand in front of Paula Berge's building door. And don't let anyone leave.'

Zander looked alarmed. 'Suppose he's in there. The man's a murderer. He's got a gun, hasn't he? Suppose he comes out shooting?'

'Then shoot back. You've got a gun.'

Zander pulled a face.

'Have you ever fired it before?' I asked.

'No. But how difficult can it be?'

'Not difficult at all. Just pull the trigger and the Walther will do the rest. That's why it's called an automatic.'

CHAPTER 60

April 1939

Not for one moment did I think Johann Diesbach had walked out of the bookshop and then simply ducked into his estranged sister's doorway – that would have been a hell of a gamble – but I couldn't risk the possibility he hadn't done exactly that. What seemed more probable was that my earlier suspicion had been correct, and that Diesbach's sister had been warned we were coming, and that Johann had been on his way out the door when he'd seen Zander and me walking across Markt Platz and had decided to hide in the bookshop; he couldn't ever have thought we'd step in there *before* going up to Paula Berge's apartment. For him to return to the very same address we had been heading for would have been foolhardy. Still I had high hopes of finding him abroad on Homburg's empty streets and I ran one way and then the other, like a windup Schuco toy – a short way down Klosterstrasse, then along Karlsbergstrasse, and finally north, up Eisenbahnstrasse, towards the railway station. I'd already seen the blonde climb into a green Opel Admiral driven by a man wearing the smart uniform of a naval captain lieutenant, but of Johann Diesbach there was no trace. He'd disappeared.

Nor did I find any sign of a local policeman on patrol. Of course Homburg would never be the kind of place where there were cops hanging around the street corners. It wasn't just life that happened somewhere else than Homburg; crime did as well. It had started to rain again, hard Saarland rain that was full of coal dust and the exhausting truth of ordinary German life. Any sensible Orpo man would have been wrapped up in his waterproof police cape and standing in a quiet doorway with his hands cupped around a quiet smoke, or holed up in the nearest café waiting for the rain to stop. It's certainly what I would have done. A cigarette in a doorway is usually as near to luxury as any half-frozen, uniformed cop on duty is ever likely to come.

Two-thirds of the way up Eisenbahnstrasse I found the local police station and, flashing my beer token, explained that I was on the trail of a dangerous police killer by the name of Johann Diesbach, and added a reasonable description of the man I'd seen in the bookshop at Markt Platz.

'This is a matter of the highest priority,' I added self-importantly. 'I'm acting on the direct orders of the government leader's office. The man is armed and dangerous.'

'Right you are, sir.' The sergeant had muttonchop whiskers down to his shoulders and a moustache that was as big as the wingspan of the Prussian imperial eagle. 'What do you want me to do?'

'Send a couple of your best men to the railway station to keep an eye out for him. And the local bus station, if you have one. I'll be back here in half an hour to take charge of the search.'

Then, ignoring the rain, or at least trying to, I walked back to where I'd left Wilhelm Zander. My shoes were already soaked and my feet were cold; my hat looked more like a lump of clay on a potter's wheel. Very sensibly, Zander was standing deep in the doorway of the building with one hand inside his great-coat pocket and I guessed he was holding a gun. The valise was safely between his heels. He threw away the cigarette he'd been smoking and almost came to attention.

'No one has been in or out of this building since I've been standing here,' he said.

'I've sent a couple of coppers to keep an eye on the local

railway station. So, hopefully, he won't get far. And anyone lurking in a doorway like you are is bound to stand out in this place.'

I squeezed into the doorway beside him, opened the case, and searched quickly through Diesbach's belongings: I found some clean clothes, a bit of French money, a French Baedeker, a pair of shoes, a Saarland newspaper with a number and an initial pencilled on the front page, a picture of a naked woman I didn't recognize, a travelling chess set, a tin of Wybert throat lozenges, a razor, a leather strop and some soap, a toothbrush and a tube of Nivea toothpaste, a box of Camelia, some pistol ammunition, and a spiked object that looked as if it had come from a medieval armoury.

'What the hell is that?' asked Zander.

'It's a trench mace. We used that sort of thing when we were raiding enemy trenches at night. It was a very effective way of killing Tommies quietly. And the old ways are the best.'

Zander blinked uncomfortably. 'Who's the woman in the photograph? His wife, I suppose.'

I smiled. 'No. I think that's probably his girlfriend, Pony. Lives in Munich.'

'And the Camelia – the sanitary towels? Is she with him?'

'No.'

'His sister's?'

'I expect he borrowed them from her.'

'Why on earth – ?'

'When you're on the run, your shoes get wet. I know mine are.' I showed him the spare pair of shoes in the valise and how Diesbach had tucked a towel inside each like an insole, to help dry it. 'It's an old soldier's trick. Helps keep your feet dry. Which is especially useful on a day like this. A Camelia is much more absorbent than newspaper.' I closed the valise, turned in the doorway, and rang the doorbell but if Paula Berge was at home she was sensibly not answering.

'Kick it down,' said Zander.

'I don't think so. Besides, what would be the point? We already know he was here. The street and apartment number are pencilled on the front of this newspaper. But she's going to deny he was ever with her, of course. And in the time we waste persuading Paula Berge to talk I think we could usefully return to the local police station and detail some more police to start searching the rest of this town. That's what I've told the duty sergeant.'

We climbed into the car – Zander joined me in the front seat this time – and I drove to the police station on Eisenbahnstrasse, where I now ordered the desk sergeant to deploy his entire force; but this turned out to be just three more men because – including the two at the railway station – there were only five men on duty in the whole of Homburg, and they moved at an unhurried sort of pace that only the police in small towns can achieve. What was almost as bad, they seemed to regard the very idea of a police search as some kind of jolly game and were full of chatter and jokes and eager to arrest a cop killer. I told them to pay particular attention to buses travelling west, towards Saarbrücken and the border with French Lorraine, but it was like setting a donkey to catch a hare and a poor start to a Homburg manhunt.

'I don't give much for their chances of finding so much as a broken umbrella,' I said as I returned to the car with Zander. 'Those are the doziest cops I've seen outside a Mack Sennett movie.'

'They didn't impress me, either,' admitted Zander. 'I think we'd better keep looking for him, don't you?'

We drove northeast to the railway station to check that our man was not yet arrested – he wasn't – and then motored around Homburg in the driving rain for a while, searching the deserted streets for Johann Diesbach. Homburg made Saarbrücken look like Paris. We saw only one other pedestrian who looked like it might be him; it turned out to be a woman.

'How can a man disappear like that?' complained Zander. 'The bars aren't even open yet.'

'Happens all the time in Germany,' I said. 'You might even say it's common. Only police like me don't normally go looking for them. The ones who disappear. Not least because everyone knows where they really are.'

'And where's that?'

'A KZ. Or worse.'

'Oh. I see. Then perhaps he knows someone else here in Homburg. A friend of his sister, perhaps. That man you saw at the Karlsberg Brewery. Perhaps he's hiding him. And there are plenty of places you can hide in a brewery.'

'Yes, that's possible, I suppose.'

I pulled up in front of a coffee house.

'Stay here,' I said.

I ran in, checked the lavatories, and came out again.

'Not in there, either.'

I turned the car around and once again started to drive in the direction of the brewery.

'Where are we going now?'

'The brewery.'

Zander nodded. 'I was thinking. When we were in Bormann's car, you said this man was a Jäger, trained in Hutier tactics. What are Hutier tactics?'

'Hutier tactics? You might almost call it common sense. Instead of ordering the kind of attack in which thousands of soldiers would walk across no-man's-land, Hutier trained up special storm battalions of light infantrymen, small groups of men who were specialists in carrying out surprise infiltration attacks. It might have worked, too, if someone had thought to do this a bit earlier than March 1918.'

'So he knows what he's doing.'

'When it comes to looking after himself? I should say so. Or maybe you've forgotten that trench mace in his valise.'

'Yes. I do see what you mean.'

'Look, what else can you remember about this awful place?' I asked. 'Besides what happened here in 1793.'

'Most of the furniture that was saved from the old château went to Berchtesgaden Castle.'

'Something that might help,' I said acidly.

'It's so long ago.'

'What brought you here, anyway? From Saarbrücken.'

'My brother, Hartmut, and I had a very religious childhood. He's now in Berlin, working for the Gestapo. Most people around these parts are Roman Catholics but my parents were strict Lutherans and on Sunday Hartmut and I went to Sunday school. Most of the time that was as bad as it sounds. But once a year the Church used to organize a summer picnic and it was nearly always here in Homburg, in the old gardens of Karlsberg Castle. Which for a small boy was quite exciting, as you can imagine. There were lots of games and sports. But—' He shrugged. 'I was never very good at those. Mostly Hartmut and I used to go off with a couple of friends and explore the castle ruins.'

Zander lit us a couple of the French cigarettes he favoured, and I waited patiently while he took us on a short walk down memory lane.

'Now I come to think of it,' he said finally, 'there is somewhere, perhaps. Somewhere I'd hide if it was me on the run in Homburg. Of course, you'd have to be pretty desperate.'

'You mean like Johann Diesbach.'

'Er, yes. Well, underneath the castle ruins are the Schlossberg Caves. When I was a boy we used to go in there a lot. I think everyone in Homburg knows about the Schlossberg Caves. Strictly speaking, they're not caves at all, but man-made quartz mines; the sand, you see – it was highly prized and especially useful for cleaning and grinding glass. And with at least five kilometres of passageways on at least nine levels a man could evade capture indefinitely. That's one of the reasons I'm fond of *Tom Sawyer*. Because McDougal's cave in Twain's book always reminds me of the Schlossberg Caves, here in Homburg.' He shrugged. 'Of course, it was not everyone's cup of tea. And in truth I never liked actually going into the caves much myself. Not as much as Hartmut. Although I had to, of course, for reasons of youthful bravado. I suffer from claustrophobia, you see. I hate being in an enclosed space. Especially one that's underground. I used to read Mark Twain's book as a way of confronting my phobia. After being lost in McDougal's cave for several days Tom Sawyer and Becky Thatcher find their way out again, you see?'

'That's not likely to be a problem for a man like Diesbach who owns a salt mine and who's spent half of his life underground.'

'No, I suppose not.'

'And quite a bit before that, when he was in the army, of course. I'm probably half troll myself after four years in the trenches.'

'He'd probably be quite at home in there. It's warm and dry, and I think you'd be reasonably comfortable on the sandy floor.'

'Where are these Schlossberg Caves?'

'Further up the same hill as the brewery.'

'Then that's where we're going first. And if we don't find him in the caves, we'll take a look in the brewery, as you suggested. Maybe they've got a beer barrel as big as the Heidelberg Tun and we'll find him hiding inside it.'

'I hope you're not expecting me to go in the caves with you,' Zander said nervously. 'I told you before. I suffer from claustro-phobia. Besides, it's like a rabbit warren in there, with multiple ways in and out.'

I said nothing.

'Shouldn't we go and fetch some of those uniformed policemen to help us?'

'I want to catch the rabbit. Not scare him away.'

'With one important difference surely,' said Zander. 'This particular rabbit is by your own admission armed and extremely dangerous.'

CHAPTER 61

April 1939

'He's in there all right,' I said quietly.

'How can you be sure?'

I pointed to a trail of wet footprints on the dry red sand that covered the ground near the cave entrance and led into the silent darkness.

'Those could belong to anyone,' objected Zander.

'True. But smell the air.'

Zander took a tentative step further into the cave entrance, lifted his long thin nose a little higher, and sniffed quietly, like an experienced perfumer from Treu & Nuglisch. The air inside the Schlossberg Caves was warm and dry and carried the scent of something sweet and aromatic. 'What is it?' he asked.

'Pipe tobacco,' I said. 'To be exact, Von Eicken pipe tobacco. Diesbach smokes it.'

I lit a cigarette; our previous talk about Hutier tactics had left me feeling on edge, as if I'd been about to go over the top of the trench on a midnight wire-cutting mission in no-man's-land. My hand was shaking a little as I held the lighter up to my cigarette and sucked in the volatile, hot hydrocarbon gases I needed to calm my fraying nerves. I was always better at physics than philosophy.

He frowned. 'Are you going in there?'

'That's the general idea.'

'By yourself?'

'Unless you've changed your mind about coming with me.'

Zander shook his head. 'No, this is as far as I go.'

'Sure about that?' I grinned and offered him the police torch I'd taken from the boot of the car. There were two leather tabs on the back of the light to allow the bearer to attach it to his belt or tunic so the unit could be used hands free. 'You can have this, if you like. Just button it on your greatcoat.'

'And make myself a nice target?' He shook his head firmly. 'I might as well paint a bull's eye on my chest. There are a lot of things I'll do for Martin Bormann – some of them I'm not very proud of – but I have no intention of getting myself killed for that man.'

'Spoken like a true National Socialist.'

'I'm made of different stuff than you, Gunther. I'm a bureaucrat, not a hero. A pen feels a lot more comfortable in my pocket than this stupid gun.'

'Haven't you heard? The pen is mightier than the sword, Wilhelm. Especially since January 1933. If you only knew the damage a Pelikan can do these days. Just ask Dr Stuckart. Besides, neither one of us is going to get killed.'

'You sound very sure of yourself, Gunther.'

'With any luck I'll get a chance to reason with this Fritz. Talk him out of there. Tell him that I'll make sure they go easy on his wife and son if he gives himself up. Which they certainly won't if he doesn't. I wouldn't put it past Bormann to dynamite his salt mine in Rennweg and take the roof off Diesbach's house in Kuchl. A compulsory purchase, he'd probably call it.'

'You're right. It's just the sort of vindictive thing he would do. Sell the house to some Party hack and make a nice fat profit.' Zander looked sheepish. 'I've organized one or two of those compulsory purchases myself. Frankly I was quite happy to hand over those particular duties to Karl Flex. It's not very pleasant to have to throw someone out of their house and put them on the street. Especially in a small place like Obersalzberg.' He winced. 'Believe me, I know how much I'm hated there.'

'What's this I hear? A Nazi with a conscience?'

'We all have to do things we'd perhaps rather not do, in the way of working towards the Leader. That's what Bormann calls it. You're a good man, Gunther, but before this year's out you may also find yourself having to do things you regret. We all will.'

'I'm way ahead of you there, Wilhelm.'

I slipped the torch into my coat pocket, took out my gun, worked the slide to put a round in the breech, and eased off the hammer. 'Just in case he's not open to reason.'

'Aren't you going to switch that torch on?'

'Not until I have to.'

'But it's pitch-dark in there. How on earth will you find him?'

'Very carefully. At least he won't hear me coming. This sand is like a living-room carpet.' I grinned and flicked my cigarette out of the cave into the damp undergrowth that shrouded the entrance. From the narrow path that led to it you could see the whole of Homburg laid out below like a miniature wonderland, with the accent on miniature. 'I dunno. Maybe he'll have a torch on the wall. A fire to keep warm. Some limelight and a couple of half-naked girls from the Tingel-Tangel. Any last words of advice?'

'Sound doesn't carry very far in there. Not much echo. The ceiling is vaulted and, in parts, much higher than you think. It's actually rather beautiful, although you won't be able to appreciate that much in darkness. In other places the ceiling and the ground are still joined, like a column. And here and there are some buttresses to help keep the ceiling up. But there's not much likelihood of a collapse. I certainly never heard of one when I was a boy. There are also stairs that lead down from one level to another, so watch your step. And as far as I remember there are no open holes. So it should be safe enough underfoot. There's a light switch on the wall of one of the larger, more colourful chambers but I really don't remember which one.'

I nodded. 'All right. You stay here and guard the entrance.'
I pointed at the dark tunnel in front of me. It looked like the
entrance to Helheim.

'If everything goes all right in there I'll call out the code words
"Prussian blue" when I'm about to come outside. Don't worry.
You'll hear me. I'll certainly say it more than once. But if you
don't hear me say it, then assume it's him and start shooting.
Got that?'

Zander took out his Walther P38 and thumbed back the
hammer, almost as if he knew what he was doing.

'Prussian blue. Got that.'

CHAPTER 62

October 1956

I stood outside the Karlsberg Brewery frowning and shaking my grey head in wonder as I stared up at the big blue company logo on the dirty stucco wall: a man in a leather apron shifting a beer barrel inside a blue star of David, dated 1878. On the face of it, nothing in Homburg had changed very much; nothing except me, and the surprising thing was I felt surprised by this. It seemed almost impossible that seventeen years had passed since I'd last been there and yet none of those years had had any effect on Homburg itself. It still looked like a small and very boring town in Germany and I hadn't missed the place more than I'd missed a lost sock. But time lost was something else; that was gone forever. And this brought me up short, as if I'd just driven an express train straight into the buffers of my own past. For everyone, the future arrives at a thousand miles an hour but for a moment I took that personally as if this was some kind of hilarious game the Chancellor of Heaven had chosen to play with me, and only with me. Like I was nothing more than five dice in a game of Yahtzee. I'd always thought there was plenty of time to do a lot of things and yet, now I really thought about it, there had been not a moment to spare. Perhaps that was why people chose to live in a dump like Homburg in the first place: the pace of life just seems slower in a town like that, and maybe that's the secret of a long life, to live in a place where nothing ever happens. Then something did happen; it started to rain heavily.

Of course I knew where I was going to be spending the night as soon as the police moto rider dropped me in front of the gates of the brewery. I suppose that was written on my heart in fiery letters. There was a hotel nearby and with franks in my pocket I tormented myself for a long moment by staring at it wistfully and thinking fondly about a bath, some hot food, and a bed, but I'd already decided against it. I needed to fly below the radar now, to be someone I'd never considered being before: a man without a future. The Stasi were depending on me acting as if I believed the opposite. Besides, I was hardly dressed for respectable company; any hotel manager or desk clerk seeing me would have put in a call to the local police just to be on the safe side. Playing the part of a tramp, I'd have given Charlie Chaplin a run for his money. There was a hole in my shoe to match the one in my trouser leg, my face looked like a magnet for iron filings, and the shirt on my back felt like a butter wrapper. So I trudged up the hill, to the top of Schlossberg-Höhenstrasse, admired the view for about two seconds, and made my way through thick vegetation along the same narrow hillside path I half-remembered, until I reached the entrance to the Schlossberg Caves. These were closed for the winter, and a heavy iron door that hadn't been there before blocked the way inside. According to a sign on the wall, the caves were now a tourist attraction, although it was hard to imagine anyone coming all this way to see not very much; it wasn't like the caves were home to some fascinating paleolithic paintings of ancient man and his favourite pastimes, or a series of spectacular geological formations; these weren't even proper caves, just old quartz mines, worked out years ago and then abandoned. With the rain becoming heavier and now dripping down the back of my neck, abandonment felt like a familiar story in that part of the world. I tried the door. It wasn't locked.

Inside the caves, the ground was as soft and dry under my

feet as if I'd been walking along the sands at Strandbad Wannsee in early summer. With my Ronson extended in front of me like a grave robber's lamp, I made my way to one of the larger chambers, where I found an electric light switch and flicked it on. The illumination this provided was small, meant only to be atmospheric, and that suited me fine; the last thing I wanted was to advertise my presence there. The concave vaulted ceiling was the shape of the whorl on my very dirty thumb and presented a variety of colours, mostly beige and red, but also a few blues and greens, although this might have had more to do with what the quartz did to the light, which played as many strange tricks as the immortal Chancellor himself. It was like being inside a large ant colony somewhere in the irradiated depths of New Mexico, with tunnels extending in all directions, and I half-expected a mutated giant insect to come and bite my head off. It certainly didn't feel anything like Germany. Then again, I'd seen some really bad movies since moving to France. For a while I explored the various levels – only one or two of which had electric light – and gradually figured out how the mine workings had been constructed; in some of the tunnels you could still see traces of the old tracks that had been used to transport wagons full of sand out of the caves. Everything was quiet, like a stopped clock wrapped in several layers of cotton wool, as if time itself was finally on hold. Perhaps because I desperately wanted it to be that way.

I took off my sodden jacket and hung it on the light switch in the main cavern, hoping it might dry. I also fetched the money from my coat pocket and laid it on the sand to dry. Then I sat down with my gun by my side, leaned against the rough-hewn wall, and lit a cigarette. I might have lit a fire except that I knew there was nothing outside that looked dry enough to burn. Besides, out of the wind and the rain, it was reasonably warm in the caves – warm enough to relax a little, draw a breath, and reflect on how far I'd come since leaving Cap Ferrat.

I opened the bottle of red, drank a third of it in one gulp, and ate some of the chocolate. For a while after that I wondered if I should smoke another cigarette and decided against it; making my tobacco supplies last a while seemed like a better idea. Perhaps I would smoke one after a nap. I tried to imagine what life had been like for the hundreds of quartz miners who were now my invisible companions. But instead I set myself the easier task of remembering just what had happened in those caves before the war some seventeen years ago, with Johann Diesbach and Wilhelm Zander. To think I'd risked my life to arrest that man. And as if any of it had ever mattered. Germany's invasion of Poland had been just five months away. Instead of working as a police commissar in a country where the law had ceased to matter very much, I should have been on the first train west, to France and safety. French Lorraine had been so very close to Homburg. As a senior policeman with plenipotentiary powers I could easily have bluffed my way across the border. Instead, I'd been playing the kind of hero that no one really wanted. What a fool I'd been.

I glanced around my new apartment and wondered what I could buy to make the place seem a little more congenial. That was how we made things better in the trenches: a few books from Amelang, some furniture from Gebrüder Bauer, a bit of expensive table linen from F. V. Grünfeld, a couple of silk rugs from Herrmann Gerson, and maybe several carefully selected paintings from Arthur Dahlheim on Potsdamerstrasse. All the comforts of home. Mostly we pinned a few photographs to the rough planks that were our walls: girlfriends, mothers, film stars. Just as often we didn't know who the photographs were of, since the men who'd put them there were long dead, but it never felt right to take them down. I opened my damp wallet and looked for a picture of Elisabeth I'd kept but somewhere along the way I must have lost it, which grieved me a little. And after a while all I could do was sit back and screen the movie from 1939 on the wall of the cave. I watched myself – in black-and-white, of course – like Orson Welles in *The Third Man*, gun in hand, torch at the ready, moving slowly through the tunnels in search of Johann Diesbach, one rat looking for another. Could rats see in the dark? As a boy I'd visited the Museum of Natural History in Berlin's Invalidenstrasse on many occasions and I remembered being horrified at some pictures of a naked mole rat; I thought it was probably one of the most unpleasant-looking animals I'd ever seen. Which was what I felt like now. A kind of deracinated, unloved rat who'd lost all his fur. Not to mention the only photograph of my wife.

I thought I might hole up in the Schlossberg Caves for a couple of days before making for the new German border, which was only a short way east of Homburg. Once I was properly in West Germany, I could hitch a ride to Dortmund or Paderborn, and buy myself another identity the way someone else might have bought a new hat. Lots of people had done that after 1945. Including me. It wasn't difficult to get a new name; besides, those new names were real enough, it was just some of the Germans who used them who were false.

I suppose I must have fallen asleep but I don't know for how long. When I awoke with a start it was because I was certain I was not alone, and this was mainly because the silencer on a Russian-made PM automatic was pointed squarely at my face.

CHAPTER 63

April 1939

I suppose everything began with darkness. And then God switched on the light. But still He felt obliged to hide Himself. As if the darkness comprehended not His light; or perhaps, as I suspect, He just preferred to keep his true identity, and the remarkable nature of what He'd done, a secret. You could hardly blame Him for that. Any good cabaret conjurer needs light's delay to work his magic. Imagination is built not on clarity but on its absence. Mystery needs the dark. You know you're being tricked, of course. But without the dark there would be no fear and where would God be without a bit of terror? Performing a good trick is one thing, inspiring dread is something else. What's fatal to the flickering human spirit needs palpable darkness. It's light that gives men the courage to get off their knees and tell God where to go. Without Thomas Edison we'd still be crossing ourselves in desperation and genuflecting like the most credulous nuns attending a pope's requiem mass.

In the Schlossberg Caves, darkness enveloped me as if I'd been swallowed by a whale. For several black minutes I felt my breathless way along the rough quartz walls like a blind man on a cliff edge, as if my fingers were my eyes. Now and again I pressed the small of my back hard against the rock to punctuate my progress and tiny fragments of sand adhered to my palms and worked their way under my fingernails. Once or twice I even dropped to my knees, and with the toe of one shoe pressed against the wall, I reached out to check if I was still within a tunnel. It seemed that the one I was in was less than two metres in width because it could easily be touched without abandoning the thread of the labyrinthine wall I was using as my route. I didn't care about my coat now. I was more afraid of falling than being covered in sand, or being shot. Mostly it was my nose that led me forward, because as I returned to my wall and stepped through the gently curving sable tunnels, the perfume of Johann Diesbach's distinctively sweet pipe tobacco grew ever stronger. I could also smell Zander's cigarette – my colleague's favourite French cigarettes were very pungent – I could even smell the acrid sulphur of the match that had lit it – and I cursed myself roundly for not prohibiting him from smoking. If I could smell his tobacco inside the caves, then so might Johann Diesbach. For ten or fifteen minutes I moved through the void in this flat-footed, halting way, but when I reached the end of my wall I guessed the tunnel I was in had ended. Warning myself against impatience, I dropped onto my front once again and crawled forward, but this time I realized that I must now be in one of the so-called caves and, with no sense of its size, I knew I would have to risk taking a quick glimpse of approximately where I was in order to cross it, or else risk serious injury.

My police torch was the Siemens kind we'd used during the war, with a little adjustable metal cowl to conceal the electric bulb from an enemy sniper while you were reading a map at night; more often than not we'd only ever used these cowled torches to read a map with a thick greatcoat pulled over our heads. With all this in mind – I kept telling myself that Johann Diesbach was a former Jäger and a formidable adversary, and I certainly hadn't forgotten the trench mace I'd found in his valise; a man who could pack a weapon like that next to his toothbrush was certainly to be feared – I got down on my knees and, with the torch half-buried in the sand, I switched it on for just a second in the hope I might get a better idea of my immediate surroundings. It was as well that I did: in the middle of a substantial cavern a steep stair led down to a lower level; another few steps in the dark and I'd have broken my neck. I left the light on just long enough to calculate the number of steps I'd need to reach the next tunnel and then switched it off again. A minute or two later, I'd negotiated my way across the sandy floor to the opposite wall. Gradually, I reached a second inner chamber and, on the other side of silence, a few stray sounds – a cough, a throat cleared, the scrape of a match, a sigh, lips drawing fiercely on a pipe stem – crept into my empty ears like crepuscular clues. Then, at the very edge of the darkness, black became a violet grey, and with eyes straining for something to see, the way my lungs would have needed oxygen, I saw the pale beginning of what might have been light. I took a few more tentative steps, and gradually the unfocused blur grew stronger, shifting like something that was almost alive until I perceived that it was the guttering, quiet flame of a very small candle. I lifted my gun to my face, thumbed back the hammer, slipped off the safety, and poked my head around the corner of the wall.

I saw his shoes first of all and my first thought was how big they were. The man had enormous feet. He'd taken the shoes off to allow them to dry. A green hat with a cock feather in the band lay alongside them and his loden coat was hanging on a nail in a roof prop. Diesbach himself was seated on the floor with his back to the wall, about ten or fifteen metres from where I was standing. The candle was only a few centimetres away from his stockinged foot. He was wearing a good wool suit, with plus fours I hadn't noticed before; his arms were crossed, a briar pipe was in his mouth, and his eyes were closed. From time to time his mouth twitched to let out a puff of smoke, like a sleeping dragon. He seemed like a tougher-looking version of Adolf Hitler. The moustache wasn't exactly uncommon in Germany; there were lots of men who wanted to look like the Leader. Some grew a Hitler moustache to make themselves more authoritative, and I'd even read in the newspaper about a man who'd claimed he was due a greater amount of respect just because he had a tooth-brush moustache. Apart from the long-barrelled Luger resting in his hand Diesbach appeared to be as relaxed as if he'd been on a day trip to Rügen Island and seemed very much at home in the cave, as if he'd just sat down after a good day mining salt.

I ought to have shot the bastard just for the moustache – and without warning, the way Diesbach had shot Udo Ambros and Karl Flex. Most other cops who still worked for the Murder Com-mission in 1939 would certainly have put a hole in him without a moment's hesitation. And a hole would certainly have slowed him down long enough to get the cuffs on him. In those days, however, I still entertained the foolish notion that I was better than them, and that it was my duty to give the man a chance to give himself up. But in truth, while it was a shot I could easily have made in broad daylight, in the flickering light of a solitary candle, missing him looked only too possible; and if I missed him with one shot, I knew I might not get another. From my training at the Alex I knew that most criminals were shot by police at distances of less than three metres, and at that kind of range, you couldn't get a better pistol than a Walther PPK. But at more than ten metres, it was hard to beat a long-barrelled Parabellum Luger. In the hands of a Jäger, a long-barrelled Luger had the edge on my PPK, with the stopping power of a castle door. Which made it more or less imperative that I should cross as much of the cave's floor as possible before trying to arrest him. Even then I knew I'd be taking a considerable chance. No man with an Iron Cross First Class prefers an ignominious death on the guillotine at Plötzensee to dying with a gun in his hand and a good curse on his lips. While Diesbach's eyes were closed, the one thing I had in my favour was the element of surprise; with a thick layer of sand under my feet I might easily halve the distance between us before letting him know I was aiming a gun at his beer hole. At which point he might be of a mind to give himself up. But even as I made my plan I was aware that he was too tough to quit without a fight; the muscles of his forearms bulged like ham hocks and he had a jaw that looked as if it had been cut in a quarry. Mining was probably less of a problem to a man like that than charming customers smoothly in expensive Munich restaurants. Maybe he just scared the chefs into buying his pink gourmet salt. Him and that damned tooth-brush moustache.

CHAPTER 64

April 1939

Pointing my gun at the centre of his chest I started across the cave. At fifteen metres my mouth was as dry as the sand on the ground; at fourteen metres, my heart was beating so loudly I thought he might hear it; at thirteen metres I was starting to grow in confidence; at twelve I was close enough to see the white scar on his chin; at ten I was getting ready to tell him to drop the gun and put up his hands; but at eight metres, he opened his eyes, met mine, and smiled as if he'd been expecting me.

'I think that's far enough, copper,' he said coolly. 'Take another step and you'll find out how excellent a shot I am.'

'All that salt must have dried your brain like last week's herring. If I shoot you'll be dead before you can even wave that pistol.' I threw some handcuffs onto the sand beside his leg. 'Let go of the Luger, gently, like it was one of Pony's lovely breasts. Toss it over here and then put those bracelets on.'

'How did you know about Pony?' he asked, still holding on to the Luger.

'Your wife told me.'

'I guess she told you a lot,' he said, puffing his pipe nonchalantly. 'Otherwise you wouldn't have come all this way to lovely Homburg.'

'Don't blame her,' I said. 'Blame Benno. And then blame the

Nazis. Threatening someone with a trip to Dachau is a very persuasive way to preface all sorts of pressing questions.'

'You know, I somehow think that Bormann has something far worse planned for me than that. So I should tell you now, I've no intention of swapping my best hat for a wastepaper basket in Plötzensee. Which means I've really got nothing to lose by shooting it out with you here, copper. It will be a pity if we both have to take a bullet because you want to put my neck in the lunette.'

'I can live with that. Which is more than I can say for you, Johann. The second I pull this trigger your last thought is a red mark on that wall.

'But give up now and I give you my word I will make sure that nothing happens to Eva and Benno. I'm not a vindictive man, Johann, but I'm afraid the same cannot be said for my employers. They'll treat your wife and son like the worst kind of criminals. Take the roof off your house. Dynamite your salt mine. If your wife thought your son was too warm for the army, how long do you think he'll last in Dachau? And all because you want to go out like Jimmy Cagney.'

'You're not much of a detective, are you?'

'I found you, didn't I?'

'Yes, but surely you've worked out that my wife and I haven't been getting along at all well. Not since she found out about Pony. And my son. Well, you've met Benno, haven't you? He's not what I'd call a man's man, so much as a man's boy, if you see what I mean. His mother bribing that bastard Flex to keep him out of the army was the last straw as far as I was concerned. What I'm saying is that they'll have to take their chances. Besides, I rather think that if I do have to shoot you, I'll just walk out of here and be across the border tonight. I speak French. I shouldn't think I'll have much of a problem.'

'You must be mistaking me for a cop who was dumb enough to come here on my own. This whole area is surrounded with the local leather heads. Besides, don't assume that the Franzis won't hand you over to us. They might be about to go to war with Germany, but until that happens we enjoy the total co-operation of the French police.'

'Sounds about right. The French have always been in Germany's back pocket. And I suppose you must be in Martin Bormann's. How does it feel to be just another Nazi doing the dirty work in Hitler's new order?'

'I'm not a Nazi. And I'm tired of hearing about the new order. The only shred of self-respect left to me now is to try to do my job the old way. That means taking you to jail. Alive. To arrest you for a crime I know you committed. After you're safely in the cement it's up to them what they do with you. I really don't care. But don't make the mistake of thinking I won't shoot you, Johann. What I know about you, shooting you would be a real pleasure.'

'Then we're not so very different, you and I.'

'How do you figure that?'

'I killed Karl Flex because he was a part of the same criminal hypocrisy as your police bosses. Because he had it coming. You must have known about all the rackets he was involved in, surely. Bormann's Obersalzberg rackets. Drugs, property, bribery. There's nothing that man doesn't have a piece of. Flex was one of Bormann's rats. The worst kind of Nazi. The greedy kind. Surely you can see that.'

'You can tell yourself what you like,' I said. 'And perhaps Flex did have it coming. But you can hardly say the same for Udo Ambros. Your old comrade. Your friend. A man who served with you. I don't see for a minute how he deserved to have his face blown off with a shotgun. By you.'

'Don't you see? I had to kill him. He'd threatened to go to the police and tell them about the carbine I'd borrowed from him. The one I used to shoot Flex. That was clever of you, copper – finding it down the chimney like that. Anyway, Udo said he would give me a twenty-four-hour head start out of

Berchtesgaden before he went to the police. But I had too much to lose just to let him drop me in the shit pit like that. And all because I'd wiped out a piece of dirt like Karl Flex. You saw the way Udo lived. What right did he have to wreck my life? All he had to do was keep his mouth shut. Say the rifle was stolen, something like that. I had a good life, a good business. I had to kill him. Please. You have to understand. He gave me no choice. I had to protect my family and my business.'

There was a note in his pompous Bavarian voice that hadn't been there before. It sounded like the kind of unctuous, self-justifying mendacity we'd heard just a few weeks before, when Hitler had torn up the Munich agreement and occupied what was left of Czechoslovakia after Germany had already annexed the Sudetenland. It was what happened next that convinced me I'd overestimated him: when he reached for his pipe his hand was shaking. Johann Diesbach was scared. It was in the man's eyes.

'The way you talk about it – your whining explanation for an act of cold-blooded murder – in my book, that makes you as bad as the Nazis, Johann. Worse, maybe. But I think you're losing your nerve for this stalemate game. I think that you're the kind of Fritz who only shoots a man when he's not expecting it. Am I right? Are you going to fire that Luger or use it to pick your nose?' Lowering my pistol I walked towards him and kicked his stockinged foot. 'Go ahead, tough guy. Point that Bismarck and see what happens.' Diesbach stared at me sullenly: close up, I could see now that whatever fight had been in him was long gone. Perhaps it had never really been there. Candlelight – especially in a cave – can play some strange tricks on you. 'No? I didn't think so. Maybe once upon a time, *pifke*. But not anymore. Your son Benno has more guts than you.'

I took the gun away from him and dropped it into my coat pocket. Then I dragged him onto his feet and slapped him hard. Not because of that irritating Hitler moustache but because he'd scared me and I didn't like being scared.

CHAPTER 65

April 1939

Holding the torch, I pocketed my gun and escorted my manacled prisoner back through the tunnels. As soon as he was on his feet and moving he began offering me a deal.

'You really don't have to do this, Commissar Gunther,' he said. 'You could just let me go. I have plenty of money. Back there in the caves, I have at least a thousand reichsmarks in the lining of my loden coat. And there are also some gold coins in the belt on my trousers. It's all yours the minute you agree to turn me loose. Just don't hand me over to these Nazi bastards. You know exactly what they'll do to me. They'll starve me half to death like they did to that poor bastard Brandner and when they've finished doing that they'll chop off my head.'

'You're going to need that money for a good lawyer.'

I don't know why I said that – habit, probably. I didn't think there was one lawyer in Germany able to save Johann Diesbach from the guillotine. Clarence Darrow couldn't have persuaded the People's Court in Potsdamer Platz that Karl Flex's murderer deserved anything less than a haircut. Not that I cared very much. As soon as Diesbach was safely in police custody in Saarbrücken, I could return to Obersalzberg and organize Brandner's immediate release from the RSD prison in the Türken Inn. It was *his* fate I was concerned about. I was even hoping that Martin Bormann might be so grateful to me that he would agree to commute the death sentence on the two Gestapo men from Linz. And once my business with Bormann was concluded, I would work on getting Gerdy Troost to introduce me to brother Albert; only then might it be possible to acquaint Albert Bormann with the full extent of Martin's corruption and the blatant simony of the Obersalzberg Administration.

Diesbach now turned threatening.

'You'd better watch out, copper. After what you told me back there I could land you in a lot of trouble. Just see if I'm wrong.'

'How's that?'

Diesbach grinned. 'Maybe I'll tell the Gestapo how you told me you hate the Nazis,' he said. 'Maybe I'll tell them that, copper.'

'If I had five reichsmarks for every dumbhead like you who's threatened me with the Gestapo, I'd be a rich man. Don't you think they expect people like you to say that kind of thing? To accuse cops of talking treason?'

'I bet you're not even a Party member. In which case it might strike a chord with them. Of course, if you let me go—'

I took hold of him by his jacket collar. We were nearing the exit and, after taking a great deal of trouble to capture him alive, I hardly wanted Diesbach to get shot by a man who was scared of the dark.

'Zander? It's me, Gunther. Prussian blue, okay? Do you hear me? Everything's fine. I've got the man in handcuffs. And we're coming out, do you hear? We can go back to Obersalzberg now. Prussian blue.'

'I hear you, Gunther,' said Zander. 'Prussian blue. Right. I've got that. No problem. Come ahead.'

I pushed Diesbach forward. A moment later we rounded the corner of the tunnel and stepped into the grey daylight. Zander was standing where I'd left him. He threw away his cigarette, lowered his gun, and sneered.

'So this is the damn Fritz who's caused all the trouble, is it?'

'This is him.'

'Congratulations, Gunther,' said Zander. 'I must say I admire your courage, going into the caves like that. Even with a torch I couldn't have done what you just did. I'm claustrophobic just standing here in the entrance. I'm actually finding it hard to believe I ever went in there as a boy. Yes, you're quite a fellow. I can see why General Heydrich thinks so highly of you. Now and then one just needs a useful and probably expendable man like you who can get things done, the hard way. In any normal circumstances you might expect to get a police medal for this. For bravery, I mean. It's just unfortunate for you that these are not normal circumstances. A promotion would be the very least you could expect out of this.'

'I can live with it,' I said.

'Yes, I'm sure you can live with it, Commissar. But I'm sorry to tell you that Martin Bormann can't.'

The next second Wilhelm Zander lifted the Walther from his side and shot Diesbach three times without even blinking. In the cave entrance it sounded like the metallic roar of some modern Minotaur. He collapsed onto the ground, his blood draining onto the sand as he died.

For a moment I just stood there, frozen to the spot, not least because the gun in Zander's hand was now pointed very squarely at me.

'I wanted him alive,' I yelled.

'Maybe you did. But no one else did.'

'There's a proper way of doing things,' I said. 'Otherwise the law is as bad as those who break it. Don't you see?'

'How old-fashioned you sound. And how very naïve. Can you really be so stupid? This unfortunate incident – namely Karl Flex's murder – never happened. For obvious reasons. After all, it would hardly do if the Leader were ever to find out that someone had been shot on the terrace of the Berghof, would it? That would be bad enough, don't you agree? But if other people found out, that would be even worse. I mean, if Flex could be shot on that terrace, anyone could be shot on that terrace. And can you imagine what they'd do with a story like that in the foreign newspapers and magazines? It would give all sorts of people ideas. Bad ideas. It would be open season on the Leader. Democratically minded English sportsmen with hunting rifles arriving in the area for the ultimate prey. Hitler himself.'

'I might have known you'd pull something like this, Zander.'

'This certainly wasn't done on my own initiative. Martin Bormann ordered me to kill him. So don't get all high and mighty with me, Gunther. Killing's not my thing at all. I'm just the button that Bormann pushed back in Obersalzberg before we left. Anyway, if you ask me, I've done the poor bastard a favour. They would only have chopped his head off and that's not a good way to die. From what I've heard, they've stopped sharpening the blade on the guillotine at Plötzensee on Hitler's personal orders. Just to make the whole execution process last a bit longer. By all accounts it can take two or three drops of the falling axe before the head is actually severed. Christ, I bet that makes your eyes water.'

'So what happens now?' I asked, carefully watching the gun in Zander's steady hand and more particularly his trigger finger. I knew there were at least four shots still left in the Walther's magazine. There was no trace of nerves in the little man's demeanour, which surprised me. It's not every pen-pushing German bureaucrat who can murder a man in cold blood. 'Can we go home now? Or does Bormann want me dead, too?'

'My dear Gunther, Bormann doesn't want you dead. But I do. And so do several of my colleagues in Obersalzberg. People like Dr Brandt, Bruno Schenk, Peter Högl. I suppose a fellow like you just leaves the rest of us feeling rather embarrassed by our own dishonesty. You see, as you've probably gathered, we're all in the same racket that Karl was. The ten per cent racket. All of us have been skimming off what Bormann has been making from his stewardship of Hitler's mountain. Well, that seemed only right, given that we were the ones he detailed to collect his various tributes. Not that it seemed particularly dishonest, I have to say. Bormann's been making a fortune since he came to Obersalzberg. And if it's all right for him, well – not that you could do much about our racket even if you wanted to. If you exposed us, you'd have to expose Bormann, and he wouldn't like that. But why take the risk? At least, that's what we've all concluded. You're a loose end, Gunther, and being shot while trying heroically to arrest Johann Diesbach ties that up rather nicely. One problem cancels out the other. It even makes a nice bow and, under these circumstances, I wouldn't be at all surprised if you get that police medal after all. Albeit posthumously. Those are the Nazi heroes that Dr Goebbels likes the best. The ones who are not around to gainsay what he—'

There was nothing clever or ingenious about what happened next. You couldn't even have said that I outwitted him. A typical Nazi, Zander was still giving me this long, self-serving speech when I simply turned tail and ran away, back into the Schloss-berg Caves. Usually running away is best. Cowardice only looks that way when there's someone watching closely and from a position of comparative safety. Most brave men are cowards on any other day of the week.

The next moment there was a loud bang. A piece of quartz beside my face flew off as Zander's first bullet missed me. With my head buried in my shoulders I kept moving. Another loud explosion followed and it was as if some angry cave-dwelling insect had bitten the back of my right hand. I grimaced with pain, made a fist, and ducked into the sanctuary of the darkness. Two more shots ricocheted off the wall behind me, like the blows from some invisible miner's pickaxe. But only silence pursued my last-minute escape. Silence and the sound of my own feet stumbling across the sandy floor. I guessed Zander was probably reloading the Walther and this prompted me to stop for a second before I managed to run into one of the walls, and to switch on my torch, and then to go on with all speed. I hoped Zander's fear of Martin Bormann wouldn't overcome his fear of the dark and his claustrophobia. I was counting on that. I had two loaded guns in my coat pockets, but I was never much of a shot with my left hand; my right hand was already numb and I could feel blood between my fingers, which is no way to take careful aim, even with a long-barrelled Luger. I paused for a second behind the cover of a wall and switched off the torch for a few moments so that I might draw a breath in comparative safety. It was as well that I did; a moment later the darkness was lit up in a series of brief gunpowder flashes as Zander fired six shots into the caves. They were the wild, speculative, hope-for-the-best kind of shots that men used to let off in the trenches when they got bored, but they were still dangerous if they hit something and I threw myself on the ground until the tiny bombardment was over. The air reeked of cordite and I realized he'd already tried his very best to murder me. Six in the dark had been it. If he'd had what it took to enter the caves and kill me he'd have conserved his ammunition until he had a clear target. For a moment I thought about shooting back, but I couldn't see any better than he could and, in truth, I had no wish to earn the enmity of a figure as powerful as Martin Bormann; killing his messenger wasn't likely to play well back in Obersalzberg. But I was already feeling safer. Under the circumstances it hardly seemed probable that Zander would mention trying to kill me to his master. Now all I had to do was find another way out of the caves and with nine levels to choose from, I had a pretty good chance of making good my escape. After that I had no idea what might happen beyond a cigarette and an immediate trip to the local hospital to get my hand fixed, and perhaps my jaw as well.

CHAPTER 66

October 1956

'On your feet, Gunther.'

Friedrich Korsch was stuffing the gun he'd found on the floor by my leg under the waistband of his trousers and slowly backing away. In the low light I could just make out the triumphant expression on his face, as if he was looking forward to killing me; he appeared to be alone.

'Why?' I said wearily. Once before I'd escaped being shot in the Schlossberg Caves and I scarcely thought I was about to manage it again. There's a limit to how lucky one lucky man can be. Then again, good luck is merely the ability and determination to overcome bad luck; anything else looks like capricious fortune. But my determination to do anything other than sleep inside that mountain for a thousand years was sorely lacking. 'What's the point?' I added. 'You might as well shoot me in here, Friedrich. As mausoleums go, this place is as good as any.'

'Because those aren't General Mielke's orders. I'm to make your death look like a suicide. Something the local cops can explain away. The Blue Train murderer takes his own life. Which can hardly happen if I kill you now. So please get up. I'm not a sadistic man, and I'd hate to have to blow your kneecaps off. But I can assure you, not nearly as much as you would.'

He had a point. My luck had finally run out and, as coincidences go, this one seemed more meaningful than not; it looked very much as if fate had always meant me to meet my end in the Schlossberg Caves and was determined not to be disappointed in that respect. God moves in mysterious ways but it's best to recognize that most of the mystery relates to why people still think He gives a damn about any of us. I stood up reluctantly and brushed some of the sand off my trousers. 'I expect they'll give you a promotion for this. Or a medal. Perhaps both.'

Korsch circled away some more now that I was on my feet. But he certainly wasn't about to miss me from wherever he was standing in the cavern. Not even with one eye.

'For catching an old fascist enemy of the people like you? Yes, I expect so.'

'Is that what I am?'

'It's how it will be reported in Germany, probably. And why not? These days we need our villains just as much as we need our heroes. There's a lot we can blame on the Nazis and usually do. Now, then. Do you have any more guns?'

'Sadly, not.'

Korsch moved around the wall of the cave to where my jacket was hanging on the light switch and patted it down. 'Just making sure. You always were a slippery bastard, Gunther.'

'That's how I managed to stay alive, Friedrich.'

'You can keep telling yourself that if you like. But I rather think you stayed alive by doing exactly what the likes of Heydrich and Goebbels told you to do.'

'And you didn't?'

'Sure. But you were the police commissar, not me. I was just your spanner for a short time.'

'I guess you have to tell yourself that now that you're a spanner for the Ivans. More importantly, I guess you have to tell them that, too.'

'Not the Ivans, no. There's a new Germany that's being constructed. A socialist Germany. We're running our own show, now.

Not the Russians. Us. The Germans. It's better this time because there's a proper goal we're all working towards.'

'Even in this light I can see you don't believe any of that crap. I look at you and see myself all those years ago, trying to keep my mouth close to the Party line and pretend that everything was fine with the way our masters were running Germany. But we both know it wasn't – and it still isn't. The GDR and the communists are just another universal tyranny. So how about you pretend you never saw me in here and let me go? For old times' sake. Does it really make such a difference to the new order if I'm dead?'

'Sorry, Bernie. No can do. If General Mielke ever found out I let you go it wouldn't just be me who suffered, it would be my whole family. Besides, there are a couple of my men waiting by the entrance outside, just in case you manage to give me the slip in the dark. If I let you escape, they wouldn't like it, either. You've led us on a real polka since the Riviera.'

'And why? Because I wasn't prepared to go to England and poison Mielke's own agent, Anne French. That's why. That should tell you something about your new masters, Friedrich. They're cowards. Still, it was brave of you coming in here on your own, I suppose.'

'Wasn't it? You were joking before about my getting a medal and a promotion. But that's not a joke to me. I will get both of those things now. My men will see to that. Catching you is my big chance of preferment with Mielke. I could get my fourth pip for this. Maybe even a major's whipped-cream shoulder boards.'

'You do know Erich Mielke was a cop killer. Before he became a cop.'

'I remember he shot some Freikorps police bully, if that's what you mean.'

'My, the commies really have done a good job with your re-education, haven't they? I bet you could even spell "dialectic" and "bourgeoisie".'

Korsch brandished the automatic and grinned. 'Since I'm the one holding the Bismarck, it would seem as if my re-education has turned out better than yours, wouldn't you agree?'

'Therein lies the true essence of Marxism. "From each according to his ability, to each according to his needs" only ever works with a gun in your hand. How did you find me, anyway?'

'I'd like to say I know you better than you think, Gunther. But I can't claim it was the result of any great insight on my part. That moto rider from Saarbrücken reported bringing you here to one of our police informants. It was him who told us you were in Homburg. He suspected you from the beginning, apparently. After that it was more or less obvious to me that you'd return to the Schlossberg Caves, given what happened here just before the war.'

'I was always under the impression that no one ever knew about that. Not precisely. Certainly Wilhelm Zander never talked about it, for obvious reasons. I never talked about it, either. Not even to Heydrich. For equally obvious reasons. I thought I was safer that way, given what Bormann had said about keeping my mouth shut concerning what happened on the Berghof terrace. And before he left the area, Zander removed anything that would have identified Johann Diesbach. Including Johann Diesbach, now I come to think of it. I believe Zander had some local Gestapo come to fetch the body so they could dump it somewhere else. So how did you ever think to connect me with this place?'

'Does it matter?'

'You might call it an itch on my nose that needs scratching now that I'm standing on the gallows with my hands tied behind my back. That is, if you wouldn't mind.'

'Maybe I'm just cleverer than you give me credit for.'

'It's always a possibility.'

'When you and Zander showed up in Homburg looking for Diesbach, it was his sister who suggested that he should hide in the caves. After a few days she came up here to bring him some food and found the floor of the cave entrance littered with empty cartridges. From their number she guessed there had been some sort of shoot-out and when, weeks later, Diesbach still hadn't contacted her, she naturally assumed the worst.'

'How do you know all that?'

'Because she wrote to Diesbach's wife, Eva, informing her that she suspected Johann might have met a violent end. And when Eva forwarded me the letter, asking for my help in finding out what had happened to him, I agreed.'

'I don't remember the two of you being that friendly.'

'After you left me behind in Berchtesgaden, she and I got on quite well. You might say that I was a real consolation to that woman. Very soon after her husband disappeared, Eva moved to Berlin. And, for a while, we were lovers.'

'Taking a risk, weren't you, Friedrich? Given her medical history.'

'Worth it, though. You saw what she looked like.'

'She was built, all right, if that's what you mean. But why didn't you ask me what became of Diesbach, to save you all that bother?'

'I did. On two or three occasions. Maybe you've forgotten but all you'd say was that he was dead and that I'd stay alive longer if I forgot he'd ever existed. Or words to that effect. So I did, eventually. And so did she.'

'Good advice, if you don't mind me saying so. I did you a favour there. For Bormann, the security of the Berghof was more than just a matter of guarding Hitler's life. It was also a matter of guarding Hitler's feelings. It was made very clear to me that any kind of loose talk about Karl Flex's death would be treated as treasonous. Undermining Reich security or some such nonsense.'

'Anyway, none of that matters much now.'

'And did you find out what became of Diesbach's body?'

'In time. It seems that the local Gestapo took him to a crematorium in Kaiserslautern and had him burned to ashes at midnight. Not that Eva Diesbach cared very much by then. She had other things on her mind. Her son Benno, remember him? He got himself picked up by a man in the old Friedrichstrasse arcade and was sent to a KZ with a pink triangle on his jacket.' Korsch jerked the barrel of the silenced Makarov pistol at one of the quartz tunnels leading back to the cave entrance. 'All right. Story's over. Let's go, shall we? This damned place gives me the shivers. And you're right. It is exactly like being buried alive.'

'So how are you planning that I should kill myself? Thallium poisoning, or another hanging?'

'You'll find out soon enough. Now move.'

I hesitated to move. 'May I fetch my jacket? I'm cold.'

'You won't need it where you're going.'

'My ID is in that jacket. If the proper authorities don't find that, then it won't look like much of a suicide.'

'What do you care?'

'I don't. But I really am feeling cold. Besides, my cigarettes are also in that jacket. And I'm hoping you might allow me a last smoke.'

Korsch jerked his head at my jacket. 'All right. But don't get any clever ideas, Gunther. I really don't mind shooting you. Not after what you did to poor Helmut. He was the man in the leather shorts you strangled the day before yesterday. And one of my best men.'

'It was him or me.'

'Perhaps. But he was also my cousin.'

'Well, I am sorry about that. Cousins are hard to come by these days. But I really don't think he was a very nice person, Friedrich. Before I killed Helmut I watched him shoot a cat for sport. What kind of a sick bastard does something like that?'

'I don't care about cats very much. But that makes two of my men you've killed since we met again. There's not going to be a third.'

I went to retrieve my jacket.

'Slowly,' said Korsch. 'Like tree sap in winter.'

'Everything I do now, I do slowly. As a matter of fact, Friedrich, I'm exhausted. I couldn't run another step, even if I wanted to. And I'm all out of clever ideas on how to evade you and your men.'

This was true. I'd had more than enough of running. My neck ached and my feet were damp. My clothes were sticking to me and I smelled almost as bad as the cold andouillette I'd eaten in Freyming-Merlebach. All I really wanted to do was smoke a last cigarette, face up to whatever was coming to me from the Stasi, and get it over with. They say a cornered rat will attack a dog and deliver a nasty bite, but this particular rat felt like it was finished, and it was as well for me that Gunther's luck wasn't feeling the same way because, as I tugged my jacket off the electricity switch on the quartz wall, I managed, quite accidentally, to turn off the light, plunging the cavern into complete darkness. For a millisecond I wondered what had happened. I think I may even have asked myself if someone else had killed the light. I expect we both did. And in the half second it took Friedrich Korsch to pull the trigger of the Makarov, I recognized the broken shard of a chance the gods had capriciously tossed my way and threw myself onto the thick sand. I scrambled away from the splinter of flame that punctuated the inky air with harmless delicacy, once, twice, and then a third time.

I heard Korsch curse and then fumble with a box of matches, and since it's impossible to strike a match and pull a trigger at the same time, I stood up and launched myself desperately at the spot in space where I'd last seen the flame from the silenced automatic, hardly caring if I was injured or not. Half a second later I collided heavily with Korsch and the two of us crashed hard against the quartz wall, with him taking the full force of the impact and seemingly coming off the worst as he let out a loud groan and then stopped moving altogether. Breathlessly, I lay on top of his silent, motionless body for a full minute before realizing that I couldn't hear him breathing.

I rolled off him and, finding my lighter, I saw that far from being unconscious, Friedrich Korsch was dead – that much was clear even in the flickering light of my Ronson. His single bulging eye stared straight at me and for a moment I thought he was wearing a red hat until I realized that the top of his head was cracked like an egg and covered with blood. More quickly than his life had been engendered between some greasy sheets in Kreuzberg, it had now abruptly disappeared, almost as if it had been turned off like the lights on the cavern floor, and all Korsch's hopes of a captain's pip or a major's shoulder boards were gone as if with the flick of a switch. I held his stare for a while. For a moment I thought of all we'd been through together in Kripo, and then I pushed his horribly fractured head away with the heel of my shoe.

I didn't feel sorry for him. Just as easily my life could have ended in the same way, and I thought it as well Korsch had used a silencer on his pistol, otherwise the Stasi men outside would have been summoned to the scene by the three shots he'd fired. I won't say I planned to erect an altar to luck any time soon, like Goethe, but I did feel absurdly fortunate.

Now all I had to do was go to one of the other nine levels and make my escape, probably the same way I'd done in 1939.

CHAPTER 67

April 1939

Until 1803, Berchtesgaden had a college of Augustinian canons, whose priors were granted the rank of princes of the empire at the end of the fifteenth century. The Schloss, once the monastic buildings, was now the property of the ex-crown prince Rupprecht. But neither a king nor an emperor could have penetrated the tight RSD security cordon around Obersalzberg now in place following the Leader's arrival there; I certainly couldn't. My own clearance was revoked indefinitely and it was explained to me, in person, by Colonel Rattenhuber, that this wouldn't change until the Leader had left the area and returned to Berlin.

I was installed in my new lodgings at Berchtesgaden's Grand Hotel & Kurhaus when Rattenhuber came to see me, full of apologies for this apparent slight and desperate for a cigarette but unable to have one in case Hitler smelled tobacco on his breath.

'You must understand that there are lots of people in Berchtesgaden to wish Hitler a happy fiftieth birthday and that it would be impossible to accommodate you now in the Leader's Territory. The Villa Bechstein is full.'

'I'll try to contain my disappointment.'

'I only just succeeded in getting you in here, at the Grand. I've never seen so many people in Berchtesgaden. It's a real carnival atmosphere.'

I wondered how many carnivals Rattenhuber had been to;

the prospect of a war in Poland surely wouldn't make anyone inclined to run around a maypole.

'On behalf of Martin Bormann I'm authorized to congratulate and thank you for your excellent work, Herr Commissar. Not to mention your bravery. He's already telephoned General Heydrich in Berlin to express his gratitude that this whole business has been handled with such enormous discretion on your part and is now concluded satisfactorily.'

'Who told you that?' I asked bluntly.

'Wilhelm Zander, of course.'

'So he's back in Obersalzberg, is he?'

'Yes.'

'Exactly what did he tell you, Colonel?'

'Only that the two of you traced Johann Diesbach all the way to Homburg, and that when he resisted arrest you were obliged to shoot and kill him. He said you acted with great bravery.'

I smiled thinly. 'That was kind of him.'

'No doubt about it, you acted for the best. A public trial would only have drawn unwelcome attention to this regrettable lapse in security. For the Leader's sake, it's expedient that we should now proceed on the assumption that Karl Flex was never shot on the terrace of the Berghof. That no one was. That there was no sniper on the roof at the Villa Bechstein. And that Johann Diesbach never even existed. As a corollary of all that, we should like to make it quite clear that your investigation never took place. Indeed, that you were never really here in Berchtesgaden. So as not to alarm the Leader unnecessarily. For this reason, the fewer people who see a Kripo detective from Berlin's Murder Commission around the Berghof and the Villa Bechstein, the better for all concerned. And even though you can't talk about this matter – no, you really shouldn't talk about this, and perhaps I need to remind you of the confidentiality agreement you signed up at the tea house – you still have the satisfaction of knowing that you have given a great service to the Leader and to Germany. So then, your orders are to return to Berlin as soon as possible and report to General Heydrich. Your assistant, Korsch, has already left by train, on Arthur Nebe's orders.'

Wilhelm Zander had done his job well. I saw that my earlier plan – to confront him in front of Martin Bormann – was now pointless. After all, I could hardly accuse Zander of the murder of someone no one was prepared to admit had ever even existed; besides, Martin Bormann had sanctioned Diesbach's murder. As for Zander's attempt on my own life, it would be his word against mine, and it wasn't difficult to see who would be believed: an expendable Berlin cop who wasn't even a Party member, or Martin Bormann's trusted servant? I guess I wasn't surprised by any of that. After all, I wasn't even there. Never had been. I already felt like the Invisible Man.

'How is your jaw, by the way?' asked Rattenhuber.

'Better, thanks. I had a doctor in Kaiserslautern take a look at it. It's not broken. Just badly bruised. Like my feelings, I guess.'

'You're tougher than you think, Gunther. But what happened there?' He pointed at the bandage now swathing my hand.

'I was shot,' I said lightly. 'It's just a graze really.'

'Shot while you were arresting Diesbach?'

'You might say that.'

'Foolish fellow.'

I smiled again, uncertain if Colonel Rattenhuber was talking about Diesbach or me.

'It's an occupational hazard for a man like you, I suppose, Herr Commissar. Being shot.'

I changed the subject. 'What about the widow?' I asked uncomfortably. With three men in the Türken Inn already facing a firing squad it didn't take much imagination to see that a fourth name could easily be added. 'Surely Frau Diesbach will have something to say about her husband's disappearance from Berchtesgaden.'

'She's to be resettled,' said Rattenhuber. 'Permanently. In Berlin. The house in Kuchl and the salt mine are to be purchased by the OA. In a few weeks no one will know they ever lived in the area.'

'I suppose that's an occupational hazard, too. But suppose she doesn't want to move?' In view of what I already knew about the OA, this was a naïve question, perhaps, but I still wanted to see how Rattenhuber dealt with it. 'Suppose she wants to stay put exactly where she is.'

'She doesn't have a choice in the matter. There's her son, you see. Shall we say he's not like other men? I think you know what I mean by that. And I'm sure I don't have to remind you about what paragraph 175 of the German Criminal Code says about acts of severe lewdness, Herr Commissar, and those who are likely to commit them. Major Högl has already informed her that it would be best, for both mother *and* son, if they didn't make any waves.'

'I agree about that, anyway.'

I lit a cigarette, blew some of the smoke at Rattenhuber's desperate nostrils and, more important, onto his uniform, and went to the window of my hotel room. Outside, it was busy with black staff cars going up and down the left bank of the Ache. I might have been looking at the Wilhelmstrasse in Berlin; Berchtesgaden really did look more like Germany's second capital city than a sleepy little market town of just four thousand natives. I wondered how long it would take Bormann to get rid of them, too. I said, 'I don't much care what happens to mother or son, to be honest. All I care about is that an innocent man is released. I'm referring to Johann Brandner. There's absolutely no reason to hold him now the real culprit is dead. Frankly, he belongs in a hospital. Besides, Bormann promised to let him go. He also promised to consider releasing those two Gestapo officers from Linz, who are also being held in the Türken Inn cells under sentence of death.'

'It's very magnanimous of you to plead for them,' said Rattenhuber, 'in view of the fact that they meant to kill you.'

'They made an unfortunate mistake that can be cleared up

very easily. It was nothing personal, I'm sure. With so many different agencies for law enforcement now operating in the new Germany, these things are bound to happen, wouldn't you agree? Gestapo, Abwehr, Kripo, SS, SD, RSD – it's not just the left hand that doesn't know what the right is doing, it's all the fingers and toes as well.'

Rattenhuber looked awkward. 'Yes, I do agree. Policing is a bit of a jurisdictional mess. But I regret to have to inform you, Commissar Gunther, that all three of the men you mentioned were shot by a firing squad at six o'clock this morning. Major Högl took charge of the execution. It was carried out before the Leader's arrival. The two Gestapo men were shot on Heydrich's explicit orders, of course, and, given the exemplary service afforded by his office to the government leader, Martin Bormann hardly wished to disappoint him in this respect. As for Brandner, Bormann felt that he already knew far too much about Karl Flex and the shooting on the Berghof terrace, if only because of the questioning to which he'd been subjected by myself and Peter Högl. We could hardly go to such enormous lengths to ensure Frau Diesbach's silence if Johann Brandner were allowed to remain in the area and say what he liked to anyone who cared to listen. As he has done on previous occasions. Besides, it has since been discovered that his release from Dachau was an administrative error. He was supposed to have been transferred to Flossenburg concentration camp. So you see, really, there's not much harm done at the end of the day. The status quo is restored.'

'Is that what you'd call it?'

'This is all that one requires in a case like this, is it not? For the furniture to be put back the same way it was arranged before. These days it's only the lawyers and the pedants and the foreign correspondents who worry about how one conducts a case. The proper procedures, the gathering of evidence – these things mean nothing, not anymore. Not since Hitler. He cuts through these decadent superfluities and shows us that the conclusion is everything, Gunther. You of all people should understand this. The important thing in concluding a case successfully is actually concluding it. Not postponing it. Not allowing for the possibility of compromise, or appeal, or a faulty verdict. The end has to satisfy everyone, does it not?'

This 'everyone' didn't include me, obviously, but I nodded all the same. What would have been the point of arguing? I could even see how they'd shot the three men in the Türken before Hitler's arrival so as to spare the Leader the distressing sound of loud gunshots from across his back garden. The Nazis were never very difficult to understand; their logic was always impeccably fascistic.

'But most of all it has to satisfy Martin Bormann,' said Rattenhuber. 'And by extension, the Leader, of course.'

Of course I was angry, and tremendously sorry, and as I stood there brooding on the true nature of the new order that was being created in Germany I felt a haunting sense of the man I'd once been – the detective who would have protested such an outrageous demonstration of tyranny, at the expense of his own career, perhaps even at the expense of his own life – and all I kept thinking was, *You have to do something to stop these people, Gunther, even if it means shooting Adolf Hitler. You have to do something.* Rattenhuber's mouth was still moving inside his fat red face and I saw that what had happened to Diesbach and the two Gestapo men from Linz and Brandner was, to him, entirely justifiable. It was also very brutal and ruthless. These were brutal and ruthless men, Martin Bormann and his dwarves – they destroyed people and then they sat around the red marble fireplace at the tea house or wherever they talked about such things, and planned the destruction of others. No doubt the subject of a Polish invasion would be part of the Leader's fascinating table talk at his own birthday party. To think I'd been so close to Hitler's study at the Berghof. Couldn't I have done something then? Planted a bomb, perhaps, or placed a land mine under his bathroom rug? Why hadn't I acted then? Why had I done nothing?

'I daresay Heydrich will congratulate you in his own way,' said Rattenhuber. 'But Bormann and I were discussing how he might honour you and we concluded that this was perhaps the most appropriate way of recognizing your excellent work.' He started to fumble in his tunic pocket for something. 'After all, you did exactly what you were asked to do, in double-quick time, and against considerable odds. I still find it hard to understand how you worked out who the culprit was. But then I'm not a detective. Just a policeman.'

'A detective is just a policeman with a dirty mind,' I muttered. 'And maybe mine is dirtier than most.'

Rattenhuber removed a shiny leather medal-presentation case from his pocket and handed it to me. On the velvet cushion was a little bronze badge featuring a sword placed down across the face of a swastika within an oval wreath.

'It's the Coburg Badge,' he explained. 'The Party's highest civilian order. It memorializes the famous date in 1922 when Hitler led eight hundred stormtroopers to Coburg for a weekend rally where a very important battle was fought with the communists.'

He made it sound like Thermopylae but I had no memory of such a significant historical event.

'I take it we won,' I said drily.

Rattenhuber laughed nervously. 'Of course we won. Did we win?' Rattenhuber laughed again and clapped me on the shoulder. 'You're such a joker, Gunther. Always kidding. Look here, at the top of the wreath you can see Coburg Castle and village. And the wreath contains the words "With Hitler in Coburg 1922–32." Of course, that's not literally true in your case, but the great honour is in the implied assumption that you were there after all, do you see?'

'Yes, I do see that. I think Leibniz had a word for that.

Fortunately I don't remember what that word is. Anyway, thanks a lot, Colonel. Whenever I look at it I shall always be reminded of exactly how great a man Hitler is.'

I closed the box and laid it on the dresser, telling myself that in the Bavarian Alps at least there were plenty of good places to throw away my Coburg Badge so that it might never be found.

'Also, I have a railway warrant for you,' said Rattenhuber, laying an envelope on the sideboard beside my decoration. 'And some expenses. There's a train to Munich first thing in the morning, and then the express to Berlin. Might I recommend the Hofbraustübl for your dinner tonight? The pork knuckle is excellent. As is the beer, of course. There's nothing to beat Bavarian beer, is there?'

'No, there certainly isn't.'

But my plans for the evening didn't include pork knuckle and beer. I had an appointment with Gerdy Troost and Martin Bormann's brother, Albert. I don't know how else I could have listened to Rattenhuber's bullshit and kept my mouth shut.

CHAPTER 68

April 1939

I drove west out of Berchtesgaden towards the suburb of Stanggass. The new Reichs Chancellery stood at the end of the Urbanweg, off Staatsstrasse, a three-storey Alpine-style building about the size of an aircraft hangar, with a red-shingled roof, a parade ground, and a flagpole. It was after two a.m., but important-looking cars were still coming and going and the lights in several high windows were burning; smoke billowed from several squarish chimneys and somewhere a dog was barking. It seemed as if the whole area was now on Hitler time, and that until he decided to go to bed, nobody else would, either, even down here at the Chancellery, which was almost eight kilometres away from Obersalzberg and the Berghof.

I found Gerdy Troost standing inside the main entrance in an arched doorway as big as a U-Bahn tunnel. Above the doorway was a large red eagle holding a wreath that displayed a swastika. She was wrapped in a thick white fur that must have troubled the tenderhearted, animal-loving Hitler, and smoking a cigarette that would have troubled him even more. On her head was a white beret and over her arm a cream-coloured ostrich leather handbag. Being that I am a shallow sort of fellow who always appreciated the scent of expensive perfume and the sight of a perfectly straight stocking seam, the fashionably groomed Gerdy reminded me strongly of why I was keen to return to Berlin.

We went and sat in my car to get out of the cutting east wind and to talk for a few moments in private and, for no good reason I could think of, other than my most recent brush with death in the Schlossberg Caves, I kissed her almost as soon as my car door was shut. Gerdy tasted of white wine, lipstick, and the cigarette that was still burning between the fingers of her white-gloved hand. She felt slight in my arms, like a child, and almost breakable, and I had to remind myself that it had taken a lot of strength and courage to do what she was doing, that this was a woman who – by her own account anyway – had contradicted Hitler, and that wasn't something you did without pause for thought. The thin and very bony back I could feel against the palm of my hand must have been made of iron.

'You're full of surprises, do you know that?' she said. 'I certainly wasn't expecting that, Gunther.'

'Neither was I. I think the absence of any SS guards on duty here probably went to my head. Either that or I'm just pleased to see you again.'

'You're just nervous,' she said. 'It's not every day you enter a conspiracy to bring down the second-most powerful man in Germany. And not that I'm complaining, mind. But it's been a while since anyone held me like that.'

'I'm not surprised, given the company you keep and the place where you sleep.'

'You don't know the half of it. I had to sneak out the back door and collect my own car from the garage. But the Leader's full of plans tonight, which makes him very exhausting. Of course, he doesn't get up until midday, so it's all right for him. But everyone else at the Berghof is now operating on half as much sleep as before.'

I almost felt sorry for them.

'Did you catch your murderer?' she asked.

In view of Colonel Rattenhuber's warning I thought it best I didn't tell her too much about what had gone down in Homburg;

even at this late stage when we were about to present the evidence of Martin Bormann's corruption in Obersalzberg to his brother, Albert, I thought the less she knew about what had happened, the better. So I just nodded and changed the subject quickly. 'When the Leader was talking about his plans, did he say anything about Poland?'

'Only that the British and the French have failed to secure an alliance with the Soviet Union against Germany, and that if he could, he would form one himself, with the Russians against the Poles. So that doesn't look good for peace, does it?'

'Stalin would never make an alliance with Hitler,' I said.

'That's what people probably said about Sparta's deal with the Persian emperor Darius.' Gerdy took a long puff of her cigarette and then tossed it out the window.

'I don't know. Was Darius planning to betray the Poles, too?'

'Everyone hates the Poles,' she averred. 'Don't they?'

'I don't hate them. At least no more than I hate anyone else. I agree, that's not saying much. Not these days.'

'Don't you want Danzig back?'

'Not particularly. It wasn't mine to begin with. Besides, that's not the real issue here. The real issue is that Hitler just wants a real issue to make trouble, so he can expand our borders to include the rest of Europe. It's what Germany always wants. Hitler. The Kaiser. There's not much difference. It's the same old chestnut.'

'I can see we're not going to agree about that, anyway.'

'Probably not.'

'So. Are you ready to do this?'

'I think so. But you were right, of course. I am nervous.'

'You should be. What we're doing is not to be done lightly.'

'You don't hear me whistling.'

'We're about to walk into that building and give Albert Bormann the most dangerous weapon there is. Knowledge.'

'I know.' But still I hesitated. The Chancellery looked like it was recent, so, changing the subject again, I said, 'Is that one of your late husband's buildings, or Speer's?'

'Neither. Alois Degano designed this place. In common with Speer, he has only one design in his head. If you asked him to redesign the Reichstag it would probably look like this.'

I smiled. I always enjoyed hearing Gerdy's scathingly candid opinions of her colleagues' abilities.

'Having said all that, this is probably the most important building in Germany,' she added. 'Much more important than any building in Berlin, although it may not look like it. You're looking at the place where all of the Leader's executive orders are put into action. If Nazism has an administrative centre, this is it.'

'Hard to believe,' I said.

'Berlin's just for show. Big speeches and parades. Increasingly, this is the place where things get done.'

'That's depressing. Speaking as a Berliner, that is.'

'Hitler has no love for our capital.'

I wanted to tell her that Berlin had no great love for the Leader, but after giving her my thoughts on Danzig I thought it best to reserve my opinion in this matter at least; without Gerdy Troost I hadn't a prayer of even seeing Albert Bormann.

'Did you bring the ledgers?' she asked.

'In my briefcase.'

'Now, let me tell you what's important, which is how to deal with Albert. He's a modest, cultured sort of man, and a strict Lutheran. He's meeting us because he trusts me and because I vouched for your honesty. I told him that you're not in Heydrich's pocket. That you're old-school Kripo for whom justice still means something. Honesty and integrity count high with Albert. Very probably he's checked you out himself. Albert's not without his own resources. So, then; he hates his older brother, Martin, but that hatred certainly won't extend to allowing you to speak badly of him without hard evidence. Martin exercises no such restraint in talking about Albert, however. Albert is everything that Martin is not. And yet they are noticeably brothers. Jekyll and Hyde, you might say. Martin calls Albert the Leader's valet, or sometimes, "the man who holds Hitler's coat". He's even spread some rumours that Albert's Hungarian-born wife is a Jew. It's strange. When they're together you would think they don't even see each other. If Albert made a joke the only person not laughing would be Martin, and vice versa.'

'What does Hitler have to say about that?'

'Nothing. Hitler encourages rivalries. He believes it makes people try harder to gain his favour. And he's right. Speer is the living embodiment of what constantly trying to please Hitler can do to a man. Hitler relies on Martin but he trusts and admires Albert. So don't forget: Albert loves the Leader. Just like me.'

'Why do Martin and Albert hate each other?'

'I don't know. But the curious thing is not why they hate each other – brothers are often this way – but why Martin hasn't tried to get rid of Albert. No, not even to have him posted elsewhere. It's almost as if Albert is holding something incriminating on Martin. Something that guarantees his place here in Berchtesgaden. Anyone else would have been sent away by now.'

'It's all one big happy family, right enough.'

'Here, Gunther. Kiss me again, for courage. I liked it the first time. More than I thought I would.'

I leaned across the front seat and kissed Gerdy fondly on the cheek. Both of us knew that it wasn't going to come to anything but sometimes those are the sweetest kisses of all. There was another reason I kissed her, too, and probably why she let me. Whatever she said about Albert Bormann, he was still Martin's brother. Maybe they did hate each other; then again, maybe they'd made things up, the way people do when they're blood relations. Stranger things have happened. Then, after she'd fixed her make-up in the rear-view mirror and wiped my face with her breast-pocket handkerchief, we got out of the car and hurried towards the main entrance, where the eagle looked as if it was going to come alive, drop the swastika, and make a grab for Gerdy's white fur coat, like something in a fairy tale. It certainly felt like we were walking into real danger. But a hungry eagle was probably the least hazardous thing we were likely to encounter in Stanggass. Albert Bormann may have hated his brother but he was an SS general who loved Adolf Hitler and that made him very dangerous indeed.

CHAPTER 69

April 1939

Albert Bormann stood up to greet Gerdy Troost and when he came around the desk to kiss her, I saw that he was several centimetres taller than his older brother, although not as tall as me. His features were finer, too, although maybe that was more to do with how he looked after himself; he looked fit and his waistband was probably a couple of sizes smaller than Martin's. All that tea and chocolate cake in the tea house were bound to take their toll. Albert Bormann was wearing the uniform of an SS general and a Party armband, and although it was past two a.m. his white shirt looked as immaculate as his light brown neatly combed hair. The red Party armband gave me pause for thought, although not as much as the Coburg Badge on his left breast pocket; and given what I now knew about Martin's contempt for his brother, I had the sudden idea that the reason I'd been given the same badge was, perhaps, to devalue it; probably if Martin Bormann awarded enough of them, the Coburg Badge his brother wore would cease to be 'the party's highest civilian honour'. It looked like just the kind of spiteful thing that one brother would do to another.

When he and Gerdy had finished embracing each other, he helped her off with her coat, hung it up behind the door, and bowed very politely in my direction as she made the introductions. The office was large but simply furnished: on the desk next to an Erika five-tab and a rather loathsome book by Theodor Fritsch was a small photograph of the Leader, and on a wall a cuckoo clock. Outside the window you could hear the Nazi flag snapping in the breeze like someone shaking out a damp towel.

He drew up an easy chair in front of the fire for Gerdy, invited me to sit with them, and came straight to the point.

'You report to Heydrich, do you not?' asked Bormann.

'That's right, sir. Reluctantly.'

'Why do you say so?'

'I'm just not the thumbscrew type, I guess.'

'Really? Tell me about yourself, Commissar Gunther.'

'I'm nobody. Which is the way my superiors seem to like it.'

'Nevertheless you are a commissar. That's a little more than just nobody.'

'You would think so, wouldn't you? But these days rank doesn't count for much. Not since Munich. All kinds of important people are treated like nobodies now.'

'So you don't think the Sudetenland belonged to Germany?'

'It does now. And that's all that seems to matter. Otherwise we'd be at war with England and France.'

'Perhaps. But you were telling me about yourself. Not the situation in Europe. For example: Why should I trust you?'

'It's a good question. Well, sir, I resigned from Kripo in 1932. I was a member of the SPD, and I'd have been sacked before very long, anyway – for my politics, not my investigative record. You'll remember how the National Socialist Party used to think that to be SPD was almost as bad as being a communist. Which I never was. After I left the Alex I worked at the Adlon Hotel for a bit before setting up on my own as a private detective. I was doing all right at it, too, until late last year, when Heydrich drafted me back into Kripo.'

'Why did he do that?'

'There had been a series of brutal murders of young girls in Berlin that were allegedly committed by Jews. Heydrich wanted the case investigated by someone who wasn't a Nazi Party member and consequently had no racial axe to grind, as it were. He wanted the true culprit caught and not someone who'd been framed to suit the requirements of prevailing anti-Semitic propaganda. I believe the general felt that my previous record in the Murder Commission meant I was the best man for the job.'

'In other words, he thought you were an honest cop.'

'For what that's worth these days, yes, sir.'

'In the present circumstances, it's worth quite a lot. And did you catch the true culprit? I mean, the person who'd murdered these girls?'

'Yes, sir. I did.'

'And because he still thinks you're a good detective he sent you down here to investigate the murder of Karl Flex, is that right? Because my brother had asked him to send his best detective.'

I nodded. Albert Bormann's voice was almost the same as his brother's except for one thing: there was no rough edge in it, just courtesy. Gerdy had been right: it was indeed like meeting Dr Jekyll after one had first met Mr Hyde. I wondered that two brothers could look so similar and yet be so different.

'But you don't like working for Kripo now any more than you like Heydrich. Is that fair?'

'That's exactly right, sir. As I already said, I don't like his methods.'

'Nor my brother's, if Gerdy is to be believed.'

'That's right.'

Bormann now listened patiently while Gerdy explained how I had amassed a considerable amount of evidence that showed his brother, Martin, was corrupt and operating numerous schemes under the aegis of the Obersalzberg Administration to profit himself. Bormann listened patiently and even made a few notes with a gold pencil in a leather notebook.

'What kind of evidence have you found?' asked Bormann.

'Mainly there's this ledger, sir,' I said, handing it over. 'Kept by

Dr Karl Flex, and which records a whole series of payments on rackets that he and several others were running on behalf of his master, Martin Bormann. Rackets that have been set up to take advantage of the Obersalzberg Administration.'

'What sort of rackets?' asked Bormann.

I told him about the rackets in Pervitin and Protargol. 'But the most egregious one I've found so far is a scheme to give employees of OA deferment from military service. For approximately one hundred reichsmarks a year, virtually anyone can pretend to be employed by OA and thus avoid the call-up. On top of the local property empire that Martin Bormann has amassed, also corruptly, these payments are worth hundreds of thousands of reichsmarks per annum.'

Albert Bormann let out a sigh and nodded as if it was something he'd always suspected. I watched him find a pair of reading glasses and turn the pages of the ledger for a while before he told me to continue.

'There are also a couple of bankbooks for the Wegelin Bank of St. Gallen in Switzerland,' I said. 'One of these was in Flex's own name and the other is in the name of Martin Bormann. These accounts show exactly how much money your brother has amassed, sir. Once a month Karl Flex drove to St. Gallen, where he deposited checks and large sums of cash into both of these two accounts. Smaller sums for himself. Massive ones for your brother.'

'May I see these bankbooks, Commissar Gunther?'

I handed them over and waited while Albert Bormann scrutinized the Wegelin Bank passbooks.

'Astonishing. But I see that my brother's passbook has a second signatory: Max Amann.'

'Yes, sir.'

'Do you know who Max Amann is, Commissar Gunther?'

'I believe he's an associate of your brother, sir. A newspaper publisher and president of the Reich Media Chamber. He's also the Reich press leader. More than that I really don't know.'

'Yes, but none of those positions you mention is very important. Do you know what else he does?'

'Not exactly, sir.'

'Max Amann is the chairman of Centralverlag NSDAP.'

I bit my lip hard, suddenly understanding that none of my evidence was worth a spit; not anymore. 'Shit,' I said quietly.

'That's right, Commissar.'

'I don't understand,' said Gerdy. 'I've never heard of Max Amann.'

'Yes, you have,' said Bormann. 'Do you remember meeting a man with one arm in Munich at the Braun Haus?'

'That was him?'

Bormann nodded.

'I still don't understand why he's important,' she admitted.

'Centralverlag is the Party's publishing arm and in case you didn't know it, they're Hitler's own publishers. In other words, Max Amann is the man who publishes *Mein Kampf*.'

'Oh,' she said.

'Now you're getting it, Gerdy. And judging by the size of sums involved and the fact that Amann is also a signatory, I should say that the bulk of this money in Martin's Wegelin bank account probably comes not from these illegal activities you describe but from the royalties on Hitler's book. Which are considerable, as you can probably imagine. Does Hitler know that my brother has a Swiss bank account? Almost certainly. If there's one thing the Leader is careful with it's his own money. For some time I've been aware that my brother has absolute control not just of the Leader's Reichsbank chequebook, but also of his Deutsche Bank chequebook. Clearly Hitler already trusts my brother with his royalty money, too.

'Having said all that, is the Leader aware that Martin has been topping up some of the royalties from *Mein Kampf* in this Swiss account with money received from the corruption you've described here in Berchtesgaden? Not being a National Socialist yourself you will, doubtless, have your own quietly held opinion about that. Speaking for myself, I very much doubt that he does know. But I don't think there's any way of finding out for sure. Not without causing enormous embarrassment to the Leader. Which is perhaps why my brother's done it. Do you see?'

'Because if he mixes illegally obtained funds with ones that are legally obtained, then he can't very well be held to account,' said Gerdy. 'Yes, I do see.'

'It's the perfect cover for corruption,' said Bormann. 'All Martin has to say is that the money in the Swiss account is held for the Leader and with the Leader's full knowledge. And if the ledger was kept by Karl Flex, then my brother can deny all knowledge of it or any of the corrupt schemes he very likely masterminded himself. Yes, I'm quite sure you're right about this, Commissar. My brother's fingerprints are all over this loathsome scheme you describe. But sadly, I don't think this is quite enough proof to destroy him.'

There was another possibility, of course – that Hitler knew of Martin Bormann's corruption and tolerated it – but it wasn't one that I was prepared to moot in front of Albert or Gerdy. That would have been asking too much of their loyalty.

'Oh, don't get me wrong, Commissar. There's no one in the whole of Germany who would like to see the end of my brother more than me. But there's just not enough in what you've brought me to do that. I thank you for your courage in coming here tonight. I appreciate it can't have been easy. Nor for you, Gerdy. I know you love the Leader as much as me. And for the same reason you hate my brother.'

'Yes,' she said. 'I do hate him. I hate the way he's always there. I hate his increasing influence over the Leader. But most of all I hate his brutality and contempt for people.'

Albert Bormann handed back the ledger and the passbooks. 'Perhaps Himmler and Heydrich will know how best to use these. But I'm afraid I can't help you with this, Commissar. Pity.'

I nodded dumbly and lit a cigarette. For a minute there was silence.

'I am right, aren't I?' said Bormann. 'Himmler and Heydrich would like to get rid of my brother, wouldn't they?'

'I don't know about Himmler. But Heydrich likes to gather information on people so he can use it against them when it suits him to do so.'

'Including me?'

'Including me, including you, including everyone, I think. Even Himmler is afraid of him. But he didn't mention you when last we spoke. Only your brother, sir. I think he believes that you may have some secret information on Martin that prevents him from getting rid of you.'

'And he's quite right, of course. I do. And I am now going to tell you what that secret is.'

In life there are some secrets you never want to know and this certainly felt like it was going to be one of those. I was already regretting coming back to Berchtesgaden. 'Why would you do that, sir?'

'Because it may be that Heydrich can eventually achieve what I have signally failed to do, which is to destroy my brother. In my opinion, to do this he will need to assemble a wall of evidence, one brick at a time. Your ledger will help. But on its own, it is not enough.'

'If anyone can do it, he probably can,' I said. 'I've seen him do it. Look, perhaps you need to have a meeting with him, sir. A private meeting. Just the two of you. I'll tell him of your willingness to help when I get back to Berlin. But I'm not sure that I should be the middle man in this fraternal feud.'

'In case you hadn't realized it, Commissar, you already are. As for meeting Heydrich, no. I dislike Heydrich and Himmler almost as much as I dislike my brother. But they are a necessary evil, I think. Now and then we have need of thumbscrews, perhaps. Their motives would be different from mine, but the result would be the same. A corrupt, venal man whose influence over the Leader is fast becoming dangerous would be removed from high office. But I need to do this silently and from behind the scenes. To be a grey eminence myself, perhaps. So here's what I want you to tell your boss. "Help me to get rid of my brother. I will assist you in any way I can." Will you do that, Gunther? Will you give him that message?'

'Yes, sir.'

'Your master will need to go carefully. Both of you will. But there is also a need for some urgency here. Because my brother's power grows by the day. In case you hadn't yet realized it, Commissar, he's close to becoming Hitler's gatekeeper. And when that finally happens it will be too late to do anything. In my opinion Heydrich needs to make this happen before there is another European war. After that happens, my brother's position will be unassailable. You need to tell Heydrich that, too.'

Albert Bormann stood up and fetched a bottle of good Freihof from the desk drawer and poured three stemmed glasses to the brim. The glasses had little Nazi eagles etched on them like the one over the Chancellery entrance, just in case anyone stole them. I guess that happened a lot. Most Germans like a nice souvenir.

'And now I will tell you what I have known for fifteen years and what has, until now, prevented Martin Bormann from being able to get rid of me, his little brother, Albert. Now I will tell you the Bormann family secret.'

CHAPTER 70

April 1939

'In 1918, after briefly serving in the Fifty-fifth Field Artillery Regiment, my brother, who'd studied agriculture at high school, became the estate manager of a large farm in Mecklenburg where, as thousands like him did, he joined an anti-Semitic landowners association and the Freikorps. If you remember, food after the war was very short and many estates used to have Freikorps units stationed on them to guard the crops from pillagers. Also belonging to the local Freikorps was a man called Albert Schlageter, who – you may remember – led several sabotage operations against the French who were then occupying the Ruhr under the aegis of the Treaty of Versailles. One such operation involved the derailment of the train from Dortmund to Duisburg. Several people were killed. Following this, in April 1923, Albert Schlageter was denounced to the French and, on the 26th May, 1923, he was executed as a saboteur by firing squad. Of course, for this reason, he is generally regarded as a Nazi hero today; Hitler mentions Schlageter in *Mein Kampf*, and there's even a memorial to him in Passau, although my own opinion is that he was an honourable but misguided figure.

'Immediately after Schlageter's death the local Freikorps set out to discover the identity of the traitor who had denounced him. An investigation ensued and suspicion soon fell upon another member of the local Freikorps, a sixty-three-year-old local schoolteacher by the name of Walther Kadow, whose right-wing credentials were otherwise impeccable. He was also a dedicated anti-Semite. But importantly he was already known to and hated by two other members of the Freikorps – a twenty-three-year-old man called Rudolf Höss, and my twenty-four-year-old brother, Martin. Walther Kadow had taught the young Rudolf Höss at an elementary school in Baden-Baden and it's my impression that the old man was, like many gymnasium teachers, a bit of a martinet and gave Höss a pretty hard time of it. Meanwhile, my brother was closely acquainted with Kadow's underage daughter.

'Much too close for any father's liking, and when my brother seduced and impregnated her, Kadow wrote several letters to the owner of the estate where Martin was employed as the manager, denouncing him as a statutory rapist and demanding his immediate dismissal. The estate owner showed the letters sent to Martin, who then alleged, quite outrageously that, thanks to the local police, he'd had sight of the letters to the French denouncing Schlageter and that the handwriting in them was identical. It seems to me, having reviewed all of the facts of the case, that my brother's hatred and desire to get even was the one and only reason that suspicion ever fell on Kadow. But the logic of this hatred was simple: Albert Schlageter's death had to be avenged and therefore Walther Kadow was to be killed. My brother asked Rudolf Höss and two others to help him carry out the murder and subsequently, Kadow was kidnapped, taken to a forest near Parchim, stripped, humiliated, and then beaten to death with shovels. It was not, perhaps, the most glorious moment in the history of the Freikorps.

'Soon afterwards, one of the other murderers, a man named Schmidt, keen to deflect any suspicion that it was really him who had denounced Albert Schlageter to the French, confessed to the killing of Walther Kadow. Kadow's body was dug up by the local police, and Schmidt and Rudolf Höss were arrested, interrogated. In spite of Höss's strenuous denials that my brother had had anything to do with the murder, so was Martin. All of them went to trial and were found guilty in May 1924. Höss and Schmidt were sentenced to ten years in Brandenburg Prison. But thanks to Höss's willingness to take nearly all of the blame, my brother was sentenced to just one year in Leipzig Prison and, after nine months, was released. He promptly joined the Nazi Party and soon achieved an important position within the SS simply by virtue of the heroic status that was conferred by his act of politically motivated revenge against Kadow. Indeed, Adolf Hitler praised my brother so warmly for this action that Himmler conferred on him an early SS number to reflect his Old Fighter status. In other words, all of his current high standing within the Nazi Party rests on a lie told to the Leader himself. Kadow was murdered not because he had betrayed the Freikorps and informed upon a freedom fighter but because he objected to my brother's rape of his only daughter. What could be more understandable than that? It probably wasn't even Kadow who denounced Schlageter but Schmidt, the same man who had confessed to Kadow's murder.

'Now, while Martin was still serving his sentence in prison, the estate owner in Mecklenberg, understandably anxious not to fall foul of the Freikorps who'd been guarding his crops, sent the letters of complaint he'd received from Walther Kadow to Martin, care of my parents in Wegeleben, which is how I come to have them now. And my brother Martin isn't the only man with a safety-deposit box in Switzerland. They're part of my own insurance policy. These days everyone needs such a thing. Especially here in Berchtesgaden. Those letters from Kadow and certain other items the foreign press would love to publish are one reason that Martin doesn't dare to try to get me sacked. Because if he did, he knows I would show them to the Leader, and my brother would be revealed for the rapist and murderer he is. And now you know everything. Almost everything. This is what I would like you to tell Heydrich. That I will put the considerable resources of the Reichs Chancellery at his disposal in this respect.'

'But I don't understand, Albert,' said Gerdy. 'Why don't you do just that? You don't need Flex's ledger or those blue bankbooks to bring him down. You don't need Heydrich. Surely those letters are enough to destroy Martin's reputation on their own. Your brother isn't just a rapist, he's also a murderer. All you have to do is show those letters to Hitler.'

'You would think so,' admitted Bormann. 'And I might have done just that, but the plain fact of the matter is that murder is hardly uncommon in the higher reaches of the Party hierarchy. I'm sorry to say, several members of the present government have committed murder. Not just my brother. And I don't mean they killed someone in the war. Although there are some among us who would argue that Germany was in a state of near anarchy, not to say civil war, in the early years of the Weimar Republic. And that some murders were justifiable. Isn't that right, Gunther?'

'I'm not one of those,' I said. 'For all its faults, the Weimar Republic was at least democratic. But yes, you're right. Political murder, like that of Kurt Eisner, was common. Especially in Munich.'

'Bravely spoken.'

'What happened to Eisner was regrettable,' said Gerdy. 'But the man who shot him was an extremist, wasn't he?'

'Indeed he was,' said Bormann. 'But I'm afraid what happened to Eisner was not atypical. Those were extremely difficult times and it's almost impossible to say now with any degree of certainty which murders were justified and which were not. Indeed, it would be pointless even to try. Which is why I'd be wasting my time showing those letters to the Leader. He knows very well who has blood on his hands and who does not. For example, Julius Streicher murdered a man in Nuremberg, in 1920.'

'Oh well, Streicher – Streicher's mad,' said Gerdy. 'Even the

Leader says so. And thankfully, there are now moves to remove him from office.'

'Then there's our present Reich sports leader, Hans von Tschammer und Osten,' Bormann continued, smoothly. 'He murdered a thirteen-year-old boy in Dessau, did he not, Commissar? Beat him to death in a gym with his bare hands.'

'Hans? I don't believe it.'

'General Bormann is right,' I said. 'Von Tschammer und Osten is also a murderer.'

'But why would he do such a thing?'

'Because the boy was a Jew,' I said.

'And I'm afraid that Julius Streicher and von Tschammer und Osten are hardly unusual in this respect,' said Bormann. 'There are others. Significant others. Powerful men whose previous homicides give a smaller man like me, intent on accusing his own brother of committing a serious crime like murder, some serious pause for thought. The fact is, I'm not sure anyone in Germany apart from the commissar cares very much about murder these days. Least of all the Leader. Presently he has other things on his mind. Avoiding another European war, for one thing.'

'Nonsense,' said Gerdy. 'Murder is the most serious crime there is, everyone knows that.'

'Not anymore,' said Bormann. 'Not in Germany.'

'What do you think, Commissar?' asked Gerdy. 'That can't be right. You're a policeman. Tell him it's not true.'

'He's right, Gerdy. Eisner's murderer got just five years in prison. Murder's just not the serious crime it used to be.'

'But who are you talking about, Albert?' demanded Gerdy. 'Who are these people – these murderers among us?'

'I couldn't say,' said Bormann. 'But the fact remains that I do need Heydrich's help to have my brother removed from office. It will have to be something else. Some greater disloyalty. Espionage, perhaps. The crime of murder just isn't enough anymore.'

'Oh come on, Albert, don't be so mysterious. Who? Göring?

Himmler? Tell us. I can believe anything of Himmler. He's such a nasty little man. He at least looks like a murderer.'

'No, really, Gerdy, this isn't a game. Look, it's best I don't say anything. For all our sakes. I may be a general but I'm of no real importance. Yes, the Leader listens to me, but only because I don't tell him anything he doesn't want to hear. I'm afraid I wouldn't last very long if I started dragging up some of the Party's inglorious past. A past from which no one – no one – comes out very well.' Bormann shook his head. 'I suspect none of this is news to Gunther. But look, Gerdy, all I'm trying to do is tell you why things are not nearly as black and white as you seem to imagine they are. Why I can't act on my own. Why I do need Heydrich's help.'

'I think it's very unfair of you,' she said petulantly. 'Leading us on like that. And then telling us you won't say who among us is a murderer. Do you mean people who are at the Berghof now?'

Of course, I was thinking about Wilhelm Zander and Dr Brandt and the murders they'd committed, and how they would almost certainly get away with it, too; but I had already guessed that Albert Bormann wasn't talking about them. He didn't even know about the murders of Johann Diesbach and Hermann Kaspel, and nor did she. I hadn't told her.

'Most certainly,' said Bormann, answering Gerdy's question.

'Well, I for one should like to know with whom it's safe to go for a cigarette. No, really, I would, Albert. Your brother is one thing – I never liked him and it doesn't surprise me at all that he's a murderer. But really, this is too much.'

'I can't say,' said Bormann. 'Because sometimes words aren't enough and sometimes they're too much. But since a picture is worth a thousand words, there is this.' And after a long pause he opened his desk drawer, pulled out a manila file, and handed it to me.

'What's that?' asked Gerdy.

'It's a copy of a report from the Munich police,' said Bormann. 'The original is in the same safety-deposit box as those letters about my brother. The report concerns the murder of a Jew that took place at Stadelheim Prison in July 1919, following the short-lived Bavarian Soviet Republic. The Jew's name was Gustav Landauer, and apart from his left-wing politics and the historical event that brought about his death, he is perhaps best known for his translations of Shakespeare into German. Let me add also that I don't personally question the killing of this man, merely the wisdom of the photograph that was taken of it and which the report includes. Landauer was a communist agitator and a dedicated Bolshevik who would have had no compunction in murdering his own right-wing enemies. As I said, these were extremely violent times. My aim here is merely to point out the complete futility of making any noises at the Berghof concerning who's a murderer and who isn't.'

As I moved to open the file, Albert Bormann laid his hand firmly on mine and added, 'It's not pretty, Commissar: the man was kicked and stamped to death. However—'

'I've seen worse, I can assure you.'

'In your line of work, I'm quite sure you have, Commissar. But I was about to add that, in life, sometimes it's best not to know what we know. Don't you agree? Gerdy? Certainly it's not the sort of thing that the electorate would ever be allowed to see, for obvious reasons. Which is why this particular photograph has been so carefully suppressed.'

'Now I really am intrigued,' said Gerdy.

'Gerdy. Please take a moment to think about this very carefully. Once you've seen what's in that file, I promise you won't ever be able to forget it. Neither of you will.'

But when he took away his hand I opened the file. You can call it a cop's curiosity if you like, or something else. Maybe it was curiosity that made me a cop in the first place, and maybe it's curiosity that would one day get me killed, but he was right of course – as soon as I saw the contents of the file, I wished, like Pandora, I'd left it closed.

Attached to the typewritten police report were three photographs. Two were autopsy pictures of a bearded man in his forties or fifties. And I *had* seen worse, much worse. For every cop, the sight of violent death is the carpenter's plane that shaves away our ordinary human feelings until we're almost desensitized and close to becoming unfeeling planks of wood. In the third photograph a group of four grinning Freikorps were standing beside the same man's lifeless body; they looked like a group of big-game hunters on safari, posing proudly with a trophy animal they had bagged. One of the men, who appeared to be the leader, I recognized immediately: he was wearing a short leather coat, a tin hat, and puttees and he had one boot resting on the dead man's badly contused face. I hadn't seen a photograph like that before; no one had. And of course I was lost for words, as Albert Bormann had predicted. I heard a distant voice from my own past that seemed to say I told you so. For a moment, a sentence took shape in my buzzing head and I felt my lips start to move like a ventriloquist's dummy, but all that came out of my gaping mouth were a few syllables of startled surprise and horror as though I'd lost the power of speech. And after what seemed an eternity, I closed the file and handed it back to Bormann before it could contaminate me, and it was probably just as well that what I'd almost said to Martin Bormann's brother, Albert, and Hitler's close friend Gerdy Troost was left unsaid forever.

CHAPTER 71

October 1956

Even after seventeen years I remember that photograph very well, and how it was enough to overshadow the remainder of my time in Berchtesgaden like a glimpse into some devil's private nightmare. Seeing it made me regret my curiosity and I was more than glad to return to Berlin, as if merely being near the Berghof knowing what I knew about the Leader would cause me trouble. I can't say that it ever did. Nor that it changed my opinion of Hitler very much. But I could easily understand why it wasn't the sort of thing any chancellor would have felt comfortable sharing with the German folk, and why Albert Bormann treated it like a great state secret. It's one thing to murder a man in cold blood; it's something else to have your picture taken while standing on his face with a big grin on your own. Gerdy Troost chose not to look at the picture after all, on my advice, which I now regret having given her, since she remained loyal to the Leader right up until and well after the end. Given the hell Hitler unleashed upon the world, it might have been better if she'd seen him for what he was: a political criminal. Everyone knows that now, of course; Hitler's name is a byword for mass murder, but back in 1939 it was still shocking to realize that the head of the government was capable of such barbarous behaviour. Until then all I'd heard had been rumours that he'd been in charge of a Freikorps death squad in Munich, but these were nothing more than that: rumours. Bormann's photograph was the first time I'd seen actual evidence and when you're a cop, that's really all that's supposed to matter.

The last I heard of Frau Troost, she'd been ordered not to work as an architect for ten years and fined five hundred deutschmarks by some Allied denazification board. But I liked Gerdy, even admired her, which, at the time, was probably why I thought it best to talk her out of looking at the picture. I was more thoughtful then. Like the way I made sure that the one thing I did before I left the Bavarian Alps was to seek out Dr Brandt at his little home in Buchenhohe and let him know I'd guessed it was he who'd cut the brake hoses on Hermann Kaspel's car, he who'd murdered him, and that I knew all about his crummy little racket in Pervitin and Protargol, not to mention those illegal abortions. He arched a dark eyebrow and smiled thinly as if I'd told him a very vulgar joke, said I was sadly mistaken, and then closed the door in my face like someone who was absolutely certain that I couldn't touch him. He was right about that, of course. I'd have had a better chance arresting Josef Stalin. But still, I wanted to say my piece and not to let him think he had gotten away with it entirely, for Kaspel's sake and, I suppose, because I felt it was my duty. No one else was interested – interested, I mean, in the kind of justice to which everyone in a decent society is entitled. I saw Major Peter Högl again, too. He turned up at the hotel in a nice little blue sports car and cheekily offered to drive me to the local railway station – I suppose he just wanted to make sure I actually left Berchtesgaden; I let him drive me, too, just so I could tell him what I thought of him and the whole rotten operation on Hitler's mountain, and when I finished he told me to disappear, or words to that effect.

Would that I had disappeared, in which case perhaps the war might have worked out differently for me; if Heydrich hadn't drafted me into the SD from Kripo I might never have gone to France and seen Erich Mielke again, nor saved his life. Not that the comrade-general thought himself in my debt; not anymore, that much was certain. And while I was hopeful that having at last got rid of the tenacious Friedrich Korsch permanently I might escape the now leaderless Stasi hounds Mielke had sent after me, I can't say I was certain. But I did at least feel a greater sense of confidence that it would be a long time before they caught up with me, especially given that I was back in West Germany. I slipped across the new border soon after leaving the Schlossberg Caves and made my way via Cologne and Dortmund to Paderborn in the British zone, which I'd heard was now Germany's number one dirty-laundry centre for 'Old Comrades' seeking new identities. I don't think the poor Tommies suspected such things as laundries for old Nazis even existed, least of all that one would have operated out of a second-hand bookshop next to the university. And seventy-two hours after arriving there, I was checking into the local Hotel Löffelmann as Christof Ganz, with one hundred and fifty deutschmarks in my pocket, a passport, a railway ticket to Munich, and a new driver's licence. I even managed to knock a few years off my age and instantly became a much more youthful fifty. At this rate I could go back to Paderborn in ten years, get another new identity, and not age at all.

A few days later I arrived in Munich. Of course, I'd have preferred it to have been Berlin I was returning to, but home was out, possibly forever; surrounded by the GDR, it was pointless even thinking about it. Berlin looked like a pearl of freedom in a bucketful of ball bearings and, probably, was the second-most beleaguered place on earth. I might as well have tried to get into Budapest, which the Red Army's tanks were currently blowing to pieces following the Hungarian uprising. Besides, I knew lots of people in Berlin and what was worse they knew me, so I thought Munich was best. It wasn't like it used to be, but it would do. Besides, Munich was in the American zone, which meant there was always money to be made there. And while Bernie Gunther and Walter Wolf may have been wanted by the Amis and the

French, Christof Ganz was a man without a past, which suited me very well because without a past I at least had a fighting chance of having a future.

On my first night back in Munich my aimless footsteps led me from the Christliches Hospiz in Mathildenstrasse, where I was staying, to Odeonsplatz and the Feldherrenhalle, which was a copy of the Loggia dei Lanzi in Florence. While I haven't seen the original building myself I can easily imagine that it probably contains some beautiful Renaissance marble statues and works of art in bronze – all very Italian. The Munich copy contained a monument to the Franco-Prussian war and a couple of heavily oxidized statues to some now forgotten Bavarian generals. All very German and, once, very Nazi, too: on the left of the Feldherrenhalle, in Residenzstrasse, there had been a memorial to the so-called beer-hall putsch, but that was now gone and so, thank God, was the misguided man who'd instigated this doomed attempt at a coup d'état. But the jackboot echoes were still there and probably so were a few of the ghosts. And as I stood there brooding on the old Germany, I managed to forget the foreign tourists who were still milling about. Gradually they melted away and, perhaps more important, so did I. Then a dark cloud shifted, revealing the bright moon, and I was suddenly able to picture the scene that had existed there on that fateful day back in November 1923, as if I'd been in a cinema theatre. Theodor Mommsen probably puts it better than Christof Ganz, but for a brief, enchanted, almost transcendental point in time, I perceived how history was nothing more than an accident, a fluke, a matter of a few centimetres here or there, a head turned, a sudden gust of wind, a dirty gun barrel, a misfired cartridge, a breath held for a second too long or too little, an order misheard or misunderstood, an itchy trigger finger, a second's delay, an instant's hesitation. The idea that anything is ever meant to be seemed nonsensical; small causes can have large effects, and some words of Fichte came to mind, about how you could not remove so much as a grain of sand from its place without changing something in the immeasurable whole.

When Adolf Hitler, Ludendorff, and more than two thousand SA men had marched to this spot from the Bürgerbräukeller some two kilometres away, they encountered a blockade made up of a hundred and thirty policemen armed with rifles. The stand-off that took place ended when one of those guns – history doesn't tell us to which side it belonged – was fired, after which there was a lot of shooting on both sides. Four policemen and sixteen Nazis were killed. By all accounts Göring was struck by a bullet in the groin, while some of the men standing beside Adolf Hitler were killed outright, so perhaps it was hardly surprising he thought he had been picked by God to lead the country. Had he, I wondered, ever really believed that what he was doing was right? Or was it that he had been possessed by a misplaced and overriding devotion to pan-Germanism, which is to say he was infected with too much Germany as an idea, in inverse proportion to no Germany at all, which was the situation that existed until the unification that followed the conclusion of the Franco-Prussian war of 1871? It was of course unfortunate that the outcome at the Feldherrenhalle had not produced an alternative result. History would certainly have been very different. But I could hardly argue with the blockade or the decision to shoot, only the marksmanship.

It seemed that for once the Bavarian police had been doing their job properly.

AUTHOR'S NOTE AND ACKNOWLEDGEMENTS

Following **Heydrich's** assassination in June 1942, **Ernst Kalten-brunner** became the chief of the RSHA, which comprised Kripo, the Gestapo, and the SD, in January 1943; he was tried as a war criminal at Nuremberg and hanged in October 1946.

Hans-Hendrik Neumann remained Heydrich's adjutant until the capitulation of Poland in 1939, when he was sent to Warsaw to set up the SD office there. Subsequently he became police attaché at the German Embassy in Stockholm in 1941, again on Heydrich's orders; and then served with the SS in Norway. After serving a short prison sentence he joined Philips Electrical GmbH in Hamburg where he worked for the rest of his life. He retired in 1975, and died in June 1994.

Gustav Landauer was a leading anarchist at the beginning of the twentieth century. He was stamped to death by members of the Freikorps in May 1919. His last words were, 'To think that people like you are human.'

Colonel Johann Hans Rattenhuber's RSD units murdered hundreds of Jews at Hitler's Werewolf HQ in January 1942. He was captured by the Russians in May 1945 and served ten years in prison before being released by the Soviets in October 1955. He died in June 1957.

Major Peter Högl followed Hitler into the Führerbunker in early 1945. It seems probable that he commanded the firing squad that executed Himmler's liaison man and Eva Braun's brother-in-law, Hermann Fegelein, on the 28th April, 1945. Högl was killed on the 2nd May, 1945, while crossing the Weidendammer Bridge under heavy fire in Berlin.

The fate of **Arthur** and **Freda Kannenberg**, who were the house managers at the Berghof, is unknown.

Martin Bormann became Hitler's private secretary and the most powerful man in Germany after Hitler himself. He died while making his escape from the Führerbunker on the 2nd May, 1945. His co-conspirator in the murder of Walther Kadow in 1923, one Rudolf Höss, was released from prison in 1928; he joined the SS in 1934, and subsequently became the commandant of Auschwitz concentration camp. He was hanged as a war criminal in Warsaw in 1947.

Albert Bormann flew out of Berlin in April 1945. He was arrested in 1949 and, having served six months' hard labour, was released that same year. He refused to write his memoirs and never ever spoke about his elder brother, Martin. He died in April 1989.

Wilhelm Zander accompanied Hitler to the Führerbunker in early 1945. Zander was one of three men Hitler entrusted to take his political testament and effective command of German forces to Admiral Doenitz in April 1945. He survived the war and died in Munich in 1974.

Wilhelm Brückner was sacked by Hitler in October 1940 and replaced as chief adjutant by Julius Schaub. He joined the German army and by the end of the war held the rank of colonel. He died in Chiemgau in August 1954.

Dr Karl Brandt took charge of the Aktion T4 Euthanasia Programme in 1939, which gassed some seventy thousand victims. He was one of the defendants in the so-called Doctors' Trial, which began in 1946. Charged with carrying out medical experiments on prisoners of war, he was found guilty and hanged in June 1948.

The **Krauss brothers** were Berlin's most famous burglars. They really did burgle the police museum. Their fate is unknown to the author.

Gerdy Troost resumed her design work in Haiming, Upper Bavaria, in 1960. She died in Bad Reichenhall in 2003 at the age of ninety-eight.

Polensky & Zöllner continued in business long after the war. In 1987, the German arm of the construction company went bankrupt. But an arm of the company continues to exist today under the old name, in Abu Dhabi.

Erich Mielke served as the head of the Stasi from 1957 until after the fall of the Berlin Wall in November 1989. Prior to this, in October 1989, Mielke had ordered the Stasi to arrest and indefinitely detain eighty-six thousand East Germans in what he considered was a state of emergency. But local Stasi men refused to carry out his orders for fear of being lynched. Mielke resigned on the 7th November, 1989. He was arrested in December 1989 and went to trial in February 1992. Suffering from the effects of old age, he was released in 1995 on compassionate grounds and died in May 2000.

The tea house at the **Kehlstein** exists to this day and is a popular visitor attraction, as is the excellent **Hotel Kempinski** in Obersalzberg, which is built on the site of Hermann Göring's house. The ruins of both the Berghof and Bormann's house are still visible. The Türken Inn continues in business as a hotel and may be visited throughout the year. The Villa Bechstein no longer exists, but Albert Speer's house is still there and was sold recently to a private buyer for several million euros.

Albert Speer was tried as a war criminal at Nuremberg and sentenced to twenty years in prison. He died in London in 1981.

I am grateful for the help of Marie-Caroline Aubert, Michael Barson, Ann Binney, Robert Birnbaum, Robert Bookman, Paul Borchers, Lynn Cannici, J. B. Dickey, Martin Diesbach, Gail DiRe, Abby Fenneweld, Karen Fink, Jeremy Garber, Ed Goldberg, Margaret Halton, Tom Hanks, David Harper, Ivan Held, Sabina Held, Kristen Holland, Millie Hoskins, Elizabeth Jordan, Ian Kern, Caradoc King, John Kwiatkowski, Vick Mickunas, Simon Sebag Montefiore, Christine Pepe, Barbara Peters, Mark Pryor, Jon Rinquist, Christoph Rüter, Anne Saller, Alexis Sattler, Stephen Simou, Matthew Snyder, Becky Stewart, Bruce Vinokaur, Thomas Wickersham, Chandra Wohleber, Jane Wood, and, above all, Marian Wood, as always.